THE MAJOR EFFECT

THE
MAJOR
EFFECT

Dennis Kavanagh
AND
Anthony Seldon

MACMILLAN
LONDON

First published 1994 by Papermac

an imprint of Macmillan General Books
Cavaye Place London SW10 9PG
and Basingstoke

Associated companies throughout the world

ISBN 0 333 62276 6

1 3 5 7 9 8 6 4 2

A CIP catalogue record for this book is available from
the British Library

Photoset by Parker Typesetting Service, Leicester
Printed and bound in Great Britain by
Mackays of Chatham plc, Chatham, Kent

CONTENTS

Acknowledgments   vii

Introduction by the Editors
Dennis Kavanagh and Anthony Seldon   ix

Part 1: Politics and Government

1 A MAJOR AGENDA? *Dennis Kavanagh*   3
2 THE PRIME MINISTER *Hugo Young*   18
3 THE CONSERVATIVE PARTY *Anthony Seldon*   29
4 MAJOR AND PARLIAMENT *Peter Riddell*   46
5 THE CIVIL SERVICE *John Willman*   64
6 LOCAL GOVERNMENT *Ken Young*   83
7 ELECTORAL BEHAVIOUR *Ivor Crewe*   99
8 LAW AND THE CONSTITUTION *Simon Lee*   122
9 OPPOSITION *Dennis Kavanagh*   145
10 POLICY MAKING AND CABINET *Anthony Seldon*   154

Part 2: Economics and Finance

11 THE ECONOMY 1990–94 *Peter Jay*   169
12 INDUSTRY *Nicholas Crafts*   206
13 FINANCIAL SECTOR *Peter Sinclair*   223
14 EMPLOYMENT AND INDUSTRIAL RELATIONS
      POLICY *Robert Taylor*   246

Part 3: Policy Studies

15 DEFENCE POLICY *Lawrence Freedman*   269
16 FOREIGN POLICY *William Wallace*   283

17 CRIME AND PENAL POLICY *Terence Morris*   301
18 HEALTH AND SOCIAL POLICY
   Howard Glennerster   318
19 EDUCATION POLICY *Peter Scott*   332
20 THE FAMILY AND WOMEN *Ruth Lister*   351
21 COMMUNITY CARE *Jane Lewis*   365

Part 4: Wider Relations

22 THE NATIONAL QUESTION *Andrew Gamble*   383
23 MASS MEDIA *Colin Seymour-Ure*   399
24 THE ARTS *Robert Hewison*   418
25 SCIENCE *Tom Wilkie*   431
26 SPORT AND LEISURE *Richard Holt and*
   Alan Tomlinson   444

Epilogue
Dennis Kavanagh and Anthony Seldon 459

Appendix A: Chronology of Main Events 464
Appendix B: Cabinet Office-Holders 481
Appendix C: Notes on Contributors 483

Index 485

ACKNOWLEDGMENTS

A number of people have worked hard to produce this book. We would like to thank first our secretaries, April Pidgeon and Annemarie Weitzel for their efficiency in a wide field.

Our appreciation is due to Tanya Stobbs, our editor at Macmillan, for her good cheer and diligence; to Stephanie Darnill for her copy-editing; to Oisin Commane who compiled the chronology, and to Roland Phillips for initial backing of the project.

Anthony Seldon would like to thank colleagues at the Institute of Contemporary British History for their constant support and enthusiasm; colleagues at St. Dunstan's, principally Chris Muller and David Norris, for stimulating discussions, and to participants at the Hansard Society at Tonbridge for a bracing seminar on the ideas expounded in this volume. He would also like to thank his wife Joanna whose editorial skills and patience reached new heights. She also produced the index.

Finally, the editors would like to thank the contributors for their exemplary speed and efficiency in the execution of their assignments.

INTRODUCTION

Dennis Kavanagh and Anthony Seldon

The Major Effect follows up the *Thatcher Effect*, which tried to assess the changes in various policy areas and institutions in Britain under Mrs Thatcher, and the role of the government, and especially the Prime Minister, in promoting them. At that time, and still more so since, Mrs Thatcher had become the most studied of all post-war premiers. Our claim to originality was partly our focused approach, and also the breadth of the coverage of our areas of interest, with twenty-five chapters all dealing with different subjects.

The case for a similar approach to John Major's government is even more compelling. He has failed so far to attract a single serious book analysing his own contribution and the work of his government. The highly partisan media treatment in much of the press has served further to obscure a balanced understanding of the years since the fall of Mrs Thatcher in November 1990.

It is difficult to recall any other prime minister in the post-war period who has been subject to such a bitter and sustained media attack as John Major. After Britain's departure from the ERM in September 1992, until Major's perhaps short-lived recovery of nerve from July 1994, the press painted a picture of almost unrelieved woe. Yet there is a case for saying that *any* leader who came to power in November 1990 would have faced considerable problems. Europe would have been a deeply divisive issue for any Conservative Party leader to confront. The recession has dogged the government. Longevity in office has been a profound source of malaise. Remaining in power for the longest continuous period for any party this century has had its costs. Any leader taking over from such a dominant personality as Mrs Thatcher would have suffered by comparison and a parliamentary majority of 21 at the 1992 election, cut to 15 after the Eastleigh by-election in June 1994, has not provided a platform for heroic leadership.

John Major's fourth anniversary in office is a good time to review his record to date over a broad front. He will have served longer in office than eight premiers this century (Arthur Balfour, Henry Campbell-Bannerman, Andrew Bonar Law, Neville Chamberlain, Anthony Eden, Sir Alec Douglas-Home, James Callaghan and Edward Heath). That John Major's is a very different Britain from Margaret Thatcher's is apparent from the book. His premiership has lasted as long as a term of an American president. It merits full-length examination.

We asked our contributors to organize their essays around the following themes:

- What was the Thatcher legacy?
- What had been the amount of change since the arrival of John Major?
- What factors had facilitated or arrested change?
- What was the contribution of John Major to the change?

The writing of contemporary history labours under certain handicaps. These include lack of access to key documents, over-reliance on oral sources, a dearth of published literature and lack of perspective: only with the passage of time can the consequences of events be fully assessed. The Institute of Contemporary British History (founded in 1986 and the sponsor of this volume) acknowledges the force of many of these handicaps. But there is *never* an ideal time to publish a book of history, still less the study of a political figure or an administration. There is no definitive verdict of history. Every age will reinterpret the past, as new sources, writers, approaches, questions and preoccupations appear.

The value of the book is in line with the ICBH's own

objective, to provide an account and analysis of the recent past that gets beyond the coverage of the media and is more even-handed than the parties' own versions. Of all periods of history, it is most important to have good analyses of the very recent past, because it is upon readings of that past that decisions will emerge that will affect the future, whether by government or at the ballot box. Scholars undoubtedly know much more about the Attlee government of 1945–50 than they do about the Major government of 1990–94. Much research time and money is expended each year on investigating the minutiae of Attlee's ministry. But the practical importance of yet more work hardly compares to the value of a good analysis of Major's government. Having twenty-five authors, all specialists in their fields, further combats some of the problems of 'instant' history. The authors have monitored and interpreted developments more closely and authoritatively as they have unfolded than any single author could have done.

Finally, even when subsequent books appear, *The Major Effect* will still have value in showing what twenty-five very different men and women thought at one particular point in history. *The Major Effect*, like any book published on the tip of the events described, will be a product of the period in which it is written. It is nothing more or less than the first serious attempt to bring the events of 1990–94 into focus.

July 1994

Part 1

POLITICS AND GOVERNMENT

Chapter 1

A MAJOR AGENDA?

Dennis Kavanagh

POSING THE question about a Major effect on the political agenda is a compliment to Margaret Thatcher. Nobody doubted that she had an agenda or a 'big idea'. In fact she had lots of ideas and lost no opportunity to propound them. She is the only Prime Minister to have had an 'ism' named after her and, as a conviction politician, has probably set impossible standards for any successor. From the start, however, John Major rejected the comparison, going out of his way not to be identified with an 'ism'. Being a Conservative has been enough for him.

This modesty stems partly from John Major's personality and partly from his approach to party management. Some politicians are interested in political ideas and philosophies. Of the remarkable post-war politicians, Macmillan, Butler, Joseph, Crossman, Jenkins and Crosland stand out. More recently, Hailsham, Gilmour, Hurd, Lawson, Howe, Heseltine and Patten all expressed, in pamphlets or books, their visions of Conservatism, usually before reaching high office. They have a reflective side to their character, happily quoting Burke, Hume or Butler. John Major is not of this type. One looks in vain for a statement of his political beliefs before 1990.

In this John Major is not unusual – one thinks of Attlee, Eden, Home, Callaghan or even Wilson. He entered

Parliament in 1979, gained experience as a whip and, following a brief spell as a junior minister, joined the Cabinet in 1987. Nothing in his background suggested that he was going to promote a new agenda when he became Prime Minister in 1990. Indeed, providing continuity of policy with a change of personality was a significant factor in his election as party leader. As Hugo Young observes in the next chapter, the party deliberately passed up the opportunity to choose a different ideological direction. Major may also have calculated that to cultivate his own 'ism' would not only ape his predecessor but also, because it would be distinctive, accentuate discontinuity with a leader who was irreconciled to her downfall.

Apart from the emphasis on social citizenship it is difficult to discover a distinctive Major effect on the agenda. He has presided over the Thatcher legacy and not been unhappy with the lack of a 'Majorism'. Indeed, for much of the time, Majorism equalled the absence of Thatcher. Chris Patten's elegant essays and speeches in 1991 on the social market and attempts to reconcile post-Thatcherite Conservatism with Christian Democracy were rebuffed by Number 10.

HOW AGENDAS CHANGE

It is not surprising that there has not been a Major effect. Big movements in the climate of political ideas occur rarely in Britain. The normal pattern of policy development is for change to be incremental; the lessons learned from shortcomings of existing policy produce marginal changes to the status quo.

There have perhaps been three occasions this century when the agenda of politics has shifted, in 1906, 1945 and 1979, years which produced the elections of Liberal, Labour and Conservative governments respectively. The dates coincide with changes of government and are significant primarily as registering variations in mood which were already under way. In each case a party, long considered to be the minority, displaced the normal party of government; the new government was backed by a large House of Commons majority and a change in the climate of opinion; the governments introduced far-reaching reforms which set the agenda for their successors. The first combined social liberalism with constitutional reforms, the second a mixed economy with the welfare state, the third a New Right agenda of free market economics and a strong state.

The idea of cyclical change in the public mood has been an extremely powerful one, more so than the idea that history moves in one direction. Economists study the alterations of economic booms and depressions, political scientists the swing of the pendulum between left and right, and philosophers the interaction of thesis and antithesis. Each new *Zeitgeist* appears to start out with strong support and high expectations but over time loses popularity and credibility.

In Britain political agendas seem to change only when certain conditions are met. One is circumstances, the emergence of pressing new problems or the deterioration of old problems to crisis proportions, demanding solutions which existing policies cannot provide. Such crises may include the collapse of government authority, mass unemployment, or soaring inflation. The second is when a new set of ideas, sometimes stimulated by the discrediting of existing policies (for example, academic selection for schools in the 1960s or incomes policies in the 1980s), acquires respectability and an appreciative audience. To have an impact ideas have to combine with circumstances; there are lots of attractive ideas, but few which are achievable, timely and relevant. The expression, 'an idea whose time has come', is a comment on the circumstances as much as on the quality of the ideas. This certainly helped the reception of many 'New Right' ideas from the mid 1970s on. A third is the availability of leaders who want to change the agenda and are in a key position (i.e. in government) to do it. These three conditions were broadly met in 1906, 1945 and 1979.

The effect of these changes is to undermine existing policies, elites and procedures; expectations are altered and new goals set. They provide a window of opportunity for leaders to alter the agenda. If successful, the new dominant party takes advantage of the mood for change, shapes the agenda and influences the policies of opposition parties and the other elites. This occurred with the New Deal of the Democrats in the United States after 1932, the 'middle way' of the Social Democrats in Sweden after 1932, the social market approach of Christian Democracy in post-war West Germany and Thatcherism in Britain after 1979.

THE THATCHER IMPACT

The main features of the domestic political post-war agenda are well known. They included full employment through Keynesian demand management; state provision of welfare; consultation between the trade unions and employers and government, increasingly so over time as a result of incomes policies and the social contract; the mixed economy, including state intervention through outright ownership of utilities and a private sector constrained and cushioned by a mix of regulation, subsidies and sanctions. Whitehall was confident that the centre knew best, that its decisions, taken in conjunction with the major interests, would lead to superior outcomes than those created by the play of market forces and collectivism. The thrust of public policy was broadly redistributive.

The heroes of this package of policies were Keynes, Beveridge and the Fabians – all high-minded paternalists. These policy entrepreneurs believed that getting the right policies and giving power to the 'right sort' of people (like themselves) provided the best government. Their views were broadly shared across the political spectrum – frontbenchers in the main political parties, Whitehall, academe and opinion forming organs such as *The Economist* and *The Times*. The Labour left was a minority, never more so than when the party was in government, and free-market Conservatives were a beleaguered rump. Conservative leaders from Macmillan to Heath regarded a body such as the Institute of Economic Affairs as rather odd or at best old-fashioned.

That agenda of 1945 broke down in the 1970s. One can disagree about the exact date – the defeat of the Heath

government in 1974, Healey's budget in 1975 which abandoned full employment, the IMF rescue in 1976 or the Winter
of Discontent in 1979. The consensus had few credible defenders by 1979. Circumstances were crucial in its undoing.
Governments increasingly found it difficult to maintain free
collective bargaining, low inflation and full employment. The
first of this trinity was regularly abandoned in the 1960s and
1970s, the last by 1975, both in the quest for low inflation.
Governments virtually collapsed in 1974 and 1979 in the face
of trade union resistance to incomes restraint. Government
could neither work with, nor break, the unions. The British
economy was in a fragile state; attempts to boost growth
regularly ended in a balance of payments or sterling crisis.
Fears of ungovernability were expressed across the political
spectrum.

It was then an easy step to undermine the legitimacy of
the collectivist ideas. Between 1974 and 1979 this was done
initially and most boldly by Sir Keith Joseph. He did this
against the wishes of, at first, Heath, and then many of Mrs
Thatcher's senior colleagues. Sir Keith attacked the commitment to full employment on the grounds that it was beyond a
government's power to achieve; the welfare state, which
failed to do enough for the deserving poor and, by encouraging dependency, undermined the work ethic; trade union
privileges which distorted the working of the market; high
levels of public spending and taxation which 'crowded out'
investment; and the pursuit of equality, which weakened
incentives and penalized success. Sir Keith and Mrs Thatcher
attacked virtually the entire thrust of the post-war social and
economic policy. It had failed. There must be a better way.

The alternative agenda was developed largely after 1979,
when the new ideas marched alongside the policies, sometimes preceding them, sometimes following them. The market was preferred to the public sector as a provider of
solutions, even to the extent of privatizing state owned industries. The conquest of inflation as an aim of economic policy
took priority over the pursuit of full employment; there was
no longer a trade-off between these two goals, for achieving
the former was a means to achieving the latter. Control of the
money supply replaced prices and incomes controls as the

means to squeeze inflation. Curbs on the trade unions would provide a better 'balance' between employers and trade unions. Cuts in income tax were preferred to increases in public spending; allowing people to keep and spend more of their own money was essential to freedom. In education and health there was a squeeze on resources and the introduction of more market mechanisms. Mrs Thatcher was fully committed to the new agenda.

The Conservatives' landslide election victories in 1983 and 1987 may convey the impression that the Thatcherite project won the hearts and minds of the people. But the public appears to have been less moved by it than was elite opinion. Surveys showed that the public moved steadily against key elements of the government's programmes in the 1980s, particularly on tax cuts versus more state spending on public services, on the government's disavowal of responsibility for full employment and on further privatization. Interestingly, in the second half of the 1970s public opinion had also moved against the Labour government's positions on welfare, trade unions and public ownership. Shifts in public attitudes also preceded changes of government at general elections in 1964, 1970, 1974 and 1979, and, in each case, soon turned against the new government. British governments seem to have short-lived honeymoons. Studies of Conservative MPs, conducted before Mrs Thatcher's downfall in 1990, also suggest that there were a limited number of true Thatcherites on the Conservative backbenches; most of them were middle of the road. Philip Norton prophetically entitled a study of MPs: 'The Lady's Not for Turning, But What About the Rest?'.[1]

MAJOR'S IMPACT

It is difficult to make the case that the conditions for agenda change, outlined on page 5, were present when John Major became Prime Minister. A number of Conservatives thought that Thatcherism as a continuing agenda was finished. But beyond repealing the poll tax there was little support for rolling back its main planks. Rather, there was a general feeling that the voters had had enough of curbing public spending, shaking out surplus labour, privatization, and bashing the unions. There was nothing comparable in 1990 to the call for a sharp change of direction in 1945 or 1979 or the availability of leaders who promised to carrry it out. Most Conservative MPs wanted a change of leader, one who would bring about a victory at the next election. John Major seemed to provide change with consolidation; 'Thatcherism with a human face', in the words of Kenneth Clarke.

Thatcherism in the 1980s had been largely applied to the economy, increasing take-home pay for those in work, extending private ownership and implementing direct tax cuts. Major has continued with much of that Thatcher legacy. The government is planning to privatize British Rail and British Coal and part of the Post Office but this effectively ends the list of utilities which can be sold off. The agency principle in the civil service has been continued and by the end of 1994 some three-quarters of civil servants will work in agencies. There has been a continuation of market testing in Whitehall and contracting out in local government. In principle, the reforms will both scale down government and make it more businesslike. The wages councils have been abolished and further restrictions imposed on the unions. There was much fuss about the decision to wind up the National Economic Development Office in 1992 but it was more symbolic than substantive; corporatism had already died. The big change has been the increase in direct taxation, a consequence of Lamont and Clarke budgets.

Major's main impact has been on the public services. Under the third Thatcher government the Education Act (1988) and student loans had been introduced, the health service reforms had just started and the Housing Act allowed council house tenants to opt for private landlords. John Major's search for mechanisms other than privatization to empower people, giving them more opportunity and choice, resulted in the Citizen's Charter in early 1991. Mrs Thatcher's notion of empowerment had not extended beyond giving people property rights. She showed little interest in providing means of redress of grievances beyond facilitating opting out of schools, council housing and the NHS.

Having rejected privatization of health and education, John Major's task has been to import the best of private sector practice as a means of improving the performance of these services. This includes performance pay, audit, competition and more information about performance. The government has tried to mobilize consumers to expect and demand a level of performance comparable to what they would expect from say, Marks & Spencer. In health, the devices have been internal markets, hospital trusts and fund-holding doctors, in schools, core curriculum, opting out and local budgets. These were all set in train by 1990 but John Major has implemented them energetically.

The Charter has been John Major's initiative, and Britain's precursor to *Reinventing Government* in the United States.[2] It is a philosophy of administration, an attempt to change the culture of public services. Consumers are provided with more information about their rights and about the performance of services; there is more regulation of the providers, targets for improved performances, more competition between service providers, more choice for consumers, independent inspection and better complaints procedures. There are sharper divisions now between consumers on the one hand and the producers and professionals on the other.

It is too early to state whether the Charter will mark a revolution in Whitehall. The steps are small and John Major lacks the gift for dramatizing his initiatives; plans to hold a press conference on the Citizen's Charter during the general election were abandoned. At the heart of the Charter is the notion of the citizen as an individual consumer of public services and a new relationship between the client and the provider of the service. The election and accountability of government are missing from this equation, with services being contracted out to such bodies as grant-maintained schools and hospital trusts.

The new heroes in the post-Thatcher age are businessmen, accountants, consultants and managers. Optimists might hope that, given the decline of local government, these quangos may become independent intermediaries between citizen and government, examples of Burke's 'little platoons'.

More realistically, the cult of managerialism will win out.

A key test of the enduring impact of a shift in the government's ability to change the agenda is that many of its ideas are accepted by the opposition. Just as the Conservatives came to terms with the programme of the 1945 Labour government, so the Labour party has moved a good deal since 1983 or even 1987. In some respects Mrs Thatcher had more effect on the Labour party than she may have done on the Conservative party. Labour is now in many respects a party of European social democracy. It speaks cautiously on public spending and taxes, has abandoned unilateralism, accepted many of the changes in industrial relations, is steadily weakening its connections with the trade unions and has given up on public ownership. The leadership's rhetoric now invokes 'consumers' or 'citizens' not 'workers'. Socialism, on the rare occasions that the word is uttered, is not about public ownership but about supply side socialism, diffusing power, giving people more choice and freedom. Labour is now virtually the catch-all social democratic party that the revisionists sought to promote after 1959, the party that the Social Democrats wanted to become.

Labour has responded to four successive election defeats and changes in the real world. The modernisers in the party know that society has changed radically and the party must change also. Its core vote in the working class and trade unions has shrunk and many of its associated interests, notably the trade unions, local government and public sector, have been weakened. Many of the economic and social measures of the 1980s will be too firmly entrenched for a future Labour government to reverse anyway.

LESSONS FROM ABROAD

Any study of changes in the policy agenda needs to look beyond Britain. Many of the concerns of policy makers in Britain are found in other industrial societies. An international market in policy ideas has also developed with the proliferation of conferences, working parties and exchanges between countries and political groups. Many of the New Right ideas in the 1970s and 1980s originated in the United States and were "brokered" here by think-tanks. At times, different national governments have worked independently towards broadly similar solutions. In the United States the best-selling text *Reinventing Government*, by David Osborne and Ted Gaebler, has promoted the idea of government as an entrepreneur, one which encourages competition in service provision and consumer choice, prefers market over bureaucratic solutions, and explores ways of measuring and publishing performances. The ideas have been welcomed by Republicans and Democrats, but much of the spirit and a number of the proposals resemble John Major's Citizen's Charter.

Thatcher and Reagan may have stolen the headlines in the 1980s but many of their policies and even their rhetoric had echoes elsewhere. Indeed much of Thatcherite economics was a British response to wider changes in the international economy, notably the loss of competitiveness. Social Democratic parties in most countries have undergone versions of a Bad Godesberg and absorbed a good part of the message of economic liberalism. In the second half of the 1980s leftist governments in France, Spain and Australasia ended up with recognizably New Right policies and even the Social Democrats in Sweden, for long the model of active and redistributive government, had to adapt.

Economic management is increasingly influenced by outside forces; a nation's macro-economic policy has to satisfy the 'good housekeeping' expectations of international markets. As Britain becomes more enmeshed in the European Union so more of the parameters are set in Brussels and national policies increasingly converge with those of our partners, notwithstanding the British opt out from the social chapter. In Eastern Europe the change has been spectacular, with the collapse of communism and disillusion with the results of years of central planning and state ownership. Throughout much of Western Europe in recent years there has been a move to the deregulation or privatization of public enterprises, extension of markets, abandonment of full employment budgets, provision of more selective or constrained welfare, lower marginal rates of income tax, cutbacks on subsidies or tax breaks, and in health and education the recruitment of managers who are charged with making the services more responsive to the consumer and delivering greater value of money. Britain has been at the forefront of many of these ideas.

EXPLANATION

The lack of a new agenda since 1990 is not, I have claimed, unusual. There was not massive dissatisfaction with the *status quo*, the availability of a persuasive alternative agenda, or the emergence of a leader who wanted to break with Thatcherism. But it is worthwhile considering the secondary causes that have constrained the emergence of new thinking since 1990. The first has been the general sense of the need for consolidation after a decade of radical changes. Few would deny that there has been a demonstrable need to cope with the consequences of radical legislation and to correct ill-considered or rushed measures, notably in local govern-ment finance, the school curriculum and criminal justice; witness the numerous revisions of policies in these areas. John Major did not see the Conservative party, as some Thatcherites seemed to do, as the party of permanent cultural revolution, dedicated to the disruption of complacency in a variety of interest groups. He cares more about continuity, community and stability than his predecessor. His liking for the traditional and the familiar is one reason why he is reluctant to disturb institutions or raise questions of constitu-tional reform.

A second cause is that the Thatcher governments may have tackled the easier, or at least the more obvious, targets. These included inflation, the trade unions, an expanding public sector, the nationalized industries and high spending local authorities. If the agenda in the 1980s was largely economic, in the 1990s it is largely social. Such problems as soaring crime figures, family breakdown, a growing under-class, poor schooling and run-down inner cities did not start in 1979 but it is an open question whether the policies of the

1980s, the soaring unemployment and growing inequality of incomes exacerbated them. The encouragement of individualism, private ownership, efficiency savings (or job cuts), and enterprise created their own pool of casualties. These problems are more complex than those of the 1980s, and require multi-faceted and multi-agency solutions.

A third reason is that Thatcherism was defined to a significant degree by what it was against. It had a long list of enemies – inflation, the 'dependent society' and the undeserving poor, corporatism, left-wing local authorities, the EC Commission, trade unions, and much of the non-market public sector. Conquering these 'dragons' (a Saatchi term), called for a determined, even abrasive, leadership. An apparent unwillingness to listen or to compromise was a virtue when dealing with Scargill, Foot, Delors and Galtieri. It is less clear what or who the dragons are in the 1990s.

Finally, one has to take account of the very different personality and political style of John Major himself. One can make a plausible case that circumstances have inhibited him from promoting a distinctive agenda. At first, he had to heal the scars of a divided party, and since the 1992 general election his room for manoeuvre has been limited by a small parliamentary majority, the dominance of Maastricht and Europe (an issue that could split the party), the economic recession and a succession of accidents and scandals affecting ministers. He inherited problems, commitments and policies; his scope for choice has been narrow. But, compared to Mrs Thatcher, he is less insistent on *the* one way, believes in and practises Cabinet government, is more concerned to conciliate and reach agreement, and does not have an agenda so clearly separate from that of his principal Cabinet colleagues. Sir Ronald Millar, a speechwriter to the two Prime Ministers, doubted that John Major would ever ask 'Is he one of us?' but would say 'I'm one of you'. Major has not used Downing Street as a pulpit to lecture and chastise the nation. He is happy to be a 'healer' rather than a 'warrior'.

British politics now appears to be going through one of its eras of 'good feelings' in which many policy goals and views are broadly shared across the political spectrum. In other words, after the polarization of the 1980s we might be returning to less ideological politics. Such a claim can only be made with confidence after a future spell of Labour government – to see whether its actions on tax and markets match its present rhetoric. But in a post-socialist post-Thatcherite era both parties have moved to the metaphorical centre ground. The common ground includes the following:

- a narrowing of choice in macro-economic policy. Britain's membership of the ERM between October 1989 and September 1992 largely determined macro-economic policy; policies on public spending, interest rates and borrowing had to be made with membership in mind. Even out of the ERM, however, economic policies have to take account of the views of financial markets.

- a greater reliance on the markets for wealth creation and, to a lesser extent, allocation of welfare. The leaderships in both parties still remain tentative in pushing the idea of markets because of perceived public resistance and Labour prefers more management of markets. But all main parties clearly accept the market as more effective in promoting greater choice. The privatization of most utilities is now common ground; the divide is between pro-competitive regulation and more 'dirigiste' regulatory agencies.

- a need for public services to be more responsive to consumers. Conservatives think of consumers more as individuals while Labour is more willing to recognize groups such as trade unions. But there is a shared concern with promoting the rights of consumers of services, emphasizing the importance of delivering satisfactory services and establishing more equal relations between consumers and producers. A century ago Lord Harcourt said, 'We are all socialists now.' Today it would be more accurate to say that 'We are all consumers'.

- an emphasis on cost-containment and value for money in the public sector. The new public management strategies are here to stay, given the voters' demand for better public services, alongside a resistance to pay more income tax and constraints on increased public spending in the near future.

- a rethinking of the range of services and benefits which

the state provides (e.g. through more selectivity and opting out) and of new ways to finance them (e.g. through increased charges and private provision). The right regards vouchers or transfer payments as more efficient as well as a means of reducing the role of the state, while for Labour's modernisers some means have to be found to get it off the indictment that it is the party of high spending and high taxes.

- a concern at how some of the social and economic policies of the 1980s have actually weakened the sense of community. It is not surprising that the left makes this charge. But the right has also complained that the economic changes ignored the 'civic virtues' of solidarity, self-sacrifice and service for others (David Green in his IEA pamphlet *Reinventing Civil Society*) and weakened the social fabric (John Gray in *After the New Right*).[3]

- a turning away from top down provision in universal services; greater flexibility and variety, as in schools and higher education, is the order of the day. In some ways, this is less a European than a North American model of government (partly because of federalism, partly because of a more modest state role in the provision of welfare, and partly because of the lower social and political status of the federal bureaucracy).

These new concerns have gone hand in hand with the rise of a new group of opinion formers and think-tanks since 1990. The IEA and Centre for Policy Studies have fewer listeners. Most ministers are more attentive to the Social Market Foundation and the European Policy Forum, as well as the Adam Smith Institute from the 1980s, and Labour to the Institute of Public Policy Research. These are addressing cross-party concerns in reinventing government, measuring the outputs and performance of government departments and public services, studying the consequences of the European Union for our political institutions and rethinking the funding of welfare services.

One policy paradigm suggests that we have arrived at an *end* state (*The End of History* for Fukuyama).[4] Reinventing government belongs to the school that says liberal capitalism has won, socialism is dead and ideological conflict has ended.

Government is seen as a business; departments and agencies have missions, government institutions should be decentralized, play the role of an enabler rather than a provider, and be judged by results and customer satisfaction. An alternative paradigm is that public policy moves cyclically between a focus on private concerns and a focus on public issues (Hirschman in *Shifting Involvements*).[5] As disillusion builds up with, for example, the pursuit of private interests so the public responds more favourably to leadership calls to correct the neglect of the public concerns. The Major years have seen some reaction to the privatizing cycle of the 1980s, but this is more of a correction than a repudiation. The Thatcher administrations moved the centre of political gravity firmly to the right. John Major's style and emphasis differ from his predecessor – he is a reconciler, not a warrior – but he has largely accepted the Thatcher inheritance.

Notes

1. Philip Norton, 'The Lady's Not for Turning, But What About the Rest? Margaret Thatcher on the Conservative Party 1979–89', *Parliamentary Affairs*, 43, 1990; pp. 41–58.
2. David Osborne and Ted Gaebler, *Reinventing Government* (Penguin, 1993).
3. David Green, *Reinventing Civil Society*, (IEA, 1993).
   John Gray, *After the New Right* (IEA, London 1993).
4. F. Fukuyama, *The End of History?* (IEA, London 1993).
5. A. Hirschman, *Shifting Involvements* (Blackwell, 1985).

Major had to contend with Gulf war
Poll tax
Europe.

Bottom 19.

Chapter 2

THE PRIME MINISTER

Hugo Young

PRIME MINISTER MAJOR was oppressed from the start by a contradiction that sprang directly from his inheritance. He was selected by a Conservative party that had just ousted a leader as much for her rebarbative personality as for her unacceptable policies. It thought itself in danger of losing power through the unpopularity of an autocratic politician whose wilfulness, on a series of issues, had rendered her incapable of supposing she might be wrong. The party therefore wanted an emollient, listening figure, and in John Major it found him. At the same time, it was determined to elect a leader who was in substance a follower of Margaret Thatcher. It rejected the opportunity to make an ideological break with the past. It wanted Thatcherism pursued by non-Thatcherite means, neglecting to consider the possibility that this might be an unattainable ambition. Mr Major personifies a dilemma that four years have failed to resolve. The fault-line between these two objectives has reached into most of the areas that mattered.

This fresh climate, and the exultant welcome it received, had a variety of causes connected to the personality and provenance of the new leader. He was, by historical standards, a remarkable choice. While parties in opposition had sometimes reached across the generations to pluck a tyro from obscurity, no governing party had ever selected such an

inexperienced leader as John Major. His three months as
Foreign Secretary and year as Chancellor represent a thinner
record in high politics than many of his ministers. In Parliament for barely a decade, he drew his strength not from an
imposing series of political triumphs but from his appearance
as the man with the fewest enemies in the party. While being
a creation of his predecessor and therefore a rightist, he was
by temperament a conciliator and by experience a whip. This
preordained the character of the only kind of government he
could run, and so did the personal relations he enjoyed with
the important people who put him where he was. They liked
him. He liked them. His was an administration built on an
instinctive preference for the lowest common denominator of
agreement.

WHIP'S RULE

To begin with, this unexpected Prime Minister was surprisingly successful. To those who knew hardly anything about
him he revealed an impressive professionalism. Landed in the
middle of the Gulf War, he remained cool under fire and used
the opportunity for swift promotion into the echelon of
world leaders who could stand shoulder to shoulder with the
American president and suffer little by comparison. The Gulf
was a hardening experience. So was grappling with the two
chief political problems that seemed likely to settle the Tories'
fate at the next election. The poll tax and relationship with
Europe were the focal points of backbench panic, and
although they had been the source of most MPs' apprehen-
sion about the next election, there was no agreement about
how the new man should redirect them. But taking his time,
and deploying his whip's calculation of the mood of the Tory
party, Major presided over a replacement of the poll tax and
a re-ordering of the grammar of Europe. Converted into a
'council tax', the poll tax vanished from politics: an improbable achievement. As for Europe, in place of the embarrassing
shrieks of Mrs Thatcher as she approached oblivion, Major
offered calm deliberation and a promise, couched in shrewd

state of feeling
2 conflicting emotions at same time

ambivalence, that Britain's ambition was to remain at the heart of things. He found a language hardly anyone disagreed with. Between continuity and a subtly new direction nobody important was prepared to drive the obvious wedge. They were all too busy preparing to win an election, which was the pretext for Major's unlikely presence in the first place.

There was also a formal loosening on some of the reins of prime ministerial power. Ministers mattered more, both collectively and individually. Along with the passing of an autocratic temperament went the retrieval of more conventional, and possibly more accountable, modes of government. A disease of the Thatcher years had been ad hoc decision-making in the Prime Minister's office. The back door of Downing Street was ever open to favoured ministers wishing to press for the overturning of a decision of the collective. In a lecture given in 1993, Major's Lord Privy Seal, Lord Wakeham, gave authoritative evidence of the change of style. Wakeham was a veteran of the Thatcher court. After three years of Major, he reported that 'The move towards the use of ad hoc groups appears to have been halted . . . My impression is that the balance has shifted back towards greater reliance on the Standing Committees.' As chairman of half the committees in the Cabinet, Wakeham set his privy seal on the kind of development – the retreat from presidential government – that the country was looking for when Mrs Thatcher fell.

THE ELECTION WON

What the party was looking for also happened. Its desire, in sacrificing the winner of three elections in order to win a fourth, was satisfied. Here was the greatest vindication of that unprecedented process but also, arguably, of John Major's specific elevation. By ruthlessly changing leaders, the party distracted people from the impression that it had been in power too long. By hoisting to the top a man of the people, Brixton-born and standing on a simple soap-box, it found someone who came across as enough of a popular hero to carry the election. By general consent it was he and not the party that triumphed in April 1992. He came from behind because, in the end, he and not Neil Kinnock was seen as the man to trust. Most objective evidence was against him. Though personal incomes were rising, the economy was in recession. Most opinion polls predicted failure. But doggedness and quiet decency, the anti-Thatcher side of Major, the part that helped the voters forget the past, saw him through.

RULING BY DEFAULT

It was the last time that happened. Victory was astounding and, in the hands of a larger man, could have begun a resolution of the contradictory demands he had to satisfy. Certainly its psychological value was as great as its political importance, and remained a vital private prop to Major's survival through the troubles he now began to face. But seldom has a decisive mandate from the voters bestowed as little vitality as this one did on the Major government. Instead of resolving the post-Thatcher dilemma, it exposed the frailty of the future the Tories thought they had arranged. The anti- or non-Thatcherite attributes Major brought with him were immediately eclipsed by the discovery that the conflicts inherent in Thatcherism lived on. The leader himself turned out to have no clear vision he could call his own. The most divisive problem associated with Mrs Thatcher, moreover, had not been answered by the lady's departure. Finally, what had once been seen as the chief of Major's virtues – his preference for moderate and agreed solutions to hard questions – now became, in the eyes of fickle Tories in and out of Parliament, proof of a weakness that left him ruling more by default than by irresistible presence.

THATCHERISM CONTINUED

It is not quite true to say he had no vision. He did have an idea of the kind of Britain he wanted to encourage, which was in an important respect the reverse of Thatcherite. He had a feeling for the public weal that repudiated the most famous phrase Mrs Thatcher ever uttered: 'There is no such thing as society'. Major's invention of the Citizen's Charter was an attempt to marry the concepts of the consumer society and customer-driven markets with the provision of services which were always going to be, in his view, public rather than private. In place of the Thatcherite premise that all public services were suspect, he started from the assumption that many were an unavoidable obligation of the modern state. He thought they could be reformed, and placed no restraint on the turmoil already let loose in schools or on the introduction of quasi-market principles into the National Health Service. He was also a benign anti-traditionalist in his attitude to openness, permitting, usually against civil service advice, publication of a fair amount of material that might be inconvenient to public servants, from ministers downwards. But the world Major summoned up when speaking from the heart was intensely traditionalist. He liked school uniforms and the three Rs, old regiments and the Great Western Railway, warm beer and a constitution that gave Scotland nothing.

The overwhelming thrust of his policy was, nonetheless, Thatcherite. Although apparently promoted in order to make a fresh start, he was found to have nothing big or new to say. The Conservative party could think of little more than continuing what Mrs Thatcher had begun. It produced yet more anti-trade union legislation, and took privatization into parts of the economy that even she had not tried to reach. The political and practical problems of privatizing British Rail far exceeded any demonstrable economic or social gain from its accomplishment, but the ideological engine could not stop itself going forward. The novelty of a new leadership turned out to be largely cosmetic, a disguise applied to a leader who had rather little of his own substance underneath. In one respect, Major was what he was mean* to be: the nearest available thing to a new front-man for the Thatcher years, the only era he had known as a national politician.

MAJOR THE EUROPEAN

Most of his own administration, however, has been dominated by another left-over from those years, the problem of Europe. This, the issue that drove five men from the Cabinet between 1986 and 1990, proved, after the initial emollience, to be even more problematic for Major than it had been for Mrs Thatcher, its last and most resplendent victim.

Major was a 'European'. He had none of the hang-ups of the post-war generation, nor was he engaged in any of the Euro-arguments of the early Thatcher years. He was too junior and too canny. But he saw Europe as an inescapable framework for real life and proposed, as mentioned, to put Britain at the heart of it. He had already shown his hand as Chancellor, conducting a long campaign for the ear of Mrs Thatcher to persuade her of the case for entering the exchange rate mechanism of the European monetary system. It was one of the few matters about which, at that time, he seemed to care with passion. But when entry was effected, little more than a month before his accession to leadership, he had made himself responsible, prospectively, for one of the events that was to undermine most lethally the credibility of his 1992 election triumph. Only five months later, sterling was forced out of the ERM in circumstances that were not only humiliating but made the Prime Minister and the Treasury look alarmingly incompetent. British membership of the ERM was Chancellor Major's baby. Leaving the ERM was Prime Minister Major's catastrophe. Its consequences for economic recovery, with a helpfully devalued pound, were favourable. But its impact on Major's reputation, and on his strategy for the wider European venture, was grievous for the next year and is unlikely to be erased.

It was also his misfortune to be in post for the final eruption of the Conservative party's conflicted attitudes to the broad question of European integration. Contemporaneous

with the short sharp shock of 16 September 1992, the day the
ERM eviction occurred, was the long-drawn-out punishment
the government endured through much of 1992 and 1993 in
the process of writing and ratifying the Treaty of Maastricht.
The treaty was in many ways a natural extension of the
European venture, its formation of a European Union pre-
figured in the Treaty of Rome, its moves to broaden the field
of integration already exceeded by those put in place under
the Single European Act. Major had succeeded a Prime
Minister who, behind a barrage of anti-European propaganda, bound Britain more closely into the Community than
ever before. Upon him, however, was turned the odium of the
Euro-phobes, led by Lady Thatcher herself, who were in
significant part seeking vengeance for decisions to which they
had been party over the previous twenty years but, it trans-
pired, with which they had never entirely agreed.

Major was fully sensitive to this history. He did not want
a Treaty of Maastricht or any other place. The British
thought most of its likely provisions would be objectionable
or unnecessary. But they knew they could not resist the
continental impulse to have a treaty of some kind, and set
about negotiating one that they could live with. This brought
out one of Major's genuine strengths as a Prime Minister, his
capacity as a man of detail who could rely on being better
briefed than most of his counterparts in an international
forum. Skilful chairmanship – one climax coincided with
Britain's presidency of the Council of Ministers – and clear-
sighted tactics enabled Britain to secure, at modest cost, the
right to opt out of those sections of the European future the
Tory party did not like. Both the social dimension and the
single currency were set aside for future consideration by the
British Parliament, as and when it suited the national interest.
It should have been enough to satisfy all but the most incor-
rigible anti-Europeans, and certainly all Thatcherites with
any respect for consistency.

To expect this, however, was to underrate the power of
history. Enough Conservatives saw Maastricht as the last
chance to set back the European tide, irrespective of what
had been agreed to long ago, for this to become an argument
that almost engulfed not only the Major premiership but the

continuing life of the party itself. Through the first half of 1993, Parliament attended to nothing else. Night after night, the harangues continued and the votes were won and lost. More than once the Government was beaten. By the end it could secure ratification only by putting its existence on the line, and demanding a vote of confidence which even these party rebels, who numbered anything up to fifty, were not prepared to withhold if the price of defeat was a general election.

MASTERY VANISHES

Given the scale of dissidence, this could be considered a success for Major the Whip. It did succeed in burying the ferocities of Euro-antagonism for the next few months, until the 1994 European election came into view. But Maastricht had a strong after-life. The contamination seeped into many corners of the party. What it fostered was a habit of disagreement, which spread through other issues and, more important, into the topmost governing circle. Intermingled with the ideological crisis of Maastricht was the personal crisis of Major. Disagreements over Europe were magnified by a growing belief that he was insufficiently masterful on many other matters as well. Encouraged by strident voices in the Tory press, elements in his Cabinet grew bolder in their expressions of dissent. They sought to set themselves apart. Within a couple of years of taking over, in short, Major's original claim to preside over a unified college of like-minded ministers was set at nothing. His government was riven by faction, ranged on either side of the European divide but spreading wider, into the camps of left and right that Major had not, after all, managed to liquidate.

BASTARDS AT LARGE

Owing his place, originally, to right-wing support, he had been careful to promote its spokesmen. Managing the Tory party in the post-Thatcher period resembled nothing so much as managing the Labour party in the Wilson era, when every reshuffle was inspected for the doctrinal balance it revealed. Michael Portillo and John Redwood joined Peter Lilley as representatives of the unambiguous right, a breed that only made itself felt in copious numbers in the parliamentary party after Mrs Thatcher had gone – such are the time-lags of politics. Junior though they were, these three were bold to make known their view on Europe. Their operations destroyed Major's reputation for equability. Late in the summer of 1993, he was overheard calling them 'bastards' and vowing to undo them. Earlier, there had been a more poignant revoking of what began as a different era. Norman Lamont, Major's campaign manager in November 1990, had been so universally derided in the press and the City after the exit from the ERM that he had to go. The leader waited many months before doing the deed. He did the same with other colleagues, like David Mellor, who got into different sorts of trouble. The delays, perhaps born of too much human decency, did further damage to his reputation in the eyes of a party which, once so relieved to be free of Thatcherite abrasions, now decided it needed more of them. But the dominant aura of Lamont's departure was, once again, European. Furious at being made the scapegoat for the collective failure over the ERM, he marked his departure with a series of sneering attacks on the competence of the man for whom he had once campaigned. His own dismal repute ensured that these were less than lethal. But the danger to Major remained. When Europe reappeared on the agenda, he could no longer rely on emollience or loyalty to guarantee his survival.

Survival, not triumph, will be the leitmotif of the Major administration until its second election. It is banking heavily on economic recovery to float it off the rocks. Resumed growth and gently falling unemployment, against a background of low inflation, offer at least the opportunity for it to re-establish the Conservative reputation for sound economic management. But it contends with massive unpopularity. In February 1994, according to opinion polls, Major was by almost every measure more lowly regarded than Mrs Thatcher had been only a few weeks before she was removed. Fewer than 20 per cent of voters thought he even understood the problems facing Britain. In June 1994, the European election produced the Conservatives' lowest national vote since the beginning of universal suffrage. The famous likeability, the down-to-earth Englishness that won the 1992 election, had evaporated into the blandness of a low achiever about whom, at best, people couldn't give a damn.

Alternative conclusions were drawn from this. One was that the political consequences of economic recovery might be helpfully accelerated by the removal of the leader and his replacement by yet another one. Just as no leader has been promoted so fast in government as John Major, no leader has been identified as a candidate for sacking so soon after victory in an election. The grey man presided over coruscatingly volatile times. Within months of a propaganda exercise to ensure that Labour was not elected, much of the Tory press was shamelessly campaigning on the proposition that the leader they had helped return to Downing Street was incompetent. As well as living through a Parliament bent mainly on his government's survival, Major could seldom escape from daily questions about his own. This was a permanently contingent leader. Whether he could actually be removed was another matter. This is where the prevailing ambivalence came to his rescue. Although it was the anti-European right that manoeuvred against him, the legacy of Mrs Thatcher had conspicuously excluded a field of inheritors to choose from. The potential successors with election-winning potential, Heseltine and Kenneth Clarke, were on the left. In default of a plausible alternative, Major could still expect to survive, if only in the inglorious role of least reviled enemy of the party. Such was the net effect of the Major phenomenon four years on.

CONCLUSION *political domination.*

This, however, is a poor account of his predicament. The truth is that the Major effect is being made in the last four years of a fifteen-year hegemony. It is an appendix to the earlier years and, just as important, suffers from a law of diminishing political returns. Conservative government has lasted a very long time. No government's energy is inexhaustible, and changing the leader, whether for the first or second time, cannot alter that elementary truth. Such a government tends to lose its intellectual vitality, its moral impulse, its political drive. It also grows corrupt. A political system built on the premise of alternating governments suffers strange deformations when no alternative presents itself. The fourth year of Major was marked by a series of discoveries, from the Scott inquiry to the Pergau Dam, all dating back to earlier years, which showed a state of governance that had slipped below the vaunted British standards of probity. Whitehall, like Westminster, was feeling the effects of a party in power too long. So, to judge by opinion polls and by-elections, were the people. They no longer expected much of Mr Major's government. And he expected of the people little more than the chance to remain in power.

Chapter 3

THE CONSERVATIVE PARTY

Anthony Seldon

THE CONSERVATIVE PARTY has dominated the twentieth century, and has been in effective power for all but thirty years of it. It is an electoral force which hungers for office and changes policies, leaders and interests to retain or regain it. The party has experienced four periods of dominance (1886–1905, 1924–40, 1951–64 and 1979 onwards), each of which have been characterized by a degree of decay and conflict towards their ends. The party John Major took over as leader in November 1990 was already in downturn. This position was compounded by the malaise affecting political parties throughout the industrialized world, manifesting itself in a reduced ability to deliver core functions, namely securing members, formulating policy, raising finance, aggregating diverse wishes, delivering the vote and political education. Parties have also failed to perform in two further areas, staffing the government and providing cohesion in the political process between the different branches and levels. These problems were all in evidence before 1990. Under John Major the party has gone some way towards addressing them.

ORGANIZATIONAL CHANGE

Margaret Thatcher had appointed six party chairmen. Her last, Kenneth Baker (1989–90), has been criticized, or scapegoated, by many in the party for his failure above all to control finance. 'Central Office was in a terrible mess by 1990' is a widely-held, and largely fair, view. John Major's brief to Chris Patten as chairman (1990–92) covered politics and finance, not organization, though he quickly appreciated with Sir Hector Laing (joint treasurer, 1988–93) that streamlining the organization would be necessary. Patten's prime objective was to prepare the party to win the general election. In the wake of electoral victory, Norman Fowler arrived as chairman in May 1992 with a clear brief from Number 10 to institute reform to the party organization, the first chairman for fifteen years to have such a mission, as well as to tackle finance. Major gave him *carte blanche* in these tasks. Here was another clear break with Mrs Thatcher, who usually appointed a lightweight chairman for the first two years after a general election (John Selwyn Gummer, 1983–85, Peter Brooke, 1987–89). Unlike Major, she never deep down wanted changes in the party organization, but was constantly interfering with it. Major saw that change was needed, yet rarely troubled those carrying it out. To spearhead the organizational review, Arthur Andersen Consulting were appointed, and from May to October 1992 they conducted over 300 interviews before making their final report. The party boasted that this was 'the widest consultation in the history of the party'.[1]

Fowler himself believed that the two core problems were lack of management and financial control. Andersen's report concurred, and one of its principal recommendations was to appoint two new officers, a director general, in overall charge of the party, and a finance director. Mrs Thatcher had never wanted a general manager at Central Office, and resisted attempts by Tebbit (chairman, 1985–87) to create one. Major had no such qualms. Paul Judge, a highly successful businessman in the 1980s originally from the food industry, was appointed director general in November 1992, and Martin Saunders became finance director. Judge promptly set about his own review, which formed an important part of the report 'One Party', published in February 1993. Published at the same time was 'Working Together', a report into the voluntary party, the National Union, prepared by a working group under the chairmanship of Sir Basil Feldman, chairman (since March 1993) of the National Union.

Central Office slimmed down as a result of the changes. Total staff in Central Office and the regions, numbering 372 in April 1992 during the general election, and about 300 in February 1993, were cut to some 230 by June 1994. Central Office's area offices in England were cut from ten to six, with corresponding staff savings. The Treasurers' Department was brought firmly within the control of Central Office; before it had direct responsibility to the party leader. A new Board of Treasurers was established with a tough-minded financier, Charles Hambro, as chairman. The Campaigning and Constituency Services Departments were separated, the former (under Tony Garrett, chief agent from 1993) to concentrate on campaigning, and the latter to coordinate all constituency needs from the central party, including constituency fund raising, speakers and computer advice. A new Financial and Administrative Department was set up, under Saunders. The two other principal departments, Communications and Research, remained unchanged.

To improve the party's voluntary organizations and its links with other sections of the party, an important new Board of Management was unveiled in February 1993. Appointed by the party chairman, it is in effect the Board of Directors, including senior figures from the parliamentary party, National Union and Central Office. Its aim, to 'bring together the elected, voluntary and professional parts of the party', was a small step also in the direction of party democracy, but not nearly as far as many activists wanted. As with the reorganization at Central Office, the motive for this new structure was financial. The Board of Management has major roles in fundraising and overseeing budgets (although excluded from political matters). Other aspects of the reforms to the voluntary side of the party included the adoption of new titles of 'President' and 'Chairman' of the National Union, opening up the Executive Committee to more constituency chairmen, and an aim to expand party membership, all of which again fell a long way short of the demands of those who wanted to see the party made more democratic.

What has been the impact of these reforms? The improvement in the party's financial position, discussed below, is beyond doubt. Opinions differ, however, about the wider impact. Any initiatives in the early 1990s would have had to labour against the widespread disaffection among activists in constituencies, most of whom did not want to see Mrs Thatcher go. Reconciling themselves to her loss has not been eased by her successor's tangible unpopularity with the media and electorate since 1992. John Major worked very hard to improve links between the voluntary and professional party, and in autumn 1993 went on a number of visits around the country to meet area chairmen and other key activists. His attention bore fruit in warmer relations seen at the 1993 annual party conference and at the Central Council in March 1994 (though the party remains notoriously unwilling to voice discontent, at least in public).

On the other hand, unrest on the line over Europe came sizzling to the fore at the October 1992 party conference; in March 1993 constituencies refused the requirement to submit fuller financial information to the National Union, and in January 1994 criticism of the leadership surfaced again strongly in the comments of Tim Yeo's Suffolk South activists. Membership has continued to decline, from an estimated 1.2 million in 1982 to about half a million in 1994, with an above average decline among the young. At the same time financial support to Central Office from constituencies has fallen markedly. Numbers of full-time agents in constituencies have fallen from 506 in 1959 to 299 at the time of the 1992 general election and 230 in January 1994. Activists reported difficulty finding sufficient volunteers to campaign in the local government and European elections in May and June 1994.[2] Within Central Office itself, morale suffered due to the staff reductions and familiar protests were heard about new bureaucratic and management procedures. One can of course argue that morale throughout the party might have been even lower had the reforms not been instituted. The malaise might indeed be too deep for any structural reform to help. Time alone will tell whether Norman Fowler's successor as Party Chairman can improve the position.

FINANCE

Financial concerns underlay much that the party has done or not done under John Major. In the latter 1980s, the party had received large sums, but it had spent at an even quicker, some would say extravagant, rate. Successive party treasurers had failed to match income (about £50m in the four years to April 1992) to the very high expenditure (about £65m). John Major's arrival at Number 10 came soon after the publication of the party's financial results for 1989–90, revealing the gravity of the cumulative deficit. Central Office received £9.1m in that year, but spent £13.5m. In 1990–91 income rose to £13m, but was insufficient to match spending, which was £18.1m. The annual party conference in 1991 saw widespread concern at the lack of financial control; only part of the high spending could be put down to the expansion and refurbishment of party headquarters (at £3.8m, thought by some in the party to be a reckless figure) and the installation of a new mainframe computer.[3]

The general election in April 1992 further drained resources and left an even higher deficit than before. This was despite curtailed expenditure in the campaign (compared to 1987 levels) resulting in Labour being outspent by as little as £1.5m. Despite considerable efforts, Chris Patten was unable to reduce the deficit, and it was left to his successor, Norman Fowler, to tackle the problem.

The deficit had risen to £19m by March 1993. At the same time the Smith Square headquarters had dropped in value from £12m to about £7m by the end of 1993, causing a severe credit crunch. Fowler adopted a number of strategies to combat the problems. Organizational reform led to some savings. Cutbacks also fell on current expenditure, reduced to the lowest levels in real terms since 1979, severely curtailing the party's propaganda activity. Corresponding efforts were made to increase corporate funding, helped by the improved climate between the party and the business community. Both the rhetoric and substance of government pronouncements were felt to be far more friendly to business than in the mid to late 1980s, particularly towards manufacturing. The CBI published an open letter in 1992, strongly endorsing Conservative achievements. But efforts to increase funding during 1992–94 were still hampered by recession, with little spare cash for industry to give (British Airways was not the only company to suspend payments), and also by industry's perception of the electoral cycle, which disinclined it to be generous without a general election in sight. Donations to the Conservative party came under close Opposition and media scrutiny in 1993–94 as a result of investigation by the Home Affairs Select Committee, in the wake of accusations in 1993 over donations by Asil Nadir. The efforts overall since 1992 to improve the financial position of the party bore fruit in the results for 1993–94, which revealed a surplus on the year of around £2m, the first since the 1980s. The huge deficit of over £16.5m, however, remains.

POLICY-MAKING AND NUMBER 10 –
CENTRAL OFFICE RELATIONS

The formulation of policy is one of the key functions of a political party in opposition, with a reduced role when the party is in government. In the opposition periods 1945–51, 1965–70 and 1975–79, the Research Department (CRD) orchestrated fundamental reappraisals of policy. After the mid 1970s, the role of stimulating new ideas and formulating proposals fell increasingly to the right-wing think-tanks, the Institute of Economic Affairs, the Centre for Policy Studies and the Adam Smith Institute, although their influence can be exaggerated and declined after 1990 (see pp. 155–6).

Who and what filled the vacuum left by the think-tanks for much of 1990–94? Not the party machine, in the main. The Research Department's importance as an independent agent of policy advice had been diminished when in 1979 it moved from its office in Old Queen Street into Central Office, and has been further restricted by the economy-driven reduction of desk officers (the policy staff) from 17 in 1989 to 11 in 1994. The CRD largely confined itself to the task of briefing MPs for parliamentary debates, and support for ministers' campaigning efforts against Opposition policies, an increasingly prominent part of the CRD's work since 1990, as seen in the 1992 election campaign. The Conservative Political Centre, connected to the CRD but a part of the voluntary party, is responsible for running 750 discussion groups nationwide. But their influence, though significant, rarely shifted policy in new directions. The same is true of annual conferences in the early 1990s which, with rare exceptions such as helping to bring about the climbdown in 1992 over pit closures, made little policy impact. Ministers did, however, use it as the forum to announce policy they knew would be popular, as Howard with his crime plan at Blackpool in 1993.

No long-term policy planning took place in the party following the 1987 general election until the summer of 1990, when Mrs Thatcher decided that, with a maximum of two years before the next election, policy groups should be convened. Little progress was made until John Major's succession in November, which unleashed a temporary burst of ideas, including some 'unthinkables' under Mrs Thatcher, such as the further reform of local government finance. John Major also stimulated policy with ideas of his own, principally reflected in the introduction of citizen's charters heralded in his white paper *The Citizen's Charter* of July 1991 (cm.1599). With an election possible at any time from the moment Major took over, the policy groups, meeting under the secretary of state responsible for different areas, worked with some urgency but also conventionality (policy groups chaired by secretaries of state rarely produce radical ideas). The CRD, under whose auspices the policy groups met, produced a first draft of the manifesto in the summer of 1991. But when an election in the autumn of 1991 did not transpire, with Major himself favouring delay, the draft became redundant (to the CRD's chagrin). The Policy Unit at Number 10, under Sarah Hogg, then took over responsibility for producing it, subcontracting some parts out to

Whitehall departments. The final version, approved by a group of senior ministers chaired by John Major, was very much the work of Sarah Hogg, its managing editor, with 'topping and tailing' alone from Chris Patten.

The 1992 manifesto, 'The Best Future For Britain', contains some 350 policy pledges, over twice as many as in 1987, itself a policy-heavy manifesto. The bias in favour of pragmatic and programmatic content reflected the thinking that the election would be won more on the promise of solid and sensible policy pledges than on the offer of further doses of ideology or doctrine. Another motivation was to rebut the expected charge that the party had run out of steam and new initiatives. The principal items in the manifesto included the promise of increased competition in public utilities, the privatization of BR and British Coal, encouragement to home ownership and widening of the EC.

From 1992–94 the small role the party organization earned in policy formation during 1990–91 disappeared again. Policy was made, not by the party, but by and within Whitehall. The origin of 'back to basics' at the 1993 party conference illustrates the hectic nature of Major government decision-making. The plan was to go into the conference fighting on three issues of the Conservatives' choosing, the economy, law and order, and education. But Number 10 produced the words 'back to basics' in John Major's keynote speech, a phrase intended to pull together the broad drift of the strategy. Insufficient thought had been given to the words, which were subsequently invested with interpretations that the hurried process of speech-writing and policy-making had overlooked.

Relations between Central Office and Number 10 fluctuated in warmth. The nadir had been mid 1986. John Major's arrival produced a honeymoon which lasted some months, but feelings cooled considerably during the 1992 election when Number 10 felt that Central Office (and Chris Patten) had fought the campaign very poorly. Relations since were helped by the close personal contact between Major and Fowler, who met formally on party business once a week, and at a lower level by the presence in Number 10 of Jonathan Hill, Major's political secretary since March 1992, one of whose tasks is to provide the bridge between the PM and the party machine. But some other factors militate against the relationship being so effective. Norman Fowler did not sit, at his own request, in Cabinet (he was the first chairman since Peter Thorneycroft, 1975–81, not to have had a paid sinecure job in the government).[4] His absence from Cabinet was a disadvantage in facilitating coordination, as he was unable to represent the party viewpoint in Cabinet deliberations, and vice versa. But the use of 'political Cabinets' (see p. 165) compensated. John Major does not hold regular meetings with the key Central Office heads of department as Mrs Thatcher did to discuss and review political business. Senior staff in Central Office feel to some extent marginalized by Number 10, and the wounds of the 1992 election have still not finally healed. Fowler increasingly found himself called on, as Baker and Patten before him, to defend government policy on the media. His lack of flair at inspiring the party faithful (he was not a popular Chairman), and his own feeling that he had done the job asked of him, informed his decision in June 1994 to resign.[5]

PROPAGANDA

John Major was also one step removed from discussions on propaganda, although in this area it was deemed a relief that the Prime Minister, in stark contrast to Mrs Thatcher, did not interfere. Money, or the lack of it, was the principal factor determining the party's publicity effort after 1990. Even without television advertising, the single most expensive item in campaigning in the US, the costs of publicity in Britain were very high relative to the parties' ability to pay.

The contract with Saatchi and Saatchi had been terminated after the 1987 general election, and for the next four years the party did not enjoy a relationship with a single agency, but hired different production and advertising companies for different contracts. It also consulted Mrs Thatcher's public relations favourite Tim Bell, in particular over the European elections in 1989, for which it employed the agency Allen, Brady and Marsh. Chris Patten wanted to clear away old-style personnel such as Brendan Bruce (communications director) and Harvey Thomas (director of presentations), both of whom left in early 1991. He also wanted to distance himself from Tim Bell, and at the same time to revert to the use of a single agency.[6] A competition was duly held, which Saatchis won convincingly. Maurice Saatchi has since taken a very close personal interest in the account. The 1992 Saatchi campaign, widely criticized at the time for being too negative (e.g. about Labour's taxation plans) has been more favourably regarded since the successful election result.

For almost two years after the 1992 election, there were no newspaper or poster campaigns, and spending on party political broadcasts was reduced. After the election, the experienced TV producer Shaun Woodward gave up as director of communications, and the youthful, though highly competent, Tim Collins took over. The party girded itself carefully for the local and European elections in mid 1994. Analysis by the party of the previous European election in 1989 revealed that despite heavy expenditure, the message was blurred, largely due to party wranglings. The party was still handicapped by divisions, especially over Europe, five years later. It also needed to find cost-efficient strategies for both mid-1994 contests, and decided to opt for greater prominence for the senior ministers most concerned in the campaign, including Major, to show their personal involvement, and to give them a higher profile in the regions and exposure to local media. Two or three press conferences a week were also held from March 1994. But continued restrictions on funding meant that Labour outspent the Conservatives in the European elections, the first time they had done this on a national election campaign. Financial stringency also meant a cutback on the employment of new campaigning techniques (which had been partly stimulated by the Republican Party in the US) of direct mail and greater use of sophisticated computer programmes, prevalent in the 1980s.

PARTY POPULARITY

Measured by the party's popularity ratings, the publicity effort has not been conspicuously successful. The tables reveal a remarkable record of prolonged unpopularity since November 1990, with only two peaks. The first came with Major's initial arrival, when a Labour lead over the Conservatives of 16 per cent in October 1990 was changed to a Conservative lead of 5 per cent in January 1991. In March the Conservatives lost the Ribble Valley by-election to the Liberal Democrats, as the party's lead in the national polls disappeared. The second peak came in April 1992, at the election, when the party reached their high point of an 8 per cent lead, which continued for a further three months.

Party popularity plummeted in the autumn of 1992, and has remained low since. In September the government left the ERM (on 'black Wednesday') and David Mellor resigned, despite Major's attempts to save him. The party conference in October saw Norman Tebbit leading a revolt over the Maastrict bill and the leadership forced into a retreat over pit closures. In November 1992, with Labour's lead rising to a high of 13 per cent, Major only narrowly avoided defeat in the House of Commons over Maastricht.

Fortunes improved in January and February 1993, but then Labour's lead rose to 15 per cent, and the government suffered its first parliamentary defeat on the Maastricht bill, unemployment rose to over three million, and the budget announced that VAT would be imposed on fuel. The Newbury by-election and local elections in May brought little relief, and Major's sacking of Lamont later that month was widely judged to have come too late. The results of the local elections in particular, which saw the party relinquishing control over several shire counties it had held for a hundred years – Kent, Norfolk, Surrey – led to widespread grassroots unrest. In July Major survived a Commons confidence vote on Maastricht in which he threatened a general election if he was defeated, but only days later the party lost the Christchurch by-election to the Liberal Democrats with the biggest swing of the century (35.4 per cent). Media speculation about Major's personal survival due to his lack of leadership skills

VOTING TRENDS

	Con %	Lab %	Dem %	Con Lead +%
1990				
Oct 18–22	33	49	14	−16
Nov 15–19	38	46	12	−8
Dec 27–28	41	45	9	−4
1991				
Jan 18–21	46	41	9	+5
Feb 22–25	44	41	11	+3
Mar 21–25	40	40	16	0
Apr 18–22	42	40	15	+2
May 24–28	37	43	16	−6
Jun 21–24	39	41	15	−2
Jul 19–22	38	43	15	−5
Aug 23–27	42	40	14	+2
Sep 20–24	39	39	17	0
Oct 18–21	39	45	12	−6
Nov 22–25	40	42	15	−2
Dec 27	38	44	14	−6
1992				
Jan 17–21	42	39	16	+3
Feb 21–25	39	40	18	−1
Mar 20–24	38	41	17	−3
Apr 9 (GE result)	43	35	18	+8
Apr 25–28	43	38	16	+5
May 21–26	43	38	16	+5
Jun 19–23	42	39	16	+3
Jul 23–28	39	43	15	−4
Aug 27–Sep 1	41	44	13	−3
Sep 25–29	37	43	16	−6
Oct 23–27	35	45	15	−10
Nov 27–Dec 1	34	47	15	−13
Dec 11–15	34	47	16	−13
1993				
Jan 21–25	37	45	14	−8
Feb 18–22	34	46	16	−12
Mar 25–29	32	47	17	−15
Apr 22–26	32	46	20	−14
May 20–24	28	44	24	−16
Jun 24–28	28	46	23	−18
Jul 22–26	27	44	25	−17
Aug 19–23	28	42	25	−14

	Con %	Lab %	Dem %	Con Lead +%
Sep 16–20	29	43	25	−14
Oct 21–25	29	45	23	−16
Nov 18–22	29	47	22	−18
Dec 9–13	29	47	20	−18
1994				
Jan 20–24	28	48	20	−20
Feb 24–28	28	47	21	−19
Mar 24–28	27	49	20	−22
Apr 21–25	26	47	23	−21
May 19–23	27	46	23	−19
Jun 16–20	24	52	20	−28

Source: MORI

became intense for the first time, as he became the least popular Prime Minister since Gallup began polling in 1938.

The party conference in October 1993 was widely seen as a personal test for John Major's continued leadership. He rebounded with his 'back to basics' message. Kenneth Clarke's November budget, the conclusion of a GATT agreement, and the Major-Reynolds joint declaration in December were all well received, and the Conservative MPs went off for the Christmas recess with a confidence, in particular about the economy, unseen for eighteen months.

Labour's lead in the polls, however, remained high throughout the autumn (16–18 per cent) and soared further in 1994. A series of difficulties, beginning with Tim Yeo's affair in January, the 'climbdown' over the EU enlargement and qualified majority voting in March, which brought press hostility to new heights, and the introduction of tax increases in April, brought little relief. But the local elections in May and the European elections in June and the five by-elections held on the same day produced the worst results for the party since 1945. Cecil Parkinson, a former Party Chairman, described the June 1994 results as very poor. Few Conservatives, in their hearts, would have disagreed, especially as Labour's lead that month soared to a high of 28 per cent.

RIFTS AND DIVISIONS

The party lacked ideological cohesion under John Major, but he was not responsible for the deficiency. The party had lacked ideological cohesion from the moment of Mrs Thatcher's election as party leader in February 1975, and it remained divided ever since. In his senior appointments, John Major has reflected his own essentially pragmatic approach to politics, and has a Cabinet slightly to the left of the Parliamentary party. He has been reluctant to sack discredited ministers (e.g. Mellor, Michael Mates and Lamont) and not loath to promote two men seen at the time as his two main rivals, Kenneth Clarke (Chancellor of the Exchequer) and Michael Portillo (Employment Secretary).

The parliamentary party has been more divided than the voluntary side of the party. Three main divisions can be discerned in the parliamentary party.

1. Europe. The divide between those who resist European integration and those who welcome it, or see it as inevitable, is the deepest divide, and since the late 1980s has cross-cut all other divisions in the party (left/right, wet/dry, etc.).[7] Among those strongly hostile to closer links with the EU are a group of 30 to 50 MPs, including those in Conservative Way Forward, almost all of the 92 Group and No Turning Back, and powerful voices in the House of Lords, including Lord Tebbit and Lady Thatcher. In March 1994, the arch anti-European Sir George Gardiner was re-elected chairman of the 92 Group, seen as a further challenge to Major's line on Europe. The divide is the most serious since tariff reform (1903–24) and the repeal of the Corn Laws in the 1840s. Any Conservative Prime Minister, however brilliant his leadership, would have been severely damaged by it. Major was at least felt to have been tactically astute in the June 1994 European elections in aligning himself more closely with Euro-sceptics. But in doing so he angered some of the party's European enthusiasts, including unsuccessful candidates in the June elections. Peter Riddell discusses the whole issue further in Chapter 4 on Parliament.

2. Reformers versus consolidators. The reformers want to continue maintaining the momentum of the previous fifteen years, when the Conservatives set the agenda on trade unions, privatization and tax. The consolidators are concerned that the pace does not become too frantic, and resist further doses of radicalism, e.g. privatizing the Royal Mail and London buses. They want to see more thought given to policy-planning, and to see legislation better prepared. Among the former in 1994 are natural activists such as Kenneth Clarke, Michael Heseltine and David Hunt, as well as the few Thatcherites in Cabinet, Michael Howard, Peter Lilley, Michael Portillo and John Redwood. Among the latter are Douglas Hurd, Peter Brooke and the three business managers, Tony Newton (leader of the House of Commons) Richard Ryder (chief whip) and Lord Wakeham (leader in the House of Lords).[8]

3. Traditionalists versus modernisers. This is the traditional division within the party between those who wish to see the consensual values to which the party adhered since the war (full employment, welfare state, etc.) followed, and those economic liberals who see the state as hostile, not benign. Among the former are the Lollards and One Nation Tories such as Virginia Bottomley, John Patten and Douglas Hurd. The latter include the Thatcherites in Cabinet and backbenchers such as Edward Leigh. To an extent this divide had been superseded by events, but it is still a deep-seated polarizing force in the party.

All three factions of course overlap. Major could be strongly assertive (pushing ahead with scrapping the community charge) but in general his way of handling the dissent was tactical manoeuvring, not open collision. The existence of these factions caused him difficulties (he is instinctively in the middle of most divides) but also relieve him of anxiety: with so many deep divisions in the party, agreement on a successor remains that much harder to obtain.

CONCLUSION

The Conservative party changed considerably after 1990. Some of the alterations were in train before 1990 (ideological lack of cohesion, loss of membership, minimal party role in policy-making). Others were caused primarily by financial problems (i.e. organizational change, slow-down on adoption of new technology) or a less assertive premier (open challenge to the policies, and personnel, of the leadership). John Major himself has had little detailed impact on internal party organization (in common with most other party leaders), although he empowered the chairmen to make the changes. He is seen as being partly responsible for the decline in the party's popularity, although many other factors contributed to this as well, including the prolonged recession, boredom and staleness after so long a period in office, the unsettling effect of losing such a dynamic leader as Mrs Thatcher, and internal party divisions. The continuous speculation over the leader's future has been unprecedented this century (despite the tightening of the rules, from two MPs to 10 per cent of the parliamentary party required to support a challenger). Some aspects of the party changed little from 1990–1994, including constituency associations, annual party conferences and the limited extent of democracy in the party. The most important factors causing the changes that have occurred are finance, longevity in office, the fact of having a leader without strong authority, and ironically, the legacy of Mrs Thatcher.

Notes

1. Sir Norman Fowler in *One Party* (Conservative Central Office, 1993), p. 6.
2. Interview with Christopher Muller, 24 March 1994.
3. Simon Burgess in Peter Catterall, ed, *Contemporary Britain, An Annual Review 1992* (Basil Blackwell, 1992), p. 39.
4. Stuart Ball in Anthony Seldon and Stuart Ball, eds. *Conservative Century* (Oxford University Press, 1994), pp. 75–76.

5. *Ibid.*, p. 179. *Sunday Telegraph*, 6 February 1994, p. 2.
6. David Butler and Dennis Kavanagh, *The British General Election of 1992* (Macmillan, 1992), pp. 33–34.
7. Andrew Gamble, PSA Paper, March 1994.
8. Peter Riddell, 'Managers versus Meddlers', *The Times*, 21 March 1994.

Chapter 4

MAJOR AND PARLIAMENT

Peter Riddell

THE REAL problem is one of a tiny majority, John Major claimed in his leaked remarks about 'bastards' at the end of the Maastricht saga in July 1993. But he was only partly right. A smaller majority than during the eleven and a half years of the Thatcher era – indeed the smallest Conservative majority in the Commons since the 1951 Parliament – has been only one of his problems. The others have been his own background and temperament and, most important of all, the growing tensions and strains produced by one party being in office for so long.

Parliament could be taken for granted for most of the Thatcher years. But Mr Major has paid, and been forced to pay, far more attention to both the Commons and the Lords, especially since the April 1992 general election. The question 'will the backbenchers accept it' has been heard much more often. The long-established tendency towards greater back-bench independence and assertiveness has continued under the Major government on a range of issues from Europe, via pit closures, to the allowances of MPs and their staffs. Not only have Tory MPs been more fractious and unsettled than before, but the Labour opposition has, at least from time to time, shown more energy and vigour than it did during the long years of three-figure majorities in the middle and late 1980s.

Yet if more of the drama and melodramas of politics have been played out in Parliament than during the 1980s, little of substance has changed in the balance of power between the legislature and the executive. What has mattered has essentially been internal Tory dissent rather than any challenge from the opposition or from Parliament as an institution. The government has still been able to get its programme through Parliament largely unchanged, even if more time has had to be spent cosseting troublesome Tory backbenchers and rebellious peers. Virtually all the lengthy legislative programme outlined in the Queen's Speech after the 1992 election had become law by the end of the long session eighteen months later. Parliament has remained an obstacle course to be circumvented, rather than an insurmountable barrier frustrating the executive.

ROOTS IN THE COMMONS

Mr Major has been particularly sensitive to the mood of Parliament in part because his rise up the ministerial ladder during the 1980s was based upon his ability to read the mood of his fellow Tory MPs. He was extremely skilful in handling MPs, understanding their personal and constituency interests. He has often been described as one of nature's whips, with his preference for conciliation rather than confrontation. During his period in the whips' office from January 1983 until September 1985 he was reckoned to be one of the shrewdest and most effective whips in recent memory.[1] Later, he was favoured by some, including Lord Whitelaw and John Wakeham, to take over from the latter as chief whip after the 1987 general election. Initially, Margaret Thatcher as well had wanted him to take the post. However, Nigel Lawson had been impressed by his work as Treasury whip. So after Mr Wakeham had said he was not interested in becoming chief secretary to the treasury, Mr Lawson asked for Mr Major to become his deputy. If Mr Major had become chief whip, as he himself initially wished, he would not then have had the chance of becoming Prime Minister and he might even have helped to defuse the tensions which ultimately forced Mrs Thatcher out of Downing Street. Throughout his period as a departmental minister, both at social security from 1985 until 1987 and then at the Treasury, Mr Major carried his whip's instincts with him. He always paid close attention to the views of MPs. These were not just his fashionable colleagues and fellow ministers in the Blue Chip Group, but, more significantly, the obscure and unfashionable backbenchers. The respect, contacts and debts which he built up during this period proved to be the bedrock of his support during the second ballot of the Conservative leadership contest in November 1990. He was the ordinary backbenchers' choice.

Since then, as Prime Minister he has similarly taken a close interest in what happens in the Commons: the results on particular votes and the strengths and weaknesses of individual Tory MPs. If some Prime Ministers are still at heart Chancellors or Foreign Secretaries, Mr Major has, at heart, been a chief whip *manqué*. He has been accused of paying too much heed to the views of MPs, of making too many concessions and of not confronting troublesome backbenchers often enough. His critics claim he delayed the final showdown over the Maastricht bill for too long.

In his defence, Mr Major points to his small majority. This has been a constraint but not just in a straightforward arithmetical way. Throughout the Thatcher years, the government could brush aside abstentions and votes against it by a hard core of, say, a dozen of its own backbenchers. Such revolts were usually ignored in the press unless they were on an important issue. It only became a matter of minor note when in a debate on the poll tax in early December 1990, a week after Mr Major became Prime Minister, the government majority fell below 60, compared with its then paper margin of more than 90. Such a drop would have been sufficient to wipe out the government's majority after the 1992 election. However, the 21 majority over all other parties following April 1992 has been less of a constraint than it has appeared for most of the time, even though it fell to 15 in 1994 when the Conservatives lost the Newbury, Christchurch and Eastleigh by-elections.

In practice, the majority has usually been more comfortable since the Tories started the parliament with 65 more MPs than Labour, a larger margin than they had, for example, in 1970. Moreover, the Ulster Unionists and the other minority parties have not often all turned out together to vote against the government. During the final Maastricht bill crisis of July 1993, the nine Official Unionist MPs promised to support the government on votes of confidence and the like. The government whips have, however, had to tighten up to prevent any slip-ups, particularly after December 1993 when Labour suspended normal cooperation in the Commons in a row over the guillotining of two bills. As part of the action, there was an abandonment of normal pairing arrangements which allow Tory and Labour MPs to be away from Westminster on a particular evening. While this meant that some ministers had to cancel visits away from the Commons and MPs without obliging friends on the other side had to hang around late at night in case of an ambush, the breach made no difference to the government's majority.

The drop in the majority has represented more of a potential than an actual threat. It has forced ministers and whips to be more attentive to backbench pressures. A group of would-be rebels could always point out that only a dozen of them would have to vote against the government for it to be defeated. Since there have always been a hard core of half a dozen permanent rebels (starting with Nicholas and Ann Winterton), it is in theory easy to reach that figure. But the threat has seldom materialized. There have been few occasions when ministers have had to make significant concessions to their own backbenchers: the handling of pit closures, some details of rail privatization and the impact on the elderly and less well-off of the extension of VAT to domestic fuel being the main exceptions. Otherwise, Tory MPs have continued to vote for the legislative programme they were elected to support.

PERILS OF LONGEVITY

More important than the reduced size of the Conservative majority has been the fact that the Tories have been in office for so long. It is much more difficult to move from a series of big Commons majorities to a much smaller one than it was for the Tories to move from opposition to relatively small majorities in 1951, 1970 and 1979. In the latter cases there was still the coherence and shared objectives of an opposition team eagerly moving into office. That has not applied since 1992. Rather, the whips have had difficulty persuading MPs to change their habits from the more relaxed days of the 1980s when it did not matter whether a few MPs rebelled.

The longer a party is in power, the greater the number of disenchanted and disaffected MPs there are. There is a growing group of ex-ministers who feel they should never have been dropped and bitter middle-aged members who resent never being asked and who realize that their opportunity has passed. Norman Lamont, for instance, made a resignation statement highly critical of Mr Major's style shortly after he was dropped as Chancellor of the Exchequer in May 1993. Edward Leigh, who was sacked as a junior trade and industry minister in the same reshuffle, turned overnight into a rebel over Europe. As Mr Major vividly remarked in his leaked July 1993 comments: 'Where do you think most of this poison is coming from? From the dispossessed and the never-possessed. You can think of ex-ministers who are going around causing all sorts of trouble. We don't want another three more of the bastards out there.'

The pool of fed-ups grows year by year, and can usually only be cleared out through a period in opposition. The problem has been associated with the growing restlessness of backbench MPs since the 1980s. More and more MPs are now career politicians rather than what have been described as spectators.[2] More depend on politics not just for their livelihood but also for their purpose in life. They want to be something in politics. This is not just reflected in those ambitious to become ministers. The perpetual backbenchers, the rotarian populists, are equally committed to the political life. One outlet for that is being awkward, forcing the whips to acknowledge your existence and attracting media attention by rebellious actions or words. Few of the permanent rebels or the Masstricht opponents have exactly shunned publicity.

THE MAASTRICHT SAGA

These tensions and constraints have come to the fore most over Europe. Disagreements within the Tory party over Europe have dominated Mr Major's premiership as they did the last two years of Mrs Thatcher's. This has in a sense been a mirror image of Labour divisions over Europe during the 1970s and the first half of the 1980s, which were one of the main reasons for the decision of thirty MPs to break away and form the Social Democratic Party. In both cases, the issue of Europe has overridden normal party loyalties. Some MPs have felt so strongly that no amount of cajoling, threats and persuasion by the party whips could induce them to support their party line. In the case of Maastricht, at least two dozen Tory MPs were willing to vote against the Government on all but the final vote of confidence on 23 July 1993. The rebels included a mixture of some of the original opponents of British entry into the then European Economic Community, such as John Biffen, Sir Teddy Taylor and Sir Richard Body; long-established critics of a loss of sovereignty to Brussels, such as Nicholas Budgen (the heir to Enoch Powell's first seat at Wolverhampton); and more recent entrants to the fight, such as William Cash and Michael Spicer, together with the two unofficial whips of the battle, James Cran and Christopher Gill, and Ian Duncan-Smith, one of the few 1992 entrants to stay the course. None were susceptible to pressure from the whips and most faced no difficulties from their local constituency associations.

The Labour party supported the main thrust of the Maastricht bill, though they opposed the negotiated British opt-outs from the social chapter on employment laws and from a fixed timetable towards economic and monetary union. Consequently, Labour felt no obligations to assist the government to get the bill through faster. So an alliance operated between Labour, including both its pro- and anti-European wings, and the Tory rebels. Labour could have got nowhere without the Tory rebels. They voted against both the second and third readings; and with Labour very nearly defeated the government in a key procedural vote to resume the committee stage of the bill implementing the Maastricht treaty. Twice they did help defeat the government (once on a relatively minor matter to do with the composition of the committee of the regions and the other time on a crucial vote in July on the social chapter). Throughout the lengthy committee stage, which dominated the first four months of 1993, the government was constantly in danger of defeat. Hence at various times it avoided confrontations by, for example, not pressing the 10 o'clock motion needed for business to continue beyond 10 p.m. in the evening. On other occasions it accepted amendments in order to avoid the threat of defeat, notably over the social chapter and on some details of parliamentary monitoring of economic policy.

Consequently, as Mr Major argued from time to time, the government was, in effect, in a minority on the bill. He and his whips had to tack and weave, avoiding defeats where they could and occasionally securing alliances with other groups. The Liberal Democrats supplied the votes necessary to carry the paving motion to resume the committee stage by a margin of only three in November 1993. That slim victory also required all kinds of blandishments from the Tory whips, both behind the scenes and on the floor of the chamber as the vote was under way. That prised away some of the more peripheral rebels but it also led to complaints about bullying tactics by the whips, threatening MPs personally and even seeking to influence them via their constituency parties. But there was little that had not been seen many times before, during the Labour minority government of the late 1970s. The overall result was to make the government look weak and not in control, particularly in early March 1993 when Mr Major and other party leaders had criticized the rebels and appealed for unity at a meeting of the Conservative Central Council in Harrogate, only to be rebuffed two days later when 26 Conservative MPs voted against the government and a further 16 deliberately abstained. The willingness of the rebels to push the issue to the brink was shown in July 1993 when 23 Tory MPs voted against the government, and one other abstained, on a key motion on the social chapter which had to be approved if the Maastricht treaty was to be ratified by Britain. This was on one of the most dramatic nights in recent parliamentary history when the first vote was tied, and decided in the government's favour on the Speaker's casting vote (though it later turned out that the government had won by one vote). Then came the government defeat and Mr Major immediately announced that there would be a motion of confidence the next day on the social chapter question. Once that vote was announced, the rebels came back into line, recognizing that the fight was over – though Rupert Allason, a maverick Tory MP, was absent and subsequently faced temporary withdrawal of the party whip.

At the end of the day, the bill was passed – with the British opt-outs intact – and the treaty was ratified.[3] And despite a chorus of demands from usually Tory-supporting newspapers and from Lady Thatcher, the government easily defeated calls for a referendum on the treaty. Most of those involved knew the government would get its bill. Indeed, the Labour leadership privately accepted that all they could do was to delay passage of the bill and cause the government maximum embarrassment, which they duly did. But the Maastricht debate cannot merely be dismissed as a lengthy, and somewhat tiresome, charade which baffled ordinary voters outside the political world. The saga not only seriously weakened Mr Major's authority and leadership but it showed that, on a few, rare issues, the executive can be constrained and restrained by the legislature. However this only applies on occasions when the government cannot rely on the full support of its own backbenchers.

Europe, and the Maastricht bill, were in a sense the exceptions that underlined the general rule: governments can usually have their way. The revolt over pit closures is generally cited as another example of the power of Parliament, but this again was a highly unusual event. The outcry over the scale of pit closures announced in mid-October 1992 was much more to do with the general collapse in public confidence in the government following the humiliation of sterling's forced withdrawal from the exchange rate mechanism than with the future of the coal industry, which served as a lightning rod for public frustration and anger with the government. But these protests, expressed as much from the rural shires as from coal mining areas, had a greater impact when the government's majority was small. Therefore, concerned Tory MPs, such as Winston Churchill, Elizabeth Peacock and Richard Alexander, had much greater leverage by threatening to rebel, and doing so amid great publicity. The government only headed off defeat then by withdrawing some of the closures and promising a review, in conjunction with the Trade and Industry Committee of the Commons. The laborious consultation and discussion certainly forced ministers to pay more attention to the views of MPs than usually happens, but the final package in spring 1993 and the pace of pit closures thereafter were in line with the originally announced plan. This did not really mark a change in the balance between the executive and legislature.

The chief impact of the smaller majority was that the government had to consult more. The main example was over the extension of VAT to domestic fuel. Unusually, the proposed extension was announced a year before it was due to come into effect and without any indication of offsetting measures to reduce its impact on the less well-off. This provided ample political ammunition to Labour and the Liberal Democrats and was widely regarded as an important factor in the Conservative defeat at the Christchurch by-election in July 1993. Consequently, nervous Tory MPs warned of the need to reduce the impact of the tax change and Kenneth Clarke, the Chancellor of the Exchequer from May 1993, and Peter Lilley, the Social Security Secretary, engaged in extensive consultations with Tory MPs about what could be done. The package announced in the November 1993 budget reduced the cost of the extension of VAT for the elderly in particular and ensured that there was no significant rebellion over the measure. But the price was substantial, both in reducing the net gain in tax revenue to the Exchequer and in further eroding political support for the government.

The government had had difficulties over these and other issues, such as rail privatization, not because of the opposition but because of dissent among Tory MPs. The unease of Tory backbenchers also helped force the resignations of David Mellor in September 1992, following revelations about his private life, and of Michael Mates in June 1993 over disclosures concerning his personal links with Asil Nadir, the businessman wanted on serious criminal charges in Britain. A lack of confidence among Tory MPs also contributed to the removal of Norman Lamont as Chancellor of the Exchequer in May 1993. It has remained relatively easy for ministers to brush aside attacks from their Labour shadows.

THE OPPOSITION REVIVES

Nonetheless, the Labour opposition has been more vigorous than at the start of previous Parliaments since 1979. This was partly because of the election of John Smith in July 1992 to replace Neil Kinnock. Mr Smith was a much duller platform orator than Mr Kinnock, but he was a more competent and sharper Commons performer. He showed this during his rare set-piece confrontations with the Prime Minister, notably in the emergency debate on the economy after the Commons was recalled in September 1992 following sterling's forced departure from the European exchange rate mechanism. Mr Smith sparkled then, though his performances were patchier in the twice weekly Prime Minister's questions when Mr Major always has the last word. Overall, however, Mr Smith's interventions in the Commons boosted the morale of his own MPs more than Mr Kinnock's more erratic performances did. That also helped to raise the spirit of Labour supporters out in the country. The record of the Labour shadow team has been mixed. There have been strong performers such as Robin Cook, Gordon Brown, Tony Blair, John Prescott, Donald Dewar, Jack Straw and George Robertson (belatedly rewarded for his skill in handling the Maastricht bill by election to the Shadow Cabinet in October 1993). But others, such as Tom Clarke (first at Scotland and then at Overseas Development) and Ann Taylor (at Education) have been much weaker, providing an easy ride to the ministers they have been shadowing. The Labour effort has been helped by the high quality of many of the new intake first elected in April 1992. The biggest spur to activity has been the government's vulnerability, especially over Europe and the Maastricht bill. This has reduced, but not eliminated, the frustrations of life in opposition. The sudden death of Mr Smith in May 1994 not only stunned Labour but also forced a change of approach. He was the last high level link with the Callaghan cabinet. He also personified reassurance. No potential successor had his experience or could put forward a similar image. Tony Blair, the new Labour leader, had to take more risks: safety-first and personal decency would not be enough. Labour would have to show how it would change Britain.

The other opposition parties have had more impact than their numbers might suggest, mainly because of the government's small majority. The Liberal Democrats, twenty strong at the start of the Parliament and rising to 23 in 1994 after by-election victories, played a key role during the passage of the Maastricht bill, both in sustaining the government on some key votes and opposing it on other occasions. But, in general, the Liberal Democrats have been squeezed out of the limelight at Westminster by the dominance of the two main parties. They have had, as in the past, to look to success in local government and parliamentary by-elections to raise their public profile and opinion poll ratings. The Ulster Unionists have also mattered. The nine strong Official Unionist group under James Molyneaux offered their support to the government in confidence votes following discussions in July 1993 as the Maastricht saga was reaching its climax. The existence of any formal deal has always been denied but Mr Molyneaux has at least been assured of an open door at Number 10. Their role became even more important at the end of 1993 when Mr Major and Albert Reynolds, the Irish Prime Minister, launched their joint initiative to break the deadlock in peace talks.

SELECT COMMITTEES

Away from the floor of the chamber, the government has also had to spend more time dealing with the activities of select committees. The post-1979 system of departmental select committees has now become fully part of parliamentary life. But a number of changes occurred after the 1992 election, largely reflecting alterations in the organization of central government. For instance, the Energy Committee disappeared along with the Energy Department, only to be subsumed into the Trade and Industry Committee, which had a prominent role during the lengthy dispute over the future of the coal industry during the winter of 1992–93. A National Heritage Committee was created along with the department of the same name. To monitor the work of the Office of Science and Technology, now part of the Office of Public Service and Science with its own Cabinet minister, a new Science and Technology Committee was established. After a stalemate during the 1987–92 Parliament when the reduced number of Scottish Tory MPs prevented its formation, a Scottish Affairs Committee was also formed. However, its size was reduced and to make up the number on the Tory side a parliamentary private secretary had to be included, contrary to the normal convention, and Sir Nicholas Fairbairn only agreed to serve if he was also allowed to sit on the Defence Committee. And, in March 1994, a Northern Ireland Committee was established after a lengthy argument which had more to do with the politics of the province than with scrutiny of the executive of Westminster.

The committees were not selected without a furious argument about their membership.[4] The Committee of Selection usually nominates MPs to reflect the overall balance of parties in the Commons. Moreover, understandings are reached between the whips about the balance of chairmanships. But all this was complicated by the government's small majority. The creation of new committees permitted a shifting around of the chairmanships with Labour taking Trade and Industry and the new National Heritage Committee. There were also disagreements about whether former ministers who had recently resigned, or shadow spokesmen, should serve. But more controversial was a suddenly devised rule that no MP could serve on a committee for more than three Parliaments. This was widely seen as an attempt by the Conservative whips to prevent the rebellious Nicholas Winterton from continuing to hold the chairmanship of the Health Committee. An unintended result was to prevent Sir John Wheeler from remaining as chairman of the Home Affairs Committee, though he later became a Northern Ireland minister following the resignation of Michael Mates in June 1993. The whole affair exposed the messy way in which the select committees were chosen and the desire of the whips to retain a continuing influence on behalf of the executive.

There has been less change in the impact of these select committees. The prominence which the Trade and Industry Committee achieved as a participant in the review of the future of the coal industry over the winter of 1992–93 was exceptional and reflected the weakness of the government at the time. Nonetheless, under the chairmanship of Labour MP Richard Caborn, the committee undertook a thorough review despite the sharp party differences over the issue. But in virtually every other case, the rule has remained that the more controversial the subject the less influential is a select committee report in view of the priority of party loyalties. The hearings when ministers and civil servants have been questioned have been far more important. For instance, no one paid much attention when in spring 1993 the Treasury and Civil Service Committee produced a report calling for the resignation of Norman Lamont as Chancellor of the Exchequer. That recommendation emerged because of the absence of several Tory MPs at the crucial drafting session. In general, select committees have had more impact on subjects of less partisan controversy. The Treasury Committee, by contrast, made an impact in December 1993 with a largely bipartisan, well researched and balanced report on the accountability of the Bank of England for monetary policy. The Social Security Committee has, under the chairmanship of Frank Field, influenced the debate on pension funds following the Maxwell affair. A significant change since the April 1992 election has been the higher profile taken by the Public Accounts

Committee under Robert Sheldon, its chairman since 1983. The committee has taken a close interest in allegations of incompetence and sleaze in government, particularly problems in some of the new semi-independent executive agencies created by the reorganization of central government, as well as the changes in the health service and in the running of schools. Its inquiries, supported by the work of the National Audit Office, have identified a number of shortcomings which the committee, unusually, brought together in early 1994 in a report on the conduct of public bodies which attracted widespread attention.

The work both of select committees and of the Commons chamber has been changed by the presence of television cameras. The experiment which started in November 1989 is now irreversible. Its impact may have been as great on the work of committees as on the floor of the House. Mr Major's handling of the Commons has been more exposed to public scrutiny than his predecessors' ever were. He took office a year after televised proceedings began. While the appearance of the cameras has made much less difference to the general behaviour of MPs than many of them had previously feared, or hoped, it has had a greater effect on the party leaders. The main confrontations between the Prime Minister and the Leader of the Opposition, particularly the twice weekly questions, now appear as leading items on the evening news bulletins. This has reinforced the existing tendency towards sound bite partisan politics, with each side cheering on its champion.

The other new feature of parliamentary life has been the election of the first woman Speaker of the Commons after 154 men. Betty Boothroyd was chosen in April 1992 in the first contested election since 1951 with the backing of many Tory backbenchers as well as opposition MPs. She defeated Peter Brooke who left the government at the election in the hope of becoming Speaker. Mr Brooke was informally backed by Mr Major. Within five months he was back in the cabinet as National Heritage Secretary after David Mellor's resignation. Miss Boothroyd has proven to be a firm, and rather earthy, occupant of the Chair with her trademark 'Time's Up' at the end of questions. She has only made one significant slip-up, in her handling of the tense resignation statement of Michael Mates over the Asil Nadir affair in June 1993. Her election has helped to humanize Parliament and make it less remote from the public at a time when there has been growing criticism of Westminster politics and politicians.

THE HOUSE OF LORDS

The government has faced continuing difficulties from the House of Lords. The increased rebelliousness of their lordships which developed in the mid-1980s has continued. This has partly reflected the increased role, and prominence, of life peers, particularly former members of the Commons, who have carried some of their partisan habits over to the Lords. This has been reflected in the expansion of oral questions at the beginning of each day's sitting, as well as in more intense battles over parts of the government's programme. The Lords includes representatives of institutions which the radical policies of the Conservative government have been challenging. Several peers have had close links with the universities, judges, chief constables, rural interests, the disabled and so on. This has produced resistance to, and questioning of, some of the government's more radical legislation.

The classic example came in early 1994 when the government was forced to back down and introduce a series of concessions on the Police and Magistrates' Courts Bill, particularly over proposals to reorganize police authorities. A group of Tory and crossbench peers, initially involving even Lord Whitelaw, the Tory elder statesman, objected to the proposal to confer greater powers on the Home Secretary to appoint members of police authorities, which would reduce the representation of local councillors. But faced with the prospect of five defeats on one night, the government backed down. Conflicts also occurred over the rail privatization bill in the 1992–93 parliamentary session, even though amendments had earlier been made in the Commons.

The House of Lords may have become bolder because of

the unpopularity of the government, but the impact of its protests and rebellions should not be exaggerated. The conclusions drawn by Andrew Adonis[5] still broadly apply: that the Lords has not provided anything but minor obstacles to the Conservative government's legislative programme. There is a distinction between the working and voting Lords. The latter is still dominated by the Conservative party. Opponents of the government are more vocal among the working and speaking peers, while its supporters, both those taking the Tory whip and on the crossbenches, turn out on most key votes. In that respect, the occasional, high profile rebellions are exceptions, however irritating they are to the ministers concerned. Nonetheless, these are exceptions which were virtually unknown during the long period of Tory dominance in the 1950s and early 1960s.

CONCLUSIONS

The impact of Parliament has been different during the Major premiership. This has been more to do with the continuation of the party in office for so long than just the result of the smaller Conservative majority in the Commons after 1992. The factional fighting within the Tory parliamentary party has increased – as shown in the battles each autumn for election to the chairmanship and other offices of the party backbench committees, between the 92 Group on the right and the Lollards on the left. These are largely symbolic posts with little real influence, though the winners have greater credibility with the media to deliver sound bites. The real significance has been that the right has proved to be consistently better in organizing its supporters. The Tory party has become more difficult to manage and that has been compounded by Mr Major's style of leadership, preferring tactical manoeuvring to outright confrontation. While this has sometimes been of necessity, as over Europe, where the government did not have a majority in the Commons for much of the Maastricht bill, it has compounded the party's overall political problems. This has created an opportunity for the opposition to exploit Tory divisions.

The basic character of Parliament has, however, altered little. Philip Norton has argued[6] that despite backbench independence, no significant reforms have been achieved. Though many MPs – though by no means all – favour change, the leadership and authoritative reform proposals necessary for change have been lacking. Just before the 1992 election, the Select Committee on the Sittings of the House, chaired by former Tory chief whip Michael Jopling, recommended a reduction of late sittings and called for timetabling of bills. The report was backed by MPs of all parties, though opposed by traditionalists, including some Labour whips. Tony Newton, the leader of the Commons after the 1992 election, also proved to be cautious and reluctant to move without all-party support, which disappeared when Labour started its campaign of non-cooperation in December 1993 which lasted for more than four months. So little altered in either the procedures or the working conditions of the Commons. This was despite the frustrations of many younger members, particularly those used to different conditions and better resources in local government.

The position of the House has also been under challenge in a different way from the growing powers of European law and institutions following both the Single European Act and the Maastricht treaty. Both increased the powers of the European Parliament, much to the anger of many Westminster MPs. But, apart from protesting, the Commons did little to ensure it had a greater say over developments in Europe. The work of European scrutiny committees in the Commons has been changed since the late 1980s, but they are still largely ineffective, commenting on directives after they have been put forward, rather than when they are being prepared. Westminster MPs are mainly determined to keep their European opposite numbers at a distance. As in so many other aspects of British political life, the Commons has not yet satisfactorily adjusted to Britain's involvement in the European Union.

The Major Effect has been to increase the importance, or at any rate the prominence, of Parliament, but it has not altered the fundamental balance between the executive and the legislature. The executive can still get its way most of the

time, even if it has had to pay more attention to the legislature than during the Thatcher years.

Notes

1. Further discussion of Mr Major's rise in the Commons
   hierarchy is in Bruce Anderson, *John Major* (Fourth Estate,
   1991).
2. For a detailed examination of the motives and attitudes of the
   new generation of MPs see Peter Riddell, *Honest
   Opportunism, the rise of the career politician* (Hamish
   Hamilton, 1993); and Donald Searing, *Westminster's World,
   Understanding Political Roles* (Harvard University Press,
   1994).
3. The parliamentary manoeuvring over the Maastricht bill is well
   covered in David Baker, Andrew Gamble and Steve Ludlam,
   'The Parliamentary Siege of Maastricht', *Parliamentary Affairs*,
   vol. 47 no. 1, January 1994.
4. The debate over the composition and record of select
   committees is discussed by Matthew Cremin, 'Departmental
   Select Committees after 1992', *Parliamentary Affairs*, vol. 47
   no. 3, July 1993.
5. The most balanced view of the House of Lords, puncturing
   much of the hype of recent years, is in Andrew Adonis,
   Parliament Today, 2nd ed. (Manchester University Press,
   1993).
6. Philip Norton discusses the pressures for reform in his chapter
   on the 'Reform of the House of Commons' in B. Jones, ed.,
   Political Issues in British Politics (Manchester University Press,
   1994).

Chapter 5

THE CIVIL SERVICE

John Willman

THE ARRIVAL of Mr Major in Downing Street in late 1990 was greeted with relief by many civil servants. They hoped it would bring to an end eleven years of permanent revolution in Whitehall, with privatizations, staff cuts, pay restraint, efficiency drives and institutional reform.

They could hardly have been more mistaken. Majorism has intensified the pace of change in the civil service. Far from stilling the revolution, Mr Major has spurred it on and backed more radical measures. Indeed, one of his most significant bequests to his successor is likely to be a civil service vastly different from that created by the Northcote-Trevelyan reforms 140 years ago and largely unchanged until recent years.

THE CITIZEN'S CHARTER

At first, Mr Major seemed to speak a language congenial to civil servants. He talked of his commitment to public services and his concern for improving their quality. His big idea was the Citizen's Charter, a campaign to raise the standard of public services.

This was in marked contrast to Mrs Thatcher, who never

troubled to conceal her contempt for the public services. She wanted to roll back the state, to reduce the size of the public sector. The 'entitlement state' was an anathema, part of the British disease. Public services should be cheap and basic, for people who could not afford to provide for themselves.

But while Mr Major differed in believing in high quality public services, he did not accept the traditional view of those who worked in such services that improvements required only an infusion of funds. As he told the Conservative Central Council in Stockport on 23 March 1991, when he first mentioned the idea of a charter, it was the attitude of those who worked in the public services that needed to change.

'People who depend on public services – patients, passengers, parents, pupils, benefit claimants – all must know where they stand and what service they have a right to expect,' he said. 'Where necessary, [we will] look for ways of introducing financial sanctions, involving direct compensation to the public or direct loss to the budgets of those that fall down on the job.'

When the Citizen's Charter white paper[1] was published in July 1991, it was made clear that no new money was available. The aim was to improve standards without extra resources. Each service would be required to set itself performance targets and publish them to users. Independent inspectorates would be created to monitor performance. Managers would be expected to deal sympathetically with complaints. There would be redress for poor service (though not the generous compensation anticipated by some proponents).[2]

There was intense cynicism about the charter in Whitehall, often with open scepticism from ministers. But Mr Major's commitment to his 'big idea' could not be doubted. Like Mrs Thatcher, he paid attention to creating the mechanisms to see through change, in the form of a special unit to implement the programme. Its first head, Brian Hilton, enjoyed the direct access to Number 10 that had made Lord Rayner, Mrs Thatcher's first efficiency adviser, so effective. Regular Downing Street seminars were held to review progress and push forward recalcitrant departments. Those who greeted the charter with cynicism soon found Mr Major breathing down their necks.

MARKET-TESTING

The charter also promised to return to old Thatcherite themes of privatization and competition as engines of efficiency and effectiveness. That Mr Major was serious about introducing market forces into the civil service became clear later in 1991 with the publication of a second white paper, 'Competing for Quality'.[3] This sought to introduce both privatization and contracting-out into Whitehall.

Where services could not be privatized, competition was to be introduced by means similar to the compulsory competitive tendering imposed on local government. This forced councils to put services such as refuse removal and street cleaning out to tender. Henceforth, government departments and agencies would be required to do the same, to see whether private sector contractors could do their work more cheaply and to a higher standard.

At first, progress was slow in drawing up lists of activities to be 'market-tested'. The mandarins saw contracting-out as threatening their empires and challenging established procedures. Companies in the private sector were increasingly constructing flexible relationships between their core businesses and their contracting partners. The approach was, however, alien to the monolithic and centralized civil service.

The closing date for submission of lists was in March 1992, close to the expected general election. Senior mandarins dragged their feet on a policy they had little time for. The anticipated Labour victory in the 1992 election would, of course, remove the threat of market-testing. The political will to drive it through – and Mr Major's attention – was missing.

But after the election, the civil service found that the threat had not gone away. Mr Major had been returned to power fired up with determination to see through public service reform. Indeed, he created a special section of the Cabinet Office to give it teeth, headed by a full Cabinet minister. The Office of Public Service and Science (OPSS) took over responsibility for the Citizen's Charter, executive agencies and market-testing. At its head was Mr William Waldegrave, with the title of Chancellor of the Duchy of

Lancaster. For the first time civil service reform was considered important enough to be represented at the Cabinet table.

THE SACKING OF SIR PETER KEMP

An early setback in the new world of the OPSS came with the breakdown in the relationship between Mr Waldegrave and the man appointed as its first permanent secretary. This was Sir Peter Kemp, the mandarin who had been responsible for the creation of executive agencies to deliver central government services. Kemp was an unconventional civil servant: he was not a graduate and had joined the civil service from the private sector; he was a rare accountant at Grade 1 level. As Next Steps project manager, he had successfully cajoled departments into creating executive agencies along the lines set out in the 1988 Next Steps report.[4]

However, even his admirers felt that the mercurial Kemp was temperamentally unsuited to running a department, and that his skills would be better used elsewhere. The final cause of the breakdown in his relationship with Mr Waldegrave may be established only when the relevant papers emerge into the public domain in 2022. That it did break down is indisputable, as was the failure of Sir Robin Butler, Head of the Home Civil Service, to find an alternative billet acceptable to Kemp. The upshot was that a Grade 1 permanent secretary was effectively sacked, a rare (though not unprecedented) occurrence at such a senior level of the civil service.

The immediate effect was to send a frisson through Whitehall over the relationship between top mandarins and their ministers. But it sent another signal that was perhaps more subversive to Mr Major's reforms; the chief advocate of change had been sacked. Or, as Kemp put it with his customary sharp humour, 'The guards are in charge of the escape committee ... The only heads that have rolled have been among the revolutionaries.'[5] His sacking was widely seen as the revenge of the college of cardinals, the twenty or so permanent secretaries at the head of Whitehall departments whose empires he had threatened.

If they thought that they had seen off the threat, Whitehall's finest were quickly disabused. The OPSS's new permanent secretary was Richard Mottram, an iconoclast from the Ministry of Defence. Mottram was one of the 'Keele connection', a group of Keele graduates now reaching the top of the Whitehall machine, displacing the cream of Oxbridge on the way. With his eye firmly fixed on the top job at Defence, Mottram was keen to make a success of civil service reform.

Mottram, Waldegrave and Sir Peter Levene, the Prime Minister's efficiency adviser, pressed ahead with drawing up lists for the first tranche of market-testing. They were more successful than many had expected: the first programme, published in November 1992,[6] promised to put almost £1.5bn of civil service work out to tender. This would force 44,000 civil servants to compete for their jobs. Mr Waldegrave predicted that the programme would cut costs by 25 per cent.

Progress on this first tranche of market-testing was slow initially, partly because it represented a new world for departments unused to contracting out work. There were also difficulties over European legislation that protected the terms and conditions of those whose jobs were contracted out. But by the end of 1993, around £1.1bn of the programme had been completed.[7] Some £850m of work had gone to outside contractors, with just £190m going in-house. Savings of over 20 per cent were claimed. A further programme worth £830m covering another 35,000 civil servants was announced for the second tranche.

Market-testing was here to stay as a tool for improving civil service efficiency. Apart from the cost-savings, many departments were also able to demonstrate improved service quality. The very act of calling for bids forced managers to define the service they were providing and to set performance targets for the successful bidder. Traditional ways of doing work were questioned. The civil service was moving towards 'government by contract', a concept urged upon it by Graham Mather, president of the European Policy Forum and an influential Conservative adviser.

THE PRIVATIZATION OF AGENCIES

One by-product of market-testing was a move to privatize some of the executive agencies created by Mrs Thatcher under the Next Steps programme. The creation of agencies had accelerated under Mr Major, with more than half the civil service now in around a hundred agencies. They had become relatively uncontentious politically, enjoying cross-party support from the House of Commons Treasury and Civil Service Committee.[8]

The market-testing exercise had, however, led to the privatization of DVOIT, the Department of Transport's IT agency. This had been sold off to EDS-Scicon, the US contracted services company, with several contracts to provide IT services to various parts of the department and its agencies. Other agencies, such as the Transport Research Laboratory, the Patent Office, Companies House and various DTI research laboratories, were expected to follow.

The increasing role of the private sector in taking over government services was recognized explicitly in a December 1993 white paper on executive agencies.[9] This pointed out that with another fifty or so executive agencies in the pipeline, around three-quarters of civil servants would soon be in agencies. Each agency was operating as a discrete organization, with its own chief executive and board, delivering services under contract to Whitehall. If some agencies had already been privatized or identified for privatization, others ought to be similarly considered.

The mechanism for this was to be what Whitehall called the 'Prior Options Review', carried out before setting up a new agency. The questions which formed the basis of the review ran as follows:

- Was the activity really necessary at all? If not, the civil service should stop doing it.
- If the activity was necessary, could it be privatized?
- If it could not be privatized, could it be contracted out to the private sector?
- If none of these options could be followed, only then should an agency be created.

In the past the answers to the first two questions had

often been cursory and agencies had been formed as a matter of course. In future, alternatives to agencies were to be examined much more carefully, with the private sector invited to come in and advise during the prior options exercise. Existing agencies and quangos would face similar questioning at their periodic reviews which normally occur every three years. There was now a stronger presumption that more would be sold off or otherwise privatized.

It was an open secret in Whitehall that Number 10 had pushed the OPSS into this more radical strategy. Mr Major and his advisers feared that agencies had become an end rather than a means to an end. The white paper made clear that the creation of agencies was only a step towards further change in which public services would be increasingly provided by private sector organizations. Privatizing the utilities during the 1980s was seen to be a singular success that would now be repeated for core public services.

CHANGE AT THE TREASURY

There was backing for this more radical approach from the Treasury. Stephen Dorrell, the Financial Secretary, had launched what he described as 'a long march through Whitehall' in a November 1992 speech. His thesis was that the government had tended to look at the civil service and ask itself what should be privatised. The real question to be asked, he said, was why any agency should not be privatized – what was there about it that meant it had to be done in the public sector?

Previous Treasury ministers may have paid lip service to the creation of agencies and the privatization of government activities. But under Sir Peter Middleton, permanent secretary between 1983 and 1991, the Treasury had been highly sceptical about the creation of agencies. It saw them weakening budgetary control over important parts of the civil service. Agency chiefs complained bitterly of interference in their activities by Treasury officials who seemed unwilling to let them run their own shows.

The mood changed, however, when Sir Terry Burns took over as permanent secretary at the Treasury in 1991. Burns, a laid-back northerner, had joined the civil service only in 1980 from the London Business School where he had been an influential economic forecaster. Not only was he non-Oxbridge, he eschewed the traditional Treasury desire to keep its fingers in every part of the public expenditure pie. He saw the Treasury's role as akin to the corporate headquarters of a business conglomerate: it should exert strong financial discipline over departments and agencies by allocating budgets and setting challenging performance targets. But it should leave management to get on with the job, with incentives for success and penalties for failure.

With Burns in charge at Great George Street and Dorrell anxious to establish his radicalism, the Treasury began to lose its reputation as the bank that liked to say 'No'. The message coming from corporate HQ was that privatization and government by contract were now in.

THE CORE CIVIL SERVICE

Market-testing also demonstrated another trend. In almost a third of market-tests, the work had been put out to tender without an in-house bid.

With the Inland Revenue IT division, for example, a ten-year contract worth around £200m a year was awarded to EDS-Scicon after a bidding round that excluded the existing management team. Those tax staff who wished to continue in the IT field were offered the opportunity of transferring to EDS. But Revenue management had taken a strategic decision to contract the work out, mainly because they felt that future IT development would be better done by private sector specialists.

It was clear that market-testing was beginning to make senior civil service managers think more like private sector managers who had been refocusing their businesses on core activities for over a decade. Ministers and their top civil servants could be heard saying that data processing, systems development, property management and a raft of other activities were not core work for the civil service. Increasingly, civil servants would stick to what they were best at – giving policy advice to ministers and implementing their decisions.

The November 1993 white paper gave form to this trend with the concept of a core civil service in which all but the core activities would be contracted out. It sketched out a vision of the civil service of the future in which just 50,000 civil servants – 10 per cent of the total – would do the jobs traditionally associated with Whitehall such as policy making and policy execution. Around them would be a penumbra of organizations, contracting to provide services. Some of these would be agencies, others private sector contractors. Increasingly, there would be several organizations competing for contracts.

To give the mandarins an incentive to think radically, Kenneth Clarke, the chancellor, announced a three-year freeze in civil service running costs in the November 1993 budget.[10] The £20bn allocated for Whitehall's running costs would not increase before 1997 (and perhaps not even then). Funds for pay rises, extra staff or higher costs would have to be found from within existing resources. To help them manage this tough task, departments and agencies were to be given control over staff pay, their biggest cost. The notion of a unified civil service, based on common pay and grading, would gradually fade as top managers re-engineered their empires to cope with this new pressure.

One other nugget was also buried in the November 1993 budget, the introduction of resource-based accrual accounts to replace the traditional civil service cash accounting. This would make it much easier to compare the costs of the public and private sector, since both would account for costs and assets using similar rules. Many parts of the public service that had sat on hitherto 'free' land and buildings would find that their costs under the new accounting system were hugely uncompetitive. The pressure to streamline – or contract out activities – would become irresistible once such figures were available.

CIVIL SERVICE MORALE

Not surprisingly, this ongoing revolution hit the morale of the civil service. The most obvious manifestation was the strike against market-testing called by five unions on 5 November 1993. Around half the civil service took part in the biggest industrial action since the 1981 pay dispute.

Less public had been the demoralization at the most senior levels. Top civil servants were not prone to strike action, but they had made their unhappiness felt through their trade union, the Association of First Division Civil Servants. The First Division Association, under its energetic and telegenic general secretary Elizabeth Symons, publicly raised the concerns of top mandarins over the direction of the reforms.

Unhappiness at the highest levels was confirmed with the premature resignation of two high-flying permanent secretaries. In November 1993, Sir Geoffrey Holland announced his departure from the Department for Education after barely ten months in the post and a glittering career as head of, first, the Manpower Services Commission and, then, the Department of Employment. It was widely reported that he had fallen out with John Patten, the Education Secretary. Too much time was spent fire-fighting, dealing with problems over issues such as school testing which many in the department felt were self-induced.

In March 1994, Sir Clive Whitmore, top man at the Home Office and a former principal private secretary to Mrs Thatcher, announced he was also off before retirement age to an unspecified 'well-paid' job in the private sector. Unlike Holland, Whitmore circulated a memo to his officials denying a rift with his secretary of state, Michael Howard, the Home Secretary. But there was no doubting the unhappiness among many senior Home Office mandarins over the Home Secretary's robust approach to law and order.

Even the Foreign Office, in the safe hands of the unflappable Douglas Hurd, was not immune from fear and loathing. An unprecedented meeting of London-based staff was summoned in January 1994 to hear the Foreign Secretary attempt to soothe fears about the future of the diplomatic service.

The anomie in Whitehall was amplified by the progress of

the Scott inquiry into the arms-for-Iraq scandal. The interrogation of civil servants in public by Lord Justice Scott and Presiley Baxendale, his steely counsel, set what many saw as a dangerous precedent. Senior mandarins such as the urbane Sir Robin Butler seemed ill at ease in trying to account for their actions on a public forum. The time-honoured traditions of Whitehall, of economy with the truth and loyalty to the government of the day, appeared to be under attack.

PUBLIC ACCOUNTABILITY IN WHITEHALL

Behind such sentiments lay a recognition that Mr Major and his colleagues had inherited one central assumption of Mrs Thatcher's administration. This was that the performance of the civil service had contributed to Britain's decline. Politicians could not be blamed for all the country's ills: civil servants must also take their share of the blame. A new culture was needed in which the civil service was much more openly accountable for its performance.

One aspect of this was a drive for greater openness in government, something that Conservatives had instinctively shied away from in the past. But government by contract involved giving much more information about what was expected of different parts of the public service. Agencies, for example, were set performance targets in their framework documents, and encouraged to produce annual reports describing their achievements. Other public services were required by the Citizen's Charter to define the standards they aimed for and to publish their success in achieving them.

This openness was further extended in a white paper on open government published in July 1993.[11] It introduced a code of practice on the provision of government information that would require departments to publish facts and analysis behind major policy decisions. Subject to a list of exemptions to cover matters such as security and commercial confidences, the presumption was to be that official information should be provided unless there were good reasons for withholding it.

It was not the Freedom of Information Act that many had campaigned for, and the degree of change involved would depend on the interpretation of the exemptions. Internal discussion, opinion and advice were still to remain confidential, for example, because it was 'widely accepted as being consistent with the public interest'! But the white paper clearly committed the government to 'a more open administrative culture' and to much greater openness than ever before.

There was no doubt, either, that it was Mr Major who was behind the move. As a symbol of the new era, several veils around the security services were lowered in 1993, including the publication of a guide to the three main intelligence services. Stella Rimington, head of MI5, the security service, staged a photo call for the press. And Sir Colin McColl, then head of MI6, the secret intelligence service, was the first 'C' to give a press conference (though he refused to be photographed).

CHANGES AT THE TOP

Exposing the workings of Whitehall was only one element in increasing the public accountability of Whitehall. The other was the process by which top mandarins were appointed and their performance monitored. Radicals, such as Graham Mather of the European Policy Forum, looked enviously towards New Zealand, a Westminster-style democracy that had gone much further in moving towards government by contract. There, permanent secretaries were now employed on three- or five-year contracts, with explicit performance targets and rewards linked to their achievement.

In Whitehall, the top positions were still filled by prime ministerial appointment, largely on the recommendation of the head of the civil service. This secretive approach left the civil service strangely out of kilter with the rest of the public sector where open advertisement of top jobs – and rigorous procedures to ensure that they were filled on merit – were routine.

Even after fifteen years of radical reform, it appeared that Whitehall was still controlled by the old establishment. Despite the arrival of men such as Sir Terry Burns and Richard Mottram in key permanent secretary jobs, most of the Whitehall departments remained under the sway of men educated at public school and Oxford or Cambridge. The generalist remained in control, moving from job to job without ever being required to demonstrate a track record in a specific discipline.

In practice, this caricature probably underestimated the degree of change at the top in Whitehall. Many of the public schools attended by the twenty most senior permanent secretaries were formerly direct grant grammar schools which had been in the state sector when they passed through them. Since Oxford and Cambridge routinely cream off many of the most able university entrants, it would have been strange if many of the top mandarins did not come from them (as do many top business executives). And several permanent secretaries could now include substantial non-civil service jobs in their CVs.

Yet the senior open structure of the civil service remained largely a closed caste. Sir Robin Butler, the man at its very top since 1987, in many ways epitomized this: a former head boy at Harrow, he took the traditional generalist's Double First in Mods and Greats at Oxford. He had never worked outside Whitehall, and was steeped in its culture and practices. The idea of bringing a complete outsider in to run a Whitehall department – as is commonplace in business – was still unheard of.

The same was not the case, however, in the executive agencies. Most of their senior posts were already advertised openly and filled by open competition. A growing number had gone to candidates from outside the civil service, bringing in talented managers from business and other parts of the public sector. In 1992, for example, Derek Lewis, the former chief executive of Granada, the leisure group, was appointed director of the Prison Service agency, one of the most challenging and high-profile jobs in the civil service.

Mr Major was keen that something similar should happen in Whitehall departments, to bridge the divide between the civil service and the rest of society. A report from the Cabinet Office efficiency unit on top appointments in the civil service[12] promised to open many more top posts to outsiders. All top jobs were to be considered for open competition and publicly advertised. Personal contracts were to be introduced for the most senior mandarins, with pay linked more closely to success in meeting objectives such as greater efficiency.

POLITICIZATION OF WHITEHALL

Such changes again raised the threat that the appointment of top civil servants could be politicized, 140 years after the Northcote-Trevelyan reforms had eliminated political placemen. It was not that ministers openly sought to appoint political supporters to top jobs (though some did). Rather, it was the new performance culture which encouraged top managers to take a leadership role in agencies and departments, with hefty performance bonuses for pushing through controversial reforms. It was hard for senior officials to avoid becoming overly identified with their ministers in such circumstances.

This concern was voiced repeatedly during the inquiry of the Commons Treasury and Civil Service Committee into the role of the civil service in 1993 and 1994. Its interim report expressed fears that the essential civil service values of objectivity, independence and political neutrality were being undermined.[13] The final report, due in the autumn of 1994, was expected to call for some sort of code of conduct for civil servants to spell out their duties and values in an era of change.

There was also growing concern over the consequences of the reforms for the public service ethos. One symptom was an adverse report from the powerful all-party Commons Public Accounts Committee on the conduct of public business.[14] This warned that the pace of change in the public services threatened traditional values of probity and accountability in the handling of public money.

Critics used the PAC report to imply that there was a

fundamental incompatibility between the values of the private and public sectors. The former, with its emphasis on profit, was unaccustomed to public scrutiny and justified the spending of money by the bottom line it achieved. The latter had to be accountable to the taxpayers for how money was spent – and those taxpayers were entitled to demand equality of treatment in its use.

In fact, the report was worded carefully to avoid saying that, but its message that efficiency and effectiveness could be increased without throwing out traditional public sector values was drowned out by the political skirmishing. Furthermore, a series of reports from the National Audit Office highlighting shady practices and waste of public money indicated that some of the reforms had been rushed through with inadequate attention to the traditional demands of public accountability.

PARLIAMENTARY ACCOUNTABILITY

One other concern over the direction of reform was a weakening of the mechanism of parliamentary accountability. Some MPs – notably Labour's Gerald Kaufman – protested that the creation of agencies was letting ministers escape their responsibility to Parliament. Parliamentary questions on agency performance were routinely passed directly to the agency chief executive for reply. The minister became involved only if an MP was unhappy with the answer. Many MPs found this procedure preferable, since it cut out the middleman: answers were given, and complaints cleared up, often more promptly by going direct to the agency.

But it was ministers who were accountable to Parliament, not civil servants, the critics pointed out. This was more than a constitutional nicety: if ministers no longer dealt with MPs' letters, they would become out of touch with what was going on. Alarm bells would take longer to ring when something went seriously wrong. Indeed, this is exactly what happened when the Benefits Agency became swamped by claims for a new benefit for the disabled in 1992: it was some weeks before the situation was brought under control, while MPs' mailbags bulged with constituents' complaints.

Another symptom of the decline in accountability was the proliferation of quangos, quasi-autonomous non-governmental organizations set up to deliver public services. Mrs Thatcher had waged war on quangos, cutting the number of non-departmental public bodies (NDPBs) from 2,167 in 1979 to 1,539 in 1990. But reforms of the public services created a new generation of quangos such as the NHS trusts, grant-maintained schools, independent further education colleges, Training and Enterprise Councils, housing action trusts and the rest. Overall, the number of quangos was rising again, to 2,134 in 1993, with 1.2m staff spending £43bn a year. They accounted for one fifth of public expenditure, a larger share than in 1979.

Many of these new quangos fulfilled functions previously carried out by elected local authorities. In most cases, their members were appointed by ministers and accountable to Whitehall, rather than the local people whose needs they were supposed to meet. The fact that some of these quangos provided the worst instances of waste of public resources in the PAC report added to the view that they were not really accountable to anyone at all.

HOW MUCH HAS CHANGED?

Whatever the pessimists said about the demise of the British civil service, it was still possible to arrive at very different conclusions. There were critics on the right of the Conservative party who maintained that too little had been done to shake up Whitehall. They saw it as the last bastion of privilege, left relatively unscathed by fifteen years of Thatcherism and Majorism. After the initial surge of Mrs Thatcher's onslaught, the machine had fought off or neutralized the Conservatives' reforming zeal.

Evidence in favour of that thesis was provided by civil service numbers. Mrs Thatcher had succeeded in cutting the civil service from 730,000 in 1979 to a post-war low of

562,000 by 1990. Since then, the number had barely fallen to 554,000 in 1993.[15] All of the drop in later years had been in the blue-collar civil service, the industrial civil servants who worked mainly in defence establishments. The number of white collar civil servants, 503,000, had scarcely fallen since 1984.

This was in strange contrast to what had happened in other parts of the economy, as a study by the European Policy Forum pointed out.[16] The civil service had fallen in numbers by 7.3 per cent between 1987 and 1993. Banks, similar people-intensive, administrative organizations, had cut their staff by 16 per cent between 1989 and 1993. Both had experienced rising workloads over these periods. The EPF's conclusion was that the civil service had yet to adopt the efficiency standards of the private sector.

Yet a new determination was apparent in the way that the reform programme was being pursued. Ministers were now looking to much more radical steps forward in the civil service, with privatization, contracting-out and a refocusing on core activities. Top civil servants, too, would be forced to adopt those methods if they were to live within their frozen budgets. For all Mr Major's smooth talk about the importance of public service, he had shown a determination and single-mindedness in reforming the civil service that was often absent in other policy areas.

Mr Major could claim that his period as premier had not only consolidated the Thatcher reforms, but had taken them much further forward. A new model of the civil service was emerging, which had already been seen in prototype in some local authorities. This was the 'enabling state', the core of central decision-makers who funded public services, set standards and monitored performance. Unlike the civil service of the Northcote-Trevelyan reforms, this reformed civil service did not aim to also deliver those services itself. Instead, it bought them in from competing organizations in the public, private and voluntary sectors – government by contract, in other words.

It remains an unfinished revolution. It is also not yet irreversible: a Labour government would be able to call a halt to the process of change and reimpose a measure of centralized planning on the civil service. Whether it would be wise to do so is another matter: public administrations around the world are 'reinventing government' along similar lines to the UK Conservatives. And there is no evidence that lower standards of public administration are a necessary consequence of such reforms, properly implemented.

However, the real test of Mr Major's success in changing Whitehall would be judged from the response of top mandarins to any attempt to reverse the forward march of reform. If they become convinced of its advantages for clarity in policy-making and standards in public services, then they would be the most effective opponents of counter-revolution. That point has not yet been reached, however. Mr Major could be right in his repeated assertion that it will take a decade for his reforms to make a lasting impact.

Notes

1. *The Citizen's Charter – Raising the Standard*, Cm 1599 (HMSO, London, July 1991).
2. For example, in the collection of Adam Smith Institute essays edited by Dr Madsen Pirie: *Empowerment – The Theme for the 1990s* (ASI, London, 1991).
3. HM Treasury: *Competing for Quality – Buying Better Public Services*, Cm 1730 (HMSO, London, November 1991).
4. Efficiency Unit, *Management in Government, the Next Steps* (HMSO, London, 1988).
5. Sir Peter Kemp, *Beyond Next Steps* (Social Market Foundation, London, November 1993).
6. *The Citizen's Charter – First Report: 1992*, Cm 2101 (HMSO, London, November 1992).
7. *The Citizen's Charter – Second Report: 1994*, Cm 2540 (HMSO, London, March 1994).
8. See, for example, Treasury and Civil Service Committee, *The Next Steps Initiative, Session 1990–91, 7th report* (HMSO, London, July 1991).
9. *Next Steps Agencies in Government – Review 1993*, Cm 2430 (HMSO, London, December 1993).
10. HM Treasury, *Financial Statement and Budget Report 1994–95 (The Red Book)*, HC 31 (HMSO, London, November 1993).

11. *Open Government*, Cm 2290 (HMSO, London, July 1993).
12. Efficiency Unit, Cabinet Office, *Career Management and Succession Planning Study* (HMSO, London, December 1993).
13. Treasury and Civil Service Committee, *The Role of the Civil Service – Interim Report*, Vol. 1: Report, Session 1992–93, 6th report (HMSO, London, July 1993).
14. Committee of Public Accounts, *The Proper Conduct of Public Business*, Session 1993–94, 8th report (HMSO, London, January 1994).
15. HM Treasury, *Civil Service Statistics, 1993 Edition* (HMSO, London, December 1993).
16. European Policy Forum, *Civil Service Numbers* (London, October 1993).

Chapter 6

LOCAL GOVERNMENT

Ken Young

T HE FALL OF Mrs Thatcher and her replacement by John
Major – the first ex-councillor to attain the premiership
since Clement Attlee – might well have been expected to have
immediate effects upon local government. The contrast
between Mrs Thatcher's long-standing antipathy to local
councils and her successor's personal experience of and
apparent sympathy towards them could not have been
greater. Moreover, Michael Heseltine's challenge to her
leadership, which culminated in John Major's succession,
had drawn considerable impetus from hostility to the poll tax
among Conservative MPs, a tax which Heseltine, and in turn
Major, pledged to abandon. This pledge, above all others,
would have to be honoured, and quickly.

Anxious nonetheless to dispel any impression of poll tax
abolition as a politically convenient quick fix, Heseltine
presented it as one arm of a three-part strategic review of
local government. The search for 'accountability' which had
fuelled the poll tax fiasco could be diverted into a plan to
restructure on the basis of 'unitary' authorities (thus avoiding
the weakened accountability of precepting), with clearer
management and more identifiable leadership.[1] Such sentiments scarcely amounted to a policy. Yet, against all reasonable expectation, and perhaps against reason itself, they led
the Major government to involve itself in a tortuous

approach to an historically intractable problem: the reform of local government structure.

The ultimate political consequences of this episode will not be apparent for some years. In other respects Michael Heseltine's zeal for administrative reform and new initiatives had more immediate effects. One such was the much-publicized City Challenge scheme, which marked the Environment Secretary's return to his old stamping ground of urban policy with the diversion of urban programme and other funds into a new national competition. Instead of comparative need, the ability of local authorities to spend imaginatively in support of economic regeneration and community development was to be rewarded. To many, City Challenge seemed a short-lived programme, unlikely to outlast its author. But the principle of competition and the emphasis upon developmental capacity have all the signs of a genuine innovation.

These new ventures compounded rather than replaced the pressures of the Thatcher years on local authorities. None of the requirements of the pre-Major period were abated: the scope of compulsory competitive tendering continued to be extended and financial stringency became still tighter, while important changes in community care and education were pressed forward. Overall, the first years of Major government coupled new initiatives to an acceleration of policies which were already in place when he entered 10 Downing Street.

POLL TAX AND AFTER

Few major policies in modern times have been so hurriedly adopted, and as promptly abandoned, as the community charge or poll tax, and none with greater political consequence. The poll tax debacle underlay the ebbing of Mrs Thatcher's support and thus Major's triumph in November 1990, even if it played a lesser role in precipitating the fateful contest than the more elevated debates over Europe. The tangible relief of Conservative MPs in marginal seats made this first consequence of John Major's election the most remarkable instance of the politics of instant gratification.

The effects of the introduction of the poll tax in April 1990, the huge expense of transitional relief at £3 billion, the vigour, even violence, of the reaction against the tax, and the wild inaccuracy of its predicted levels, all served to demonstrate that its proclaimed virtues of fairness and accountability were largely discounted by the public, if they were perceived at all.[2] Within the party many of those who, like Sir Rhodes Boyson, had originally applauded the poll tax scheme were, in the space of eighteen months, pushed by the mechanics of its introduction into opposition.

With at most two years to run to the next general election, a sizeable minority of Conservative MPs recognized that their political futures were linked inextricably to the poll tax.[3] The 1990 leadership stalking horse, Sir Anthony Meyer, was a poll tax rebel who had voted against the second and third readings; Heseltine's views were well known. Former local government minister Sir George Young ensured that the case against the poll tax was put from the back benches with unanswerable authority. Thus, the question of the poll tax came to permeate the mounting speculation over the alternative to Mrs Thatcher.

RIGHT THIS TIME? MAJOR'S COUNCIL TAX

The poll tax played no particular part in Michael Heseltine's campaign in the first of the leadership ballots, although he was on the record as promising a review of this Thatcher 'flagship'. But by the time the three candidates – Heseltine, Major and Hurd – contested the second ballot, there was nothing between them on the need to replace it. Major had been advised to follow Heseltine's position on this critically important issue for, in Norman Lamont's reported view, a commitment to abandon the poll tax would be crucial to victory.

Dropping poll tax was, then, the first and most unequivocal of the 'Major effects'. Apart from Heseltine himself, who accepted the offer of a cabinet post as the price for withdrawing from a punishing and unwinnable third ballot, other notable poll tax rebels were to join the Major government then or soon after: Sir George Young, Michael Mates, Robin Squire, Tim Yeo. Commentators dwelt lovingly on the irony of Mr Heseltine rejoining the cabinet in his original place at Environment, being thus responsible for delivering a more acceptable alternative to the tax he had long opposed. But, in the event, the Major cabinet was prepared to lubricate the process with such generosity that Mr Heseltine had scarcely too much discomfort.

On 17 January 1991 the government announced a further £11m support to keep poll tax levels down in what was hoped to be its second and final year of operation in England. This stopgap move was followed by the budget statement in March which announced an across-the-board reduction in poll tax bills of £140, to be funded by a 2.5 per cent increase in value added tax. The sting was drawn, though at the price of a further shift in the balance between the central and local sources of revenue in favour of the centre.[4]

A week after the budget, Michael Heseltine unveiled his proposals in 'A New Tax for Local Government'. Significantly, the illusion of a 'charge' was dropped. A hybrid of the rating and poll tax systems, the new council tax would consist in equal parts of a property and a personal tax, the former based on capital value, the latter on a presumed two-person household, with a discount for single persons. The business rate, already nationalized and redistributed to local authorities as grant, would remain unchanged.

The strongest objections to the poll tax were met at a stroke by this announcement. There would be no need for a register. The notion of a universal charge with a fixed 'floor' was abandoned in favour of rebates. The property basis gave an element of stability and predictability, while easing collection. Michael Heseltine made considerable play of these virtues in his 21 March announcement, urging that the new tax met the requirements of accountability and fairness better than its short-lived predecessor.

Yet it was not to be all plain sailing. The banding of

property values did rough justice, and reproduced some of the earlier anomalies of the rating system, with high valuations in the Conservative south. In April the government announced a seven-band scheme; at the end of the month it abandoned consideration of a possible nine-band scheme; in July the scheme was finalized at eight bands.[5]

So rapid a pace of policy development was bound to leave the government exposed to critics. The transition, with introduction in 1993 coming on top of increasingly desperate efforts to collect the residue of the vanishing poll tax, would be predictably difficult, although this was not a point which had much electoral force. Neither did the overall outcome – an 80:20 division of central and local funding of local government – although it recognizably locked the government into a system of virtual direction of local expenditure, and thus troubled some critics.

The Heseltine rescue operation was celebrated, even by his critics, as one of political astuteness tempered by high financial and constitutional costs. Would it work? Was it, in the words of the formidably expert Institute of Fiscal Studies, 'right this time'?

The doubts soon set in, partly because the council tax enjoyed the advantages, and suffered the disadvantages, of both the systems – property and per capita tax – of which it was a hybrid. Michael Heseltine made much of the by-now obligatory claim of enhanced accountability when announcing the changes, although the council tax was not evidently superior to the universalist doctrine that underlay the poll tax.

As to his second criterion of fairness – by which he had consistently implied relation of the tax level to ability to pay – the new tax, while preferable to the poll tax, nevertheless has less margin of superiority than at first appeared. The value of property occupied is a poor indicator of personal resources, while the banding of values provided for only modest progressiveness. The verdict of the IFS was that council tax was a highly regressive system, made palatable only by virtue of the system of benefits. But with poll tax safely buried, these shortcomings were of more interest to political and professional commentators than to the Major government itself.

CONTROLLING LOCAL EXPENDITURE

Whatever the score on the criteria of fairness and accountability set down by Heseltine for a better local tax, the council tax and its associated adjustments secured the government's over-riding aim: the tighter control of local authority spending. In this regard John Major and Michael Heseltine shared Mrs Thatcher's preoccupation with restraining spendthrift, generally Labour, local authorities.

'Restraint' was the fifth of the five criteria for an acceptable tax which Heseltine set out in March 1991. Clearly, the steeper the gearing, the more marked the restraint. Following the introduction of the council tax, the gearing ratio averaged 7:1 nationally; that is to say, it would require on average a 70 per cent increase in council tax to fund a 10 per cent increase in local expenditure. But reliance upon this relationship is in actuality the least important of the restraining bonds which the Major government has placed upon the local authorities.

First – and here the trade off between accountability and restraint is at its most evident – local tax levels are crucially affected by the standard spending assessment (SSA), whereby central government determines how much a local authority should spend, service by service, to provide a standard level of service nationally. From this total is subtracted the distribution of the business rate (NNDR) and the level of council tax necessary to achieve the standard spend, and the balance is met by the government in the form of revenue support grant (RSG). The SSA is not only a powerful mechanism of control, it is open to political manipulation to ensure that the electoral effects of the annual expenditure round are as beneficial as possible.

Secondly, the council tax level itself is open to being effectively set by ministers through the powers of universal capping taken in April 1992. When the provisional SSAs are announced around December each year, the Secretary of State announces the criteria he will use to decide whether or not a particular authority's budget is 'excessive'. Authorities are then expected to regulate themselves by working within these limits; to do otherwise is to risk having the minister's figure substituted for their own.

Introduced by Michael Heseltine and further refined by Michael Howard and John Gummer, these new arrangements represent a tighter control on local authority expenditure than existed previously. For example, for 1994–95 the local authority associations argued for a total standard spending settlement (TSS) of £46.2bn. Treasury pressure pushed the DoE down to an even lower figure than hoped for, £42.7bn, a figure substantially less in cash terms (once the earmarked community care funds are subtracted) than the 1993–94 budget totals. The result has been to bring most authorities close to the risk of council tax capping and budget cuts.

Finally, control over borrowing for capital expenditure has been further tightened, with basic credit approval (BCA) forced down dramatically between 1992–93 and 1993–94, and with the option to fund capital projects out of local revenues effectively precluded by the council tax capping arrangements. From the point of view of the Treasury (and Mr Major's own term of office there was of formative influence upon him) the Major government has scored considerable success in achieving tighter control of local expenditure.

The settling of the poll tax issue has made this easier to attain; it is no exaggeration to say that the principal effect of John Major has been to realize the aspirations to constrain local expenditure which Mrs Thatcher voiced when she first assumed the leadership of the party in 1975. Yet, paradoxically, her ends were achieved by Major through the abandonment of her means. The failures of the fumbling attempts at financial control from 1980 had led directly to the logically appealing – because notionally self-regulating – poll tax as a system 'without "targets" ... "penalties", "holdback", "slopes" or "thresholds"'.[6] The difficulties of making poll tax work, together with backbench inclination to abandon it when the going got rough, led inescapably back to direct control.

REDRAWING THE MAP

If John Major's abolition of poll tax was the apogee of
political good sense, the accompanying local government
review certainly balanced the account. There was no demand
for local government reorganization and while the Heath
government's reforms in 1972 had greatly weakened the
party at the time, there was no reason to suppose that
undoing them now would bring much advantage.

The origins of the local government review appear to be
threefold. Firstly, there was Michael Heseltine's predisposi-
tion to action, for which local authorities, with their complex
structures and cumbersome processes, provided an irresistible target. Second was the persistent search for accountability, in which the division between revenue collection (at
the district level), and the greater proportion of spending
(through precepting, at the county level), was inferior to the
unitary pattern found in London and the metropolitan areas.
Third, Environment Secretaries since Nicholas Ridley were
not disposed to tolerate the Labour-controlled artificial
'counties' of Avon, Cleveland and Humberside. Although
they already possessed the power to guide the Local Government Boundary Commission towards abolition (and had
used it in the case of Humberside), the existing review process
was laborious, and its outcome uncertain. The temptation to
seek more immediate and certain results, and to do so across
the country, was compelling.

The essence of the structure proposals which followed the
advent of the Major premiership can be briefly summarized.
In Scotland and Wales the respective Secretaries of State
published proposals for comment, aiming to achieve a
rationalization into a smaller number of single tier or 'unitary' authorities. Particular political advantage was seen to lie
in the abolition of the Scottish regions, especially the huge
and powerful Strathclyde Regional Council. The proposals
were published in January 1992, and firmed up for Scotland
in October 1992 and for Wales in March 1993. Legislation
was introduced in the autumn of 1993.

In England an independent Local Government Commission was established with a brief to review the entire country

(outside London and the metropolitan areas) in stages, producing locally-appropriate solutions, but with a presumption in favour of a unitary structure. Within this framework an improbable blend of Majorite sentiment was developed (a rather gushing emphasis on community, on parish government, on choice, on letting local people decide) and Heseltine style (the extensive use of consultants to formulate guidance for the English Commission and the appointment of former CBI director general John Banham to lead it). There was never much doubt as to which would prove the more powerful force.

The Banham Commission was given some easy targets for the first phase of its work, including the Isle of Wight, where the case for a unitary authority was almost self-evident, and the artificial counties of Avon, Humberside and Cleveland. Thereafter, a rather leisurely process of review in a further series of four 'tranches' was envisaged, the end-date of 1997 reassuring some authorities that the tide of change was unlikely ever to reach them.

If this starting point for the review process seemed uncontentious enough, it nonetheless soon began to disintegrate under the pressure of its own contradictions. Either unitary authorities were everywhere appropriate or they were not; and either it was for the Commission to judge this or it was not. Unhappily for the government, and infuriatingly for Commission members, these ambiguities clouded the relationship between them, to the delight of their critics in local government.

In May 1993 the Commission proposed replacing Cleveland with four unitaries, and in June the twenty-three authorities in Avon, Gloucestershire and Somerset with eight. In November the Commission proposed a mixture of two-tier and unitary authorities in Derbyshire and in Durham, claiming that a unitary model alone was inappropriate to the more rural parts of these counties. In that same month local government minister David Curry warned of a 'strong chance' that the Commission's recommendations might be 'some distance' from the government's wishes, and in December Environment Secretary John Gummer tossed the Avon/Somerset/Gloucestershire proposals back to the Commission, asking them to think again.

The original commitment to enhance community, elegantly expressed by Lady Blatch in the second reading debate on the Local Government bill, quickly became the target of widespread scepticism, not least because initial consultants' work on identifying community areas seemed to offer little practical guidance. The use of consultants to write guidance for the Commission had from the first seemed curious, and by the summer of 1993 the central role of the several consultancy firms involved was drawing considerable criticism.

By mid 1993 the review process had few friends, and the conflicts between John Gummer and John Banham – who was reported as hovering on the brink of resignation – were well-publicized. Kenneth Clarke's PPS accused the Commission of misleading MPs. *The Guardian* reported that Conservative backbenchers were calling for the review to be abandoned. That the 1993 elections virtually wiped out Conservative control in the English counties, leaving them with the sole bastion of Buckinghamshire, scarcely weakened the gradual rise of Conservative indignation.

Recognizing a losing position when he inherited it, John Gummer sought to wind down this unpopular and uncontrollable initiative by putting the review on a voluntary basis, with councils opting-in. However, in September 1993 *The Independent* reported that Major had overruled Gummer; instead, the timescale was to be foreshortened, and the Commission asked to complete its work by the end of 1994. To the critics, this simply compounded the error, raised the stakes, and ensured that the political backlash would come with full force this side of the general election.

The Association of County Councils, speaking for the most obvious losers, warned that the end result of the review would be a loss of efficiency and higher costs. The insistence on creating unitary authorities clearly spelt doom for the county councils, which in the past had proved the backbone of Conservatism. In the spring of 1994 Douglas Hurd dramatically rocked the boat with his public support for retaining the county of Oxfordshire, while Conservative peers comforted themselves with the knowledge that proposals to dismember the historic county councils would be difficult to get unscathed through the House of Lords.

The English review process was, then, a precarious undertaking from the outset. Indelibly identified with Michael Heseltine, few other ministers took much interest when it was launched. That John Gummer should have wished to dilute its force suggests that he was in touch with grassroots party feeling on the issue; Major's own determination to drive it forward suggests that he was not. The local government review promises John Major no political gains, but contains the potential for repeated humiliations in Parliament.

MODERNIZING MANAGEMENT

If the abolition of poll tax and the launch of the local government structure review distinguished Major's approach to local government from that of Mrs Thatcher, the third new initiative, the review of local authority management, appeared to signal a still more radical break by taking local government seriously and seeking to strengthen its leadership and authority.

The consultation paper on the internal management of local authorities, which Heseltine published in July 1991, set out the government's objective of promoting more effective, speedier and more businesslike decision-making; strengthening scrutiny and enhancing public interest in local government; and enabling councillors to devote more time to their constituency role.[7] To these laudable ends a series of options for internal structural change were proposed, including a shift to a 'Cabinet' type system of local government, or even the creation of elected mayors to provide a focus of executive authority.

These ideas were not new. They had been bandied around by Peter Walker a quarter of a century earlier, and were generally dismissed by Conservatives with an understanding of local government.[8] The justifying references to the practices of other countries giving rise to greater effectiveness merely underscored their author's unique combination of Europhile sentiment and American style. Civil servants thought the proposals scarcely credible and, after Heseltine made his hoped-for move to the Department of Industry to be replaced by Michael Howard, were no longer obliged to pay homage to them. Referred instead to a worthy joint working party of officials, the sublime rhetoric of the original Heseltine conception was soon reduced to modest municipal dimensions.[9]

A CHARTER FOR CONSUMERS

In yet other respects the local government management initiatives of the Major government converged with, and took forward, the Thatcher legacy. Indeed, the greatest impact upon local government management is to be found in Major's continuation of Mrs Thatcher's approach to local service delivery. This emphasized strengthening parents, tenants and service users against providers, opening out the decision-making process by 'empowering customers', and pressing still further with the requirement to submit local service provision to the disciplines of compulsory competitive tendering.

The cumulative effect of the reorganization of housing, education and social services has been profound, and would not have occurred without the Major government's apparent zest for management and service reform. They have brought about a transformation of structure, process and style in the great majority of authorities, a transformation which is almost exclusively attributed to central government's recent requirements.[10] Rightly anticipating the force of continuing change under Major, Keiron Walsh writes that

> In future the vast majority of services will be affected, in one way or another, by contracting and market mechanisms. Financial and accounting systems will need to change, and organisational structures will be transformed. The local authority will become a network of overlapping and inter-linked contracts.[11]

The underlying principle which runs through these changes in management is the separation between purchaser and provider roles. Its effect has been to promote the development of internal markets within local authorities, to sharpen awareness of value for money on both sides of the purchaser/provider divide, and insinuate the language of consumerism into public service provision.

Nevertheless, most public service providers remain monopolies, and it is in recognition of this feature that Major launched his own personal initiative – the Citizen's Charter – to strengthen the hand of consumers. In his foreword to the published Charter document, the Prime Minister generously recognized that many developments in improving public services and making them more responsive to their users occurred during the 1980s; his new initiative was intended, he wrote, 'to carry these reforms further and onto new territory'.[12]

That new territory was at first more easily reached in central government than at the local level, and all national public bodies were required to frame a response to the demands of the Charter. Local authorities' own responses were generally lukewarm, not least because Labour local authorities were more attracted to developing local charter initiatives along the lines of that pioneered at York. Accordingly, the Major Charter was not reckoned a great force for change within local government, although the principle of locally-originated charters rapidly gained ground.

If Labour in local government was hoping to thereby deny John Major a propaganda victory, the party was doomed to disappointment. In 1992 the government placed a statutory requirement upon the Audit Commission to issue a legal direction to local authorities to report 'Citizen's Charter Indicators' in a form prescribed by the Commission. Neatly reflecting the prime minister's own concerns, the Commission warns that

the Citizen's Charter presents local authorities with a challenge they should not ignore. It offers them an opportunity to use the publicity generated to develop an informed dialogue with their residents about the services they offer and the policies they adopt. This is the start of a process which could help to strengthen local democracy, by empowering people with information and increasing their interest in local affairs.[13]

THE MAJOR EFFECT ON LOCAL GOVERNMENT

One particular expression of interest in local affairs, the propensity to vote against Conservative candidates, has proved uncomfortable for John Major. Indeed, one of the most direct effects that any Prime Minister has on local councils is to produce an election outcome that, for better or worse, reflects his or her own national standing. Major's electoral honeymoon proved shortlived, but few observers were prepared for the scale of the defeat which the Conservatives suffered in the May 1993 county council elections.

The party lost control of fourteen counties, including flagship Kent CC, in what was conceded to be a disaster beyond all expectation. Once the heartland of Conservatism, the polls left the party with only 968 county councillors on the 47 councils (a net loss of 473), with the Liberal Democrats close behind at 874 and Labour well ahead with 1,388 councillors. The district, London and Metropolitan borough elections in May 1994 provided a reverse of similar proportions. The Conservatives lost 428 seats and control of 18 councils. However else these results may be read, it is clear that they represent no kind of judgment on Conservative policies for local government. Their significance is to the contrary: the fewer Conservative councillors there are to offend, the fewer the inhibitions on radical action.

The track record so far suggests that there is little to distinguish between the actions taken under Major and those which might have been expected from a fourth Thatcher government, as far as pressing ahead with the competition requirements and thus continuing the Thatcher revolution is concerned. On local finance, the abolition of the poll tax has enabled John Major to out-perform his mentor and establish an unprecedented degree of central control over local spending. Only the local government review, with all its potential for embarrassment and acrimony, stands out as the kind of institutionalized indecisiveness that Margaret Thatcher could not have contemplated.

All Prime Ministers are prisoners of circumstance to some degree, and the presence of Michael Heseltine at Marsham Street was a circumstance of particular force in shaping the Major administration's initial approach to local government. In one particular, however, the Prime Minister's own personal stamp has been unmistakable: the launch of the Citizen's Charter. The Charter requirements for local authorities, which come into effect in 1994, represent the most personally attributable of all the Major effects on local government. Unlike the abolition of poll tax and the achievement of greater central control over local spending, they are unambiguously this former Lambeth councillor's *own* achievement. Like their author, they are modest, but by no means insignificant. There is little doubt that they will outlast his premiership to leave an enduring mark on the relationships between local authorities and the people they purport to serve.

Notes

1. Department of the Environment, *The Structure of Local Government*, (HMSO, London, 1991); *The Internal Management of Local Authorities*; (HMSO, London, 1991).
2. John Gibson, *The Politics and Economics of the Poll Tax: Mrs Thatcher's Downfall* (Warley, EMAS Books, 1990).
3. Alan Watkins, *A Conservative Coup: the Fall of Margaret Thatcher*, 2nd edition (Duckworth, London 1992).
4. Financial details in this chapter are largely drawn from the *Council Tax Guide* (1994) and the periodic *Council Tax Facts* published by the Local Government Information Unit. See also 'From Rates to Council Tax', *INLOGOV Informs*, vol. 2, No. 2, 1992.
5. Keiron Walsh, 'Local Government', in *Contemporary Britain: An Annual Review, 1992* ed. P. Catterall, Blackwell, (Oxford 1992).

6. Margaret Thatcher, quoted in Shirley Robin Letwin, *The Anatomy of Thatcherism* (Fontana, London, 1992), p. 187.

7. Department of the Environment, *The Internal Management of Local Authorities* (1991). Similar papers were published by the Scottish and Welsh Secretaries.

8. For evidence as to the absence of support for these proposals among councillors of all parties, see Ken Young and Nirmala Rao, *Coming to Terms With Change? The Local Government Councillor in 1993* (Joseph Rowntree Foundation, 1994).

9. Department of the Environment, *Community Leadership and Representation: Unlocking the Potential* (DoE, London, 1993).

10. For detailed survey evidence gathered across the country in 1992/3, see Ken Young and Liz Mills, *A Portrait of Change* (Local Government Management Board, Luton, 1993).

11. Keiron Walsh, 'Local Government', in *Contemporary Britain: An Annual Review, 1993* ed. P. Catterall (Blackwell, Oxford, 1993).

12. *The Citizen's Charter: Raising the Standard*, Cm 1599 (HMSO, London, 1991).

13. Audit Commission, *Citizen's Charter Indicators: Charting a Course* (The Commission, London, 1992).

Chapter 7

ELECTORAL BEHAVIOUR

Ivor Crewe

THE BRITISH electorate has presented two contrasting faces during John Major's four years as Prime Minister. The period up to 15 September 1992 ('Black Wednesday'), when the foreign exchanges bundled Britain out of the European exchange rate mechanism, was the longest electoral honeymoon for a post-war British prime minister. Despite the deepening recession, Conservative support bounded back and remained remarkably buoyant up to and through the election it unexpectedly won in April 1992. John Major himself was widely liked and trusted, despite – or perhaps because of – his grey ordinariness. The period after Black Wednesday, by contrast, has turned out to be the longest electoral nightmare for any post-war British premier. Conservative support has plummeted in the polls. The government was humiliated in local and Euro-elections and crushed in every by-election. Voters decided that Major was not decent and dependable but weak and useless. Conservative backbenchers and editors blamed their party's misfortunes on him and called for his head.

This electoral transformation has led to two connected assumptions about a 'Major factor'. The first is that Major was the architect of the Conservatives' recovery in 1991 and victory in 1992; the second is that he was the architect of the Conservatives' slump in 1993 and 1994. The rest of this chapter charts the turnaround in voters' attitudes, examines a range of explanations, and questions the assumed importance of the Major Factor.

THE LONG HONEYMOON, NOVEMBER 1990 TO MARCH 1992

John Major's replacement of Margaret Thatcher transformed the Conservative party's electoral position overnight (see Table 1).[1] Although the party did poorly (but not disastrously) in the 1991 local elections and lost four by-elections – Ribble Valley, Monmouth, Kincardine & Deeside and Langbaugh – its standing in the polls recovered dramatically. In the Gallup 9000 poll for October 1990, just before Geoffrey Howe's resignation triggered the leadership crisis, the standing of the parties was Conservative 34, Labour 46, SLD 13. In the Gallup 9000 poll for December 1990, after Major's accession, it was almost reversed: Conservatives 45, Labour 39, SLD 11 – a 9 per cent swing from Labour to Conservative. Thereafter Conservative support was remarkably stable, rising slightly during the Gulf War in early 1991, ebbing back in the summer and autumn. It stayed ahead of Labour in ten of the fifteen months, the parties' average standing being Conservative 40, Labour 38. In the fifteen months prior to Mrs Thatcher's downfall, Labour had led the Conservatives throughout, and the average was Conservative 34, Labour 46. Thus voters continued to use by-elections and local elections to protest against the government's performance, but their attitude to a fourth term of Conservative government was open-minded. The electoral atmosphere was completely different.

The shift of electoral mood owed far more to Thatcher's departure than to Major's arrival. Major was an obscure figure to the voters, an unexceptionable politician who had risen without trace. Before the leadership election, according to contemporary polls, Major was, on balance, an electoral liability: his becoming leader would make 11 per cent 'more inclined' to vote Conservative but 19 per cent 'less inclined'

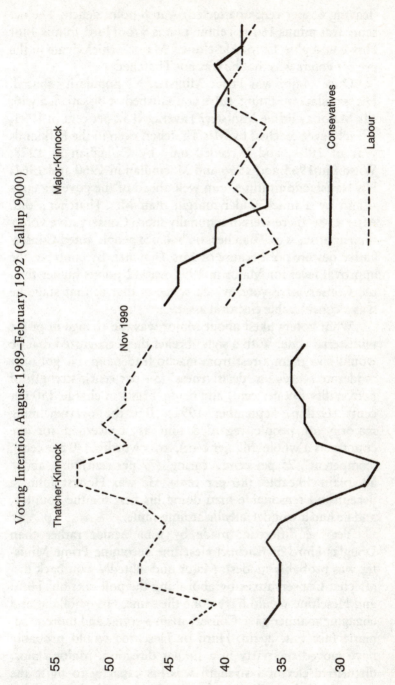

Voting Intention August 1989–February 1992 (Gallup 9000)

Conservatives

Labour

Major-Kinnock

Nov 1990

Thatcher-Kinnock

55

50

45

40

35

30

25

(leaving 65 per cent unaffected) – an 8 point deficit. The net score was minus 16 for Tebbit, minus 8 for Hurd, minus 4 for Howe and plus 17 for Heseltine.[2] Major's chief virtue in the eyes of voters was that he was not Thatcher.

Once Major was Prime Minister, his popularity soared. His 'satisfaction rating' ('Are you satisfied or dissatisfied with Mr Major as Prime Minister?') averaged 52 per cent in 1991, a level never reached by Mrs Thatcher, even in the Falklands year of 1983, and exceeded only by Callaghan in 1978, Wilson in 1965 and 1966 and Macmillan in 1960 and 1961. His 'satisfaction ratings' ran well ahead of the government's – and by a much wider margin than Mrs Thatcher's did. After 1986 there were fractionally more Conservative voters than approvers of Thatcher: on balance people voted Conservative despite not because of Mrs Thatcher. By contrast, the approval level for Major in 1991 was 12 points higher than the Conservative vote, which suggests that at that stage he was a considerable electoral asset.

What voters liked about Major was the change in prime ministerial style. With a sigh of relief they recognized that he would give them a rest from macho leadership. He got only moderate scores on 'decisiveness' (54 per cent), strength of personality (49 per cent) and being 'firmly in charge' (50 per cent) (Gallup, September 1991). But the overwhelming majority of people regarded him as 'concerned for the country as a whole' (67 per cent), 'trustworthy' (70 per cent), 'competent' (75 per cent), 'caring' (77 per cent) and, above all, plain 'likeable' (86 per cent). He was Honest John, a decent and reasonable man doing his best for the country; and he had a wonderfully disarming smile.

Yet the difference made by John Major rather than Douglas Hurd or Michael Heseltine becoming Prime Minister was probably modest. Major undoubtedly won back disaffected Conservatives by abolishing the poll tax; but Hurd and Heseltine would have done the same. His emollient and engaging manner gave Conservatism a softer and more pragmatic face but, again, Hurd or Heseltine would probably have moved the party in a similar direction. Major's most distinctive electoral strength was his capacity to unite the party. He belonged to no faction, bore no ideological label and had made few enemies. He was an instinctive healer and party broker (he had, after all, been a whip). Most crucially, as the contender favoured by Thatcher, his election helped to reconcile Thatcher's supporters to her downfall. But as a general election approached, the party would probably have closed ranks irrespective of the leader, at least temporarily.

Conservative support would almost certainly have recovered under any of the contenders to replace Thatcher. When Thatcher was Prime Minister voters thought in terms of 'Mrs Thatcher's government' as much as 'the Conservative government'. By changing the Prime Minister, the Conservative party could present itself to the electorate as a wholly new government. At the general election sixteen months later, when Gallup asked people 'who or what is most to blame for the recession?' 48 per cent replied 'the worldwide economic recession', 43 per cent 'the Thatcher government' and only 4 per cent 'the Major government' (6 per cent said 'don't know'). By changing their leader – albeit for the former Chancellor of the Exchequer – the Conservative party was absolved of past sins and given a new period of grace.

THE 1992 ELECTION: MORE CONTINUITY THAN CHANGE

Favourable comparisons of Major to Kinnock played a prominent part in the media's coverage of the 1992 election campaign and its immediate verdict on the unexpected outcome. 'If you want fireworks,' the *Daily Mail* advised its readers, '– Kinnock. But for guidance and judgment, Mr Major looks a good deal safer.' 'When the chips were down,' the *Daily Express* gloated, 'it was John Major the voters knew they could trust.' Major's sincere, un-flashy style of campaigning, it was argued, eventually got through to ordinary voters. Kinnock's strobe lights were no match for Major's soap-box.

It is true that voters decidedly preferred Major to Kinnock as prospective Prime Minister. Gallup asked: 'Leaving aside your general party preference, who do you think would make the best Prime Minister?' People replied: Major 52 per cent, Kinnock 23 per cent, Ashdown 24 per cent – a much larger advantage for Major than Thatcher had had over Kinnock in 1987 (42 per cent to 31 per cent) or over Steel in 1983 (46 per cent to 35 per cent). Moreover, whereas the proportions preferring Thatcher and voting Conservative were almost identical in 1983 and 1987, the proportion preferring Major as Prime Minister was substantially *higher* than the proportion who actually voted Conservative on the day. John Major was a stronger electoral asset than Margaret Thatcher and it seems plausible to infer that were it not for his leadership the Conservatives would have fared worse.

In fact, Major's personal boost to the Conservative vote was probably very small. His lacklustre campaigning – so heavily criticized by the Conservative press *before* election day – did not impress voters at the time: asked immediately before the election to say which leader had 'campaigned most impressively so far', people's replies were: Ashdown 41 per cent, Kinnock 30 per cent and Major 17 per cent.[3] A detailed analysis of the vote of those who preferred the leader of another party to the leader of the party they normally supported – including the substantial minority of Labour and Liberal Democrat supporters who nonetheless preferred Major as a prime minister – concludes that the *net* impact of Major's popularity was minuscule.[4]

Detailed accounts of the 1992 election result can be found elsewhere.[5] The main explanations can be summarized as follows:

1. The baseline vote continued its glacial shift to the right. Social demography, notably the contraction of the working class, council housing and trade unionism, and the aging of society, continued to benefit the Conservatives.

2. The four-week campaign made very little difference, although in the last two days there was a small surge to the Conservatives and a small tactical shift from Labour to the Liberal Democrats.

3. The opinion polls consistently underestimated Conservative support, mainly because Conservative voters were less willing to be interviewed or, if interviewed, to reveal their voting intentions. In reality the Conservatives were

ahead throughout the campaign, and probably in the run-up to it.[6]

4. The main factor behind both the late swing to the Conservatives and the Conservatives' recovery prior to the campaign was the broad sense that the Conservatives were more capable than Labour of managing the economy at a time of recession. This overrode recriminations against the government for the recession, concern about unemployment and the public services, and the belief that, other things being equal, a Labour government would be better for jobs, the health service, education and pensions.

5. The greater confidence in the Conservatives' economic competence was helped by the gradual reduction of interest and inflation rates in the nine months prior to the election. Personal economic optimism – a crucial factor among uncommitted voters – increased sharply in March and April 1992.

6. Voters did not trust the Conservatives so much as distrust Labour. A lack of confidence in Kinnock, the belief that a Labour government would raise income tax, and the anti-Labour campaign of the Conservative tabloid press all contributed to this distrust of the Labour party – although the separate importance of each has been exaggerated. The Conservatives did not win the election. Labour lost it, and had lost it before the campaign began.

7. The Liberal Democrat vote declined from 1987 because the electoral damage inflicted by the botched merger of the SDP and the Liberals could not be wholly mended by Ashdown's energetic four-week campaign. The belief that a vote for the Liberal Democrats was wasted and that it would 'let Labour in', reinforced perhaps by talk of a Labour-Liberal Democrat coalition in the final week of the campaign, helped the Conservatives.

None of these explanations are particular to Major's short period as Prime Minister. Most of them applied equally to the Conservative victory in 1987 and reflect enduring features of British electoral behaviour whose origins go back to the Thatcher era – or beyond. Social demography has been undermining Labour's base for two decades. Perceptions of the government's economic competence, judged by trends in the economy, have always been important, and usually decisive. The centre party suffers from the 'wasted vote' argument at every election.

Inevitably, the 1992 election was not a photocopy of its immediate predecessors. Firstly, the North-South polarization of the vote that characterized the Thatcher years went into reverse. The largest anti-Conservative swings were in the Midlands (3.8 per cent) and the South (3.0 per cent), while smaller swings were recorded in the Northern (1.6 per cent) and North West (2.0 per cent) regions and Scotland swung marginally to the Conservatives. The geography of the swing reflected the geography of the recession: areas with particularly sharp rises in bankruptcies and unemployment swung furthest against the Conservatives and they tended to be in the South and Midlands.

Secondly, there was a small but clear increase in anti-Conservative tactical voting. In Conservative-Labour marginals the Liberal Democrat vote fell by more than average, to Labour's benefit; in Conservative-Liberal Democrat marginals, it generally held up or increased.[7]

The third unusual feature of the 1992 election was a product of the first two. Two of the regions with above average swings to Labour – London and the East Midlands – contained a disproportionate concentration of Conservative-held marginals. Moreover, tactical voting by Liberal Democrats pushed the Labour vote up by more than average in Conservative marginals. As a result Labour's gain in seats was disproportionate to its gain in the popular vote: hence the Conservatives' overall majority was reduced to 21 even though they were fully eight percentage points ahead of Labour in the national vote. For the first time since the 1950s Labour's national vote was more efficiently distributed than the Conservatives'.

Fourthly, the largest swing to Labour (5.5 per cent) occurred among the 'ABs' – the professional and managerial classes – where non-Conservatives abandoned the centre for Labour, apparently unconcerned by Labour's plans to raise taxes and national insurance for high earners. This continued the steady erosion of Conservative support in the salariat, which goes back to 1983 for reasons that probably include the spread of higher education and the growing rift between the Conservative government and many of the professions, especially those working in the public sector.

Finally, the gender gap reopened, having narrowed in the three elections won by Mrs Thatcher. It widened particularly among the old, where women swung sharply to the Conservatives. The probable cause was John Major's replacement of Margaret Thatcher as Conservative leader. In the 1980s Mrs Thatcher's 'macho' leadership appealed to men (especially young working class men) and repelled women. John Major's gentler style appears to have had the opposite effect. Among women Kinnock trailed Thatcher as preferred Prime Minister in 1987 by 28 per cent to 44 per cent, but trailed Major in 1992 by 21 per cent to 50 per cent. Among men the gap also widened, but by less.

Of these special features of 1992 only the last can be plausibly attributed to John Major's leadership. The others have their origins in the Thatcher years – the 1989 recession, the assault on the professions, the alienation of the public sector, and the effect of the sheer longevity of Conservative government on tactical voting.

THE ELECTORAL CONSEQUENCES OF BLACK WEDNESDAY

Within months of the 1992 election the deepest and longest electoral slump in modern British politics began. Table 2 shows that on every indicator public confidence in the government – vote intention, approval of the government's record, preference for Prime Minister, perceived economic competence – sank to unprecedented depths. Previous administrations had had crises of public confidence: the 1963 Profumo scandal, the 1967 devaluation, the 1973–74 miners' strike and three-day week, the 1979 Winter of Discontent, the 1981–82 recession, the 1990 poll tax furore. None were as severe or prolonged as the confidence crisis of 1993–94.

Table 2: Public confidence in the government and Prime Minister: Comparison of 1993 with three previous worst post-war years

	1993 (mean)	Lowest previous years
% intending to vote Conservative	27%	1981: 31% 1985: 34% 1986: 34%
% who 'approve of the government's record to date'	14%	1968 (Lab) 21% 1981 (Con) 25% 1992 (Con) 26%
% who believe that the government 'is handling the economic situation properly'*	14%	1990 (Con) 19% 1992 (Con) 22% 1981 (Con) 22%
% who are 'satisfied with _____ as Prime Minister'	23%	1990 (Thatcher) 29%** 1981 (Thatcher) 31% 1968 (Wilson) 32%

* This question was asked only from 1980 onwards

** December 1990 is excluded

Source: Gallup polls

Questions: 'If there were a general election tomorrow, which party would you support?'

'Do you approve or disapprove of the government's record to date?'

'Do the government's plans for tackling the economic situation give you the feeling that they are or are not handling the situation properly?'

'Are you satisfied or dissatisfied with _____ as Prime Minister?'

The slump occurred in two stages: after the government's undignified scuttle from the ERM on 'Black Wednesday'; and after its by-election and local election humiliation in the summer of 1993.

Black Wednesday was, in effect, a devaluation of the pound, symbolizing national humiliation and a failure both of macro-economic strategy and of short-term currency management. It contradicted the traditional basis of Conservative claims to superiority over other parties: the defence of sterling, financial discipline, an understanding of the City, a safe pair of hands. As Thatcher's Chancellor John Major had propelled Britain into the ERM; in the election he had repeatedly insisted on the long-term necessity of ERM currency discipline; in the summer, he mocked the policy of withdrawal as 'fool's gold'. Who were the fools now?

The impact of 'Black Wednesday' is obvious from a casual glance at the monthly polls. In the three months from June to August 1992, the average standing of the parties was Conservative 39.1 per cent, Labour 41.5 per cent, a Labour lead of 2.4 per cent. In the three months from October to December 1992, the figures were Conservative 31.5 per cent, Labour 49.3 per cent, a Labour lead of 17.8 per cent. Confidence in John Major, the government's overall record and the future of the economy collapsed in tandem (see Table 3).

Table 3: The impact of 'Black Wednesday' on public confidence in John Major, the government's record and the future of the economy

	June–Aug 1992	Oct–Dec 1992	Change	Jan–Dec 1993
% 'satisfied' with Prime Minister	49%	25%	−24	23%
% saying Major would make best Prime Minister	41%	23%	−18	20%
% who 'approve of the government's record to date'	30%	15%	−15	14%
optimism index about 'general economic situation'*	−3	−27	−24	−4
optimism index about 'financial situation of your household'*	0	−13	−13	−8

* per cent replying will get 'a lot better' or ' a little better' *minus* per cent replying will get 'a little worse' or 'a lot worse'.

Source: Gallup polls

Most significantly of all, the Conservatives' reputation for competent economic management was shattered. This had been a priceless electoral asset in the 1980s, when it trumped the public's preference for Labour's social policies. Even during their mid-term doldrums the Conservatives were preferred to Labour as the party for the economy. All this changed after Black Wednesday. In 1993 and 1994 Labour was consistently regarded as the better party for handling 'Britain's economic difficulties' and by the largest margins ever recorded (see Table 4).

Table 4: Perceived economic competence of the
Conservative and Labour parties

With Britain in economic difficulties, which party do you think could handle the problem best – the Conservative party under John Major or the Labour party under (Neil Kinnock) John Smith?

	1992 Jan–Mar %	1993 Jan–Mar %	1994 Jan–Mar %
Conservatives/Major	42	30	25
Labour/(Kinnock) Smith	(31)	40	43
Con–Labour	+11	−10	−18

Source: Gallup poll

COLLAPSE IN THE COUNTIES, NEMESIS AT NEWBURY

The depth of public dissatisfaction suggested by the polls was put to its first nationwide test at the county council elections on 6 May 1993. The Conservatives were routed (Table 5). They lost control of every county council except Buckinghamshire. Hitherto impregnable Conservative shires such as Dorset, Kent and Norfolk – Conservative-run throughout their 105-year history – fell. The Conservative vote crumbled to the national (Great Britain) equivalent of 31 per cent, its lowest level in any nationwide election in modern history. The primary gainers were the Liberal Democrats, the Conservatives' main challengers in rural and small town England. They did particularly well in the West Country, taking control of Cornwall, Somerset and, a few weeks later, Dorset, and became the largest party in eight other counties. For the first time since the war the Centre could be said to have captured a regional base. With an additional 400 councillors, and over 4,000 local councillors altogether, the Centre had never been as strong in local government.

Table 5: The county council election results,
England and Wales, 1993

	Council control	Seats	% vote
Con	1 (−16)	966 (−478)	34 (−8)
Lab	14 (+1)	1389 (+94)	32 (+1)
Lib Dem*	3 (+3)	867 (+392)	27 (+7)
Ind/Other	1 (−1)	279 (−34)	7 (−1)
No overall control	28 (+13)		

* including SDP in 1989

Source: Colin Rallings and Michael Thrasher, *Local Elections Handbook, 1993*, Local Government Chronicle Elections Centre, University of Plymouth, 1993.

On the same day as the local elections a by-election was held in Newbury, a prosperous market town and rural seat in Berkshire. It was a lucky break for the Liberal Democrats, who were strong locally: they had nearly won the seat in 1974, had progressively squeezed the Labour vote, and ran the local council. They campaigned on the recession, which had hit the town badly. The result was even more dramatic than the local elections (see Table 6): the Conservative majority of 12,357 was turned into a Liberal Democrat majority of 22,055. The Conservative vote plunged from 56 to 27 per cent, the largest by-election drop in a Conservative seat since the war. The Labour vote, already reduced to 6 per cent at the previous general election, was squeezed down to a mere 2 per cent, the lowest ever recorded for any Labour candidate at a by-election or general election. Tactical voting reigned supreme.

A second by-election was held on 29 July at Christchurch, an affluent retirement area on the South Coast. It was the Conservative party's fifteenth safest seat at the general election, with a majority of over 23,000. Unlike Newbury, the local Liberals had always been weak, yet the result was even more spectacular than in Newbury. On an unprecedented swing of 35.4 per cent, the Liberal Democrats won with a majority of over 16,000. The Conservative vote collapsed from 64 to 32 per cent. Once again the Labour vote was squeezed to almost nothing (2.7 per cent) by ruthlessly tactical anti-Conservative voting. Christchurch confirmed

Table 6: The Newbury and Christchurch by-elections

Newbury 6 May 1993

	By-election result	%		1992 general election result	%
Lib Dem	37,590	65.1		24,778	37.3
Con	15,535	26.9		37,135	55.9
Lab	1,151	2.0		3,962	6.0
Green	341	0.6		539	0.8
Others*	3,156	5.5		–	–
Majority Lib Dem	22,055	38.2	Con	12,357	18.6
Turnout	71.3%			82.8%	
Swing, Con to Lib Dem: 28.4%					

Christchurch 29 July 1993

	By-election result	%		1992 general election result	%
Lib Dem	33,164	62.2		13,612	23.6
Con	16,737	31.4		36,627	63.5
Lab	1,453	2.7		6,997	12.1
Others~	1,951	3.7		418	0.7
Majority Lib Dem	16,427	30.8	Con	23,015	39.9
Turnout	74.6%			80.7%	
Swing, Con to Lib Dem: 35.4%					

* 16 other candidates
~ 10 other candidates 1993, 2 others 1992

that the government's unpopularity had penetrated deep into Conservative territory.

The county council elections and by-elections gave the Liberal Democrats a burst of publicity and demonstrated to disaffected Conservatives nationwide that a vote for the Liberal Democrats was an effective form of protest. The Newbury result had, after all, ended Norman Lamont's ministerial career. There followed a surge in the polls for the

Liberal Democrats, primarily at the expense of the Conservatives. Party support in the Gallup 9000 polls for February to April 1993 stood at Conservative, 30.9 per cent, Labour 47.7 per cent, Liberal Democrat 15.7 per cent – a Labour lead of 16.8 per cent. In the Gallup 9000 polls for June to August 1993 they stood at Conservative 24.4 per cent, Labour 44.5 per cent, Liberal Democrat 25.8 per cent. The centre had overcome the trauma of the breakup of the Lib-SDP Alliance and re-emerged as a serious threat to the Conservatives.

In the year following the Conservatives' local election débâcle public opinion barely moved. The series of sexual incidents that embarrassed the government in early 1994 and the wide-ranging tax rises that came into effect in April prevented the growing evidence of economic recovery from translating into political recovery. The 1994 local elections proved to be even more humiliating for the Conservatives than the previous year's (see Table 7). Their estimated share of the national vote was 27 per cent, 4 points down on the previous year. In terms of councils and seats the Conservatives came third in England, fourth in Scotland. A third of all the Conservative councillors who stood lost their seats. The Conservatives were defending the fortresses to which the poll-tax local elections of 1990 had confined them but they surrendered many of these too. Outside London they retained control in only 11 out of the 162 councils being elected; in London they were swept out of such impregnable suburbs as Barnet and Croydon, their power base reduced to Bromley, Kensington and the low-tax flagships of Wandsworth and Westminster. It was certainly the worst local election performance by a major party since at least 1945. It was probably the worst ever.

Table 7: The 1994 local election results

	Councils	Seats
Conservative	15 (−18)	888 (−429)
Labour	93 (+4)	2769 (+88)
Liberal Democrat	19 (+9)	1098 (+388)
Independent and Others	6 (−1)	220 (−34)
No overall control	65 (+6)	–

Further humiliation was heaped on the Conservatives in the European elections on 9 June, when five by-elections were also held. The Conservatives not only lost the one seat they were defending – Eastleigh, an affluent suburban and service sector town outside Southampton – but suffered the unique ignominy of coming third behind Labour. In the four by-election seats it was defending the Labour party substantially increased its majorities and the Conservatives fell back to third place in three of them. The most noticeable feature of all five by-elections was the unprecedented collapse of the Conservative vote (see Table 8). In the lowest mid-points of the Thatcher governments, the Conservatives normally forfeited about a third of their general election vote when they lost a by-election. They had lost 58 and 54 per cent respectively in Newbury and Christchurch. In Eastleigh they lost an unprecedented 65 per cent and in the other by-elections – where their organization and support was weaker – they lost over 75 per cent. Many Conservatives switched to Labour or, in Eastleigh, to the Liberal Democrats. But many more simply stayed at home.

Table 8: The collapse of the Conservative vote in the by-elections of 9 June 1944

	Anti-Con swing	Fall in Con share of vote since general election (% points)	Con vote loss*
Eastleigh	21.5% (to Lib D)	−26.6%	65%
Barking	22.0% (to Lab)	−23.5%	84%
Bradford South	14.2% (to Lab)	−20.6%	73%
Dagenham	23.1% (to Lab)	−26.4%	86%
Newham North East	16.3% (to Lab)	−15.9%	74%

* i.e. the fall in the Conservative vote as a proportion of the Conservatives' vote at the 1992 general election.

The European election results were not declared until three days after the by-elections, in line with other member countries of the European Union. The government knew that it was in for a mauling; the only uncertainty was its severity. Estimates based on some polls suggested that the Conservatives might be reduced to as few as six seats. The media speculated on the number of seats the Conservatives would need to hold for John Major to avoid irresistible pressure on him to resign, a game played skilfully by the Conservative whips, who deliberately lowered expectations. In the event the Conservatives held on to 18 seats, all but two in the South (see Table 9). The result was received with some relief and attributed to the dogged European campaigning of John Major and the temporary truce between anti- and pro-Europeans within the party. But the result did, in fact, mark another calamitous slump in the Conservatives' popularity. They won only 27.8 per cent of the vote, the lowest share obtained by either major party in any nationwide election this century. As in the county council elections a year earlier, they yielded to Labour rural and suburban areas such as Herefordshire and Shropshire, Lincolnshire, Norfolk and Suffolk which have been overwhelmingly Conservative in general elections for time immemorial. Moreover, they were lucky: of the 18 seats they held, 10 were retained with majorities of under 3 per cent and 14 with majorities of under 5 per cent. The Conservative party was within a whisker of wipe-out.

Table 9: The European elections of 9 June 1994

	Seats*	Share of GB vote (%)	Change since	
			1989 Euro election	1992 gen election
Conservative	18 (−16)	27.9	−6.8%	−14.9%
Labour	62 (+13)	44.2	+4.1%	+9.0%
Liberal Democrat	2 (+2)	16.7	+10.5%	−1.6%
Scottish Nationalist	2 (+1)			
Irish parties	3 (−)			

* The number of European constituencies in the UK was increased from 81 to 87 between 1989 and 1992. The change in the number of seats for each party is based on estimates of which of the 1992 constituencies the parties would have held in 1989.

THE CONSERVATIVE SLUMP, THE 'MAJOR FACTOR' AND OTHER EXPLANATIONS

Previous governments have presided over recessions, sterling crises or other national traumas and suffered mid-term electoral reverses as a result. Yet none have sunk so low in public esteem. What was different about Major's post-1992 government?

One answer is the complete absence of scapegoats. The 1976 sterling crisis could be traced back to the Yom Kippur War and rise in world oil prices. The 1980–82 recession could be partly blamed on the previous Labour government, a decade of irresponsible trade unionism and the world economy. The high rate of poll tax could be pinned on to profligate Labour councils. The onset of the 1990 recession could be charged to the Thatcher government. But the fault for Black Wednesday, the perpetuation of the recession and the sharp tax rises lay with nobody but the government – the Major government. One year after campaigning on the promise of currency stability, low taxes and imminent economic recovery ('green shoots') sterling was outside the ERM, VAT had risen sharply, a new fuel tax was being introduced and recovery was still over the horizon. The government's credibility was in shreds.

The second answer is the conspicuous disunity which has overcome the Conservative party. It is a Conservative article of faith that splits spell electoral suicide, which is why the party traditionally conducts its quarrels in private or in code. Voters expect Labour, not the Conservatives, to brawl in public. But not since the schism over appeasement in the 1930s have factions been as rife, former ministers as disloyal, and backbenchers as openly hostile to the leadership. Voters have noticed. In 1981, when the fierce but contained Cabinet battle between 'wets' and 'dries' was at its height, the Conservative party was still thought of as 'united' by 43 per cent of voters, while the Labour party, riven by Militant, Bennites and the SDP breakaway was considered united by a mere 7 per cent. When department was pitted against department during the Westland affair in early 1986 only 32 per cent considered the Conservatives to be united, but the figure for the Labour party, 25 per cent, was even lower. The impact on voters from the replacement of Thatcher and the connected division over Europe has been of an altogether different order. By 1993 the Conservatives were described as united by a mere 19 per cent of voters; Labour by 42 per cent. Not since polls asked the question in the early 1970s has the party been so widely regarded as split. It is now the Conservatives, not Labour, who do their brawling in public.

The third new factor in the Major period is the unprecedented hostility of sections of the Conservative press. In the 1980s, individual Conservative newspapers responded to their readers' mood and occasionally flirted with the SDP for a short period. In 1962–63 the press turned strongly against the beleaguered Macmillan government, partly out of anger at the jailing of two journalists for refusing to reveal their sources in the Vassall spy case. But the contempt of the Murdoch press for John Major's leadership and the partisan support for the Euro-rebels in the Telegraph newspapers have been of a different magnitude. The impact has been most pronounced on readers of the Tory tabloids, whose suggestibility and fickleness have made them a crucial 'swing' group in recent elections. The largest falls in Conservative support between the 1992 election and 1993 occurred among readers of the Murdoch tabloids – *Today* (minus 17 per cent), *The Sun* (minus 16 per cent) and the *Daily Star* (minus 16 per cent) – while the smallest falls (of 7 to 8 per cent) occurred among readers of the non-Conservative *Mirror*, *Guardian* and *Independent*. It was notable that the drop off in Conservative support was smallest among readers of the *Daily Express*, the one Tory tabloid to stick steadfastly by the government – and John Major.[8] 'It Was The Sun Wot Won It' crowed *The Sun* after the 1992 election. Two years later it was demonstrating that what Murdoch giveth he can also taketh away.

How far has John Major directly contributed to the Conservatives' electoral misfortunes? By any measure he has become the least respected Prime Minister since polls began. In 1993 his monthly 'satisfaction rating' averaged 23 per cent, the lowest recorded for any Prime Minister since Gallup first asked the question in 1947. To the great majority of voters he was 'incompetent' (55 per cent) and 'a loser' (58 per cent), indecisive (70 per cent), ineffective (71 per cent), 'not able to unite the nation' (77 per cent) and 'not really in charge' (81 per cent) or 'tough' (81 per cent). Asked to say which party leader would make the best Prime Minister, only 20 per cent of voters chose Major, who ran behind both Ashdown (21 per cent) and Smith (31 per cent). Comparison with Thatcher is instructive: her score never fell below 24 per cent in any quarterly period (during the Westland affair, moreover, when the SDP's existence meant that respondents had four leaders to choose from). Nor can Major's poor score be attributed to John Smith's succession as Labour leader: the decline in the proportion choosing Major has been matched by an increasing proportion saying 'don't know', not saying 'John Smith'.

Major's unpopularity is more consequence than cause of his government's unpopularity. Throughout 1993 his 'ratings' fell in parallel with the government's but they always ran above them – and by a larger margin than Thatcher's did over her government's. As Table 10 shows, Major's political reputation has declined far more than his personal one. Between the 1992 election and June 1993, the proportion who 'liked him' fell only moderately, from 63 to 52 per cent, while the proportion who 'liked his policies' fell much more sharply, from 41 to a mere 19 per cent. As a politician he has lost respect; as a man he remains liked. That perhaps is why disillusioned Conservative defectors do not put Major at the top of their list of reasons for defecting: among deserters at the Christchurch by-election his leadership (mentioned by only 15 per cent) ranked fifth out of nine factors, behind the 'overall state of the economy' (44 per cent), 'VAT on fuel' (43 per cent), 'law and order' (30 per cent) and 'government incompetence' (29 per cent).[9] Among Conservative deserters generally, it ranked only eighth out of thirteen factors: the government's overall record, the economy, the NHS and other public services and rising taxes were all far more important reasons.[10] That too perhaps is why polls in spring 1994 consistently indicated that under any alternative leader the Conservatives would probably lose rather than gain votes, the only possible (and marginal) exception being Heseltine.

Table 10: Opinions about the personal and policy dimensions of
the Prime Minister's leadership

'Which of these statements comes closest to your view of Mr Major (Mrs Thatcher)?'

| | Major | | Thatcher | |
| | June 93 | Mar 92 | Mar 90 | Jan 86 |
	%	%	%	%
I like him and I like his policies	12	36	17	18
I like him but I dislike his policies	40	27	20	17
I dislike him but I like his policies	7	5	9	12
I dislike him and I dislike his policies	36	27	51	48
Summary	%	%	%	%
Like him	52	63	37	35
Dislike him	43	32	60	60
Like policies	19	41	26	31
Dislike policies	76	54	71	65

Source: *Gallup Political and Economic Index.* Reports 395, 380, 356, 306

IRREVERSIBLE DECLINE?

No previous government has undergone a post-election reverse so early in its life and of such severity and duration. One is reminded of 1904–5: then, as now, Conservatives had been in power for a generation, were divided over Britain's position in the international economy (Imperial Preference versus Free Trade), were ineffectively led and drifted into landslide defeat at the following election. Yet it would be premature to infer that the current sea change in the public mood is permanent and that the government's position is irrecoverable. For one thing, most disaffected Conservatives have not embraced the opposition parties but turned against party politics and politicians in general. This is not reflected in the headline voting figures of the polls, which exclude the 'refusers', 'don't knows' and 'won't votes', most of whom are Conservatives who will vote loyally when the election comes. For another, most of the contributory elements in the

Conservatives' misfortunes are reversible in the short-term. The Conservative press is likely to rally round once the election is imminent: its rebellion is, after all, directed at Major, not the Conservative party. The economic upturn in 1995–96 will depend on the world economy, but as a result of a more flexible labour market could be sharper and stronger than previous cycles, giving scope for tax cuts and additional public expenditure as an election approaches. Economic recovery is a strong amnesiac: once it arrives, Black Wednesday will disappear into history, memories of bankruptcy and unemployment will fade, the fuel tax will be absorbed. With economic revival comes electoral revival, tardily but inevitably. Buried Conservative loyalties will re-surface, Conservative support will edge up in the polls, morale and discipline will return to the government backbenches. John Major's 'true' character – fortitude, patience, steadiness, moderation – will be rediscovered and his leadership reassessed. Whether the upturn in the electoral cycle will be sufficient to re-elect the Conservatives for a fifth term is impossible to predict. But mid-term electoral storms, however severe, are not earthquakes: they rarely change the party landscape.

Notes

1. Literally. In week 2 of November 1990, before Michael Heseltine formally challenged Thatcher for the leadership, Labour led the Conservatives by 16 per cent. In week 3, during the leadership election campaign, that lead fell to 5 per cent. In week 4, during which Thatcher stood down but before her successor was known, the Conservatives went into a 0.5 per cent lead. In the final three days, after John Major became Prime Minister, the Conservatives leapt into an 11.5 per cent lead. See Anthony King, 'Major restores Tories' fortunes with 2.5 per cent lead', *Daily Telegraph*, 14 December 1990.
2. *Gallup Political and Economic Index*, Report No. 363, p.2.
3. *Gallup Political and Economic Index*, Report No. 380 (April 1992), p. 8.
4. See Ivor Crewe and Anthony King, 'Did Major Win? Did Kinnock Lose?', in Anthony Heath et al, eds., *Labour's Last Chance?* (Dartmouth, 1994).

5. See, in particular, David Butler and Dennis Kavanagh, *The British General Election of 1992* (Macmillan, London, 1993), esp. chapter no. 13 and Appendix 2); Ivor Crewe, 'Why did Labour Lose (yet again)', *Politics Review*, Vol. 2(1) (September 1992), pp. 2–11; Ivor Crewe, Pippa Norris and Robert Waller, 'The 1992 general election', in Pippa Norris et al, eds., *British Elections & Parties Yearbook* (Harvester Wheatsheaf, Hemel Hempstead, 1992), pp. xv–xxxvi; David Denver et al, *British Elections & Parties Yearbook 1993*, (Harvester Wheatsheaf, London, 1993); and David Sanders, 'Why the Conservative Party Won – Again', in Anthony King, ed., *Britain At The Polls 1992* (Chatham House, Chatham, N. J., 1992), pp. 171–202.

6. See Ivor Crewe, 'A nation of liars? Opinion polls and the 1992 election', *Parliamentary Affairs*, 45 (4) (October 1992), pp. 475–95.

7. John Curtice and Michael Steed, 'Appendix 2: The Results Analysed' in David Butler and Dennis Kavanagh, *The British General Election of 1992* (Macmillan, London, 1992), pp. 322–62, especially pp. 332–337.

8. See Robert M. Worcester, 'Demographics and values: what the British public read and what they think about their newspapers', MORI, February 1994. The comparison is between the vote at the 1992 general election and the aggregate of voting intentions recorded by the monthly omnibus MORI poll for the calendar year 1993.

9. Peter Wilby, 'Economy will sink Tories', *Independent on Sunday*, 25 July 1993, p. 2, reporting a NOP poll.

10. Anthony King, 'Tories vote with their feet over economy', *Daily Telegraph*, 21 March 1994, p. 8.

Chapter 8

LAW AND THE CONSTITUTION

Simon Lee

INTRODUCTION

Law and lawyers have continued to overtake politics as a means of challenging government during John Major's premiership. This phenomenon was spotted in the mid-seventies when Lord Denning ruled OK and the judiciary began to confront the Labour government of the day over such matters as Tameside schooling and Laker Skytrain. Led by John Griffith's influential book, *The Politics of the Judiciary*[1], this judicial activism was spectacularly misinterpreted by the left, as resulting from the judiciary's right-wing political ideology. The development was more, in the literal and metaphorical sense of the word, sinister than that, arising from imperialism on the part of self-possessed (but also, critics would say, self-interested and self-obsessed) lawyers from not only the political right but also the left and especially the centre. This became evident in the 1980s when lawyers, joined by religious leaders, were the most effective opposition to the Conservative government as Labour crumbled and the media fawned on Thatcherism.

While the tabloids have had fun in the 1990s with Tory sexual fetishism, the more fundamental *legal* fetishism of our society has passed largely unremarked. Perhaps this is because part of Thatcherism's legacy was a subtle indulgence of lawyers, a world of apparently consenting adults regulating one another in private.

Indeed, as John Major became Prime Minister, there was a crisis of confidence in the legal system which, some might think, ought to have stopped the rise of lawyers in public life. At the tail-end of the Thatcher years, first the Guildford Four and then the Maguire Seven were grudgingly accepted by the system as having been the victims of miscarriages of justice. In the first year of Mr Major's tenure of office, the Birmingham Six were released and a Royal Commission on criminal justice was swiftly established, the first for ten years. Judith Ward was released the next year and three of the Armagh Four the following year, while the flow spread beyond those relating to the conflict over Northern Ireland with the quashing of convictions for Winston Silcott and others in the Tottenham Three case, the release of Stephan Kiszko, the Darvell brothers from Swansea and the Cardiff Three. As John Major took over from Margaret Thatcher, the legal system in general and the senior judiciary in particular looked tarnished by seemingly endemic injustice. Although John Griffith's new book, *Judicial Politics since 1920: a chronicle*,[2] showed some encouraging signs of revisionism, it was still damning on the quality of the judiciary, arguing of the 1980s that 'By the end of the decade, the reputation of the senior judiciary was lower than at any time this century.'

Yet four years on, lawyers have regained their own, if not necessarily the public's, confidence. A new generation, indeed a new style, of judges has taken over and one of them, Lord Justice Scott, is poised to rip apart some of the practices of government when he reports on his inquiry into the Matrix Churchill affair. Most intriguingly when one considers the cries of 'jobs for the boys' over quango appointments by the Major government, the new opposition has been appointed or promoted *by* the government. While the law remains unaccountable, then, it is increasingly calling others to account. How do we explain these features of the Major years and what are the consequences for political life in the future?

Law is overtaking politics as a way in which power is exercised and challenged. It is lawyers more than opposition

MPs or the media who call government to account, the brief as much as the ballot box which constrains government policy. Even when other political parties or the media appear to lead an attack on the government, their attention has often been focused by a court case or the threat of one. The legal system itself has so far resisted major change but the next government will have to shape a legal culture which can cope with an expanded constitutional role for law and lawyers. The first steps have been taken during the current administration with successful high profile judicial appointments. The possible legacy of the Major years will be the quasi-legalistic Citizen's Charter which may come to be seen as the precursor of constitutional reform while the Major government's nemesis may prove to be the Scott inquiry. The common themes of the law's progress are its teasing out of reasons for governmental action, its subjection of those reasons to rigorous, independent scrutiny and its ability to keep ahead of the government through drawing on a lively, if incestuous, marketplace of ideas. The right spawned many of the successes of the Thatcher years in the 1980s through creating, outside the traditional party political or university structures, a culture of think-tanks and research institutes. The centre and left have not been idle but have adapted the right's modes of operation and yoked them to another sub-culture, the intertwined worlds of academe, media and the law. These are worlds in which the mutual faxing of judgments, the circulation of academic journals and the circuit of international conferences bring bright ideas from around the world to the immediate attention of judges who launch them on the government, showing no mercy even to a government in retreat.

JUDGES

Although a Prime Minister's reputation among lawyers will depend to a large extent on the performance of the government's senior ministers with legal responsibilities (Lord Chancellor, Attorney-General and Home Secretary), the wider reputation of a Prime Minister's era for the quality of its legal system will depend on the leading judges appointed on the recommendation of the Lord Chancellor.

It would be going too far, just, to say that everyone in the senior judiciary is brighter than everyone in the government but it is fair to point out that almost every senior judge is conditioned to be excited by the quality of argument, to pay attention to the content of ideas rather than their provenance or vote-pulling power. This is why they are a more dangerous opposition than the official one in Parliament, which has to play the same vote-hunting game as the government, or the surrogate opposition of the 1980s, the churches, since religious views are more predictable, albeit challenging to the government. To understand the threat to politics from the law one has to appreciate above all this air of intellectual curiosity which pervades the work of appellate judges and those who appear before them or otherwise seek to influence them.

It is legitimate to put the judges first in an assessment of the legal system since, in contrast to what Sir Robin Day described as 'here today, gone tomorrow' ministers, the judges will still be in office in the next millennium. The two plum jobs in the English legal system, Lord Chief Justice and Master of the Rolls, both fell vacant during Mr Major's premiership. Two shrewd appointments were made. Sir Peter Taylor became Lord Chief Justice, having successfully been road-tested as a public figure and Major-esque sporting bloke by holding an inquiry into football stadiums in the wake of disasters. A Radio Five Live Lord Chief Justice, then, will outlive John Major's tenure at Number 10 and possibly, if its predecessor's swift demise is any guide, Radio Five Live itself. The intellectually brilliant Sir Thomas Bingham was appointed as Master of the Rolls, having been tried out in the more cerebral task of the BCCI inquiry, a Radio Four intellectual heavyweight. These two judges share a belief in openness, although Lord Taylor seems more easily seduced by the media, and in a bill of rights, of which more anon. Even the arch-critic of the judiciary, John Griffith, ends his recent book *Judicial Politics since 1920 – a chronicle*, with something approaching acceptance of recent appointments at this level: 'It may be that, under a reforming Lord Chancellor, a new Lord Chief Justice and a different Master of the Rolls, the administration of justice ... will ... begin to rebuild its credibility.' Every time a judge produces a report, from Woolf to Scott, one is reminded of the ability of top lawyers to master complexities, to separate the relevant from the irrelevant in a mass of material, to analyze and to criticize constructively. In contrast, it is difficult to think of any Cabinet minister who could have produced, say, the Woolf report into the Strangeways prison riots or the Bingham BCCI report in such quick time. No wonder, then, that law is taking over from politics.

At least John Major's government has picked good judges for such tasks, as it has for the two key posts. The Prime Minister can also bask in the glory of some excellent appointments as Law Lords, thanks to Lord Mackay's judgment and the willingness of both to appoint those who are not 'one of us'. The combination of judges such as the darling of the liberal chattering and chartering classes, Lord Woolf, the former European judge Lord Slynn and the razor-sharp Lords Mustill and Browne-Wilkinson, means that the House of Lords is as intellectually formidable and politically unsympathetic to a Conservative government as at any time ever. This will inevitably continue as stars like Lord Justice Hoffmann and Mr Justice Sedley ascend the judicial ladder. The appointment of the left-wing Stephen Sedley to the High Court was a coup, putting to rest the Griffithesque whinge that the judiciary is Conservative. It also stopped the trend of top QCs opting for careers outside the judiciary, an achievement akin to persuading Ian Botham to become an umpire.

LEGAL MINISTERS

Lord Mackay, the Lord Chancellor from John Major's appointment to the time of writing, has been the wisest member of the Cabinet and one whom John Major has rightly trusted. Mr Major owed his first government job to Sir Patrick Mayhew, to whom he remains close and who was his first Attorney-General. Sir Nicholas Lyell succeeded Sir Patrick in that position when the latter secured his desired post as Secretary of State for Northern Ireland. Notwithstanding a poor media reputation, Sir Nicholas is also a man of integrity and of moderate political views, like Mayhew, Mackay and Major.

In addition to his personal integrity, Lord Mackay has no political ambition, being one of the few people in the Cabinet not after Mr Major's job and the only one never to have stood for election or to have joined a political party. It was a surprise when he agreed to be Lord Advocate, the Scottish, less political version of the Attorney-General. In that position, he came to the notice of Margaret Thatcher when advising the government on Scottish legal matters. Soon after becoming a law lord, he was approached by her in the year of three Lord Chancellors, to succeed Lords Havers and Hailsham on the Woolsack. He has been trusted, relied upon and given a free rein by John Major.

The sheer variety of experience among the candidates to succeed Lord Mackay (from Lord Howe to Sir Patrick Mayhew QC to Lord Alexander) indicates that the Lord Chancellor's post pulls in different directions. Do we want a judge, a politician or someone to run a multi-million-pound business? The tensions within the office have been exacerbated during the Major years by the worthy pressure from the Courts' Charter and the mounting concern over the cost of going to law, especially when the taxpayer is financing it through legal aid. It must be difficult for the Lord Chancellor in his executive role to be urging the judges to be frugal with the public purse while still leading their commitment to first class justice for all. A flavour of the problems this can bring is given by Lord Mackay's dissent in Pepper v Hart (where the cost to the system of referring to Hansard led the Lord Chancellor to take a different view from his judicial brethren) and his disagreement with Mr Justice Wood who retired early as President of the Employment Appeal Tribunal after a difference of opinion with the Lord Chancellor over the cost of the industrial tribunal service.

There have already been minor skirmishes between the Lord Chancellor and the rest of the legal mafia although the legal profession has been remarkably resistant to change which affects its own vested interests. There have been clear signals from the Lord Chancellor that legal aid costs have to be controlled, that competition among solicitors for legal aid work, between them and non-lawyers for conveyancing, between lawyers and mediators over divorce and between solicitors and barristers for advocacy is inevitable and that courts, like trains, must run on time, although privatization is not yet anticipated for the judicial track. The Lord Chancellor favours openness where it appears innocuous, such as encouraging responsible, senior judges to speak out in public, at least to responsible, senior journalists such as Joshua Rozenberg on BBC's Newsnight (a tactic even adopted, when it suits, by the Attorney-General). Yet secrecy and lack of accountability remain the norm where it does matter, such as in judicial preferment. There is a greater awareness of the need to appoint women and ethnic minorities as QCs and judges but there is no drive for dramatic structural changes to welcome women and minorities into the professions. At the level of symbolism, lawyers in court are keeping their wigs on, after exhaustive consultation, while High Court judges are the only group to have survived John Major's classless assault on the Honours List practice of automatic knighthoods. Business as usual, then, is the Major message to the legal professions, with few bouncers delivered by Mackay, Mayhew or Lyell. When the yellow card was shown by Lord Mackay to the shameful protectionism of the legal profession, Lord Lane over-reacted. Virtually in tears, he denounced the reforms. If one may continue the football metaphor, the former Lord Chief Justice dived in to a reckless tackle, denouncing Lord Mackay's modest measures as a Nazi-like threat to the independence of the judiciary. Like Gascoigne in his FA Cup final performances, he harmed only himself and had to be carried off the pitch.

It is not only the role of Lord Chancellor but that of Attorney-General which has shown systemic fault-lines, concealed for decades by the impeccable demeanour of the incumbents but revealed in the Scott inquiry. The central problem for the modern Attorney-General is an accentuated version of that facing all ministers. In the good old days, departmental ministers had responsibilities which they or their civil servants discharged and for which they dodged questions at the despatch box. Nowadays, departmental ministers have responsibilities but fiercely independent quasi-entreprenurial agency heads run the shows. This seemed like a good idea at the time because ministers could dodge all the more easily. The difficulty is that they cannot control as much as they might like. We still have a culture, fostered by a lazy media which prefers to swan around Westminster, in which ministers are assumed to be able to influence, if not determine, events. This gap between perception and sophisticated structure is even bigger for those departmental ministers who are responsible for a big budget which they cannot control. Even with the law officers, however, similar problems have emerged. The political and legal lines of responsibility for decisions to prosecute, for example, have always posed difficulties. Now that we have a Crown Prosecution Service with a head appointed after open advertisement, a Director of Public Prosecutions likewise, and the head of the Serious Fraud Office, let alone the independent Customs and Excise team which launched the ill-fated Matrix Churchill prosecution, the Attorney-General is not clearly master in his own household.

Even within his own bailiwick as legal adviser to the government, the Attorney's job has become more complicated. On a number of fronts, but especially Europe, the public and ministers are beginning to grasp how easy it is to get in good faith contradictory opinions from different lawyers. The Foreign Office and the Attorney-General's own advisers, for example, might easily take different stances on the effect of the Maastricht treaty or of votes thereon in the Commons. The Attorney himself might even take different views at different times. Nowadays, because of this general trend for law to invade the territory of politics, these uncertainties are becoming more and more embarrassing to the government, even if cynics felt that it was convenient for it to find the Attorney's opinion contradicting that of the Foreign Office lawyers in the particular example of Maastricht. If the Lord Chancellor's post is anomalous, it is unlikely that the Attorney's position will survive a Labour or partnership government without significant alteration.

Reorganization of the legal-ish departments is needed not simply because of the arbitrary responsibilities of the Home

Office (video nasties and dangerous dogs) and the Department of National Heritage (the millennium, the lottery and dangerous TV). Nor is it desirable only because the afore-mentioned tokenism is encouraged by the need for the Home Secretary to play to the gallery at the annual Tory party conference. Nor is change required solely because the Home Office is losing other responsibilities, in that the referral of possible miscarriages of justice to the Court of Appeal is at long last to be handed to an independent review authority as recommended by the Runciman report. Again, it is deeper than any of these particular issues and is indeed the logical consequence of the Thatcherite programme of rolling back the state. Sooner or later, the great offices of state will have to be rolled back to reflect the relocation of power to various agencies. Otherwise, ambitious politicians and talented civil servants will make work for themselves to fit the media's outdated assumptions that, for instance, the Home Office is important. There are only so many refugees in the world for whom the Home Secretary can on any given day refuse asylum (and get into trouble with the courts for doing so improperly). There are only so many dangerous videos or dogs he can scrutinize. Hence it is time that the Home Office should be disbanded and the diffuse responsibilities of the Lord Chancellor, the Attorney-General and the Home Secretary rationalized. A Ministry of Justice may sound sinister but it may be desirable and it will almost certainly follow the election of any Labour-Liberal Democratic government. In sum, we are on the verge of witnessing major, but not one suspects Major, structural changes in the way the legal system is run.

INQUIRIES

The triumph of legalism over the past four years is all the more extraordinary when one considers the series of disastrous miscarriages of justice which were reluctantly, begrudgingly and belatedly admitted by the legal system in the late 1980s and early 1990s. The appointment of a Royal Commission with a limited time-frame of two years seemed to satisfy the media that something was being seen to be done. The media, and thus the public, have not yet come to terms with how to receive such reports and how to use them (for all their flaws) as a check on government. The Royal Commission made 352 recommendations to make it more difficult to secure unsafe convictions, yet the Home Secretary's response was to propose twenty-seven ways of making it easier to convict. In the two years between the Commission being established and reporting, the Major government, as noted above, had detected a gap in the market for tough talk about crime and subverted the Royal Commission into an excuse for implementing part of the programme. Since the Runciman report lacked any coherent principle, it was easy to deflect attention from its jumble of proposals but this is a trick the government has used in less propitious circumstances, such as doing the exact opposite of what the closely-argued Woolf report recommended in terms of working to reduce the prison population.

Labour has undertaken so many unsuccessful election campaigns based on pointing out ministers' inconsistencies with their own statements that it might now at last have the wit to see that a better benchmark against which to judge the government would be the independent recommendations of inquiries and commissions set up by the Government. If the opposition or the media learn how to bring ministers back to such treasure-troves of criticism then this could be the undoing of John Major.

Lawyers are the great inquirers, from Lord Scarman in the late 1960s through to the early 1980s (first class reports which stand the test of time, from Belfast to Brixton) to Lord Woolf for the late 1980s, Sir David Calcutt, QC and Sir Louis Blom-Cooper, QC at all times for all causes and Lord Justice Scott for the mid 1990s. The hallmarks of this manner of discovering the truth about the past and wisdom about ways forward for the future are to uncover as much paperwork as possible about the workings of government, to listen as carefully as possible to the opinions of those closest to the action and then to engage in rigorous questioning of those with responsibility.

There could be no better illustration of the thesis of this

article, a shift from political to legal modes of controlling government, than to contrast the poor performance of the Select Committee on Trade and Industry's investigation into Matrix Churchill with the brutal demolition of ministerial and civil service reputations by the Scott inquiry. Select committees have been heralded as a parliamentary success of the 1980s but a jolly progression round the horseshoe of MPs, each asking their pet question and conditioned to despatch-box deflections, is no match for the relentless probing by the Baxendale and Scott double-act, armed to the teeth with the information they needed to ask the right questions through the pursuit in advance of all relevant written material.

REGULATION

One reason ministers seemed to flounder when asked by the Scott inquiry to explain why they signed public interest immunity certificates is that they themselves have become conditioned to the process of avoiding personal responsibility. Agencies, quangos and regulators are the mechanisms of the modern state. Ministerial credit can be claimed for doing something about enforcing parental responsibilities but ministerial distance can simultaneously be maintained from the disasters of chasing errant fathers through the intermediary of the Child Support Agency.

Government learnt this trick a long time ago in relation to yet another of those Home Office 'responsibilities', immigration. The government can congratulate itself on keeping numbers down but decline to dirty its hands with the heart-rending details by pointing to the decisions of civil servants, then independent adjudicators and immigration appeal tribunals. The fact that the rules, and the rules about rules, have been laid down by the Home Office and the appointments made by government is largely ignored at Westminster.

The technique has become widespread, however, with the Next Steps initiative and the growing number of new dilemmas which are redirected to quangos. The problems of infertility treatment, for example, were held at arm's length by the

Thatcher government through establishing in 1982 the Warnock inquiry. That reported in 1984 and the government procrastinated until 1990, thus allowing the public to become more accustomed to the practices and the media, which had bayed for regulations in 1982, time to commission the stories of surrogate mothers. Then the Human Fertilisation and Embryology Authority was created to license infertility clinics and regulate them. Thus when tricky problems surfaced, such as sex selection, the prospect of mothers in their late fifties or the use of foetal eggs for IVF, the government could point to an independent body which had to deal with the problem. This does not stop an interventionist minister such as Virginia Bottomley from commenting on such developments, nor the hyperactive moralist wing of the Conservative party from launching backbench amendments to the law to pre-empt the HFEA. Yet it does mean that no mud can stick to the government.

It also means that it is not simply 'law' in the traditional sense of statutes and judicial decisions which governs our society but 'leaflet law', the myriad instructions from such bodies as the HFEA on what its subjects have to do if they are to get or keep licences. This in turn is affected by the choice of members, their choice of executives, and the success or otherwise of the subjects and hostile campaigners in capturing the agency's agenda. The leading commentary on the Human Fertilisation and Embryology Act notes, for example, that Penelope Keith is a member of the HFEA and lists her credentials as actress and neighbour of Virginia Bottomley.

There are other modes of regulation in Major's UK. Ombudsmen have proliferated and newly-created pseudo-markets in previously nationalized resources have an office of fair trading to watch over them, from OfWat to Ofwhatever. The law, incidentally, is fast becoming OfDem, the watchdog of democracy. Legal language is central to the new internal NHS market, for example, with providers and purchasers 'contracting' to bring us healthcare. Again, the government appears to have abdicated responsibility for decisions by independent trusts or purchasers while using what the media allows to remain as an invisible hand to shape the market. A spate of stories berating trusts for failing to treat old people properly was developed by the media without anybody observing that it is the public bodies with responsibility for commissioning or purchasing healthcare who should be called to account for any gaps in the coverage. Litigation is inevitable in this area at which point the responsibilities may become clearer.

When the regulators interfere with government policy or fail to live up to expectations, ministers will step in to try to arrogate more power to themselves (or to more 'reliable', i.e. conformist, decision-makers). This shows that the independence of other regulators is conditional on government-pleasing decisions, that is to say, it is no independence at all. It took the magisterial presence of the former Home Secretary, Lord Whitelaw, to block one such manoeuvre over changing the rules on appointing Police Authorities in England and Wales. Yet the London-based and metropolitan-myopic media failed to notice the Northern Ireland Office attempt an even more outrageous coup, for an even more important police force, along even more blatantly undemocratic lines, at the same time by neutering the power of Northern Ireland's Police Authority.

LEGAL ADVICE

A further development, alluded to above, has also been used by the Major government to abdicate responsibility for ministerial decisions. This is to blame legal advice for any dodgy decision, from signing public interest immunity certificates to deporting an asylum seeker in defiance of a court order (Kenneth Baker's spectacular achievement as Home Secretary), to changing opinions over the impact of Commons' votes on approving the Maastricht treaty to Virginia Bottomley's decision not to hold a public, judicial inquiry into the Beverley Allitt affair. It was only seven years ago that the Westland affair saw Leon Brittan resign after the leak by his department of the Solicitor-General's advice to Michael Heseltine. The law officers' advice seemed to be sacrosanct, shrouded in secrecy. In the 1990s, however, Mr Major's government regards it as second nature to pass the buck to lawyers for their advice on all manner of issues.

There is no known example of a minister telling the world that he was about to do something daft but was saved by a spirited piece of independent legal advice. Rather, the Foreign Secretary will use an alternative source of legal advice (in the Maastricht saga, the Attorney-General's rather than his own Foreign Office's) to justify a change of tack. Or the Home Secretary will accept full responsibility in name while shifting it to his lawyer in reality by observing that he only ignored a High Court order because the lawyers assured him that the judge had acted beyond his powers. The proper route, as emphasized by the Law Lords in the M case, was to have appealed the decision and to have kept the asylum-seeker in the country until the legal system had run its course.

As legal advice becomes ever more obviously a bargaining tool in politics, a deep structural problem surfaces. Is there really any need for government lawyers? Why not market-test, contract-out and privatize their work? One answer has been the need for confidentiality, especially in security matters. Another explanation has been an undue reverence for lawyers. As ministers are seen to 'betray' their legal advice to save their own skins, however, it may be less and less attractive for government lawyers to work for a fraction of the income which could be generated in private practice. Just as law becomes more and more influential, the quality of advice available to government might become more and more questionable. Hitherto, the government has been fortunate in the outstanding advice given by career government lawyers and by a succession of talented Treasury devils (such as Lord Woolf and Mr Justice Laws).

Whatever happens in the future, nobody can doubt that there has been a seachange in the public sector's attitude towards legal advice during the Thatcher and Major years. In the infamous GLC case at the start of the 1980s, Ken Livingstone's disarming honesty revealed that legal advice had not been sought on implementing a manifesto commitment to cut fares on the London Underground. Now, local authorities and other public bodies seek legal advice at every turn and even try to use it as a bargaining tool to dissuade challenge

from citizens or commercial concerns or to prompt governmental concessions. The BBC has failed to pursue the broadcasting restrictions saga through the courts on legal advice
that it would not win, convenient advice which allows it to sit
out the challenge to the government (which is considering its
funding and its charter renewal) brought by individual
journalists. That in turn makes it more difficult for the challenge to succeed (if there was a problem the BBC itself would
have come to court) so that the legal advice becomes a
self-fulfilling prophecy, at least before the domestic courts.

JUDICIAL REVIEW

Administrative law has been the most obvious example of a
legal constraint on government. Public bodies will be prevented by the courts on an application for judicial review
from acting illegally, irrationally or unfairly. In the 1980s,
the courts developed the concept of a citizen's legitimate
expectation as exercising a new constraint on government. It
would be unfair for government to renege on a legitimate
expectation generated by an explicit promise or a past practice of conduct. Thus, had it not been for the trump card of
national security (played somewhat dubiously), Margaret
Thatcher would have lost the GCHQ case in the middle of
the 1980s because her predecessors had in practice consulted
civil service trade unions about terms and conditions so her
peremptory ban on trade union membership, announced
without consultation, would have disappointed their legitimate expectations.

In the 1990s, we are seeing two other doctrines struggling
to emerge into administrative law: proportionality and a duty
to give reasons. As is the way with the common law, we are still
at the stage of judges denying that there are such principles
while in fact applying them in all but name. The first, proportionality, had a mixed reception in the House of Lords when
the broadcasting restrictions on Sinn Fein were upheld, in a
decision which (contrary to some predictions) was approved
by the European Commission of Human Rights at Strasbourg.

All the judges thought that the restrictions were proportionate even if the doctrine did apply as a distinct ground of challenge but the case serves to illustrate the enormous potential if this head of review continues to be developed. In order to decide whether ministerial action is proportionate, one has to identify the objective it seeks to achieve, a rational connection between that end and the means adopted, and then decide whether the means employed are the least possible interference with the rights of citizens necessary to achieve a legitimate goal. In other words, ministers would have to spell out much more carefully than before exactly why they are adopting certain policies and they would have to show that there were no, less draconian, alternatives which would have worked.

This is all of a piece with the second evolving principle of a duty to give reasons. The Law Lords ruled in the summer of 1993 against the Home Secretary's refusal to give reasons to all life prisoners as to why they were not being paroled. This was not because of a general duty to give reasons, they claimed, but because of the special nature of the deprivation of liberty. Nonetheless, it is clear that just such a general duty is being nursed into life by the judges. It was only in the 1970s that the courts treated prisons as a no-go zone. Now every aspect of prison life seems to be tested in court. It is not just ministers but the whole burgeoning field of public sector decision-making which now has to be much more careful about the liberties it is taking with the rights of citizens. Unless reasons can at least be adduced in litigation, the courts can draw the inference that there were no acceptable grounds for a decision. For example, the Independent Television Commission performed a difficult task heroically in allocating TV franchises under bizarre rules without any leaks or any successful court challenges. In the one challenge which reached the Law Lords, their reasons for rejecting TSW were upheld, even though it was the existing franchise-holder, passed the quality threshold and had the highest bid. The reason, revealed in litigation, was that its business plan was judged by the ITC to be unsustainable and that was another criterion which the legislation had decreed. My point is that although the legislation also absolved the ITC from giving reasons for its decisions, the course of litigation forced it to explain itself or suffer an adverse ruling.

In other words, the great legal success story of the past thirty years has been the remorseless march of administrative law calling governments to account in court. This process was what had happened in the 1970s, not some vendetta against the Labour party but a proper challenge to all in public authority. In the absence of effective political opposition, this process of judicial review had been pretty much all there was to challenge the Thatcher governments. Judges reared in that spirit have now become the leading lights in the legal system. Their enthusiasm for checking government has been reinforced by the twin streams of European law, that flowing from the Luxembourg Court of Justice and the Strasbourg Court of Human Rights.

The former has encouraged the Law Lords this year to rule unlawful the government's *legislation* which differentiated between full-time and part-time workers in the protection they received. This adversely affected women, who form the bulk of part-time workers and thus falls foul of the European Union's insistence on equality of the sexes. The latter has infiltrated the British legal systems by the back door of judicial adoption while the government is devoting its energies to keeping the increasingly irrelevant front door of domestic legislative incorporation of the European Convention firmly barred. The walls of legal isolationism will come tumbling down sooner rather than later. Indeed, they already have if one looks at recent opinions of the Law Lords which refer to Commonwealth and US legal precedents alongside European developments just as readily as they rely on their own decisions. The high point of British judicial internationalism during John Major's four years as Prime Minister came in a case which had nothing ostensibly to do with Britain at all. Towards the end of 1993, the Judicial Committee of the Privy Council ruled that the death penalty would be unconstitutional in a number of appeals from Jamaica. In the course of a wide-ranging judgment, the Judicial Committee (which sits in Downing Street) referred without a second thought to a recent analysis of USA case-law on the death penalty by the Supreme Court of Zimbabwe. This was drawn upon by British judges to resolve Jamaica's problem, interpreting a clause in the constitution bequeathed by the British upon independence and based in large part on the European Convention. It is only a question of time before British judges are performing the same role within the United Kingdom.

CONSTITUTIONAL REVIEW

Such startling constitutional change might well be the result of John Major's time as Prime Minister. One way in which this might inadvertently be achieved is that the success of the Thatcher and Major governments in economic matters has led Labour to cast around for a distinctive policy in a different area and thus to steal the Liberal Democrats' clothes as constitutional reformers. If John Major then loses the next election, and especially if he only just loses it to a combination of Labour and the Liberal Democrats, he will be giving way to a government which will be honour bound to create a new constitution for a new millennium, including incorporation of the European Convention as a domestic bill of rights and a reordering of the legal departments of the state to yield a Ministry of Justice and Select Committee scrutiny of open judicial appointments.

More positively for Mr Major, an alternative route to much the same position would be for him to extend the logic of his one good Big Idea, the Citizen's Charter, from a consumerist vision of the recipient of public services to a rights- and duties-based ideal of active citizenship. The big barrier to Conservative adoption of the bill of rights argument is that it seems to go against the grain of British common law tradition. This argument always amazes foreigners who think of the thirteenth century Magna Carta and the seventeenth century Bill of Rights as the mother and father of all constitutional guarantees.

John Major might rediscover that tradition in the context of his search for a settlement to the conflict in Northern Ireland since there have been entrenched rights in the Northern Ireland legal system from its inception. From that, it

might be but a short step to pre-empting the Liberal Democrats and the Labour party by yoking his own Citizen's
Charter to Magna Carta. This would certainly take a bold
leap of the imagination and might be undertaken in the
mistaken belief that the emperor of law has no clothes, that a
bill of rights could later be brushed aside by a vigorous
government.

For whatever reason, however, the possibility can be
glimpsed of John Major influencing the creation of a domestic bill of rights, so long as he fights the next election as leader
of the Conservative party. For if he is to last that long, he
really does need to develop his strengths such as the Citizen's
Charter and his attempts to bring peace to Northern Ireland
and if he were to lose the next general election, it would be to
a party or parties which have had to outflank him on constitutional issues. If, on the other hand, John Major were not to
lead the Conservatives into the next election, it may be that
the constitutional dimensions of his own initiatives would be
lost. It is difficult to see any of the plausible successors being
seriously interested in charterism or Northern Ireland.
Lawyers, who have not always admitted the obvious point
that they will be the beneficiaries of a shift to a bill of rights,
might therefore be keen to see John Major survive and perhaps be remembered ultimately for a Major Carta.

CONCLUSIONS

A non-lawyer's verdict on John Major's treatment of lawyers
might be that he followed Margaret Thatcher's indulgence
towards the legal professions, letting them get away scot-free
from reforms which had engulfed other entrenched interests
at least until Lord Justice Scott began the task of calling
lawyers, and the government itself, to account. Perhaps this is
because he respects lawyers, apparently for two qualities
which he admires and sees in himself: negotiating skills and
integrity. On the latter, cynics might say that he may be
relying on an unrepresentative sample – the undoubted integrity of the lawyers closest to him, his Lord Chancellor, his

former Attorney-General and his current Attorney-General. There is something appealing, however, about the Prime Minister's almost naïve belief in respect for the rule of law, which was part of what *he* meant by Back to Basics. It is in this respect that he could have focused more on the law instead of allowing others to set the pace on the sexual morality aspects of this theme from the 1993 party conference.

The trouble even had he done so, however, would have been that the basics of the legal system and legal professions have not been addressed by the Thatcher or Major governments. It is unlikely that Labour, until recently led by John Smith, QC, is going to threaten this last untouched trade union, neither would the Liberal Democrats (the lawyers' party at play) seem likely to question the advance of the legal professions.

On the contrary, the lawyers are likely to continue to flourish, pretty much regulating themselves and increasingly everyone else. As long as we remember to beware the leaders of a revolution, this is not necessarily a bad thing. For all the smallness of a very small world, and the dangers of casual conversations at cocktail parties influencing judicial thinking without it passing through the submissions of the lawyers arguing the cases, there are benefits to the recent glasnost between the judiciary and the thinking world. 'Concorde jurisprudence', which celebrates and sometimes seems to merge two cultures into "Anglo-American" law, is giving way to a truly global service in which the best ideas from what I call Celtic-Commonwealth-Continental jurisprudence are fed into the judiciary. This is particularly evident in the tours de force the Major years have seen from the Judicial Committee of the Privy Council. In their first decision on the Hong Kong bill of rights, for example, the Privy Council in 1993 analysed the Canadian approach to proportionality in a decision which then facilitates the use of that line of thinking in domestic British cases. A further example of the Jamaican death penalty case is given above. The great thinkers among legal practitioners such as Anthony Lester, QC, Geoffrey Robertson, QC and David Pannick, QC, can be relied upon to transmit the best of the latest ideas from around the world swiftly into British courts. The beleaguered Attorney-General Sir Nicholas Lyell, QC, has instructed more and more amici curiae (literally 'friends of the court', a brief not by the two parties to the dispute but to assist the court to reach a decision in the public interest by considering other arguments) in important cases, such as that by Anthony Lester, QC, in the Bland case, where Hoffmann LJ also acknowledged the assistance he had derived from conversations with a couple of philosophers.

Of course, the lawyers are self-interested and reluctant to concede the sensible demands for open scrutiny of their appointments when they call for themselves to have more power as the guardians of a new constitutional settlement. Nonetheless, the lawyers deserve praise for having used judicial review to cut significantly into the islands of unaccountable decision-making. Such areas are increasingly isolated as the law boldly goes where it has not gone before, for instance, into the heart of the royal prerogative, challenging Michael Howard's non-use of the prerogative of mercy in the Bentley case. European law makes similar waves. The difficulty facing not just Mr Major but any successor of any party is that the tides of law are in some ways beyond the control of politicians. Sea-walls can be erected, designed to regulate in a way which suits the government but there is always the danger of the water pouring through the weakest point.

The question facing John Major is whether he can emulate King Canute who knew that he could not control the sea but had to demonstrate his own ineffectiveness to his followers (ah, so that is what the Prime Minister has been doing!). Once reality is grasped, some measures can be taken to deal with the possibilities of flooding. The tides can be plotted and anticipated.

Constitutional experiments have certainly been conducted in the stormy seas of Northern Ireland. Every constitutional innovation dreamt of by the pan-legalist centre-left-front in Hampstead has been tried in Northern Ireland, not only the notion of entrenching rights but more political measures to benefit the middle ground such as proportional representation, which has been used in local and European elections in Northern Ireland for many years. More recently, the Downing

Street Declaration gave John Major a taste of what it means to draw up a new agenda for constitutional change. As somebody who went into the last election four square behind the Scottish union, he will encounter some tough questions next time round about these manoeuvres, imaginative and desirable as they are and life-saving as a settlement of the northern Irish conflict would be not only for those of us who live in Northern Ireland but, in a political sense, for John Major himself. Yet he could fashion an unlikely role as the man who heralds, in the best tradition of Magna Carta and all that, a new compact between citizens and their states to capture the mood at the turn of the millennium. Having negotiated new legal orders in Europe and Ireland, arrangements for Scotland, Wales and England itself could be relatively easy.

With or without John Major at the helm, some such new order is likely to be demanded as millennial fever grips the country. The Liberal Democrats, and their precursors, have tried and failed with this line before but now the idea of reassessing citizenship is an idea whose time has come. This is partly due to John Major's useful if tentative experiment in Citizen's Charters. The heart of that movement is the demand to make public services accountable to citizens. The further step which a genuinely *constitutional* charter of rights would take is to make government ministers accountable to citizens. This has so far been a step too far for British governments. They are being nudged in that direction, however, by legal forces beyond their control. To welcome, rather than resist, this trend towards accountability through the giving of reasons would be a mark of genius. If John Major can incorporate this into his form of charterism it would be one small step for him, one giant leap not only for the chattering and chartering classes but for all citizens.

Notes

1. John Griffith, *The Politics of the Judiciary*, 4th edition (Fontana, 1991).
2. John Griffith, *Judicial Politics since 1920 – a chronicle* (Blackwell and the Institute of Contemporary British History, 1994).

Bibliography

Ronald Dworkin, *Life's Dominion* (HarperCollins, 1993)

John Morison, 'How to change things with rules' in Livingstone and Morison (eds.), *Law, Society & Change* (Dartmouth, 1990)

John Morison & Philip Leith, *The Barrister's World* (Open University Press, 1992)

Joshua Rozenberg, *In Search of Justice* (Hodder & Stoughton, 1994)

Don Rowe, *The Citizen as a Moral Agent – the Development of a Continuous and Progressive Conflict-based Citizenship* Curriculum 1992 Curriculum 178.

Don Rowe & Tony Thorpe, eds., *Living with the Law* (Hodder & Stoughton, 1993).

Clive Walker, Introduction in C. Walker and K. Starmer (eds.), *Justice in Error* (Blackstone, 1993)

Diana Woodhouse, *Ministerial responsibility: the abdication of responsibility through the receipt of legal advice* 1993 Public Law 412

Airedale v Bland [1993] 1 All ER 821

Attorney-General of Hong Kong v Lee Kwong-Kut [1993] 3 WLR 329

M v Home Office [1993] 3 WLR 433

Morgan & Pratt v Attorney-General of Jamaica [1993] 3 WLR 995

Pepper v Hart [1992] 3 WLR 1032, and see the Lord Advocate's comments on the implications thereof (Hansard, HL Deb Vol. 231, col. 455, 3 November 1993)

R v Home Secretary, ex p Brind [1991] 1 AC 696

R v Home Secretary, ex p Doody [1993] 3 WLR 154

R v Secretary of State for Employment ex p Equal Opportunities Commission, 3 March 1994

Calcutt Report (Cm 2135, 1993)

Woolf Report: *Prison Disturbances April 1990. Report of an Inquiry*, Cm 1456 (HMSO, 1991), see also the Director General of the Prison Service's progress report on implementing the Woolf recommendations (Hansard, HC Deb Vol. 230, col. 134, 18 October 1993)

Chapter 9

OPPOSITION

Dennis Kavanagh

I F S O M E Conservatives feel that the party has been too long in office, virtually all Labour supporters feel that their party has been too long out of office. The 1980s have joined the 1930s and the 1950s as bleak periods in the party's history. If Labour had formed a government in 1992 Neil Kinnock would have selected from a shadow cabinet which included only two members who had previous Cabinet experience and then only in minor posts. John Smith's successor has none. The party's general election defeats in 1983 and 1987 were on a bigger scale than any that the party had suffered for over fifty years, and the 1992 loss was comprehensive in terms of votes, if not in seats. The average gap of 10 per cent in the shares of the vote gained by the Conservative and Labour parties in the last four general elections may justify us in talking about a dominant party system. By this we meant that a party has been in office for a long period and has a substantial margin of popular support over the second party. By 1996 the Conservatives will have been in office, alone or in coalition, for sixty-six of the years since 1900.

The relative impotence of the opposition in such a concentrated political system has had a number of consequences. The attendance of Labour MPs in Parliament for much of the 1980s was poor and the most significant opposition to the government came from Conservative backbenchers or from the Upper House. The political agenda was largely shaped by Thatcher governments and the other parties had to respond to far-reaching changes in many areas, a number of which have become so entrenched that it will be difficult to reverse them. Local government, much of the public sector, the professions and the civil service all found their working methods challenged fundamentally.

The electoral impact of the opposition was also weakened by its fragmentation, more precisely the decline of Labour after 1979 and the rise of the centre. Since 1979 the Conservative share of electoral support has been fairly steady, between 41 and 43 per cent, while elsewhere there has been much turbulence. The Social Democrats were formed in 1981, achieved stunning by-election victories, but had expired by 1989. The Alliance between the SDP and the Liberals broke up in 1989 and a new Liberal Democratic party began inauspiciously with 6 per cent of the vote, according to the opinion polls, and recovered to 18 per cent in the 1992 general election. In May 1989 the Greens came from anonymity to gain 15 per cent in the Euro elections, only to become almost extinct within twelve months. There are, therefore, two themes to the electoral politics of the 1980s. One is Conservative dominance, the other is the emergence of three-party politics and the rise of the considerable centre party vote. The bad news for Labour has been that it is not the overwhelming repository of the anti-Conservative electorate. The good news is that there is also an anti-Conservative majority.

There has been a lively debate about the extent to which the dominance of the Conservative party has been a result of demographic and value changes among the electorate, or whether it has been a result of the ineptitude of the opposition parties. Of course much of Labour's behaviour in the early 1980s was self-defeating, and a number of the party's policies frightened voters. But longer-run forces were also at work. It has been calculated that since 1964 the impact of such demographic changes as the growth of the middle class and private home ownership combined with the decline of the trade unions has added some 3 per cent to the Conservative baseline vote, and subtracted some 4 per cent from the Labour vote. It is clear that the divided opposition and the effects of the electoral system have helped the Conservative party. It gained some 60 per cent of the seats in the 1983 and 1987 Parliaments for just 42 per cent of the vote.

In the 1992 general election the proportion of voters identifying themselves as Labour was, according to Gallup, 35 per cent, compared to 39 per cent for the Conservatives. This seems to be close to estimates of Labour's 'normal' vote. In general elections since 1970 the party's average share of the vote has been 34 per cent, 6 per cent less than the Conservative average.[1] The party's core vote remains in the North and West of Britain and the inner cities, and among council house tenants and the unskilled working class. All these groups are declining in size. Since 1979 Labour has lost much support in the South and the skilled working class. To win office it has to create a broad national cross-class appeal. At the next election it will need a post-war record swing of 5 per cent to get a majority of seats.

By the end of Mrs Thatcher's tenure the Labour party had made two significant steps towards transforming itself. Following the 1987 election defeat the party embarked on an ambitious policy review which was accepted at the annual conference in 1989. The main object of the review was to remove the policies which were making the party unelectable. The party abandoned unilateralism, accepted some of the industrial relations changes, welcomed Britain's membership of the European Community, including the European Monetary System and the social chapter. In addition, it abandoned targets for reducing unemployment, moved from the steeply progressive income tax rates which prevailed before 1979 and accepted in large part the privatization of the utilities. Supply side socialism emphasized that the state's role would be less in ownership and economic planning and more in training, investment and research. The party also grasped the mantle of constitutional reform. It pledged itself to introducing an elected Scottish Assembly with tax raising powers in the first session of Parliament, an elected second chamber, a freedom of information act, and appointed a working party to examine the merits of electoral reform.

Much of this review was initiated from the top, for many of the activists were disillusioned and showed clear signs of being de-energized. Surveys of constituency members showed that they still held left wing views on public ownership, defence and public spending.[2]

Labour, like socialist parties pretty well everywhere, has moved from collectivism, and distanced itself from organized labour. It also has problems in preaching redistribution in a society in which the haves so greatly outnumber the have-nots. As noted in Chapter 1, this is part of a bigger picture throughout Europe. Parties of the left can point to the limits of markets but they also have to promise to work with them as the main engine of economic growth. Clause IV is effectively dead and buried; Labour is no longer the party of public ownership. But neither Neil Kinnock nor Margaret Thatcher killed off socialism. Rather the impact of international forces has reduced the effectiveness of state management of the economy.

As well as the policy review, after 1987 Mr Kinnock also moved to overhaul the party's structure, largely unchanged since 1918. He campaigned for one member one vote for the selection of parliamentary candidates, in face of considerable trade union opposition. Trade unions agreed to reduce the size of their block vote at the annual party conference and conference itself lost some power to a Joint Policy Commission, which gave the major say to front bench spokesmen. The party also took steps to promote the political prospects of women in NEC elections and the Shadow Cabinet. So much of Kinnock's energy in his nine years as leader was spent sorting out the party and leading it away from unpopular policies and the baggage of the past, that he failed to project a positive vision. He nearly made the party electable, but he may also have been an obstacle to getting it elected.

SINCE MAJOR

The election of John Major as party leader in November 1990 transformed the Conservative election prospects. The change from Margaret Thatcher in such a leader-dominated administration inevitably gave the impression that a new government had been formed. The Conservative party had answered Labour's appeal that it was time for a change. Labour's overwhelming lead in the opinion polls fell away, though for the rest of the Parliament the parties were still level pegging. A second consequence was the softening of the Conservative image. Mrs Thatcher had always decisively out-scored Kinnock on the qualities of toughness and decisiveness but trailed on the caring qualities. Neil Kinnock's strengths compared to Mrs Thatcher were matched by those of John Major, but he in turn never matched Major's strengths, as perceived by the public. A third consequence was that for all the emphasis which the parties placed upon policy differ-ences, the election of John Major inevitably moved the Con-servatives to the metaphorical centre ground. This had been the destination of Labour's policy review since 1987 and it succeeded. But now Labour was joined by the Thatcherless Tory party. Surveys overwhelmingly showed that the voters saw few differences between the parties, in contrast to 1983 and 1987, and regarded both as moderate rather than extreme.

Throughout much of the 1980s Labour had attacked the Conservatives for their harsh, uncaring, confrontational approach. Much of this could be personified by Mrs Thatcher. That rhetoric was no longer effective when deployed against John Major. His modest social background and many of his concerns (such as hopes for a classless society) were entirely suitable for a leader of the new Labour party. On many key issues Labour was actually preferred to the Conservatives but, crucially, on the questions of eco-nomic management, taxation and leadership Labour never narrowed the deficit with the Conservatives sufficiently to make its strengths on the social issues count.

If perceptions of John Major's premiership have been largely shaped by Britain's forced exit from the ERM in September 1992, there has been no similar turning-point in Labour's recent history. Defeat in the 1992 election and the replacement of Neil Kinnock by John Smith only reinforced the pressure for further modernization. John Smith easily defeated Bryan Gould for the leadership. Gould campaigned for a return to Keynesian techniques of combating unemployment and attacked the constraints on economic policy stemming from Britain's membership of the ERM, and he represented a change of direction. The election of Smith represented a confirmation of the old social democratic traditions of the Labour party. The party was now less factionalized. Left versus right and pro- and anti-Europe divisions remained but they were muted and divisions were more apparent between modernizers and traditionalists. Indeed the changes to party policy on defence and the EC must lead the Gang of Four to wonder why they left the Labour party for the SDP in 1981.

John Smith immediately staked his leadership on continuing to reform the party, particularly in adopting one person one vote for the selection of candidates and election of leaders. This was achieved at the party conference in 1993. Trade unions also agreed to a dilution of their role in the electoral college, reducing their original 40 per cent of the vote to a third, the same as constituency parties and MPs. He did not push proportional representation, though he was prepared to abide by the result of a referendum. Apart from this there have been few if any changes to the party structure or party policy. As leader, Smith proved to be extremely cautious from 1992 to 1994. Many of the big changes in policy and party organization had been accomplished under Kinnock. The party appears to have backed off major spending programmes which would require extra taxes. The kindly obituaries of John Smith contrasted with the disappointment of some colleagues that as leader he was failing to differentiate the party clearly from the Conservatives, and was too reliant on the blunders of the government. The left continued to decline as a force, with Smith's lieutenants, Gordon Brown and Tony Blair, both gaining election to the NEC, while Tony Benn and Dennis Skinner lost their seats. The electoral college had been promoted in 1981 to strengthen the left's grip on the party; in 1992, 90 per cent of its vote went to John Smith, the most right-wing leader since Gaitskell. It is a largely Kinnockized party that was handed to John Smith and his successor as leader.

Labour's grassroots have withered. The individual membership remains obstinately below 300,000, in spite of numerous campaigns to raise it. The number of full-time agents has remained less than 60 for two decades now. In 1951 it was near 300. The party's research department is badly run down and increasingly party leaders rely upon their own special advisers and research assistants or turn to the Institute of Public Policy Research. Indeed the Institute, with Patricia Hewitt as deputy director, has established links with social democratic parties on the Continent and has been a source of fresh thinking about the European Community, constitutional change, road pricing and new patterns of work. Since December 1992 it has also organized a potentially important commission on social justice and the welfare state. This commission and the report of the working party on electoral reform under Professor Raymond Plant are examples of the party's willingness to reach out beyond the party in search of new ideas. After all, the intellectual foundations of postwar social democracy – full employment and welfare – were laid by the Liberals, Keynes and Beveridge.

A revival of the Liberal Democrats under Paddy Ashdown ensured that Britain would still have multi-party electoral politics in the 1990s. The centre party has gained an average of nearly 20 per cent in the last six general elections. As long as this remains the case then it is difficult for Labour to break through the 40 per cent barrier. When John Major replaced Mrs Thatcher it was easier for the Liberal Democrats to be more even-handed between the two parties. Many of the Liberals' best electoral prospects are in Conservative-held seats and on many issues, notably constitutional change including proportional representation, devolution in Scotland, a Freedom of Information Act, and so on, there is little difference between Liberal and Labour. But Liberal voters are pretty evenly divided between Labour and Conservative when they are asked their second choice of vote. A move by the Liberals in Parliament to support either of the two major parties risks alienating a considerable section of their vote. This danger was perhaps seen when Neil Kinnock made his proportional representation initiative during the general election. This gave point to Conservative charges that a Liberal vote was a Trojan horse for electing a Labour government by the back door. Post-election surveys show that a number of voters were worried about the prospects of instability. One way to cope with this might be for the two parties to announce, well in advance, that in the event of a hung Parliament they would cooperate.

Research by Anthony Heath and Roger Jowell shows that the two parties were competing for the same issue space in the 1992 election and that Labour's gains in the general election largely came from the Liberals.[3] Can Labour and Liberals achieve an accommodation which will enable them to displace the Conservative party as the dominant political force in Britain? The longstanding aim of a centre left Lib-Lab coalition, dating back to before 1914, still remains a distant prospect.

CONCLUSION

One can make out a case that there has been a Major effect on Labour, although an unintended one. The events of 'Black Wednesday' and subsequent divisions, scandals and U-turns have removed the Conservative party's reputation for competent economic management and strong leadership. This has greatly improved Labour's election prospects. Labour's leader, for the first time since 1979, is no longer dwarfed by a Conservative Prime Minister. In other words, Labour's two great weaknesses in 1992 – leadership and economic management – are no longer so apparent. On the other hand, the transformation of Labour from the party that it was, even in 1987, was largely due to successive election defeats and the apparent permanence of many of the Thatcher policies. As long as Mrs Thatcher was leader there appeared to be sharp differences between the parties, not least because of her political style and ultimate goals. This is no longer the case.

What remains unclear is whether the great dissatisfaction with the Major government will be translated into support for a change at the next election. In 1992 post-election surveys revealed a strong fear of a Labour government among skilled working class voters. They feared that they would lose out from Labour's policies to help the poor; the party would 'drag down' or 'hold back' ambitious people. The Conservatives were more readily seen as the party of choice and opportunity.

A competitive opposition party presents the electorate with a realistic alternative government. Only in 1992, for the first time since 1974, did Labour do this. But the party system should also present voters with a choice of alternative visions. In many respects the party system since 1990 has failed to articulate well defined choices between the major parties on economic management, on the European Community (notably, membership of the ERM), apart from the acceptance of the social chapter, and on most of the public services (given the emphasis upon consumers). The battles of the 1980s concerning privatization, nuclear weapons and membership of the EC are dead. Although Labour is now a party of constitutional reform it is not clear how much priority it attaches to its constitutional proposals. Before 1990 it was reasonable to mourn the lack of a competitive party system, particularly in such a centralized political structure. Since 1990 critics are more likely to mourn the absence of meaningful choice between the major political parties. The first was the Thatcher Effect, the second a Major one.

Notes

1. See R. Rose, 'Structural Change or Cyclical Fluctuation?' (*Parliamentary Affairs*, 1992).
2. P. Seyd and P. Whiteley, *Labour's Grass Roots: The Politics of Party Membership* (Clarendon Press, 1992).
3. See 'Labour's Policy Review' in A. Heath et al (eds) *Labour's Last Chance? The 1992 Election and Beyond* (Dartmouth, 1994).

Chapter 10

POLICY MAKING AND CABINET

Anthony Seldon

T HE CENTRAL policy-making process and the operation of
Cabinet and its committees remain among the deepest
mysteries of British government. Even after the publication of
information about Cabinet committees in 1992, official secrecy shrouds the operation of the central decision-making
machine, yet there is no more fascinating or important part of
the constitution for the student of government to consider.
This chapter will examine briefly its operation since 1990.[1]

THE THATCHER LEGACY

Mrs Thatcher was a great centralizer.[2] In the years after
1979, she sought to drive policy herself, both in domestic and
increasingly in foreign policy. In the 1970s and earlier 1980s,
the right wing think-tanks, the Institute of Economic Affairs,
the Centre for Policy Studies and the Adam Smith Institute
had helped to prepare the ground and occasionally the detail
of the Thatcher agenda. She had very clear favourites among
ministers to whom she gave her confidence. The names fluctuated, but they all exhibited the neo-liberal reforming zeal
that informed her own thinking. Ministers deemed not to be
on side were almost invariably marginalized.

Decisions were increasingly taken in individual meetings with Mrs Thatcher and a small number of close ministerial colleagues (the so-called ad hoc bilaterals and trilaterals). Full Cabinet, and even the elaborate structure of Cabinet committees, was effectively excluded in those cases such as entry into the ERM where Mrs Thatcher believed she would not obtain her own way. Ministers, all bound by collective responsibility, would find themselves having to defend decisions to which they had not been party.

Responsibility for policy derivation, and scrutiny of policy from other departments, fell increasingly on the Prime Minister's Office in Number 10. In the first administration (1979–83), when Clive Whitmore had been her principal private secretary, Ian Gow her parliamentary private secretary, John Hoskyns her head of Policy Unit, Derek Rayner her efficiency adviser and Robin Ibbs head of the Central Policy Review Staff, this had been a relatively broad-based affair.

But by the time of her final administration (1987-90), and after the departures in 1987 of her closest Cabinet adviser William Whitelaw and Cabinet secretary Robert Armstrong, a gulf opened up between Mrs Thatcher and her Cabinet colleagues. Her network of advisers closed in, and at Number 10 influence effectively fell on Bernard Ingham, press secretary, and Charles Powell, private secretary responsible for foreign affairs, with Alan Walters an intermittent but powerful presence advising on economic and European policy and Percy Cradock, also an influential figure as her foreign affairs adviser at Number 10, chairing the Joint Intelligence Committee. Attempts by concerned ministers and officials to move Ingham and Powell had failed.

Both men became more involved in political advice and brokering than was commensurate with their status as civil servants. Not since at least 1973–74 had such a constitutional abnormality been present at the heart of British government, when William Armstrong, head of the Home Civil Service, had become too closely identified with the policies of the then Prime Minister, Edward Heath.

CONTINUED THINK-TANK AND INTEREST GROUP ECLIPSE

The decline in influence of the think-tanks, already in evidence in the latter days of Mrs Thatcher, accelerated, at least for the first two years. Major set out deliberately to adopt a different *modus operandi* from Mrs Thatcher, and distanced himself from the right–wing ideologues. Since the 1992 general election the think-tanks have been making a limited comeback, principally the Adam Smith Institute (under Madsen Pirie, whom Major finds personally congenial) and to a lesser extent the European Policy Forum (under former IEA director, Graham Mather) and the Social Market Foundation (under Danny Finkelstein). But their influence remains restricted to a narrow canvass, principally the management of the public sector and constitutional issues connected with the EU.

Interest groups, so influential in the 1960s and 1970s, were marginalized by Number 10 in the 1980s. Mrs Thatcher, influenced in part by public choice theory, was determined to separate powerful sectional interest groups from the processes of government. As a consequence of their cool response from Whitehall, pressure groups turned their attention increasingly to Parliament and indeed to the courts. In the 1990s, they have recovered some of their standing with the executive. But trade unions, even with the more amenable John Monks as General Secretary of the TUC from 1993, are still rarely consulted. John Major has more time for unions than Mrs Thatcher, but still tells them for example that unions are not acceptable at GCHQ, even though his tone in telling them is less strident. Major is keen to build up individual relations with CBI leaders and other businessmen, who have become more frequent visitors at Number 10 than in the 1980s. But the CBI and Institute of Directors still failed to win government backing for many of their favoured projects. Other non-economic interest groups are even more peripheral, though John Major remains far more receptive than Mrs Thatcher to well-organized, *ad hoc* pressure groups making a reasoned case, as the war veterans made over scrapping D-Day celebrations in the spring of 1994. But in general, the comment of one well-placed source stands: 'The policy-making process under John Major in Downing Street is totally free of the influence of outside pressure groups'.[3] Insider interest groups retain close relations with their client departments in Whitehall and in general the Major government shows more awareness than that of Mrs Thatcher of the benefits of obtaining pressure group support when passing legislation through Parliament. Where interest groups have been overlooked, as over the national curriculum and testing in education, or over Howard's police and criminal justice reforms at the Home Office, it has often been to the government's cost.

WHITEHALL DEPARTMENTS

Policy since 1990 has come from two principal quarters: Whitehall departments and Number 10, Downing Street.

Policy-making under John Major has thus devolved back more to the individual government departments, with the policy agenda being set by those departments most efficient and effective at formulating long-term plans, especially where they boasted a strong ministerial champion. Social Security under Peter Lilley after 1992 has been conspicuously activist. The Home Office in 1993-94 under Michael Howard has been responsible for producing several initiatives, as has the Department for Education under Kenneth Clarke (1990–92) and the early days of John Patten (until 1993). In both departments the reforms were pressed ahead in the face of some considerable resistance from civil servants. The Department of the Environment under Michael Heseltine (1990–92) was an activist department, but became less of an initiator after the 1992 general election, in particular when John Selwyn Gummer was minister (after May 1993).

NUMBER 10, DOWNING STREET

Departments will either work up their new ideas in tandem with the Policy Unit in Number 10, or will send them in and the Policy Unit will then proffer comments.

The Policy Unit is the heart of Number 10's policy-making capacity. Founded in 1974, its scope increased after the demise of the Central Policy Review Staff (the 'think-tank') in 1983. Mrs Thatcher's final head was Brian Griffiths, but his influence was muted, confined largely to education and limited aspects of economic policy.

Within weeks of arrival, John Major appointed Sarah Hogg head of Policy Unit, an assertive and highly intelligent figure who has aroused predictable jealousy in Whitehall and the party. An early task was to re-establish the position of the Unit, and until the 1992 election she worked closely on this with two colleagues, Nick True and Jonathan Hill. After it, True became her official deputy, and Hill became Major's political secretary, still based in Number 10. But Sarah Hogg has become unquestionably the most influential figure at Number 10 advising Major, especially on trade and economic policy.

The Policy Unit's work consists in developing the Prime Minister's ideas, commenting upon proposals put up by Whitehall departments, and disseminating the Prime Minister's approach to those developing policies in the departments. Its work was particularly felt in four key areas in Major's first two years. It helped to devise a source of local government revenue to replace the poll tax, which was the dominant problem in Major's first few months in office. The Unit acted as a bridge between Number 10, the Treasury and the Department of the Environment, out of which emerged the new council tax. It helped develop a European strategy in preparation for the Maastricht intergovernmental conference in December 1991. Thirdly the Unit worked closely on the evolution of Major's economic policy based upon non-inflationary growth. Its economic advice role has involved the Unit in establishing close relations with offices of other key heads of government, both within the EU and the wider G7 nations, in particular over GATT negotiations, which Major worked hard to see completed after earlier stallings. Finally, as discussed in chapter 3 (pp. 34–36) the Unit played a key role in developing Major's strategy for the 1992 general election, in particular his emphasis upon educational standards and training, and reform of the public service. Major's drive to improve the delivery of public services, an area comparatively neglected by Mrs Thatcher, has been very much informed by the Policy Unit. After 1992 the Unit's drive has become more diffuse, but its influence has been felt across a broad range of domestic and European policy.

With the end of Major's post-election honeymoon with the departure from the ERM in September 1992, the Policy Unit came under some fire. Some argued that Sarah Hogg had become too influential, and that short-term political advice was not her forte. Critics further alleged that John Major suffered from the lack of such an input, and indeed policy coordination, at Number 10. With an ideological and highly interventionist Prime Minister such as Mrs Thatcher, such a capability might not have been needed, but the lack has been felt since 1990. Calls, last heard in 1982-84, for a beefed-up Number 10, or indeed a full-blown Prime Minister's Department, were again heard. But with some recovery of the government's position after June 1994, such calls are likely to pass. When a government's policies are unpopular, then individuals and institutions are likely to be blamed.

Gus O'Donnell, the chief press secretary, was the other most consistently close figure to Major in Number 10. Chosen by him to succeed Ingham, and sharing similar interests, opinions of people and humble South London origins as Major, O'Donnell moved into the Number 10 press office with him from the Treasury in November 1990. A very different figure to the assertive Ingham, and indeed the more scholarly and tough Chris Meyer who succeeded him in early 1994, O'Donnell's calm and consistent influence not just on presentation but also on the substance of policy can be readily overlooked. O'Donnell received some contemporary criticism for the quality of his presentational advice to Major and for his handling of the press. Continuation of many of the same problems in Meyer's first six months suggests that there was an element of scapegoating of O'Donnell.

John Major's Number 10 was a far more fluid and informal place than it was in the later Thatcher period, which was
characterized by strong rivalries (e.g. between the press and
private office, and especially Ingham and Powell) largely
absent since. The political office provides the link between
Number 10 and the party. Run by the political secretary, its
influence extends over all party and political matters, an
influence that increased when Jonathan Hill succeeded Judith
Chaplin after the general election. Chaplin was a close Major
confidant but increasingly lacked the time (she was a parliamentary candidate at Newbury) and also perhaps the will to
be a key player in a tough environment. Major finds the style
and content of Hill's advice congenial, and again this office
has recovered some of its role since 1990, following its mar-
ginalization in the mid to late 1980s. Linkage with the party
at Westminster is provided by the parliamentary private
secretary, Graham Bright, a popular figure but not a heavyweight presence and too modest to exert much influence.
Norman Fowler (party chairman, 1992–94) was however a
powerful political influence on Major, as much as anything
by dint of their close friendship (Major had been a junior
minister to Fowler).

The private office, staffed by civil servants, links the
Prime Minister to the rest of Whitehall. It returned to its
standard constitutional role after 1990 (Powell being the
single, though highly significant aberrant figure in it under
Mrs Thatcher). Powell, who stayed on until early 1991, was
initially treated with much suspicion by Major, but his
immense skills soon won him over. His successor as overseas
affairs private secretary, Stephen Wall, rapidly became a
trusted confidant and for some time the most influential civil
servant at Number 10.

Presiding over the team of four specialist private secretaries is the principal private secretary, Andrew Turnbull,
who ran a very tight, efficient ship, as has his successor since
1993, Alex Allan, with whom Major had worked before and
whose more relaxed style appeals to him. Major has (unlike
Thatcher) an instinctive trust of civil servants, with whom,
even before 1990, he had always worked closely.

Another change is that Sir Peter Levene, head of the

Efficiency Unit, was kept at a distance from Number 10. Under Mrs Thatcher, efficiency advisers worked closely with the Prime Minister. Levene, although an effective and respected figure in Whitehall, sees John Major far less frequently. To a significant extent, this switch in practice is compensated for by Major seeing a number of new advisers in related fields, notably the head of his Citizen's Charter Panel and the head of his Charter Unit.

Major's Number 10 is no less important than Mrs Thatcher's as the key policy-making nexus in British government. Indeed, its influence, working with the Cabinet Office, is akin to the US President's White House Office. Number 10's internal operation under Major became more open, informal and broad-based. But it still arouses similar jealousies from 'outsiders' (MPs, civil servants, Central Office) as before 1990.

CABINET SYSTEM

The Cabinet system, consisting of Cabinet and a wide array of committees all serviced by the Cabinet Office, does not make policy, but it brings together all the relevant ministers who need to decide policy. Again, there have been considerable changes here since Mrs Thatcher. The principal changes are as follows:

1. Collegiate decision-making has largely returned to Cabinet discussions. The contrast was noted at Major's very first Cabinet in November 1990. Ministers began almost silently, but they gradually picked up the signal that it was safe to venture opinions, and by the end there was a crescendo of hitherto constrained voices. Major said after his first six months, 'I do encourage all ministers to express their views: if this makes for longer Cabinets, so be it.' Kenneth Clarke concurred. 'Cabinet meetings are taking rather longer than under Mrs Thatcher.'[4] Major is by instinct, and political reality, much more of a team-builder than Mrs Thatcher, and likes to get hearts and minds behind a decision. He also believes it to be a good way of pinning ministers down to a decision, thus enhancing

collective responsibility. A representative range of (unat-tributed) views on Major's Cabinet style confirms this view. 'No one would stand up to Mrs Thatcher in Cabinet: it is now very different.' 'I can recall few, if any, times that John Major has been beaten in Cabinet: the reason for this is that he carries colleagues with him, working hard beforehand if necessary to ensure he's done the groundwork on potentially difficult colleagues.' 'It is remarkable how he takes the Cabinet with him: when he sums up, he does so making people feel that they have been consulted.' 'John Major's great ability is to get consensus, a position everyone is happy to accept.' 'The big difference before and after 1990 is that now if people feel they have something to say, they say it. This explains why the Cabinet Secretariat became worried at depart-mental ministers pitching in with matters of which their civil servants had no foreknowledge.' Even allowing for a rose-tinted view of Cabinet's operation, Major's critics not being as willing to talk to me as were his supporters, and exaggerated loyalty at a beleaguered time, the broad picture from these Cabinet ministers of a restoration of Cabinet government remains. This view was confirmed in a public lecture by Lord Wakeham in November 1993.[5] The new style was seen most tellingly at the time of the Maastricht Cabinets in the summer of 1993 when Major, in a style recalling Callaghan's handling of the IMF crisis in 1976, held Cabinet together at a very difficult time and produced a passingly harmonious solution. To some, Major's collegiate approach is dictated by political weak-ness, and a desire to bind colleagues into collective responsibility. Others see it as a product of Major, unlike his predecessor, having a genuine and high respect for Cabinet colleagues. He believes that if they have made it to Cabinet then they have done so on merit and experi-ence. On the other hand, one should not overlook Major being at times sharp with colleagues in Cabinet. He has also called some of them 'bastards'.

2. There has been a move away from *ad hoc* decision-taking outside the Cabinet and Cabinet committee structure, in small, secret meetings not serviced by the Cabinet

Secretariat. John Major does not fight, as did Mrs Thatcher, to keep items which he dislikes off the Cabinet agenda. In his first two years moreover Major liked to take many final decisions in full Cabinet, but since 1992/93 more have been taken at the level of Cabinet committee. Matters reach full Cabinet if they are either deemed very important, such as commitment of troops to Bosnia, or are politically divisive, such as Qualified Majority Voting.

3. Greater openness, including the release in May 1992 of 'Questions of Procedure for Ministers', the rulebook (allegedly) of the operation of Cabinet government and ministerial-official relations, and also the names of Cabinet committees and their chairmen (their identities hitherto had been officially secret). Mrs Thatcher had been lobbied (by Peter Hennessy, among others) to release this information, but she and Robert Armstrong (head of the Home Civil Service, 1979–87) found the arguments against overwhelming. This spirit of openness was extended more widely in Whitehall with William Waldegrave's white paper on open government, which came into effect in April 1994.[6]

4. Under John Major there is an absence of a fixed group of insiders. Mrs Thatcher had an inner circle of ministers on whom she relied, including William Whitelaw until his departure in December 1987, and at different times Geoffrey Howe, Nigel Lawson, Nicholas Ridley and Douglas Hurd. An inner Cabinet was reported to have existed during the Gulf crisis and war in 1990-91, but this was in fact a subcommittee of the Overseas and Defence Cabinet committee. Major has no inner Cabinet, nor a figure akin to Whitelaw. He had hopes that Lord Wakeham would have fulfilled the Whitelaw role, but Wakeham has done this only to a limited extent. He chairs a number of Cabinet committees, as did Whitelaw, but lacks the skills and gravitas of Whitelaw at finding agreement between warring senior colleagues. Major seeks advice from a number of Cabinet colleagues, including his cautious business managers, Richard Ryder (chief whip), Tony Newton (leader of the House of Commons), as well as

Wakeham (leader in the Lords). He also pays particular attention to his most senior colleagues, including Hurd, Clarke, Heseltine, Wakeham and Howard, as well as to Norman Fowler, the party chairman (1992–94). Before the 1992 general election Major was particularly close to Chris Patten, and since his departure to Hong Kong has missed his advice, companionship and mediation with difficult colleagues. But ultimately he keeps his own counsel to an extent never realized by Mrs Thatcher.

5. The annual round on public expenditure is now conducted rather differently. The so-called 'star chamber' ('Misc 62') has been replaced by a new committee on public expenditure ('EDX') chaired by the Chancellor and containing six of the most senior ministers. In July, the Cabinet settles the remit of EDX, which then deliberates over the summer, and scrutinizes in detail the plans of spending ministers. It reports back to Cabinet in late October or early November. Ministers with spending plans still in dispute then try to persuade full Cabinet of what they want. They are seldom successful as EDX carries all the big guns. But every Cabinet minister now has a chance to express his viewpoint.[7] Those involved comment approvingly on the new system, and compare its political process favourably to the quasi-judicial process of the star chamber (which never worked well after Whitelaw's departure). Economic policy is very much controlled by the Chancellor, working closely with Major (replicating the Thatcher-Howe and Thatcher-Lawson nexus of 1979-83 and 1983-89 respectively). Following the removal of Britain from the ERM in September 1992, and Norman Lamont's alleged easing of responsibility for his work from then until his departure in May 1993, the Treasury lost a great deal of prestige in Whitehall. The key influence that the Treasury exerts in EDX, and Clarke's own style and self-confidence, have gone a considerable way to restoring the Treasury's self-esteem.

6. Cabinet committees still operate much as they did under Mrs Thatcher, but with some notable differences. The two most important standing committees are Economic and Domestic Policy (EDP) and Defence and Overseas

Policy (OPD), both chaired by the Prime Minister, who chairs a further seven committees, some much more central than others, such as Northern Ireland (NI). Another most prominent committee is Home and Social Affairs (EDH), chaired by Lord Wakeham, Lord Privy Seal. EDP, OPD and EDH replace the three Thatcher committees, 'EA', 'OD' and 'HA';. Tony Newton, leader of the House of Commons, chairs the two committees dealing with parliamentary business, Legislation (L), which meets weekly, and Queen's Speeches and Future Legislation (FLG). The two other most visible and key committees are probably EDX, discussed above, and the subcommittee on European Questions (OPDE), chaired by the Foreign Secretary.[8]

7. Major has had fewer *ad hoc* Cabinet committees (29 to July 1994) than Mrs Thatcher. In contrast he uses subcommittees of standing committees more.

8. John Major has made more extensive use of political Cabinets, where the Cabinet Secretariat withdraws and the party chairman comes. They are held about ten times a year, before party conferences, elections, or during periods of particular turbulence. First names are used, the atmosphere is less formal than in Cabinet, and purely political matters are discussed.

CONCLUSION

In stating these differences of emphasis and style, there is a danger of losing sight of the continuities. Cabinet still meets at Number 10 on Thursday mornings when Parliament is sitting, and lasts sixty to ninety minutes. The agenda is still dominated by the standing agenda items, parliamentary, home, overseas and Community affairs. Conduct is still formal, with correct Cabinet titles being employed. The 1980s and 1990s saw fewer formal papers and fewer formal decisions than in the 1970s and before. Full Cabinet had ceased to be the decision-making body in British government many years before Major came to power in 1990. It has become almost what it had been in the eighteenth and nine-teenth century, political allies meeting to review events with-out papers. The arrival of Major also has not stemmed the number of leaks from Cabinet. According to one insider 'there is now an expectation that anything controversial said in Cabinet will be in the first edition of the *Evening Standard* on Thursday afternoon'.

The central policy-making machine was much changed by Mrs Thatcher. Existing literature has barely woken up to the fact that the system has been changed radically again under John Major, with his own hand being felt in the revived collegiality in Cabinet and at Number 10, in greater openness, wider consultation and more volatility. In few areas in this book has the Major Effect been more singular.

Notes

1. Dennis Kavanagh and Anthony Seldon are writing on this subject at greater length and their work will appear in journal form. The author is grateful for comments on this chapter from John Barnes and Peter Hennessy.
2. Anthony Seldon, 'The Cabinet Office and Co–ordination 1979-87', *Public Administration* (68:1), (Spring 1990), pp. 103-121.
3. Private information. Much of the chapter is based upon private interviews and references cannot be given.
4. 'Mr Major's Number Ten', Channel 4, 24 April 1991.
5. Lord Wakeham, 'Cabinet Government', lecture delivered at Brunel University, 10 November 1993.
6. Cm 2290, HMSO, 1993.
7. Peter Hennessy, 'Central Government', in Peter Catterall, ed., *Contemporary Britain. An Annual Review 1994* (ICBH, 1994), pp. 20–21.
8. See P. Dunleavy, 'Estimating the Distribution of Influence in Cabinet Committees Under John Major', *Contemporary Political Studies 1994* (UK Political Studies Association, 1994), pp.359–82.

Part 2

ECONOMICS AND FINANCE

Chapter 11

THE ECONOMY
1990–94

Peter Jay

OVERVIEW

The contemporary economic history of the government headed by John Major from November 1990 to date naturally divides itself into two parts: before and after Black Wednesday, 16 September 1992, when the pound was unceremoniously 'suspended' from operational membership of the exchange rate mechanism (ERM) of the European Monetary System (EMS). Before that date full participation in the ERM was the centrepiece of economic strategy. After it policy-making became first a search for an alternative to this panacea and then entered a period from which intellectual content had been thoroughly purged.

The economy moved from the onset of recession in the second half of 1990 and the first half of 1991, when the severest falls in output were concentrated, to a year and a half of stagnation, followed by a year in which output rose approximately in line with the long-term growth of productive potential (as during the period for which it was most recently measurable, namely between the business cycle peaks of 1979 and 1989). The implied gap (see Table 1) between output and the sustainable long-term trend opened to about 6 per cent of GDP by early 1993 and then narrowed marginally. Inflationary pressures collapsed in the second

Table 1: GDP and GDP Gap
Actuals to 1993 Q4 / £s billion 1990, CSO Revisions to 24/3/94

	Column 1 GDP Index 1990=100	Column 2 GDP Proj'd @3%pa	Column 3 GDP Past+Fut Cols 1+2	Column 4 GDP Growth per qtr	Column 5 GDP Growth a.r./qtr	Column 6 Trend @£2.3pa from 1990 Q4	Column 7 GDP Gap % Cols 3–6/Col6	Column 8 GDP Gap £s b. pq	Column 9 GDP Gap Cumulated £s billion
88 Q1	96.50		96.50						
Q2	97.90		97.90	1.45	5.93				
Q3	99.60		98.60	0.72	2.89				
Q4	99.10		99.10	0.51	2.04				
89 Q1	99.30		99.30	0.20	0.81				
Q2	99.50		99.50	0.20	0.81				
Q3	99.80		99.80	0.30	1.21				
Q4	100.40		100.40	0.60	2.43				
90 Q1	100.70		100.70	0.30	1.20				
Q2	99.80		99.80	-0.89	-3.53				
Q3	98.10		99.10	-0.70	-2.78				
Q4	98.10		98.10	-1.01	-3.98	99.10			
91 Q1	97.60		97.60	-0.51	-2.02	99.66	-1.57	-1.88	-1.88
Q2	97.50		97.50	-0.10	-0.41	100.23	-2.63	-3.14	-5.02
Q3	97.50		97.50			100.80	-3.28	-3.92	-8.95
Q4	96.80		96.80	-0.72	-2.84	101.38	-3.83	-4.58	-13.53
92 Q1	96.90		96.90	0.10	0.41	101.96	-5.06	-6.06	-19.59
Q2	97.30		97.30	0.41	1.66	102.54	-5.50	-6.58	-26.17
Q3	97.60		97.60	0.31	1.24	103.12	-5.65	-6.76	-32.93
Q4	98.20		98.20	0.61	2.48	103.71	-5.89	-7.05	-39.98
93 Q1	98.60		98.60	0.41	1.64	104.30	-5.85	-7.00	-46.99
Q2	98.60		98.60			104.90	-6.00	-7.19	-54.17

Q3	99.40	99.40	0.81	3.29	105.49	-5.78	-6.92	-61.09
Q4		100.00	0.60	2.44	106.10	-5.75	-6.88	-67.97
94 Q1		100.74	0.74	3.00	106.70	-5.59	-6.69	-74.66
Q2		101.49	0.74	3.00	107.31	-5.42	-6.49	-81.15
Q3		102.24	0.74	3.00	107.92	-5.26	-6.30	-87.45
Q4		103.00	0.74	3.00	108.54	-5.10	-6.11	-93.56
95 Q1		103.76	0.74	3.00	109.16	-4.94	-5.91	-99.47
Q2		104.53	0.74	3.00	109.78	-4.78	-5.72	-105.19
Q3		105.31	0.74	3.00	110.40	-4.61	-5.52	-110.71
Q4		106.09	0.74	3.00	111.03	-4.45	-5.33	-116.04
96 Q1		106.88	0.74	3.00	111.67	-4.29	-5.13	-121.18
Q2		107.67	0.74	3.00	112.30	-4.13	-4.94	-126.12
Q3		108.47	0.74	3.00	112.94	-3.96	-4.74	-130.86
Q4		109.27	0.74	3.00	113.59	-3.80	-4.55	-135.41
97 Q1		110.08	0.74	3.00	114.23	-3.63	-4.35	-139.76
Q2		110.90	0.74	3.00	114.89	-3.47	-4.15	-143.91
Q3		111.72	0.74	3.00	115.54	-3.30	-3.96	-147.87
Q4		112.55	0.74	3.00	116.20	-3.14	-3.76	-151.62
98 Q1		113.39	0.74	3.00	116.86	-2.97	-3.56	-155.18
Q2		114.23	0.74	3.00	117.53	-2.81	-3.36	-158.55
Q3		115.07	0.74	3.00	118.20	-2.64	-3.16	-161.71
Q4		115.93	0.74	3.00	118.87	-2.48	-2.97	-164.68
02 Q1			0.74	3.00	127.99			
Q2			0.74	3.00	128.72			
Q3			0.74	3.00	129.45			
Q4			0.74	3.00	130.19			

half of 1990; and from the autumn of 1991 inflation as measured by the annual change in the retail price index and its sundry modifications fell rapidly to a low plateau of about 3 per cent by the end of 1992, dipping below 2½ per cent by March 1994.

The story of these four years could, indeed, be seen as little more than the inevitable counterpart to the Lawson inflation of the late 1980s. The sequel consisted of the deflation of the real economy and then of price behaviour that were the necessary consequences of the boom that preceded it and of the 15 per cent interest rates which Nigel Lawson established before his resignation in October 1989. Given that indefinitely accelerating inflation towards hyper-inflation cannot be regarded as an economic strategy – or had so few advocates as not to constitute a political option – it required no great ideological or visionary gift to perceive that by the summer of 1989 the economy had proceeded up a cul-de-sac to the limit and needed to reverse out of it before embarking upon any new direction. It was John Major's lot, when he succeeded Nigel Lawson as Chancellor in October 1989 and Mrs Thatcher as Prime Minister in November 1990, that there was neither scope nor call for historic departures or rare feats of policy creativity.

This question of context should not be ignored in any judgment of performance. One would not distort history to divide most British Chancellors of the last forty years into those (Butler–Macmillan, Heathcoat Amory, Maudling, Barber–Healey Part I and Lawson) who inherited stability and had lots of fun upsetting it and those (Thorneycroft, Lloyd, Callaghan–Jenkins, Healey Part II–Howe and Major–Lamont) who inherited a crisis and had a miserable time restoring order.

After his years at the Treasury as Chief Secretary (1987–89), John Major came upon the stage as a front-rank economic policy-maker, at the very beginnings of that phase of the economic cycle in which the dour virtues are required and great reputations are hard to make. How he would have performed – and may yet perform if internal Conservative politics do not cut short the experiment – in the reverse phase of the cycle remains speculation, though aided by examination of his handling of specific policy challenges in the most frigid mid-winter of the long battle against inflation: the entry into the ERM, the replacement of the community charge (or 'poll tax') by the council tax, the GATT negotiations, policy after the ERM, reforms of fiscal and monetary policy, public sector reform and the relationship with industry.

MAJOR'S INHERITANCE

When he first became Prime Minister John Major inherited policies and an economic conjuncture from the outgoing Chancellor, himself. He also inherited a political and parliamentary environment massively dominated by both the reality and the mythology of his predecessor's long rule at Number 10. Both inheritances conditioned subsequent events.

The economy was in the first acute phase of recession with output (real GDP at factor cost including North Sea oil) falling at annual rates of 3.5, 2.8, 4.0 and 2.0 per cent in the last two quarters of 1990 and the first two of 1991 (see Table 1). Inflation in November 1990, stood at 9.7 per cent, a month past its 10.9 per cent peak; and unemployment had risen to 1,763,100, from its boom low point of 1,606,600 in March.

Britain had since Monday, 8 October, been a fully operational member of the ERM (having been technically a member of the EMS from its inception in 1979) with a declared central rate for the pound against the Deutschmark (DM) of DM2.95. So favourable were the effects on confidence and expectations that on the day of British entry short-term interest rates had been cut by an unusual full 1 per cent from their post-boom peak of 15 per cent. Indeed, it was speculated that the prospect of this cut on the eve of the Conservative party conference had provided the clinching argument in persuading a reluctant Prime Minister finally to withdraw her long opposition to British entry despite the concerted advocacy of the senior members of her Cabinet.[1]

Advocacy of British entry had revolved round the two arguments that it would strengthen Britain's political standing in Europe and reinforce her counter-inflationary strategy by forcing any government to follow fiscal and monetary policies that would deliver as good price behaviour in Britain as in Germany. An added bonus was considered to be that the inevitability of such a non-inflationary outcome, because of the operation of the chain to the anchor currency of the system (the DM being in the non-political and therefore non-inflationary hands of the flinty Bundesbank) would itself act on the expectations of price-setters, especially in the labour market, in such a way that fewer people would be forced into bankruptcy and/or unemployment to achieve any given price performance. People would know it was hopeless to count on inflation or future devaluations to compensate them for higher costs; so they would not be incurred.

The Thatcher legacy cast John Major as the successor to an historical giant and economic miracle-worker who had transformed the direction and character of the British economy, to say nothing of its global power, but whose colossal status had been rendered intolerable by an overbearing manner, a perverse attachment to the evidently disastrous community charge and a hostility to the European Community's central institutions which, it was feared, might 'cut Britain off from the Community'. The legacy also included a governing party deeply divided between those who wanted a Major government to be the Thatcher government without the warts and those who wanted it to be profoundly different. A prevalent view in the party on economic policy was that the last few years of the Thatcher government should be rewound, like a video, to whenever it was that Nigel Lawson and she had made their fatal error and allowed the boom to get out of hand, perhaps 1987, and that the story, minus the error, should be re-run from there.

Indeed, the Governor of the Bank of England, then Robin Leigh-Pemberton, had already begun, as early as April 1990, to propagate this view of a genuine economic miracle tarnished gratuitously by an unforced error.[2] He chronicled the reasons why the boom at the end of the

1980s gathered momentum and eventually got out of control. This was virtually the first semi-official suggestion that the long run of rapid growth which followed the deep recession at the beginning of the 1980s and the conspicuous prosperity of the late 1980s might after all have been unsound, even a 'mistake'.

John Major himself took to referring to mistakes made during the Lawson period, though he was always careful to say they were visible with 'hindsight', whether out of consideration for Nigel Lawson's feelings or for his own role as Chief Secretary to the Treasury. A year and a half later Robin Leigh-Pemberton returned to his theme of bright prospects thrown away, but now again within our grasp if only temptation were more firmly resisted. The media noticed only his mandatory statement that 'the picture is undeniably improving ... company confidence, though still weak, is obviously well off the bottom'. Much more controversial was his interpretation of the previous decade as evidence that stern anti-inflationary policies had produced exceptionally impressive long-run performance, only to be thrown away at the last minute.[3]

It would be hard to exaggerate the continuing importance of the state of mind of the authorities as revealed by his speech. The Governor was much influenced in its preparation by his Deputy Eddie George. The conviction that strong anti-inflationary policies were not merely desirable and necessary for price stability, but also that they were a sufficient condition of a faster long-run growth rate and of generally superior real economic performance, was deeply felt and continued to inform the pronouncements of Eddie George after he became Governor on 1 July 1993. Nor need we doubt it is shared by some in the Treasury who lived through the double-digit inflation of the mid-1970s and early 1980s and seem to have come to feel embittered that the economy had let them down, even humiliated them in the eyes of their international peers. The desire to expunge inflation for ever had become a deep preoccupation; and there were times when it seemed some of those in authority felt that, if the process of eradicating it happened to put the economy through exceptionally brutal rigours and thereby to punish it for its shortcomings in previous decades, they would shed few tears.

It remained a tribute to the power of the Thatcher legend at the time that senior spokesmen could, without evidently expecting to be contradicted, advance a proposition about the relationship between stable prices and long-term growth for which there was next to no serious academic or international evidence. It was as though they could not bring themselves to doubt the central kernel of the Thatcher faith – that she had transformed the economy, thereby raising its long-term growth rate. They were loath to recognize that the sustained growth of the middle-late 1980s reflected nothing more than the predictable arithmetical counterpart to the depth of the recession at the beginning of the decade (plus normal trend growth).

After ten years of the propaganda machine, it simply was not possible for people who valued their reputation for good judgment to believe that nothing much had changed in long-term growth potential and that, if you took away the excesses of the boom years as an inflationary error, you thereby also took away even such superficial evidence as there was that any long-run gains at all had been made in the efficiency of the economy as reflected in its sustainable long-term growth-rate. As to the unemployment required to stop inflation accelerating, far from improving it appeared to double between the 1970s and 1980s.

Thus, John Major was expected to accomplish the projection into the future of the fruits of an imagined economic miracle – and one supposedly wrought at the necessary price of passing through the agonies of the early 1980s through which it should therefore never need to pass again – and to do this without inflation. He was thus expected to repeat the exceptional growth rates of the mid–late 1980s without any of their actual and predictable inflationary consequences (predicted by the present author from December 1985). That combination of boom and price stability was, of course, the economist's stone for which all governments had been seeking since conscious thought on these matters began.

The inheritance which John Major thus received was, in macro-economic management terms, about as poisoned as it could be:

a. his predecessor was widely credited with more or less miraculous powers, from which however the economy seemed to have enjoyed no actual benefit.

b   the conjuncture of the economy was at the moment of rupture of an over-ripe and unsustainable boom, making inevitable a prolonged period of painful disinflation; and

c   the unsustainable gains in output – and other temporary economic benefits – resulting from the boom were widely and wrongly attributed to permanent gains in the long-term sustainable growth rate flowing from the miracle-working.

John Major was not free of responsibility for the difficulties in which he consequently found himself. But the contemporary historian will wish to distinguish his culpability for myths about the Thatcher period and his responsibility for the events of his own period as Prime Minister.

DISINFLATION: NOVEMBER 1990 – SEPTEMBER 1992

The story of the economy and economic policy from John Major's appointment as Prime Minister in November 1990 until Black Wednesday in September 1992 was essentially that of waiting for the disinflation by then in place to work at whatever cost that implied in real output. The sole instruments of disinflation were: monetary policy – 15 per cent base rates from October 1989, reduced to 14 per cent a year later when the pound joined the ERM; and ERM membership at a central rate of DM2.95 accompanied by gradual reductions in base rate at ½ per cent steps in February 1991 (twice), in March, April, May, July and September of that year and again in May 1992, to 10 per cent, where it stood until 16 September.

Fiscal policy, while continuing to pay lip-service to Nigel Lawson's concept of a medium term financial strategy and to the slogan of a 'balanced budget', in practice accommodated two predominant influences: the effect on revenue and certain classes of expenditure, such as unemployment benefit, of the steep plunge into recession from the summer of 1990; and the imperatives of an approaching general election.

Public spending (technically 'general government expenditure excluding privatization proceeds as a percentage of money GDP') rose from 39¾ per cent in 1989–90 to an estimated 45 per cent in 1993–94.[4] The expenditure planned for and/or incurred in the financial year 1992–93 rose from 38¾ per cent in Nigel Lawson's last Red Book[5] to 39½ per cent in John Major's first (as Chancellor) autumn statement,[6] to 39¾ per cent in his second autumn statement,[7] to 42 per cent in Norman Lamont's first autumn statement,[8] to 45 per cent in his second autumn statement,[9] to 44¾ per cent in Kenneth Clark's first budget.[10]

The budget deficit (PBSR) moved from negative (a surplus) at −1½ per cent of GDP in 1989–90 to nil in 1990–91, to 2¼ per cent in 1991–92, to 6 per cent in 1992–93. When privatization proceeds are excluded, the deficits are about 1 per cent of GDP greater. The deficit planned for 1992–93 moved from a small surplus planned by Nigel Lawson in March 1989, to an eventual deficit of 6 per cent of GDP. The eventual deficit for the following year, 1993–94, was expected to be 7¾ per cent of GDP after Kenneth Clarke's first budget.

Accommodating though fiscal policy by itself mainly was, the government's overriding economic aim during this period was exactly what ministers, including John Major as Chancellor and as Prime Minister, repeatedly said it was: the control of inflation. Moreover, it clearly was the effect of a tight monetary policy, reinforced by whatever benign effects on expectations ERM membership might contribute, that was principally relied upon to produce the required reduction in inflation.

John Major's comment when appointed Chancellor on 27 October 1989 in Northampton that 'if policy isn't hurting, it isn't working'[11] was probably the most candid and the most accurate by any leader or observer during that period, though it was not entirely straightforward to reconcile it with the parallel refrain from 1991 onwards that the British recession was not 'home made', but instead originated in a global downturn. No one should say they were not warned, and at the new Chancellor's first opportunity, though later critics of government fiscal policy may now object to the passage in the same Northampton speech, 'The economy is not regulated by interest rates alone. Government income is many billions of pounds greater than expenditure. We are repaying our debts. And this is underpinned by firm control of public expenditure. So the Government's financial position is very sound.'

The monetary squeeze worked more or less as intended, though the depth and severity of the recession were neither expected nor intended by the authors of the policy.[12] No more was it expected by most spectators, just as the impact on the unemployment figures turned out to be somewhat less than expected and predicted by those who, like myself, relied too confidently upon the robustness of the historic relationship between changes in output (above or below the long-run trend) and lagged changes in unemployment.

There were three distinguishable phases in the course of total economic output from the onset of the recession in the third quarter of 1990: rapid fall for four consecutive quarters to the middle of 1991 at annual rates of 3.5 per cent, 2.8 per cent, 4.0 per cent and 2.0 per cent (for an annualized average of 3.1 per cent); six quarters of mainly sideways drift (annualized quarterly GDP changes of −0.4, nil, − 2.8, 0.4, 1.7, 1.2, averaging 0.0), during which, therefore, the output gap (between actual and potential GDP, which rises continuously with long-term productivity, etc.) has to be presumed to have been widening steadily; and the four quarters of the calendar year 1993 during which output rose, respectively by annualized gains of 2.5 per cent, 1.6 per cent, 3.3 per cent and 2.4 per cent, averaging 2.46 per cent. Only in the last period did output expand faster — fractionally — than the long-term growth potential of the economy here presumed to be about 2.3 per cent growth per annum in line with the measured change between the last two unambiguous cyclical peaks in 1979 and 1989 (see Table 2). The output gap remained substantially unchanged at the same high level it reached by the end of 1992, peaking in the spring of 1993.

Table 2: GDP Gap 1948–92
1985 = 100

	1. GDP Index	2. Growth % p.a.	3. Growth % p.d.*	4. Trend Peaks	5. Trend '0s	6. Trend 5–2%	7. GDP Gap (6–1) %
1948	40.5	0.0		40.5	40.5	39.7	2.0
1949	42.0	3.7		42.0	42.0	41.2	2.0
1950	43.5	3.6		43.0	43.5	42.6	2.0
1951	44.5	2.3		44.1	44.7	43.8	1.7
1952	44.6	0.2		45.1	45.9	44.9	−0.7
1953	46.4	4.0		46.2	47.1	46.1	0.6
1954	48.3	4.1		47.4	48.3	47.4	2.0
1955	50.1	3.7		48.5	49.6	48.6	3.0
1956	50.8	1.4		49.7	50.9	49.9	1.8
1957	51.7	1.8		50.9	52.3	51.3	0.9
1958	51.5	−0.4		52.2	53.7	52.6	−2.1
1959	53.6	4.1	2.4	53.6	55.1	54.0	−0.8
1960	56.6	5.6	2.7	55.4	56.6	55.5	2.0
1961	58.2	2.8		57.2	58.3	57.1	1.9
1962	59.0	1.4		59.1	60.0	58.8	0.4
1963	61.3	3.9		61.0	61.8	60.5	1.3
1964	64.7	5.5		63.1	63.6	62.3	3.9
1965	66.6	2.9		65.1	65.4	64.1	3.8
1966	67.9	2.0		67.3	67.4	66.0	2.8
1967	69.4	2.2		69.5	69.4	68.0	2.1
1968	72.4	4.3		71.8	71.4	70.0	3.5
1969	74.2	2.5	3.3	74.2	73.5	72.0	3.0
1970	75.7	2.0	2.9	75.9	75.7	74.2	2.0
1971	77.0	1.7		77.6	77.1	75.5	1.9
1972	79.2	2.9		79.3	78.5	76.9	3.0
1973	85.1	7.4		81.1	79.9	78.3	8.7
1974	83.8	−1.5		82.9	81.4	79.8	5.1
1975	83.1	−0.8		84.7	82.9	81.2	2.3
1976	85.3	2.6		86.6	84.4	82.7	3.2
1977	87.5	2.6		88.6	85.9	84.2	3.9
1978	90.1	3.0		90.6	87.5	85.7	5.1
1979	92.6	2.8	1.8	92.6	89.1	87.3	6.1
1980	90.7	−2.1	1.8	94.7	90.7	88.9	2.0
1981	89.6	−1.2		96.8	93.0	91.2	−1.7
1982	91.2	1.8		99.0	95.4	93.5	−2.4
1983	94.6	3.7		101.3	97.8	95.9	−1.3
1984	96.3	1.8		103.5	100.3	98.3	−2.0
1985	100.0	3.8		105.9	102.9	100.8	−0.8
1986	103.6	3.6		108.3	105.5	103.4	0.2
1987	108.6	4.8		110.7	108.2	106.0	2.5
1988	113.5	4.5		113.2	110.9	108.7	4.4
1989	115.8	2.0	2.3	115.8	113.7	111.5	3.9
1990	116.6	0.7	2.5	118.5	116.6	114.3	2.0
1991	113.7	−2.5		121.2	119.3	116.9	−2.7
1992	113.1	−0.5		124.0	122.0	119.6	−5.4

* Annual rate over previous 10 years

Specific calculations (see Table 1) of the output gap, seen here as conceptually and computationally the most straightforward measure of the cyclical tone of an economy – where it lies between boom and slump – suggest that it peaked at 6.0 per cent of GDP (trend potential) in the second quarter of 1993, equivalent £28.75 billion (US definition) at 1990 factor cost prices. This assumes that output coincided with sustainable long-term non-inflationary potential in the fourth quarter of 1990 (after the first two quarters of sharply falling output from the summer) and that long-term trend growth in the current cycle will be the same (2.3 per cent) as in the last (see Table 2). On that basis, if output grew at an annual rate of 3 per cent from the end of 1993, it would catch up with trend – and so the period of below-trend production, i.e. 'recession', would end – in the third quarter of 2002 (see Table 1).

A FIXED EXCHANGE RATE

Meanwhile, the ERM bomb was ticking. This author should declare his belief over more than three decades that fixed exchange rates, whether adjustable or supposedly not, are invariably an economic mistake and a political folly and that an optimum currency area will always be found to be the smallest feasible one.

Britain's entry into the ERM appeared, therefore, amongst other things, to invest the entire political capital of the government, wearing thin as it already was, in a foreign exchange market equation which could not be guaranteed against the much more powerful market forces that could be brought against it. It further appeared to plant in the foundations of any conception of a politically and/or economically united Europe an economic and social time-bomb of awesome power, namely the transfer of the burden of adjustment of competitive imbalances between member economies of the EC from simple routine daily exchange rate changes, normally unremarked in the market place, to enforced movements of population in tens of millions. These shifts would be on pain of destitution, across cultural, linguistic, national and historic boundaries, from depressed uncompetitive areas in which huge social capital and inestimable personal associations have been invested to over-competitive regions of increasing congestion where the new arrivals were likely to be bitterly resented and indeed violently attacked by the existing population.

What John Major really believed about the economics of ERM membership is still hard to say. It was during his watch as Chancellor that Britain went in. He has never said anything to contradict the speculation at the time that he had succeeded, where indeed Nigel Lawson had failed, in overcoming Mrs Thatcher's resistance; but then it is hard to see what attractions there could have been for him denying his own role, given that he was Chancellor at the time and could hardly suggest that British entry had occurred despite his doubts or indifference. The most straightforward explanation is probably that like the overwhelming majority of commentators, business representatives and politicians at the time, he accepted the argument that Britain needed to be 'in' Europe, rather than 'out' of it. (Neither of these terms was precisely defined as between being in and out of the single market, already irrevocably determined by the Single European Act, being in and out of the EMS and possible future single currency, which before and after Maastricht is a genuine choice, and being in and out of any eventual political federation, which had little logical link with the case for or against ERM membership.) He probably went along with much lay opinion in seeing membership of the ERM as part of such being 'in' and took additional comfort from the thought that an anti-inflationary anchor to the German mark could only help secure Britain's goal of price stability, possibly with less transitional pain than would otherwise be required because of the favourable effects of lower inflationary expectations on pay and price behaviour.

So believing, he worked for that end and achieved it. This at least seems the commonsense of the matter, though his work was, perhaps inevitably until Mrs Thatcher caved in, far less visible than his vigorous if brief campaign during the summer of 1990 on behalf of the 'hard ECU', a project even more evidently doomed to failure than British entry into the ERM itself. It gave vent to all John Major's exceptional aptitude for mastery of a complex subject, for persuasive advocacy and for untiring persistence. If at times this eager insistence on the 'hard ECU' had about it a whiff of the enthusiastic scout-master, that was at least in part only because he himself was so conspicuously not a cynic.

Britain remained in the ERM for three weeks short of two years. Those who wish to believe that the experiment could have been a success have a long list of 'if onlys' to which they can point, arguing that up to such and such a moment the policy was intact and capable of being sustained. There were even those in the Bank of England who maintained on and immediately after Black Wednesday that there was no serious pressure on the pound and that, had it survived three more market days until the French referendum on Maastricht, the war as well as the battle would have been won.[13]

There is no doubt that the travails of the German economy after an almost overnight unification vastly exacerbated the cyclical asynchronization of the German and the other EC economies and therefore the need for much higher real interest rates in Germany than elsewhere. Since interest rates cannot be substantially different in two economies linked by supposedly immutable exchange rates (even with a 6 per cent band) and capital movements, the EC economies outside the natural greater German economy (Germany, Austria, Holland, Belgium and Luxembourg) faced a choice between devaluing (or floating down) against the German mark and raising their interest rates to compete with German rates, thereby subjecting their already cyclically weak economies to further deflationary pressures.

It can be argued that these embarrassed countries had nobody to blame but themselves for the painful consequences of their perverse refusal to depreciate against the mark and that their attempt to blame the Germans for their difficulties was ridiculous when the remedy so obviously lay in their own hands. But, of course, these countries – France ever since the U-turn of the Mitterrand government in 1983 and Britain since its U-turn of 1990 – had invested huge economic and political capital in the notion that a strong currency anchored for ever to the German mark was the foundation stone of their economic strategies.

A devaluation to accommodate the abnormal conjuncture of the German economy may have been theoretically reconcilable with such a policy; but in practice and in politics it was completely impossible. Or so the French authorities maintained in season and out until the final bitter end on 1–2 August 1993, when the ERM finally collapsed into the comedy of 15 per cent bands. So long as the French stood firm, the British faced the fact that they could not devalue – or 'realign' – with any hope of convincing people that this was somehow a mark revaluation and not a sterling devaluation; and, if it was the latter, then inescapably it represented a failure of all the economic arguments that the government had given for adherence, namely founding a permanent defeat of inflation on an immutable link to a sound anchor currency. It happened anyway; but it still matters where the fatal error lay, in the tactics or in the very conception of fixing the exchange rate.

The argument that the failure of Britain's ERM membership was due to abnormal events in Germany presupposes the premise that nobody could reasonably have foreseen that the weapons available for upholding the policy would be unable to handle the pressures that arose because either the pressures themselves or the impotence of the defences were unforeseeable. The premise is false on either basis.

The daily size of the global foreign exchange markets was well known as reaching at least into the hundreds of billions of dollars' worth daily; and anyone who had lived through the great currency crises of the last years of the previous experiment in fixed exchange rates, the Bretton Woods system, in the late 1960s knew perfectly well that, once the word is out, the pressure which can be brought on a single currency invariably means that reserves and stand-by facilities seldom amount to more than a few hours, sometimes mere minutes, worth of a big 'run'.

The idea that the ERM's defences were limitless because the central bankers issuing all the currencies in the system were included among the defenders – and could therefore print their own currencies *ad infinitum* and fast enough to outspeculate any speculator – was fatally vitiated. Everyone knew that they, and more particularly the Bundesbank, were absolutely unwilling to be drawn down that path. Anyway, even if they had been willing, the central bank responsible for the currency supposedly being supported by such Bundes-bank operations, e.g. the Bank of England for the pound, would bear the overwhelming majority of the loss, should any realignment eventually occur. The inadequacy of the defence was therefore as foreseeable as the possibility of the pressures themselves.

Indeed, one of the most remarkable sequels to Black Wednesday was the insufficiently noticed speech not by the Deputy Governor of the Bank of England, who was expected to be giving it, but by the Governor himself.[14] Again we do not need to doubt that the Governor was attentive to his Deputy's draft in advance; but it was clearly felt in Thread-needle Street that the exceptional clout of the Governor was needed to drive home the message; and a very remarkable message it was. It set out the Bank's interpretation of the ERM experience in the light of its final collapse: essentially that 'the decision to join the ERM two years ago was right in the circumstances; that, having joined, we were right to endeavour to stick with it; and that, in the circumstances which evolved, we were also right to withdraw'. Thus might the commander of the Armada have vindicated the whole affair.

But more remarkable still were the candid statements in those parts of the speech which purported to justify the eventual capitulation to overwhelming force, while preserv-ing the Bank's perennial claim to unique understanding of 'the markets', that the Bank had never believed that either of the two defences available to the authorities to redeem the Prime Minister's and the Chancellor's monotonous refrain that they would do 'whatever was necessary' would have worked. So, intervention would never work and it did not. Raising interest rates would never work and it did not. There were no defences. The Emperor was naked.

'Whatever measures are necessary' were what John Major doubtless thought he was willing to take. But seem-ingly his advisers had not told him that there were no measures which could be sufficient and which therefore could, singly or together, be necessary. One is left wondering what advice the Bank was giving to such relative innocents as the Prime Minister and the Chancellor when in the summer of 1992 they were making the speeches which returned to haunt them so mercilessly after the *denouement* on 16 September.

'Black Wednesday' in sum was the definitive event of John Major's initial stewardship, as Chancellor and as Prime Minister, of the economy. He seemed content that he should be seen at the time as the man who got us in despite his Prime Minister's well documented previous opposition. He then gave it his all. It was the centrepiece of economic policy; and it was justified by the requirements of economic policy alone, irrespective of British European policy. Eradicating inflation, not just for now, but for good was the over-riding strategic aim; and ERM membership was its core tactic.

John Major was ready to pay any price, even an election at the depths of an unusually prolonged and very deep recession, for the sake of seeing it through. It gave him visions, shared in July 1992 with the *Sunday Times*, of a Britain finally victorious over its economic disease, with inflationary psychology and perennial erosion of competitiveness eradicated, very much as malaria or some other pestilence might be for ever eliminated from the world's stock of diseases, and even with the pound perhaps taking over from the German mark as the anchor currency of Europe. Hyperbole may have infected the Prime Minister at some points; but nobody can reasonably question the thoroughness of the commitment which John Major made to the policy of ERM membership, nor therefore the scale of the disaster for him when, apparently against his expectations at most a week before at a key speech in Glasgow[15] and perhaps even a day before, the *Titanic* sank.

AFTER THE ERM: SEPTEMBER 1992 – MAY 1993

The quality of John Major's leadership was on trial at that moment as is the quality of the leadership of few men in peacetime. The Chancellor, free now to wear his heart on his sleeve and to attempt to redeem his mortgaged soul, sang in his bath. Others like Douglas Hurd, the Foreign Secretary, Michael Heseltine, President of the Board of Trade and Kenneth Clarke, Home Secretary, yearned for an almost immediate return to ERM membership at a new parity, a tactic which I described at the time as 'Raise the *Titanic*, ram the iceberg again and hope that this time the iceberg sinks!'. The press and the financial markets were preoccupied with the question of what was to 'replace' ERM membership as the required straitjacket, anchor or other form of fetter on the original sin of all governments, namely the desire to debase the currency.

It was a comment on the success of the general propaganda in support of the ERM that, despite the dramatic demonstration of its failure as a policy, its demise was greeted with loud demands for its replacement with something else of the same character. The search was on for a new 'framework', a new 'anchor', anything to displace or minimize the dreaded 'discretion' that might otherwise creep into fiscal and monetary policy, if there were no rigid objective and visible criteria to indicate instantly any deviation from the pure non-inflationary path. The inherent implausibility of this search was, perhaps unintentionally, exposed by the Governor of the Bank of England in the same speech in which he explained that there had never been any effective defences of the pound's membership against market forces. Bursting into metaphor, the Governor said on 8 October 1992 that there could be no 'Holy Grail', no single proxy indicator or correct policy.

The Chancellor had already that morning, as the Governor acknowledged in Duxford, written to the chairman of the House of Commons Treasury and Civil Service Committee setting out the policy framework with which he proposed to replace ERM membership: publicly announced long-term inflation targets (of 1 to 4 per cent, the lower half of this range by the end of the Parliament then sitting, i.e. before the next general election) and greater 'transparency' in policy-making, including the new 'unified budget', published monthly monetary reports by the Treasury, published quarterly inflation reports by the Bank of England, convening a panel of independent forecasters to advise the Chancellor and progressively more independence for the Bank of England in commenting on and in the execution of monetary policy.

Indeed, from the morrow of Black Wednesday until the dismissal of the Chancellor on 27 May 1993, a period of rare enlightenment in economic policy-making prevailed. Any idea of re-entering the ERM in any timescale shorter than the politically infinite was wisely discarded under a rubric rather similar to that under which Mrs Thatcher kept Britain out in the second half of the 1980s, namely not until the fault-lines in the ERM have been corrected. An appropriate *de facto* devaluation of the pound was allowed to fulfil itself in the foreign exchange markets; and by February 1993, at just over DM2.30 and $1.44 the worst of the ERM over-valuation had been corrected – and, as it proved, without any of the feed-back into British pay, costs and prices that the Prime Minister had so confidently expounded in his Glasgow speech and which was embodied in the endlessly reiterated Bank of England formula whereby the competitive advantages of a devaluation would always be lost within four years. There is still no sign of that erosion at Easter 1994.

Fiscal policy was brought for the first time to reflect both a long-term requirement of 'balance' in the public finances and a short-term requirement of balance in the real economy. The recession years had forced ministers to abandon the doctrine, briefly favoured when towards the end of Nigel Lawson's period the PSBR became negative, that a balanced budget meant a nil PSBR, i.e., a precise numerical equivalence of the receipts and outgoings sides of the public sector accounts. To have cut spending to match the fall in revenues during a recession (to say nothing of making room for the increases in cyclically sensitive spending, such as unemployment benefit) would have been to repeat the errors that supposedly defined the folly of US President Herbert

Hoover and British Chancellor Philip Snowden at the beginning of the 1930s and to have frustrated the operation of the 'automatic stabilizers', or the tendency of the budget to go into deficit in recessions so cushioning the downswing.

The definition of 'balance' in successive ministerial statements became, first, equivalence of receipts and outgoings over the life of the business cycle: later, equivalence of these two at least at some point in the cycle, and finally such balance between receipts and outgoings as would maintain the ratio of National Debt to gross domestic product when the economy was operating at its long-term trend level of output, with a nil GDP gap, neither in boom nor in recession. In the course of 1993 John Major himself gave as his estimate of the cyclical element in the £50 billion PSBR for 1993–94 a ratio of 70 per cent. So, £35 billion reflected the impact on public finances of sub-normal output and spending, leaving £15 billion as the acceptable long-term average annual new government borrowing which would keep the ratio of the National Debt to the GDP stable.

This evidently assumes long-term GDP growth of between 2 and 3 per cent, which is in line with most estimates. The £50 billion deficit was set to decline, as the economy recovered from a GDP gap of 6 per cent of GDP in the spring of 1993, to £30 billion in 1997–98. Interestingly, this implies that, with the 3½ per cent annual growth assumed by Norman Lamont in the 1993 March budget, output would still not quite have caught up with the long-term sustainable trend line of output four years later, i.e., the GDP gap would not have been fully closed. The Treasury's view of the size of the GDP gap in 1993 was similar to that used here.

The device used by Mr Lamont to reconcile the need for better fiscal balance over the rest of the decade with the need in the earlier years to avoid the Hoover–Snowden error was to enact into law substantial tax increases to come into effect over one or two years. Most of this £10.3 billion was in personal direct taxation, despite the government's commitment to reduce that kind of taxation above all others; but attention was successfully diverted from this anomaly by the fuss over the extension of VAT to the previously zero-rated domestic gas and electricity. It yielded less than half of what was expected from eroding allowances against income tax and increasing employees' national insurance contributions; but politicians and journalists seldom bother to count. The innovation of a new 20 per cent reduced rate band in the 1992 budget and the fact that the increases in the income tax burden in the March 1993 budget took the form of lower allowances rather than higher rates further deceived the tabloid press into missing the true impact on typical families.

After the March 1993 budget Britain probably had a fiscal balance that left enough spending for some slow recovery from the 6 per cent GDP gap to begin (six months later it was down to 5.75 per cent), while holding out the prospect that the PSBR would fall to its long-term sustainable level by the time the recession was over in about 1998 or 1999, assuming 3½ per cent annual growth from 1993.

In addition to putting fiscal policy on a balanced footing, the government had introduced probably permanent improvements in the policy-making process. The unified budget fulfilled at last the demands of elementary rationality to examine spending and revenue together, as well as providing somewhat more opportunity for parliamentary scrutiny of tax changes before their implementation – which persuaded some government whips that the change was a mistake!

The publication of specific ultimate policy targets, for example inflation between 1 and 4 per cent and less than 2½ per cent by the next election, combined with detailed regular publication of the Treasury's monthly monetary reports and the Bank of England's quarterly inflation reports, substantially assisted the quality of public debate about economic policy, not least the government's own contributions to it, though they had the unforeseen snag that any interest rate move had to be justified by some reference to change in circumstances since the previous month; and from November 1993 this locked the Chancellor into an unnecessarily high level of interest rate, since he could not give the real reason for lowering them, namely that an error had been made in November–December in not reducing them enough around the time of the budget.

The ultimate goals, at least for inflation, though not yet for growth and the GDP gap, were known. The wealth of inter-mediate information could be taken into account on its mer-its and analysed to judge whether and how far policy was prompting the stated goals. The role of the Treasury's panel of independent forecasters further enhanced this framework, even if the most useful part of that exercise turned out to be the Treasury's conveniently standardized monthly tabul-ations of the forecasters' work rather than any original impact on official thinking.

The biggest weakness remained the lack of any explicit goal for the real economy, either its long-term sustainable growth rate or conjunctural stabilization, i.e., minimization of the GDP gap, positive or negative, over the life of the business cycle. This doubtless reflected the continuing disil-lusionment with real macro-economic management after the failure of 'planning' in the 1960s and the inflationary excesses of the mid-1970s and early 1980s. The continuing preoccupation with purely nominal frameworks, with fight-ing inflation as the only declared goal, based on the correct principle that since inflation yields no long-term benefits policy might just as well target nil inflation, further reinforced by the baseless faith that low inflation is a suf-ficient condition of faster long-term real growth, was perhaps the last vestige of Thatcherite 'monetarism'.

But doctrine, as well as political convenience, still stood in the way of at least an official target for – or even a published estimate of (apart from the one rather coyly intro-duced into the Bank of England's first quarterly inflation report in February 1993) – the GDP gap. It would indeed have been politically inconvenient to acknowledge (though this was implied by the Prime Minister's remarks about the cyclical character of the £50 billion PSBR taken with Nor-man Lamont's fiscal plans for the mid-1990s) that, given 3½ per cent annual growth, the recession would continue almost to the end of the decade – and to well into the next decade at the mere 3 per cent annual growth later forecast by Kenneth Clarke in his November 1993 budget. This was, moreover, a time when it suited ministers in other contexts to tell the public that the recession (defined as a falling GDP) was over and that 'recovery' was well established.

But given the age of enlightenment in economic policy-making which overtook the authorities after their enforced liberation from the darker mysteries of the ERM era, it must be regarded as possible that Norman Lamont would have wished to take the next logical step and announce targets for other elements in government economic policy. Though he was as serious as anyone, including the Prime Minister, about fighting inflation, he certainly also recognized other economic priorities, as for example when he took the lead on and after Black Wednesday in relaxing monetary policy in order to reverse the inappropriate stranglehold it had, in his opinion, been exerting on the real economy.

Even if the long-term growth rate of the economy were still better left to the outcome of appropriate supply-side reforms, there could have been no doctrinal objections to more explicit reporting and the progress of any government's proper attempts, indeed duty, to reduce the fluctuations of the business cycle to the irreducible minimum.

AFTER LAMONT: THE ECONOMICS OF KENNETH CLARKE

This age of enlightenment came to an abrupt halt with the dismissal of the Chancellor on 27 May 1993 and his replacement by a man who clearly saw the Treasury as a base for political operations rather than as an economic institution.

It was unfortunate that the exact moment – March 1993 – when the previous Chancellor in his budget took the appropriate action to correct the growing PSBR and to lay out a suitable path for its progressive reduction was also the moment when the political nation, in the form of government backbenchers and political editorial-writers in influential newspapers, woke up to the £50 billion deficit. Not realizing that it had just been dealt with, they turned it into a problem requiring remedial action, somewhat encouraged by City interests for whom any reason or none is always more than sufficient to justify attacks on government spending and by dark innuendos from the Bank of England, ever on the look-out for opportunities to develop its campaign for independence from the Treasury, that it might be impossible to finance the deficit (itself an impossibility in a world of free capital movement and integrated capital markets).

The new Chancellor clearly needed to overcome the personal political difficulty that, if he was perceived to have inherited an already well adjusted economic policy, his personal contribution would be hard to appreciate. The opportunity to seize on the deficit, to get off a few lines about how uncomfortable he felt at borrowing a billion pounds a week, and so to portray himself as a stern and sound financier come to cleanse the mess bequeathed by a dodgy predecessor, was not missed for more than a few hours after his appointment and was duly rehearsed at every opportunity through the summer and early autumn.

This had the unfortunate and possibly unforeseen result that, come the first unified budget on 30 November, he had to do what he had said, cutting spending and raising taxes over the next three years, so as to yield a projected PSBR of some £2 billion in 1998–99, i.e., virtual 'balance' by the crude definition of arithmetical equivalence of outgoings and receipts, by the end of the decade. The consequence inevitably was to lower the annual expansion of demand and output between now and then, from Mr Lamont's $3\frac{1}{2}$ per cent to a mere 3 per cent, and thus to postpone, until 2002, the moment when the GDP gap would fall to zero and the recession really end (Table 1) – after twelve years of sub-trend output for a cumulative GDP cost (at 1990 prices) of £185 billion or an average of £15 billion a year, equivalent to half the annual cost of the NHS budget.

The question whether, in addition to this medium-term deceleration to a mere 3 per cent annual growth while supposedly trying to climb out of a 6 per cent GDP gap with an assumed long-term underlying annual growth rate of 2.3 per cent, the 'recovery' in the short-term might be aborted and even be replaced by a second 'dip' into recession is not settled at the time of writing. The CSO's second revision of the 1993 fourth quarter GDP figures shows an annual rate of increase in that quarter of 2.4 per cent, completing a gain over four quarters of almost 2.5 per cent, reducing the GDP gap by a negligible 0.15 per cent of GDP.

In practice, the so-called recovery is, as the Bank of England quarterly bulletin said some years earlier, 'bumping along the bottom' of the downswing, if measured relative to long-term trend growth. The imposition in the November 1993 budget of a negative fiscal adjustment of £6.5 billion, balanced only by ¾ per cent cuts in short-term interest rates (½ per cent on 23 November 1993, and ¼ per cent on 8 February 1994) seems bound to leave the economy more depressed than was either desirable or necessary, even if a full-scale second 'dip' to the recession is avoided.

THE WIDER MAJOR EFFECT

What, then, can we say was 'the Major effect'? This discussion has been fairly strictly confined to macro-economics, which excludes important topics that John Major's friends might argue include some of his most noteworthy achievements:

- the replacement of the poll tax/community charge;
- the details of tax reform, including what he seriously sees as progress towards a lower basic rate of income tax, despite substantial increases in personal direct taxes, as well as in taxation as a whole;
- the Maastricht negotiations (including Britain's opt-out from economic and monetary union and exemption from the social chapter);
- the final conclusion of the Uruguay round of the GATT talks;
- reforms of the public sector to give the users of its services the power of information; and
- what he calls a 'new partnership' with industry.

There is room for only a word or two on most of these topics, which is not to imply they are necessarily less important than macro-economic policy. Indeed, some of them, like the GATT talks, are manifestly of far greater long-run importance and benign potential.

The need to replace the community charge was, after the circumstances of John Major's election as leader of the Conservative party – and particularly because of Michael Heseltine's campaign for that position – a manifest political fact of life. Nonetheless, given the manifest failure of all political parties to come up with any replacement for the widely disliked rates, it was not so easy to find a replacement for the even more widely disliked poll tax.

The key to defusing the political problem lay, as it had probably always lain from the time when Nigel Lawson made the failure of Mrs Thatcher's poll tax inevitable by his refusal to countenance any large-scale cross-subsidy from central government revenues, in shifting the burden of some billions worth of revenue from local to central taxes.[16] Norman Lamont in his first budget raised the standard rate of VAT from 15 to 17½ per cent; and community charge bills were duly subsidized.

This development provided a breathing space for the introduction of a more robust system of local taxation, which duly appeared in 1993. It took some steps in the direction of, but could not fully accomplish, the full logical reform of removing from local authorities both financial and political responsibility for those services where the public evidently will not tolerate large local variations (and treats any such as anomalies requiring to be corrected by central government intervention), while leaving responsibility for the remainder to be decided and financed locally without central interference or subsidy. But, to a degree that must have surprised many of those who lived through the heated arguments of the Thatcher era about local government finance and frequent affirmations that it was a problem without a solution, it does appear to have gone away, at least for the moment; and to that extent John Major, deploying his usual command of detail and of compromise, had clearly steered his Cabinet to a successful resolution of the problem from which they began.

The keynotes of the other tax reform measures introduced in the first four budgets of the Major administration were the steps, starting in 1992, towards the goal of a 20p in the pound basic rate of tax, cunningly approached via a new reduced rate of 20p for a small number of taxpayers rather than by progressive 1p reductions in the basic rate for very large numbers. There were elements of political conjuring on the eve of the forthcoming general election about this; but it did also open opportunities, exploited by both Norman Lamont and Kenneth Clarke, to reduce the value of some of the income tax allowances to 20p, rather than the 40p 'higher rate' or 25p 'basic rate' bands. This served to advance the cause, long advocated by economists of various political persuasions, of widening the tax base so that the burden could be more thinly spread. Reducing the value of some allowances that were allowed at the full 'higher rate' to only the 'basic rate' also helped to spread the tax burden.

John Major's key influence here was discernible in his willingness to over-ride the usual chorus of political special pleading from powerful interest groups. It takes an exceptionally broadminded politician to forgo the plaudits of satisfied producer lobbies for the sake of the rather theoretical argument of economists that greater benefits will be distributed, even if not keenly felt, over the society as a whole if special tax privileges are abolished and the extra revenue used to lower the rates of tax.

The negotiation of the Maastricht treaty, including its overtly economic and monetary provisions, was clearly one of John Major's main preoccupations in his first fifteen months in office; in Chapter 16 William Wallace examines the place of those events in the assessment of John Major's first four years at Number 10.

There was little basis for the belief of the Euro-lobby that any difficulties Britain had with Brussels or with the conception of the European Community evolving into a country called the European Union derived entirely or mainly from Mrs Thatcher's abrasive style and could therefore be easily adjusted the moment they could engineer her removal in favour of someone with a more civilized way of doing business. This created the difficulty for John Major that, once he had agreed a compromise with other European leaders, the result became *his* deal. When it was found to contain features unpalatable to members of his own party, this was unfairly ascribed to failure of his style or management rather than to the real difficulty of seeking to embrace a treaty, seen and intended by its authors as the embryo constitution of a new country, which required parliamentary approval in Britain to be based on the false belief that it was just good economic housekeeping, if not indeed a large backward step from Euro-empire-building.

The only real options, from the moment that the two inter-government conferences on political union and on economic union convened in Rome in John Major's first days in office, were either to veto the whole momentum of the rest of the European Community to forms of unity that became closer to full statehood, the consequences of which for the Community and perhaps for Britain would have been very severe, or to go along with what the rest wanted with as many face-saving gestures as could be mustered.

There was therefore no compromise outcome that could leave either wing of the Conservative party or, indeed, of the wider national debate other than deeply unsatisfied. It was in tune with John Major's rationalism to choose a course that turned aside from the head-on conflict with the rest of the European Community and then try to secure an agreement that permitted Britain to do what it most wanted to do, namely, to continue to participate fully in the free trade system of the Single Market, while having as little as possible to do with those constructions whose purpose was to erect the *de facto* government of a *de facto*, and increasingly *de jure*, European state.

Over the GATT John Major's claim to have played a brave, enlightened and eventually successful role is hard to dispute. He was present as Chancellor at the Group of Seven Economic Summit in Houston, Texas, in 1990 and, as Chairman as well as Prime Minister, in London in 1991; and he was there again at Munich in 1992 and at Tokyo in 1993. On each occasion the Presidents and Prime Ministers committed themselves to completing the round of negotiations by the end of the then calendar year and each time, until 1993, they failed.

John Major is a genuinely passionate believer in free trade principles; and, as the recession in Britain and the US, and later in continental Europe as well, bit deeper into jobs and output, he saw a good GATT agreement as the one positive way in which the leading economies of the world could be given a powerful boost without renewed inflation. The failure to fulfil the pledge given when he was Chairman in 1991 impelled him to take a high-risk, high-profile initiative on the first day of the next G7 summit, in July 1992, at Munich, demanding that his colleagues join him in a definitive attempt to break the deadlock.

As always, the French prevaricated, arguing that the time was not ripe until the French referendum of 20 September on Maastricht was out of the way. John Major received less than the full-blooded support he had had a right to expect from President Bush; and, by the second day of the summit, wags were pointing out that this southern German city was no place for British Prime Ministers to take large initiatives. But he refused to let go, even when French opposition remained undiminished by the successful conclusion of the Maastricht referendum. Britain's presidency of the EC in the second half of 1992 was used to the maximum to drive forward the necessary acceptance by the Community that its agricultural protection and dumping of food mountains on the markets of the rest of the world could not continue undiminished; and in Washington in November the EC representative finally accepted the so-called Blair House agreement with the US, putting a limit on the Community's subsidized food exports.

This proved to be a vital building block, together with the 'Quadripartite Talks' (US, Canada, Japan and the EC) agreement on tariff reductions and market access reached the following July in Tokyo simultaneously with that year's economic summit, in paving the way to the final agreement in Geneva just before the 15 December 1993 deadline and the final signatures on 15 April 1994 in Marrakesh, Morocco. John Major's role in 1992 and again at the Tokyo summit was important both in his disinclination to permit his more politically-minded peers to gloss over the intractable subject of trade, trying to pass it back to functionaries already hopelessly bogged down, and in his widely acknowledged negotiating proficiency.

He is indubitably entitled to wear a GATT campaign medal with pride and with the knowledge that it commemorates much more than his presence on the battlefield. It is even possible that without him the French might have succeeded in holding the European Community to a refusal to include trade in farm products in a GATT deal and that in consequence the round would have failed altogether, with incalculable consequences for world trade, the global economy and even for political harmony among nations.

The reform of the public sector, mainly through the media of the Citizen's Charter, market testing and contracting out, are again outside the essentially macro-economic focus of this chapter, though the micro-economics of the public sector and the modernization of its supply-side are at least as proper subjects for the application of economic thinking as the overall management of fiscal and monetary policy.

This work certainly owed much to John Major's personal vision and commitment, especially to his perception that, while the Thatcher government had put great effort into privatizing part of the public sector, it had been slower to develop ideas for raising standards and involving private sector expertise in public services for which the state would continue to take responsibility. It is early days yet; and there is at least a sceptical suspicion that some of the reforms have done little more than to breed a plague of parasitic consultants, accountants and middle managers doing everything except improving the efficiency of the services in question.

However, if it should prove that the new techniques are indeed critical to making public services as efficient as tightly managed private businesses, John Major may be able one day to claim that his vision and initiative enabled some public services to continue and even grow where otherwise financial pressures would have squeezed them out, whatever political party was in office.

The essential idea of John Major's 'new partnership' with industry was that government should examine all its policies, not just macro-economic, for their effects on industry's ability to generate wealth, going wider than simply the 1980s focus on the 'supply side' as well as the 'demand side'. It led to the deregulation initiative, to the private finance initiative, to extra purpose in seeking tariff reductions in GATT and to the focus on educational standards and vocational education set out in the 1991 white paper and also featured prominently in the white paper on competitiveness.

There are few rewards in politics for pursuing very long-term goals, however meritorious the reforms. The timescale of an economic renaissance is inherently different from the timescale of an administration, however prolonged, comprising decades rather than years, let alone weeks! John Major may one day be credited with starting the long slow climb back to ideological disarmament between the prophets of public interest and the profits of private interest, a conflict which began with *The Wealth of Nations* and was not abated by *Das Kapital*.

But it may also be that there is an irreducible minimum of conflict, even in perfect competition, and that partnership extended beyond that point becomes indistinguishable from mercantilism, corporatism or communism. It is not sufficient to ask about the effects of government policies on industry's – or indeed the service sector's – ability to create wealth unless we know whose wealth it is: the wealth of the firm or the wealth of the economy and the society. Tariff reductions are a good example of the differences; but then so may be deregulation. Deregulating fraud could benefit private wealth, but it would damage public wealth.

CONCLUSION

Inevitably, the final judgment on John Major's impact in economic policy will depend on assessments of his and his government's macro-economic performance, however often some theorists tell us that the only useful action governments can take in this field is to abstain from all conscious thought about it and, if possible, from any action.

Over-arching everything else has to be the plain fact that inflation was all but 10 per cent when he started and was by March 1994 almost 2½ per cent, however measured. Indeed, in the last nine months up to June 1994 it was running at an annual rate of between nought and ½ per cent and with no signs of inflationary pressures to come – though occasionally administrative price changes will push the official measure of inflation up.

In short John Major stopped inflation. It may sound negative and lack inspirational or heroic proportions; but it is nonetheless a towering achievement, requiring quite extraordinary singleness of purpose, political courage and almost divine patience. Of post-war Prime Ministers only James Callaghan can claim even a partially similar feat (down from 22.3 per cent 1975Q1–1976Q1 to 8.7 per cent 1978Q2–1979Q2).[17]

There can be little doubt, whether from his very first speech at Northampton on his second day as Chancellor, from his fateful Glasgow speech six days before Black Wednesday, from countless other utterances or, most decisively, from his actions as Chancellor and Prime Minister that he believed inflation to be a great evil and that it was his duty to stop it, come what may; and that included a general election at the worst possible moment. At the same time he did not seem to feel it necessary to pretend that stable prices were a sufficient as well as a necessary condition of faster growth or that they were in themselves the only goal of economic policy.

True, interest rates were already at 15 per cent when he became Chancellor; and true, inflation had just peaked when he became Prime Minister. But both of those events were just the beginning, in terms of political pain, of the long agonizing recession that went on getting deeper (measured by the GDP gap) until the spring of 1993 (see Table 1) and which was the only weapon available to the government to conquer inflation.

Exchange rate mechanism membership was not a different weapon, but just a different lever of the same weapon (give or take its supposedly miraculous effects on expectations, which hardly materialized); and it broke in the Prime Minister's hand. He can never annul the price he inevitably paid in political reputation for that catastrophe (for him, if not for the economy); but he could and he did put together a new machinery for pursuing the same goal, price stability, with the same weapon (demand starvation of the economy) and it worked.

What of John Major's personal culpability for the ERM debacle? He was Chancellor when we went in; and shortly afterwards he became Prime Minister. He used the full authority of his offices to support, uphold and, if possible, ensure our continued and permanent membership. He doubtless saw advantages of European as well as economic policy in that membership, though he probably thought that ERM membership had also been all but essential to economic policy. He certainly said in his Glasgow speech that the monetary and fiscal tightness which ERM membership required would have been necessary to keep Britain competitive in Europe even if we had been outside the ERM, a marked difference from the Governor's view nearly a month later that from the early summer of 1992 ERM membership conflicted with the policies the economy truly required.[18]

He has never tried to pretend that ERM membership was anyone else's fault or that the pound's unceremonious ejection from it was anything other than a reverse for the government. He was not singing in his bath or claiming to have known all along, or for months, that there was no effective defence against a serious speculative attack. Apart from pointing out plausibly enough that, as a supposedly mutually supportive system of fixed exchange rates, the ERM had in September of 1992 exhibited faults which needed to be remedied, he has taken the affair on the chin and got on with the job of devising a replacement policy, which in practice has turned out so far to be greatly superior to the original, despite some undue financial stringency from the new Chancellor after May 1993.

These, it appears, are the actions of a capable, honourable and straightforward man who unquestionably made one huge and recognizable mistake – putting his faith in ERM membership. Even then he was in company with the great majority of respectable opinion in the City, business and politics at the time he took Britain in, astonishing as that may seem in retrospect, and indeed, to the present author.

His position is clearly different from that of Norman Lamont, who evidently never believed in ERM membership, but accepted it as the price of office and lived like Cardinal Wolsey to wish that he had given his convictions as high priority as loyalty to his political master. To that extent Norman Lamont's economics were better, but his ethics were not. He invited his own tragedy because he who lives by political calculation must expect to die by political miscalculation, as he did just at the moment when he had got the economic policy he wanted, which was probably also as close as Britain had been to having a coherent economic strategy for about fifteen years.

John Major was not cynical in adopting the strategy of ERM membership. He believed in it; and it blew up in his face. He has carried the can; and nobody seriously expects Prime Ministers to resign because of such policy disasters.

John Major's political difficulties have little, if anything, to do with any deficiencies in his conduct of government, apart from his singleminded determination to quash inflation which is the proximate cause of all the economic adversity that the public naturally dislikes. His claim to our respect rests on that achievement combined with his persistently rational approach to his duties, despite the increasing hostility of a press which appears daily less in touch with any reality beyond the psychotic nostalgia of its editors for the days when Mrs Thatcher told them what to write and rewarded them with personal honours and ever lower tax bills.

Notes

1. Nigel Lawson, *The View from Number 11* (Bantam Press, 1992), p. 499.
2. Robin Leigh-Pemberton, Governor of the Bank of England, giving the first international Celebrity Lecture at the University of Durham on 5 April 1990.
3. Robin Leigh-Pemberton, Governor of the Bank of England, at Birmingham Chamber of Industry and Commerce/West Midlands CBI, Birmingham, on 18 September 1991.
4. November 1993 Financial Statement and Budget Report 'Red Book' (Table 2A.1, page 23).
5. March 1989, FSBR.
6. January 1990 White Paper (Cm 1021).

7. February 1991 Supplement (Cm 1520).

8. February 1992 Supplement (Cm 1920).

9. January 1993 Supplement (Cm 2219).

10. November 1993, FSBR.

11. On 26 October 1989 Nigel Lawson resigned as Chancellor. Less noticed, on 27 October 1989 a Treasury press notice headed 'Extract from a speech on 27th October, 1989, in Northampton by the Chancellor of the Exchequer, the Rt Hon John Major, M.P.' recorded that the new Chancellor's first public utterance included the words, 'The problem is inflation. I have no doubt [this sentence underlined by the Treasury] that the central task before us is the reduction and the elimination of rising prices ... Many think a little inflation does no harm. I do not share that view ... Ending it cannot be painless. The harsh truth is that if the policy isn't hurting, it isn't working ...'.

12 On the same occasion (note 11) John Major continued; 'High interest rates are working exactly as intended. Spending is slowing down – we can see it in housing and in the shops.'

13. Robin Leigh-Pemberton, Governor of the Bank of England, at the CBI Eastern Region Annual Dinner in Duxford, Cambridgeshire, on Thursday 8 October 1992.

14. Robin Leigh-Pemberton, Governor of the Bank of England, as in note 13 at the CBI Eastern Region Annual Dinner in Duxford, Cambridgeshire, on Thursday 8 October 1992.

15. 10 September 1992, John Major said at a CBI Dinner in Glasgow, 'Two years ago, before we joined the Exchange Rate Mechanism, inflation was over 10 per cent and seemed to be rising. We forget too readily the alarm that that caused. Now inflation is 3.7 per cent and falling, and we overlook too readily the opportunities that that offers. We saw such figures before. We saw them briefly in the mid-1980s but they didn't last. This time I am determined that that regime of low inflation will last.'

16. Nigel Lawson, *op. cit.*, page 582. Christopher Patten wanted £2 billion to cushion the effect of the 'Poll Tax' on those living in low-rated property. Nigel Lawson confined it to £345 million.

17. Economic Trends, Annual Supplement 1994 Edition (Table 2.1, pp. 150–1).

18. Robin Leigh-Pemberton, Governor of the Bank of England, CBI Eastern Region Annual Dinner, Duxford, Cambridgeshire,

on 8 October 1992: 'Belonging to the ERM is not, therefore, a *necessary* condition for a successful monetary policy . . . for eighteen months after we joined, the ERM was in my view indeed helpful . . . during that period, therefore, membership did not seriously conflict with our domestic monetary policy needs. But over the summer [of 1992] a conflict began to emerge and it became increasingly severe.'

Chapter 12

INDUSTRY

N. F. R. Crafts

INTRODUCTION*

The Conservatives came to power in 1979 determined to end a long period of relative economic decline in the UK by breaking away from the interventionist economic policies of the 1960s and 1970s and by ending the trade unions' veto on economic reform. The emphasis of policy switched towards putting greater pressure on managers in both public and private sectors to increase efficiency, epitomized by the high-profile privatization and deregulation programmes. Under the new regime there was a surge in manufacturing productivity but a continuing, and at times very rapid, process of de-industrialization. The long-run implications of these developments have been hotly debated.

During the early 1990s a wide cross-section of informed opinion appeared to be worried by the decline in Britain's industrial base and to believe that the government should adopt a more pro-manufacturing policy stance. The House of Lords Select Committee on Science and Technology spoke for many when they claimed, 'Manufacturing industry is vital to

*I am grateful to Peter Law, Anthony Seldon and Mark Williams for very helpful discussions and suggestions. I am responsible for all errors.

the prosperity of the United Kingdom ... Our manufacturing base is dangerously small' and concluded that 'The present lack of Government commitment, support and assistance to industry are damaging to our national interest'.[1]

The Prime Minister responded with a change of rhetoric and, following the election, by giving the DTI portfolio to Michael Heseltine, who, while out of office, had published a book that argued the need for 'industrial policy'.[2] At the Conservative party conference in October 1992 Heseltine promised 'to intervene before breakfast, lunch, tea and dinner' to help business. The new Chancellor of the Exchequer, Kenneth Clarke, declared shortly after taking office that 'I should like to be remembered as a Chancellor who helped British industry and commerce'.

What follows focuses on three questions which arise from this.

1. How good was the legacy of the Thatcher years?
2. Has policy towards industry changed significantly during the Major premiership?
3. How does industrial performance since 1990 compare with that of the 1980s?

In seeking answers it will be important to bear in mind the wide array of policy decisions, both macro- and microeconomic, which impact on manufacturing's prospects and also to distinguish longer-term trends from short-term cyclical fluctuations.

THE THATCHER YEARS

The hallmark of the 1980s was the adoption of policies which seriously intensified the pressure on industrial managers to cut costs and raise productivity.[3] In terms of supply-side policy there was a move away from subsidizing investment, supporting lame ducks and picking winners towards cutting direct taxes, deregulating and privatizing. On the macro-economic front Keynesian demand management was scorned, unemployment was tolerated and exchange rate policies left industry exposed for most of the 1980s to severe import competition.

At the same time, the new policy stance substantially reduced trade union bargaining power and permitted greater flexibility in work arrangements. This partly resulted from the long series of reforms to industrial relations law but stemmed much more from rapidly rising unemployment and greater competition in product markets. Initially the main impact was felt on the conduct of industrial relations but by the later 1980s reforms in structure were also evident with reductions in the prevalence of the closed shop and multi-unionism.[4]

The new supply-side policies certainly addressed important aspects of industrial performance. Research during the 1970s had highlighted widespread problems of inefficiency and wasteful use of both labour and capital.[5] Econometric investigation of the industrial pattern of productivity improvements confirms that the 1980s saw a strong impact from changed trade union bargaining power resulting from both employment shocks and increased competition.[6] Indeed, although there was relatively little tightening of competition policy, there does seem to have been a notable reduction in industrial concentration in the 1980s, thus reversing the trend of the 1950s and 1960s. The average share in employment of the top five domestic firms in 100 industrial sectors fell from 45.6 in 1979 to 39.1 in 1989.[7]

Table 1: Growth of Output/Person Employed in
Nationalized/Privatized Enterprises (% per year)

	1970–80	1980–90
British Airways	8.1	6.0
BAA	0.6	2.7
British Telecom	4.3	7.2
British Coal	−2.4	8.1
Electricity Supply	3.7	2.5
British Gas	4.9	4.9
Post Office	−0.1	3.4
British Rail	−2.0	3.2
British Steel	−1.7	13.7

Source: Taken from M. Bishop and D. Thompson, 'Regulatory Reform and Productivity Growth in the UK's Public Utilities', *Applied Economics*, 24 (1992), p.1187.

The tougher policy towards nationalized industries and privatization seems to have promoted a faster growth of productivity following the very weak performance of the 1970s, as Table 1 reports. Nevertheless, the utilities' privatization programme (notably gas and electricity supply) attracted widespread criticism from economists for failing adequately to restructure production, for unduly weak regulation of market power and for missing opportunities to promote competition.[8] The consequences of key decisions concerning the energy industries, taken with an eye to short-term pressures in the 1980s, would come to pose difficult questions for the Major government.

Other weaknesses were not tackled so effectively and the economic environment of the early 1980s was notably inhospitable to investment. By the late 1980s business investment was booming but continued severe criticism of human capital formation was directed at a shortfall of skills and inadequate training, especially by writers from NIESR. Only in 1987–88 with the Technical and Vocational Education Initiative and the Education Reform Act were serious policy steps taken in this regard – too late to have any impact in the Thatcher period.

Table 2: Productivity of Labour in Manufacturing, 1987: Sources of German Lead Over UK (%)

Human Capital	13.4
Physical Capital	10.1
Research & Development	5.8
Efficiency	−7.5

Source: Derived from M. O'Mahony, 'Productivity and Human Capital Formation in UK and German Manufacturing', National Institute of Economic and Social Research Discussion Paper No. 28 (1992), p. 17.

A recent econometric comparison of British and German manufacturing, summarized in Table 2, gives a perspective on productivity performance. This reinforces the suggestion that Britain did well during the 1980s in cost-cutting but not in capital accumulation. In the cross-section an average British productivity shortfall of 22 per cent appears to be entirely due to relatively low investment per worker, particularly in training. Once this has been taken into account, the efficiency of factor use by 1987 actually appears to have been superior in the UK.

In fact, productivity was the high point of manufacturing performance. The mid-decade type of a 'productivity miracle' was, of course, overdone but, even so, there was a substantial improvement. By 1989, manufacturing labour productivity was 50 per cent above the 1979 level and the French and German leads over the UK had fallen from 34.1 per cent and 51 per cent respectively in 1979 to 20.4 per cent and 17.4 per cent respectively in 1989.[9]

Other parts of the picture were the source of the worries reflected by the House of Lords Select Committee on Science and Technology. These were the rapid deterioration of the balance of manufacturing trade to a deficit of 3.6 per cent of GDP by 1989, the fall in the share of industry in employment to only 29.4 per cent in 1989 and the slow rate of growth of industrial output at 1.2 per cent per year during 1979–89. Econometric analysis shows that the shortfall in skills in the British manufacturing labour force had a strong impact on exports.[10] Higher productivity had resulted much more from fewer jobs than from greater sales.

Pessimists interpreted these developments as merely a one-off boost to productivity and to imply a future balance of payments constraint on growth. Optimists saw a framework in place which would deliver additional productivity gains in the 1990s together with a further strengthening of invest-ment. As the economy moved from boom to recession, the latter view struck a growing number of pundits as too com-placent – something must be done, it seemed.

POLICY TOWARDS INDUSTRY
SINCE 1990

The most obvious change in industry policy during the Major years has been the arrival of Michael Heseltine as President of the Board of Trade in April 1992, something which would have been inconceivable had Mrs Thatcher remained as

Prime Minister. Soon afterwards the DTI produced a new mission statement, including amongst other items the promises that the DTI will:

- seek to identify the needs of UK business through a close dialogue with individual sectors and an understanding of what influences competitiveness at home and abroad;
- ensure that those needs are taken into account by government and within the European Community;
- stimulate innovation and encourage best practice throughout business in quality, design and management;
- respond flexibly to the needs of different regions and areas with special difficulties.[11]

Coming shortly after the government's debacle over pit closures, many commentators suspected that this heralded a return to an industrial policy reminiscent of the corporatist 1970s.[12] Lobbyists were, no doubt, encouraged and the CBI's newly established National Manufacturing Council promised to obtain real action from government. In its 1993 report this body declared that 'The manufacturing message appears to be much more widely understood and accepted at the most senior levels' and that 'industry is gaining increasing confidence in the DTI's ability and commitment to be seen as the champion for industry within Government'.[13] This may have been overreaction as in March 1993 the Prime Minister affirmed that his policy for assisting manufacturing mainly comprised further trade liberalization, an appropriate macro-economic policy framework, staying outside the EC Social Chapter and cutting back red tape.[14]

There have been some signs of a 'pro-business' shift in competition policy since Heseltine took over at the DTI. For example, the Secretary of State decided not to refer the Airtours/Owners Abroad and GEC/Philips Electronics mergers to the Monopolies and Mergers Commission (MMC) against the advice of the Director General of Fair Trading and overruled the MMC's recommendation that British Gas should be split up. Anticipated revisions to the Restrictive Practices Act and a new law on Abuse of Market Power similar to Article 86 of the Treaty of Rome have been shelved, whereas priority is apparently being given to reducing the costs of compliance with competition policy for firms.[15]

By May 1994, Office of Fair Trading officials were complaining to the *Financial Times* that the DTI had gone soft on competition policy.[16]

In most, if not all, respects the key elements of supply-side policy towards industry remain very similar to those of the late 1980s and the circumstances of the 1990s are fundamentally different from those of the 1960s and 1970s. Thus, since 1990, privatization has continued with proceeds averaging £6.7bn per year compared with £5.3bn in the previous four years. The top rate of personal income tax remains at the 40 per cent level adopted in 1988, a rate unthinkable in the early post-war years. Tax disincentives ('wedges') to investment as measured by OECD and reported in Table 3 are now fairly similar to those in France and Germany. Industrial relations reform is still in place and there is no evidence that trade union leaders have regained their influence in Downing Street.

The Queen's Speech in November 1993 stressed deregulation rather than new industrial initiatives. In early 1994 the sale of Rover to the German firm BMW was allowed to proceed unimpeded. Spending on old-style industrial support policies has continued to be cut, as Table 3 shows, although the new found enthusiasm for subsidizing training has been maintained. The European Commission's calculations, also shown in Table 3, indicate that at the end of the 1980s the UK had the lowest level of subsidies to manufacturing in the EC and it seems probable that this has continued to be the case.

In the high-profile area of the energy sector, important decisions have been required in the aftermath of the privatizations of the 1980s. In the case of British Gas, the government has effectively admitted that it made serious errors in the 1980s by announcing the opening of the household sector to full competition in 1998 while the price cap was substantially tightened in 1992.[17] This can be seen, however, as reaffirming a policy of intensifying the pressure on management to increase efficiency.

The greatest embarrassment arose, of course, when the implications for coal output of the 1989 electricity privatization became apparent in 1993. Commentators generally

Table 3: Industrial Subsidy and Tax Policies

a) *UK Government Spending (£bn)*

	1986/7	1990/1	1993/4	1996/7
Regional & General Industrial Support	1.5	0.8	0.7	0.7
Support for Ships, Steel, Aerospace, Coal, Vehicles	2.2	0.4	0.1	0.0
Scientific Assistance, Trade & Technological Support	1.3	1.2	0.7	0.5
Training	1.8	2.4	2.0	1.9

b) *Corporate & Personal Income Tax Wedges Combined (%)*

	France	Germany	Japan	UK	USA
Buildings	2.3	1.2	3.4	1.7	3.7
Machinery	1.4	1.2	2.4	1.5	2.5

c) *State Aids/Manufacturing GDP (%)*

	1981/6	1986/8	1988/90
Belgium	6.4	4.4	4.1
Denmark	2.8	2.0	2.1
France	4.9	3.7	3.5
West Germany	3.0	2.7	2.5
Greece	12.9	15.5	14.6
Ireland	7.9	6.1	4.9
Italy	9.5	6.7	6.0
Luxembourg	7.3	2.3	2.6
Netherlands	4.1	3.3	3.1
Portugal	na	8.3	5.3
Spain	na	5.3	3.6
UK	3.8	2.7	2.0

Source: Derived from Cmnd 1520, *Public Expenditure Analyses to 1993/4* (HMSO, 1991); Cmnd 2519, *Public Expenditure* (HMSO, 1994); OECD, *Taxing Profits in a Global Economy* (Paris, 1991), p.106; CEC, *Second Survey on State Aids* (Luxembourg, 1990); CEC, *Third Survey on State Aids* (Luxembourg, 1992).

agreed that serious mistakes had been made in the creation of a duopoly in non-nuclear generation and a regulatory structure which tended to promote a too rapid switch into gas-fired power stations.[18] Nevertheless, the die was cast and the DTI accepted the consequent rapid rundown of coal while making only the minimal concessions necessary to appease back-bench opinion.[19]

Indeed, it should be remembered that, over a wide area, the government's hands have been tied by previous decisions and it has had a good deal less room to manoeuvre than some interventionists might like. Thus, tariff policies are decided at the level of the EU, the Single Market (1992) Programme has reduced the ability to impose non-tariff forms of protectionism, international capital mobility has increased and privatizations have led to declining influence over investment decisions.

These points were all reinforced by the publication of a long-awaited White Paper, *Competitiveness: Helping Business to Win*, in May 1994.[20] The rhetoric confirmed the change of tone and repeats the DTI's mission statement. The policy announcements offered little new, continuing to stress the importance of training, contained no hint of a return to 1970s' style industrial policies and implicitly confirmed the continuing decline in DTI spending. There were no concessions to critics such as the House of Commons Trade and Industry Committee who had called for greater research and development spending by government, a return to training levies on business and action to curb hostile takeovers and other alleged encouragements to 'short-termism' in industry.[21]

By contrast, the change in macro-economic policy since 1990 has, of course, been dramatic and may lead to a rebalancing of the economy in which growth is rather less skewed towards services than in the 1980s. The big news here was the forced exit from ERM in September 1992, together with an eventual realization that mistakes in macro-economic policy during the Lawson chancellorship had left a legacy of 'twin deficits' in the balance of payments and the government's own finances requiring a serious adjustment of policy.

As Figure 1 shows, the devaluation coming at the end of a recession, with weak trade unions in product markets generally characterized by heavy import competition, led to a substantial improvement in cost competitiveness which does

Cost Competitiveness[1]

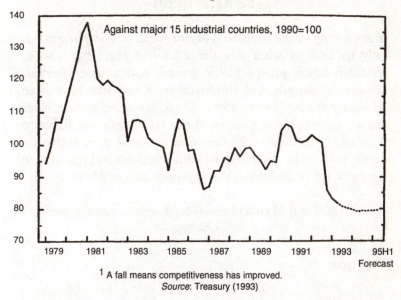

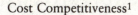

Against major 15 industrial countries, 1990=100

[1] A fall means competitiveness has improved.
Source: Treasury (1993)

not appear vulnerable to rapid erosion from wage inflationary pressures. Nineteen ninety-three saw industrial cost
competitiveness at a higher level than at any time during the
1980s and over 20 per cent above the average for that
decade.

At the same time, freed from ERM, the government has
been seeking to tighten fiscal policy and relax monetary
policy, in effect accepting a relatively low exchange rate. The
probable implication is of a relatively high rate of export
growth relative to that of domestic consumer spending, particularly against a background of heavy household indeb-
tedness left over from the 1980s credit boom. If sustained,
which may be difficult given mid-1990s electoral pressures,
this policy stance should calm some of the fears over the
contraction of the manufacturing base.

INDUSTRIAL PERFORMANCE IN THE EARLY 1990s

In reviewing recent industrial performance it is important not only to look at what has already taken place but also to consider future prospects for growth and competitiveness. Obviously, output and employment in industry have been adversely affected by the 1990–92 recession and comparisons drawn with the boom years of the late 1980s are liable to mislead. One way of establishing a useful perspective on events is to make comparisons with recession and recovery in the early 1980s and this is the approach adopted here.

Table 4: Real GDP, Exports & Manufacturing Output: % Changes

a) *GDP*

1980:	−2.1		1990:	0.6
1981:	−1.1		1991:	−2.3
1982:	1.8		1992:	−0.6
1983:	3.6		1993:	1.9

b) *Exports*

1980:	−3.9		1990:	4.3
1981:	2.7		1991:	1.1
1982:	−2.2		1992:	1.0
1983:	3.2		1993:	5.2

c) *Manufacturing Output*

1980:	−8.7		1990:	−0.2
1981:	−6.0		1991:	−5.3
1982:	0.2		1992:	−0.8
1983:	2.9		1993:	1.9

Sources: CSO, *Economic Trends* Annual Supplement (HMSO, 1993);
CSO, *Economic Trends* No. 484 (HMSO, 1994).

Nineteen seventy-nine and 1989 were both business cycle peak years. Table 4 traces out the ensuing paths of output and exports. The two recessions were fairly similar in terms of the overall decline in real GDP but noticeably different in the composition of the downturn. In the early 1980s the fall in manufacturing output was more than twice as big as in the

Table 5: Output/Person Employed (1990 = 100)

a) *Whole Economy*

	Index	% Change		Index	% Change
1979	82.3		1989	100.1	
1980	81.3	−1.2	1990	100.0	−0.1
1981	83.2	2.3	1991	100.5	0.5
1982	86.3	3.7	1992	102.8	2.3
1983	90.2	4.5	1993	106.2	3.3

b) *Manufacturing*

	Index	% Change		Index	% Change
1979	65.0		1989	98.1	
1980	62.4	−4.0	1990	100.0	1.9
1981	64.6	3.5	1991	101.4	1.4
1982	68.9	6.7	1992	106.3	4.8
1983	74.6	8.3	1993	112.2	5.6

Sources: CSO, *Economic Trends Annual Supplement* (HMSO, 1993);
CSO, *Economic Trends* No. 484 (HMSO, 1994).

early 1990s, while exports held up noticeably better on the second occasion.

The shocks of the early 1980s led to a large increase in manufacturing productivity which was based on a shake-out of overmanning and inefficient firms. Table 5 shows that the increase in output per worker in manufacturing between 1989 and 1993 is very similar to that between 1979 and 1983, somewhat to the surprise of those who regarded the early 1980s as a once and for all readjustment. Good productivity performance has certainly helped to underpin the competitiveness position reflected in Figure 1. Nevertheless it does seem unlikely that the productivity enhancing effects of recessionary shocks will be as powerful the second time around and there were strong signs of this in the last two quarters of 1993 when the annual rate of manufacturing productivity growth slowed to 2 per cent compared with 8.6 per cent in the second half of 1983.

Table 6 reports a continuation of the de-industrialization of the labour force which has exercised so many

Table 6: De-Industrialization, 1973–1993

| | % Employed in Industry | | |
	1973	1989	1993
Australia	35.4	26.5	24.1
Austria	43.0	37.0	35.1
Canada	30.6	25.7	22,5
Finland	35.7	31.0	27.4
France	39.7	30.1	27.9
West Germany	47.5	39.8	39.0
Italy	39.2	32.4	33.4
Japan	37.2	34.3	34.0
Norway	33.9	25.3	23.0
Sweden	36.8	29.4	25.6
UK	42.6	29.4	25.8
USA	33.2	26.7	24.2

Sources: OECD, *Historical Statistics, 1960–92* (1993); OECD, *Labour Force Statistics* (1994/1).

commentators in the last fifteen years. It should be noticed that the proportion of the labour force in industry in Britain is not exceptionally low but nevertheless those who like to compare the UK unfavourably with Germany will find further grounds for dismay in these data.

Table 7 looks more to the future by reporting on investment in both physical and human capital. Parts a) and b) of the table certainly offer some encouragement. While investment is obviously hurt by recession, levels of business investment during 1989–93 held up better than might have been expected. Similarly, expenditure on training was sustained through the recession at a considerably higher level than in the 1970s or early 1980s, although it is generally agreed that the quality of training remains much lower than in Germany and that replication of Germany's subtle institutional arrangements for the acquisition of craft skills is not immediately feasible for the UK.[22] Given this, Soskice sees as highly commendable the rapid expansion of higher education in the early 1990s through which a different type of comparative advantage in business might be strengthened.[23]

The *Competitiveness* White Paper promises to reinforce

Table 7: Some Aspects of UK Factor Accumulation

a) *Business Investment/GDP* (%)

1979:	12.4	1989:	16.2
1983:	11.4	1993:	14.2

b) *Employees Receiving Job-Related Training in Last 4 Weeks* (%)

1984:	9.2	1987:	11.9	1990:	15.4	1993:	13.4
1985:	10.4	1988:	13.3	1991:	14.9		
1986:	10.8	1989:	14.4	1992:	14.5		

c) *Vocational Qualifications* (% labour force, 1988/9)

	University	Intermediate	None
France	7	40	53
West Germany	11	63	26
Netherlands	8	57	35
Switzerland	11	66	23
UK	11	25	64

Sources: HM Treasury, Financial Statement and Budget Report (1993); Department
of Employment, Labour Force Survey No. 7 (1994); S. J. Prais, 'Economic
Performance and Education: The Nature of Britain's Deficiencies',
National Institute of Economic and Social Research Discussion Paper
No. 52 (1993).

education and training policies by pressing on to achieve
targets of 50 per cent of young people and of the workforce
as a whole at NVQ level 3 (2 A levels or equivalent) or
above.[24] Unfortunately, grave doubts continue to be
expressed about the quality of education and training for
those not in the academic elite and concerning the relative
shortfall of intermediate qualifications in the British labour
force which appear to have a sizeable impact on exporting
capabilities.[25] Notably Prais, a greatly respected analyst, is
extremely critical of a continuing deterioration in basic
mathematical skills among low achievers and of a dilution of
standards in curricula and tests for those acquiring vocational skills.[26] Moreover, the fraction of young people who
have serious problems with literacy and numeracy has risen
in recent years from 12 to 20 per cent.[27]

CONCLUSION

The answers to the three questions posed in the introduction should already be apparent. Supply-side policy towards manufacturing has not changed significantly during the Major premiership and there has certainly not been a lurch back to the 1970s. There has, however, been a change in rhetoric and something of a rapprochement between the DTI and manufacturing industry. The big switch has been the reorientation of macro-economic policy following departure from the ERM which should favour manufacturing if the lower real exchange rate can be sustained.

Underlying industrial performance does not so far exhibit any sharp break from the 1980s. Productivity growth has been respectable although there are signs that in manufacturing it will be difficult fully to match the increases made during the spectacular shakeout of the early 1980s. On the other hand, output suffered less during the early 1990s recession than ten years earlier and export growth prospects are much improved by the gains in cost competitiveness following devaluation. A key aspect of future performance turns on the success of new strategies of human capital accumulation and on this the jury is still out.

Developments during the Thatcher years probably raised growth *potential* to a small extent. Changes in industrial relations, privatization, increased competition, committing to the Single Market and the restructuring of taxation were all positive moves. The biggest failure was probably to be found in the initial neglect and then dubious reform of education and training. This assessment still seems applicable in 1994. In the short to medium term, however, *actual* growth depends much more on demand. Here for the economy as a whole it is difficult to envisage in the mid-1990s a repeat of the cyclical boom conditions of the mid-1980s and accordingly immediate growth prospects are surely less favourable than ten years ago.

Notes

1. House of Lords Select Committee on Science and Technology, *Report* (1991), pp. 3, 43.
2. M. Heseltine, *Where There's a Will* (Hutchinson, 1987).
3. An introductory overview and assessment can be found in N.F.R. Crafts, 'Reversing Relative Economic Decline? The 1980s in Historical Perspective', *Oxford Review of Economic Policy*, 7(3) (1991), pp. 81–98.
4. For a useful evaluation see J. Purcell, 'The Rediscovery of the Management Prerogative: The Management of Labour Relations in the 1980s', *Oxford Review of Economic Policy* 7(1) (1991), pp. 33–43.
5. The best starting point is in C. F. Pratten and A. G. Atkinson, 'The Use of Manpower in British Manufacturing Industry', *Department of Employment Gazette*, 84 (1976), pp. 571–6.
6. The flavour of a large body of literature on this topic can be obtained from C. Bean and J. Symons, 'Ten Years of Mrs T.', CEPR Discussion Paper No. 316 (1989) and J. Haskel, 'Imperfect Competition, Work Practices and Productivity Growth', *Oxford Bulletin of Economics and Statistics*, 53 (1991), pp. 265–79.
7. R. Clarke, 'Trends in Concentration in UK Manufacturing', in M. Casson and J. Creedy (eds.), *Industrial Concentration and Economic Inequality: Essays in Honour of Peter Hart* (Elgar, Aldershot, 1993), pp. 122, 124.
8. The classic overview is in J. Vickers and G. Yarrow, *Privatization: An Economic Analysis* (MIT Press, 1987).
9. These estimates are taken from B. van Ark, *International Comparisons of Output and Productivity* (University of Groningen, 1993), p. 90 and are purchasing power parity adjusted figures.
10. N . Oulton, 'Workforce Skills and Export Competitiveness: An Anglo-German Comparison', National Institute of Economic and Social Research Discussion Paper No. 47 (1993).
11. Department of Trade and Industry, *Trade and Industry: The Government's Expenditure Plans 1993/4 to 1995/6*, Cmnd.2204 (1993).
12. See, for example, *The Economist*, 30 January 1993.

13. CBI, National Manufacturing Council, *Making It In Britain II* (CBI, 1993), pp. 8, 34.

14. A good survey of these developments can be found in M. E. Williams, 'The Effectiveness of Competition Policy in the UK', *Oxford Review of Economic Policy*, 9(2) (1993), pp. 94–112.

15. *Daily Telegraph*, 12 March 1993.

16. *Financial Times*, 17 May 1994.

17. *Financial Times*, 22 December 1993.

18. This view seems to be widely held on the political right as well as the left; see C. Robinson , *Energy Policy: Errors, Illusions and Market Realities* (Institute of Economic Affairs, 1993).

19. Department of Trade and Industry, *The Prospects for Coal*, Cmnd. 2235 (1993).

20. Department of Trade and Industry, *Competitiveness: Helping Business to Win*, Cmnd. 2563 (1994).

21. House of Commons Select Committee on Trade and Industry, *Competitiveness of UK Manufacturing Industry* (1994).

22. See the perceptive discussion in W. Carlin, 'West German Growth and Institutions, 1945–90', CEPR Discussion Paper No. 896 (1994).

23. D. W. Soskice, 'Social Skills from Mass Higher Education: Rethinking the Company-based Initial Training Paradigm', *Oxford Review of Economic Policy*, 9(3), (1993), pp. 101–13.

24. See fn. 20.

25. See fn. 10.

26. S. J. Prais, 'Economic Performance and Education: The Nature of Britain's Deficiencies', National Institute of Economic and Social Research Discussion Paper No. 52 (1993).

27. *Sunday Times*, 10 April 1994.

Chapter 13

FINANCIAL SECTOR

Peter Sinclair

INTRODUCTION: THE TWO PERIODS

The four years from November 1990 fall neatly into two periods. Period 1 lasts up to Black Wednesday, 16 September 1992. Sterling was in the exchange rate mechanism (ERM) of the European Community's monetary system (EMS). The main priority in this period was to preserve the exchange rate link, and use it, and the high interest rates that accompanied it, to reverse the unwelcome climb to 10 per cent inflation in 1990. In period 2, sterling was floating freely. Objectives changed. Efforts concentrated upon reducing interest rates, reversing the recession and restoring order in Britain's budgetary finances.

ERM: THE FIRST PARADOX

Exchange rate matters dominated period 1. The period actually begins in the dying weeks of Mrs Thatcher's administration. October 1990 saw a final victory for the Foreign Office and the Treasury over 10 Downing Street. Chancellor Lawson had pressed the case for sterling's entry into the ERM from 1984. Lawson's predecessor as Chancellor, Sir Geoffrey

Howe, strongly supported that case from his new position as
Foreign Secretary. So did Douglas Hurd, Foreign Secretary
from 1989, and, still more significantly for our purposes,
John Major, both as Foreign Secretary in the brief interval
between Howe and Hurd and as Chancellor after Lawson's
resignation. Indeed Lawson's resignation itself was one by-
product of the chasm in financial policy towards Europe that
had opened up between the Prime Minister's Office and the
main departments in her government. The year that followed
saw Hurd and Major and their officials manoeuvre a bitterly
reluctant Prime Minister into locking sterling into the ERM,
with a central parity against its key currency, the Deutsche-
mark (DM), of 2.95.

The case for having sterling inside the ERM had four
main strands. One was the argument that Britain's exports to
the rest of the European Union – climbing to some 55 per
cent of total exports – were disrupted and weakened by
uncertainty about sterling's value in EU currencies. Secondly,
Germany had controlled inflation better than Britain. So
keeping inflation expectations down in Britain, which
became a top priority in 1990, could be much easier with a
commitment to a DM link than without it. Third, sterling's
continued absence from the ERM would deprive Britain of a
serious say in the discussions, then gathering pace, about
possible future monetary union in Europe. Fourth, if EU
countries had similar preferences and constraints, they would
want to adopt similar monetary policies; and if they did, how
silly it would be to allow exchange rates between their
national monies to wobble about.

Opponents of ERM had argued that it was unstable, that
its undoubted success in achieving some convergence in
interest rates and inflation had not been matched in other
variables (such as output growth, and 'real' exchange rates),
that the 'export disruption hypothesis' meant little if traders
had access to forward exchange rate cover, and that European monetary union was something Britain should avoid
anyway. They recalled that Britain had joined the ERM's
precursor – the snake in the tunnel – almost immediately
after its inception in March 1972, but found that a massive
speculative crisis had soon driven her out of it. They also

argued that oil price volatility (the UK exported oil, Germany imported it) would mean that the mark and the pound might need to move in opposite directions.[1]

The ERM's opponents lost their battle in October 1990 when sterling joined the ERM. A month later, Chancellor Major succeeded Mrs Thatcher as Prime Minister. Norman Lamont became Chancellor. But Major's position on the issue was not one of unqualified support, and still less for the vision of European monetary union (EMU) to which most EU governments now saw the ERM as a precursor. Sterling was given maximum permitted bands of fluctuation against other ERM currencies of 6 per cent, rather than the usual 2.25 per cent band, either side of the central parities. This preserved a measure of liberty. It represented a compromise between independent free floating and the tight-band fixed rates to which most of the other ERM currencies were subject. More important, the British government joined Germany in successfully pressing for tight conditions (on inflation, public debt and deficits) that EU countries would have to meet before they might join the EMU. In the 1990–91 Maastricht negotiations, Britain also secured the right to put her participation in any monetary union to a vote in the House of Commons.

As Chancellor in 1989, Major had already floated an interesting amendment to the EMU plan. This was the 'hard ECU' proposal. Europe's new monetary unit, it was suggested, should rise in line with whatever ERM currency happened to be the strongest at the time. The new currency would acquire an attractive reputation, and evolve spontaneously. The British view saw monetary union as a gradual, largely market-driven process with the overriding objective of price stability, and not something, like the Common Agricultural Policy, imposed from above, fixed up by questionable intergovernmental deals, and liable to be set in concrete or perverted by special interests. Although the hard ECU proposal was not adopted, some of the logic behind it was reflected in the final Maastricht blueprints.

Sterling's ERM participation proved ill-starred. Britain was slowly evolving from a condition which was thought to require exceptionally high interest rates, to one where they needed to be brought down sharply. Germany, the key ERM country, was reunifying. The boom that resulted led to over-heating, and rising inflation. Its central bank, the Bundesbank (Buba), essentially set interest rates for the whole ERM area. But the Buba's formal obligation was maintaining price stability in Germany, so the Buba held ERM interest rates up. That led all ERM currencies to appreciate in terms of others, principally the US dollar. Strengthening the pound against the dollar damaged Britain, for whom exports to the US market were important, and which was languishing in a deep, long recession.

In 1991–92, then, an overheated German economy opted to appreciate the DM against non-ERM currencies and dis-inflate. That called for high interest rates. Britain needed to cut interest rates and improve competitiveness to combat reces-sion. This marks our first paradox:

PARADOX 1: A key argument for putting sterling in the ERM was that the UK, and her EU partners, had common macro-economic interests which were best served by exchange rate union. For most of the period the UK stood aside from the ERM, they did. Once the UK joined, Britain's and Germany's interests fell into serious conflict.

It was paradox 1 that was to lead to Black Wednesday.

THE BACKGROUND TO THE RECESSION: THE SECOND PARADOX

Why did Britain suffer recession in period 1? To explain that we need to go back a little. The mid-1980s saw very rapid growth in all definitions of the money supply in Britain. For a time everything went well. Output grew at about 4 per cent per year, twice as fast as in France or Germany. Inflation stayed quite low, again averaging 4 per cent per year. Annual broad monetary growth of 16 to 18 per cent or so was excused (not wholly plausibly) as a one-off adjustment due to financial innovation, lower expectations of inflation, and government-inspired increased competition between financial institutions. The monetary splurge and the over-large tax cuts that characterized Lawson's chancellorship were all too reminiscent of Barber's boom from 1971 to 1973/4. That brings us to paradox 2:

PARADOX 2: *A Conservative government (Thatcher's) determined above all to avoid what it saw as the grave errors of the Heath administration (excessive stimuli to monetary demand) was destined to repeat them.*

Paradox 2 saw Britain's annual inflation rate climb from 1988, to peak at 10 per cent in 1990. The government responded by raising short-term interest rates substantially. The high interest rate policy began in the second half of 1988. It continued right through period 1, although interest rates were lowered somewhat during it.

THE NEED FOR HIGH INTEREST RATES: THE THIRD PARADOX

The logic behind the high interest rates that survived until late 1992 may be summed up as paradox 3:

PARADOX 3: *To keep interest rates down, you may have to start by raising them.*

The idea here is to minimize, in the long run, the distortionary tax on real money holdings that inflation represents. Low inflation means low inflation expectations, and that means low 'nominal' interest rates (on paper assets), and hence a strong demand for real money, with all the advantages that brings (fewer costly trips to the bank, fewer costly changes in the money prices of goods and labour). But keeping inflation low means keeping the nominal money supply, and its key counterpart, loans from banks, growing slowly. If these are rising too fast, you have to raise (short-term) interest rates to regain control of the growth of monetary aggregates.

High interest rates exerted a host of effects.[2] Sterling, floating until October 1990, went up. That brought import prices down, delivering a one-off bonus to the retail price index (where imports have a one-third weight). It also weakened the international competitiveness of British firms.

This curbed output and profits in those sectors, and reduced their labour demand. So unemployment rose. Workers' bargaining conditions worsened, trimming wage settlements (relative, at least, to what would have happened otherwise). So inflation slowed. On the demand side, consumer durables such as cars suddenly looked much less attractive investments for households. Again, labour demand down, slower wage increases, less inflation. Households with mortgage and other debts – and there was a record ratio of these to national income, after the Lawson spending spree – had an immediate cut in disposable income. So they spent less. And the squeeze occurred in spades in the construction sector, with large knock-on effects on bankruptcies and bad loans on the balance sheets of financial institutions.

FROM WUNDERKIND TO WHIPPING BOY: PARADOX FOUR

The UK macro-economic downturn was mirrored in North America. Here, as there, it was triggered by high interest rates. Output in Britain began to falter in 1989, and started falling in the third quarter of 1990. The recession was to sour the whole of John Major's premiership from 1990 to 1994. Yet it was uneven in its sectoral impact. It was most painful in construction and financial services; construction because it was most interest-sensitive and directly intertwined with the misfortunes of the financial sector. This brings us to a further paradox.

PARADOX 4: The financial sector was the Wunderkind of the Thatcher era (at least until 1989). Thereafter it became the whipping boy.

The decade from 1979 saw the UK's financial sector prosper. Banks expanded their product range after regulatory reforms, and extended the penetration of their services to Britain's dwindling proportion of unbanked residents. Building societies expanded still faster, with regulatory changes and a property boom. Merchant banks and management consultants prospered on various privatization fees.

Stockbrokers sold their businesses at handsome prices to foreign banks welcomed in by the 1986 Big Bang reforms. Many insurance companies enjoyed record profits. Even the 30 per cent tumble in equity prices in October 1987 was little more than a large sudden technical correction in the middle of the longest bull market in recent history.

The transformation from Wunderkind to whipping boy had two main causes. One was the need to reverse the expansionary thrust of macro-economic policy in response to the alarming climb in inflation; the other was the fact that this reversal took the form of a monetary squeeze (as opposed to a fiscal one, or some combination of the two). In the late 1980s, the budget was in surplus, buoyed up by high consumer spending in goods subject to high rates of indirect taxation, reduced calls for unemployment benefit, and strong receipts of income tax, corporation tax on profits, and privatization sales. Rises in tax rates were thought unnecessary (as well as politically damaging). And there was heavy political pressure to increase government spending on health and education. So the whole brunt of the aggregate demand squeeze fell on monetary policy. The financial sector was to be the vehicle through which these pressures were transmitted.

INTEREST RATES AND BANKS:
THE FIFTH PARADOX

It is ironic that high interest rates are damaging to banks. Banks' income comes from interest on loans. Loans rates lie above rates paid on deposits, and a Treasury command to raise short-term interest rates increases loan rates at once. This brings us to paradox 5:

PARADOX 5: Banks' profits come from loan interest, but the high interest rates after 1988 brought them to the brink of disaster.

What punished the banks was provisions for writing off non-performing loans. Higher interest rates contributed directly and indirectly to a sharp deterioration in the financial position of many of the banks' debtors, partly household but mostly corporate. The immediate response of the lending institutions is to grant overdraft increases, in the hope that their clients will take the necessary action to staunch losses and survive. Often this works. But sometimes it doesn't. And it is especially unlikely to work when the recession is protracted and the high rates are not just imposed for a few months (as had happened briefly in 1985) but last for years. The troubled debtors were heavily concentrated in the construction sector, where high interest rates brought a double-edged crisis: on top of higher servicing costs on loans, came a collapse in the selling prices or lease revenues on the properties they had built or owned.

The banks are faced with the painful decision of whether and when to pull the plug on their troubled debtors. British banks' freedom is constrained by accounting rules. Accountants require banks to classify loans according to whether they are performing or not. No grey. Just black or white. A loan is non-performing when interest due is not received. For a while, banks may preserve the fiction that a low-quality loan is performing by granting the debtor a fresh loan to cover the interest due on existing loans. But that cannot last indefinitely; nor would the bank wish it to. Behind the bank's decision on whom and when to drive into bankruptcy lies the ultimate horror of whether the accountant could qualify the bank's own accounts, provoking possible insolvency and closure for the bank itself. That is the core of the case for killing off your shaky debtors – in the end it could be suicidal not to. Against this, driving your debtor into bankruptcy today removes the option of doing that, or not doing that, tomorrow; and tomorrow you will know more than you do today. Your debtor could strike gold in the meantime.[3]

The main banks survived period 1 (and period 2). But not easily. In March 1993, Barclays recorded its first ever loss, for the year 1992, and cut its dividend. And Midland, once Britain's premier bank, was too weak to survive on its own. It had been bleeding for a decade. Crocker, its Californian subsidiary, had been expensively acquired, brought it massive unsuspected losses, and was sold cheaply. Lloyds bid unsuccessfully for Midland, which passed to the Hong Kong and Shanghai Bank. Midland joined that sorry list of distinguished

UK companies for which, like Ferrantis and Imperial Tobacco, a US venture proved ruinous.

In 1991, the four main clearing banks in Britain, Barclays, Lloyds, Midland and National Westminster, made a total of £4.9 billion in provisions against bad debt. Barclays and NatWest provided £1.8 billion (thousand million) apiece. Nineteen ninety-two was even worse. Lloyds' provisions fell by a seventh to £740 million, Midland's nearly doubled to £680 million, NatWest provided over £1.9 billion, and Barclays a massive £2.56 billion. In a normal year, banks typically write off about 0.6 per cent of their loans. In 1991 and 1992, the average exceeded 2 per cent.

Bad as these years were, Britain's major banks were already under threat. In its 8 August issue of 1992, *The Economist* published a study of the average ratio of value added to total inputs for Europe's top twenty-five banks for the four years 1987 to 1990. Value added was defined as pre-tax profits corrected for all reserve changes, net of cost of shareholders' funds measured as a long term bond yield plus a 10 per cent risk premium; inputs were defined as all other costs. On this measure, Abbey National topped the list, with a 12 per cent return. There were four other banks that recorded positive yields, none of them British. The yields for the big four UK clearers ranged from minus 5 per cent for Barclays, to minus 19 per cent for Midland.

Increased competition with building societies, the result of legislation in the Lawson period, was a factor that eroded returns. Another was the clearers' large labour and premises cost base. The Major government had little sympathy for them. The clearers responded to the crisis by raising loan rates sharply, especially for smaller indebted businesses, and by introducing a gamut of new or increased charges. The resulting public outcry found Chancellor Lamont receptive. Lamont initiated an inquiry, which gave the banks a limited and rather grudging exoneration. Bad debt provisions did not stop after 1992, but 1993 marked a turning point, and the clearers started to rebuild their shattered balance sheets.

THE CONSEQUENCES OF BLACK
WEDNESDAY: THE SIXTH PARADOX

What made the biggest difference was Black Wednesday. This marked the end of period 1. Britain, languishing in a deep recession, was desperate to reduce interest rates. Norman Lamont had used the occasion of the summer meeting of EU finance ministers, which he was chairing in Bath, to try to force the Bundesbank to lower their key interest rates. The Buba was infuriated: its constitution gave it independence from the German government, let alone a British one. The Buba enacted a trivial, token cut in one of its interest rates, but got revenge in the form of a newspaper interview with its head, who hinted publicly that a sterling devaluation would be welcome. When the interview was published, the Buba refused to give the immediate, fulsome retraction that Lamont sought. A huge speculative outflow from sterling ensued at once. Lamont fought back on 16 September by raising Britain's base rate, first from 10 per cent to 12 per cent, and then, at lunchtime, to 15 per cent. The Cabinet decided in the early afternoon to suspend sterling's participation in the ERM. This was announced in the early evening after Europe's financial markets had closed. The markets had gambled that the Major government lacked the stomach to put up with the costs of staying in the ERM. And they gambled right.[4]

Sterling quickly fell by a tenth against the German mark. The Spanish peseta and the Italian lira came down with it. Britain reversed the second interest rate hike at once, and the first a few days later. Over the next twelve months, interest rates were cautiously cut further, in a sequence of steps, to 7 per cent. The interest rate reductions and exchange rate depreciation were quick to exert beneficial effects. Unemployment fell through most of 1993. Profits and production rose, particularly in British firms competing with foreign businesses in both UK and overseas markets. The rising tide of bankruptcies and house repossessions began to turn and ebb at once. And for GDP, which had been in serious retreat in 1991 and 1992, the fourth quarter of 1992 marked the bottom. From then on GDP rose at an annual average rate of just over 2 per cent.

Black Wednesday brought substantial economic benefits to Britain. But were there political benefits? Strangely, no, or at least, not yet. That brings us to a further paradox.

PARADOX 6: The Major government's popularity remained high for much of the recession, and crumbled as the economy revived.

For over six months after taking over as Prime Minister in November 1990, John Major enjoyed a strongly favourable personal rating. The Conservatives led Labour in opinion polls for most of this period. The honeymoon effect, enjoyed by any new leader, was extended as a result of the Gulf war victory in March 1991. Although their opinion poll rating slipped back later in 1991 and early 1992, the Conservatives' surprise election victory in April 1992 brought them a 7 per cent lead over Labour in the national vote.

A deep recession may frighten voters into playing safe and not risking further trouble by throwing their government out. A small rise in unemployment angers; a large one terrifies. John Major also succeeded in holding electoral support by generous public sector pay settlements, by commitments to expansion in government spending, and by emphasizing the prospect of lower taxes (in comparison to Labour, which admitted to plans to raise taxation, especially on higher incomes). Major also retained the loyalty of much of the media. Only *The Financial Times* and *The Independent* joined the traditionally pro-Labour *Guardian* and *Mirror* in not advising readers to re-elect the Conservatives.

By the autumn, everything had changed. Black Wednesday marked the point at which Major's political popularity turned from decline to collapse. So much had been made of the ERM commitment for sterling. Any decision to depreciate or devalue had been repeatedly and insistently denied. The ERM was sold as an essential bulwark against inflation. The pain it had caused had been excused as nasty but essential medicine the patient had to have to restore his health. 'If it isn't hurting', John Major had declared as Chancellor to defend his high interest-rate policy in the run-up to joining the ERM, 'it isn't working.'

Exit from the ERM was certainly the correct medicine in September 1992, but the government would hardly say so without losing face. Why did we go through all this, the voters asked, if the ERM policy had been wrong all along? If joining the ERM and trying to hold the sterling-mark link had been right, as the government had vociferously claimed, exit was a humiliating mistake. If low interest rates and a low pound were right for Britain in September 1992, why not earlier? The government's sense of shame and bewilderment were all too plain. Ministers fled from the TV cameras. Harold Wilson had done himself little good with his 'pound in your pocket' television broadcast when the pound was devalued in similar circumstances twenty-five years earlier, but at least he had tried to explain what had happened. In the two years after Wilson's November 1967 devaluation, the opposition won nearly every by-election and control of almost all the major councils in the country. In the two years after September 1992, history repeated itself – despite the fact that the lower pound helped to bring the recession to an end.

CONTROL THE MONEY SUPPLY OR THE EXCHANGE RATE? THE SEVENTH PARADOX

Policy until Black Wednesday had been governed by a curious principle which constitutes a further paradox:

PARADOX 7: The 1970s taught that if you couldn't or wouldn't control the exchange rate, you had to control the money supply. The lesson of the 1980s was, if you couldn't or wouldn't control the money supply, you had to control the exchange rate.

Not everyone had accepted paradox 7's 'lesson of the 1980s', but Chancellor Lawson had, as early as 1984. So, soon afterwards, had all his main Treasury officials who were to convince his successors, Major and Lamont. The greater part of academic and journalist opinion concurred.[5] So did the main opposition parties at Westminster. It was widely agreed that the Thatcher recession of 1980–81 had been made much worse by the excessive appreciation of sterling at that time – an appreciation that reflected the financial markets' enthusiasm for a government determined to keep money growth down, one which had so manifestly learnt the 'lesson of the 1970s'.

So what should a government do, if it had jettisoned most of its monetary targets for a fixed exchange rate and now abandoned that, too? What was to be 'the lesson of the 1990s'? Major and Lamont trod cautiously. Little by little they copied America, which had fought its recession with low interest rates (just as Britain's National Government had done from 1932). They opted not to grant independence to the Bank of England, on the Bundesbank model, but they gave the Bank the interesting role of publishing a regular inflation report, a platform on which it could monitor the government's success in achieving its annual inflation target (now formalized, as a 1 per cent to 4 per cent range). The Bank could now criticize government publicly (or threaten to do so). It would also play a role in formulating monetary policy, in regular three-monthly talks with the Treasury. Under Thatcher the Bank's monetary powers had been sharply cut back. Under Major, the Grand Old Lady of Threadneedle Street regained some teeth.

The idea behind this turned on inflation expectations, which might jump less as the economy revived, if the government had tied its own hands somewhat. Governments always have a short-run incentive to create some unexpected inflation – if only because it helps them wipe away some of the real value of their debts, which damaging taxes are levied to service. Anything that makes a sneaky little burst of inflation more embarrassing for the government helps to make it less likely. Even the threat of a rebuke from the Bank of England could help.

INFLATION AND UNEMPLOYMENT:
THE EIGHTH PARADOX

The biggest argument for these new anti-inflation arrangements was the memory, still raw and very fresh, of the huge costs that had just been incurred in getting inflation down from its 1990–91 peak of 10 per cent. Inflation is a sluggish beast. It tends to follow monetary stimuli with quite a long lag of two years or more. Devaluation also normally triggers inflation, very rapidly in some conditions, but usually much more slowly when, as in 1992, unemployment is high. For over a hundred years Britain had displayed a rather well-identified negative statistical association between inflation and unemployment, called the Phillips Curve. At the end of the 1960s, the Phillips Curve started to break down. The 1970s oil shocks caused both inflation and unemployment to jump. Under Callaghan and Thatcher financial policies had been redesigned to take account of this. Policy-makers acted on the assumption that the Phillips Curve was dead. That gave rise to:

PARADOX 8: As soon as policy was based on the idea that inflation could change with negligible effects on unemployment, the Phillips Curve sprang back to life.

British statistics point to a surprisingly robust negative association between inflation and unemployment after 1980. The Phillips Curve revived when policy was enacted on the premise that it had disappeared.

An appealing explanation for paradox 8 is this. Monetarist policies, if consistently applied, make for stickiness in inflation expectations. Firms and workers are concerned about the purchasing power of wage rates, but the wage increases about which they bargain are expressed in money. Once the monetary standard is trusted, as it came to be after 1980, inflation expectations become rather immobile. Unemployment affects money wages and real wages in a predictable, broadly parallel fashion. When it is distrusted as it had been under Wilson and Heath, the relationship breaks down. Inflation expectations become unstable, and so does the way money wage rises react to unemployment. And if paradox 7 meant that the Major administration was believed to have relinquished both monetary and exchange rate targets, no wonder it was anxious to stabilize inflation expectations in some other way. As if to cement this determination, poor Lamont, whom the public regarded as the human embodiment of the old ERM-anchor that had been weighed so embarrassingly on Black Wednesday, had to be sacrificed. In 1993 he was replaced by Kenneth Clarke.

The biggest financial headache for both Chancellors in period 2 was the government's budget deficit. This had been in surplus in the late 1980s. By 1993, the public sector borrowing requirement (PSBR) was threatening to top £50 billion per year, or over 8 per cent of national income. If some of the cost of the early 1990s recession had been shouldered by the banks, far more was to be absorbed by the government.

From the first quarter of 1990 to the last quarter of 1993, the number of people claiming unemployment benefit went up by 45 per cent to just on three million. Each unemployed person costs the exchequer, on average, nearly £10,000 per year. This figure is made up by lost receipts of income tax, indirect taxes and national insurance contributions, and welfare benefits paid out. Nearly £13 billion of the increased PSBR is the price, then, that the government paid for the recession. But the bill for that is of course paid by the taxpayer. The PSBR is funded very largely by bond issues. Interest on increased government debt, averaging some 8½ per cent in this period, signals the need for increased taxes in the future (unless, improbably, the government were to balance its books by cutting its spending). Although the recession was to bring widespread pain to much of the financial sector, therefore, there were at least some for whom it brought extra work – not just insolvency experts, but bond dealers.

The recession was not the only cause of the spectacular deterioration in the government's finances between the late 1980s and 1993. Government spending on health and education rose sharply, partly as a result of electoral pressures in 1992 which led the Major government into additional spending commitments, and generous rises in public sector pay. There was also a fall in privatization proceeds. Strictly speaking, selling state assets is a disguised form of borrowing. But the PSBR, the cynosure on which all eyes were fixed, had the odd feature that one-off asset sales were treated as revenue for the government. Anyway, by 1993 the government had already disposed of most of its valuable assets.

Thatcher's administrations had wisely started with the most saleable. What was left by 1993 consisted mainly of a residuum of loss-making industries, such as nuclear power, the railways and the coal mines, for which privatization would be politically unpopular and financially unrewarding.

The government's response to its huge incipient deficit in 1993 was a stiff dose of tax increases. The prospective PSBR deficit was not to be eliminated, but the measures announced in the two budgets (Lamont's in March, Clarke's in November) would halve it by 1996. The tax rises in these two budgets would raise, between them, nearly £20 billion by 1995. They achieved this without changes in the key rates of income tax or VAT. The fact that they raised the average rate of tax with minimal change in marginal rates had the economic advantage that they would, in due course, prove 'supply-side friendly'. There was no serious erosion in incentives to work, invest or take risks. But they were regressive, and would aggravate the trend towards increased inequality in post-tax incomes that had been apparent since 1980.

THE HOUSING MARKET: PARADOX NINE

Those extra tax revenues came from several sources. National insurance contributions borne by employees were to go up by 1 per cent in April 1994. VAT was to be levied on fuel, first at 8 per cent from 1994, and then 17½ per cent from 1995. Allowances were frozen or cut back. But the most significant change for Britain's financial sector was to be the limitation of mortgage interest relief to the new 20 per cent income tax rate (on mortgages up to £30,000). Coming on top of the restriction to 25 per cent for top-rate tax payers that had been introduced in 1992, this would represent a serious threat to the building societies.

For every £5 deposited with a building society, about £4 is lent out in mortgages. Virtually all mortgagees pay income tax at the standard rate of 25 per cent, or the top rate of 40 per cent. Many have other assets besides the equity in their house – shares and deposits, for example. The new rules coming into force in 1994 mean that mortgagees in this position must find it tax-efficient to use up such assets to pay down mortgages. Building societies would face a trap of growing disintermediation – a squeeze on both assets and liabilities – as taxpayers learnt about this.

Mortgage interest relief was one of three fiscal privileges that had been given to housing. Others were exemption from capital gains tax for a primary residence, and the absence (since 1963) of any income tax chargeable on the imputed rent of owner-occupied dwellings. Local authority residential rates went some way to compensate for the last of these. But rates were abolished in 1990 (1989 in Scotland), to be replaced by the community charge, or poll tax. This brings us to another paradox:

PARADOX 9: The removal of residential property rates in 1989/90 could only make housing a more attractive investment, but the five years from 1988 to 1993 saw a massive 25 per cent decline in the aggregate real value of British dwellings.

House prices held up in some areas. But in London, the Home Counties and East Anglia, where houses had been on average twice as expensive as in the rest of the country, they recorded real falls of up to 45 per cent. The main factors at work here were the high mortgage interest rates imposed from 1988 to 1993, the steep recession with its main impact concentrated on South East England, and the sudden disappearance of expectations of capital gains after four decades of almost uninterrupted house price inflation. 'As safe as houses' became a sick joke. The replacement of rates by poll tax must have sustained house prices for a while, but the return to a form of property taxation, with banded council tax from 1992, will have reversed that.

The cuts in mortgage interest relief bode ill for the building societies in the late 1990s and beyond. These British institutions enjoy a low cost base, and an enviable record of financial strength which even the wave of repossessions in 1991–93 did little to dent. Their US counterparts, the Savings and Loans (S & L) Institutions, suffered disastrous losses after 1986: the US taxpayer has had to absorb actual and prospective write-offs approaching $165 billion. One weakness faced by the S & L was the fact that their assets and liabilities were unmatched – fixed interest on mortgages, but variable interest on a large tranche of their deposits – which exposed them to big losses when interest rates climbed and found them insufficiently covered by interest-rate swaps. If Britain's building societies follow the new trend towards fixed-rate mortgages, they too may face this source of risk. Ironically, both they and the banks are also at threat from falling interest rates, which are liable to undermine the 'endowment profit' gained from low-interest deposits.

Mid-1980s regulatory reforms encouraged Britain's financial institutions to diversify into each others' operations. Many acquired estate agencies. This was a sub-sector of the UK financial services industry for which the period of the Major government proved highly disagreeable. The number of property transactions in England and Wales was 2.15 million in 1988, equivalent to almost 9 per cent of the total stock of dwellings. This fell to 1.4 million in 1990 and only 1.14 million in 1992. In 1993, it recovered slightly to nearly 1.2 million, but this was still little over half the 1988 level. Coming on top of the house price slide, it meant that estate agents' real incomes shrank by over 60 per cent from 1988 to 1993. Housing was not just a depressed market. It was a thin one, too.

THE EQUITY MARKET: THE TENTH PARADOX

The UK stock market also suffered from a decline in trading volume from the heady days of 1986–88. But equity prices held up well: a further paradox.

PARADOX 10: Recessions normally display falling equity markets. But Britain's worst post-war recession in the early 1990s saw equity prices hardly wilt at all.

In money terms, the FT-actuaries all share index was surprisingly robust throughout the recession of the early 1990s. In quarter 1, 1989, it stood at 1037. Two years later it was 1099, and in the first quarter of 1993, 1384. Even when deflated by the retail price index, this share-price index barely registered any adverse effect from recession. After its peak in the third quarter of 1989, it had slid by 23 per cent by late 1990, but had more than recovered all this ground by the fourth quarter of 1993, when share prices were some 6 per cent higher in real terms than in quarter 3, 1989. In early 1994, they slipped back.

The UK stock market took a sanguine view of the 1991–92 recession. In the past, matters had often been very different. In the 1973–75 downturn, for example, the FT-30 share index slumped heavily. Peaking at 540 in May 1972, it touched 143 at one point in January 1975. This was a fall of five-sixths in real terms. Bull points in the early 1990s included the fact that the recession, deep and protracted as it was, had most of its impact on the financial, property and construction sectors; the encouraging trend for profits in the 1980s, which the recession dented surprisingly little elsewhere in the economy; the closer links between London and other stock markets abroad, many of which continued to display strength; investors' ability to look beyond current troubles at what they took to be a better future; and, after Black Wednesday, the bonus provided by a more competitive pound and lower UK interest rates.

The 1986 'big bang' had led to sharp falls in stockbrokers' commissions on large trades. Trading volume in the early 1990s was also down compared with the late 1980s. So the welcome strength of stock market prices was not matched by buoyant revenues for stockbrokers during the period 1990–94. For most of them, this was to be a time of grim retrenchment.

THE INSURANCE CRISIS:
PARADOX ELEVEN

Still worse were the troubles of the insurance industry. This brings us to our final paradox:

PARADOX 11: The world's largest and most experienced financial shock-absorber, Lloyds of London, was threatened with collapse, partly as a result of errors of its own making.

The years 1991, 1992 and 1993 saw Lloyds' 'Names' accumulate losses totalling £8 billion. Names underwrite Lloyds' insurance activities. They are arranged in syndicates, specializing in different kinds of risks. Some participated in just one syndicate. Others were members of several, as many as a dozen or more. Over forty names were sitting Conservative MPs in 1994; since any MP had to resign if bankrupt, and every Conservative seat was vulnerable in a by-election, the Lloyds crisis had serious political implications.

In good years names drew incomes from their syndicates. In bad times, the most recent occurring at the end of the 1960s, names would be called upon to contribute to cover losses. The complex business of claims settlement means that Lloyds' accounts are presented with a three-year lag.

The disasters of the early 1990s related, then, to insurance years in the late 1980s. What went wrong? There was some bad luck: the San Francisco earthquake; the Piper Alpha explosion; more crime. There was also bad judgment, reflected in the eagerness with which some syndicate agents wrote pollution and asbestos reinsurance contracts in the United States. Agents would often draw incomes in proportion to the premium income they attracted. This gave them an incentive to sell as much as they could. The risks would be borne by the names. This clash of interests – the agents interested in commission income, the names absorbing unseen risks – had always been a recurrent problem at Lloyds.[6] It had normally been compensated, in the main, by the rather stiff terms on which insurance and reinsurance contracts were written. As the 1980s wore on, it became increasingly evident that environmental policies were being sold too cheaply. The syndicates' agents were slow in reacting to this. At the same time, Lloyds had encouraged a large increase in the number of names; the newcomers were typically inexperienced and much less rich than the old hands. There was a further weakness. 'Baby' syndicates, consisting of insiders who creamed off safer business, had been banned in the early 1980s, but it was increasingly apparent that some professionals with inside knowledge were hedging bets by selling 'excess-of-loss', high-risk business to groups of names unaware of what was happening to their exposure.

Outhwaite was the first syndicate to run into serious trouble. In 1988 its names sued their agents, charging Richard Outhwaite, the syndicate underwriter in 1982, with negligence in accepting thirty-two run-off contracts from other syndicates which had been heavily exposed to asbestos and pollution risks. Four years later, a settlement gave them £116 million from the errors and omissions insurers. But that merely shunted the losses from one set of names to another, and some multi-syndicate names ended up funding their own settlement.

Since that settlement, litigation has multiplied. More than one third of the names have suits against Lloyds. Offers of compensation have been so far refused. The Major government's stance has been publicly distant: this is a private sector matter, they have claimed. But behind the scenes, the government has supported Lloyds' attempts to strengthen its capital base, by introducing a new category of corporate names (with previous losses 'ring-fenced', however). It has also urged financial settlements, supported by reserves, to preserve the institution and its normally positive and considerable contribution to Britain's invisible exports and national income. Mary Archer, the wife of a former deputy chairman of the Conservative Party and herself a name, was encouraged to administer a special fund for gravely straitened names anxious to avoid bankruptcy. But its terms were harsh. Liability extended to spouses' assets, and there was no time limitation. Few names accepted its terms. Many opted for litigation instead. Lloyds' future remains in doubt.

CONCLUSION AND VERDICT

John Major's premiership has been a troubled period for Britain's financial sector. Many of its woes stem from the financial policies pursued when John Major was Chancellor or Prime Minister. Those policies induced, or exacerbated, Britain's recession. But they succeeded in their prime objective of cutting inflation. And what made them necessary was the excessive expansion under Lawson and Thatcher. Correct or misconceived in principle, and much could be said on both sides, the ERM experiment turned out to be tragically mistimed. Departure from the ERM in 1992 was a political disaster, but in economic terms one's main complaint about it, and the interest rate cuts it permitted, was that they were needlessly delayed. The large tax increases pre-announced in 1993 were astute, courageous and necessary. Determining a country's financial policy is an extraordinarily intricate and challenging task. Our conclusion must be that Major's government acted with greater wisdom than speed, but better an intelligent tortoise than a scatter-brained hare.

Indifferently advised, fearing accusations of U-turns, and temperamentally inclined to middle paths and rubber-stamping, Major is blamed for bad luck and for matters for which he had *nominal* not *personal* responsibility. In listening to colleagues and officials and avoiding simple dogmas, he struck unkind observers as an aimless and inarticulate successor to Lady Thatcher. He has seemed to respond to events more than shaping them: 'in office but not in power'. But the quiet, unhurried style, the policy reversals, and the difficulty one has in identifying his personal contribution should not blind us from recognizing that his government has certainly shaped events, in the financial sphere as elsewhere, and by no means always for the worse. From 1992, policy improved. Yet after the April 1992 election, the popular verdict turned hostile. History's may be kinder.

Notes

1. The main arguments for and against British participation in the ERM overlap, but do not coincide with, those relating to European Monetary Union. The latter have been well explored in J. Driffill and M. Beber, *A Currency for Europe* (Lothian Foundation, 1991) and B. Eichengreen, 'European Monetary Integration', *Journal of Economic Literature*, 1993.

2. The varied possible consequences of interest rate increases are examined further in P. J. N. Sinclair, 'Output, Exchange Rates, Capital and Debt when Nominal Interest Rates are Policy

Parameters', *Economic and Social Review*, 1990, and, in the British context, 'The Interest Rate Transmission Mechanism in the United Kingdom', *Bank of England Quarterly Bulletin*, 1990.

3. The case for not bankrupting a sick debtor yet hinges on the size and chance of any good news the banker thinks he may get. It is an example of Dixit and Pindyck's 'good news principle', see A. K. Dixit and R. S. Pindyck, *Investment Under Uncertainty* (Princeton University Press, 1993).

4. But the market had not seriously anticipated sterling's departure from the ERM for more than a few days: see A. K. Rose, 'Sterling's ERM Credibility: Did the Dog Bark in the Night?', *Economics Letters*, 1993.

5. M. J. Artis and D. Currie, 'Monetary Targets and the Exchange Rate: the Case for Conditional Targets', in W. A. Eltis and P. J. N. Sinclair, eds, *The Money Supply and the Exchange Rate* (Oxford University Press, 1981) provided the seminal contribution on this.

6. This clash of interests is a classic example of the principal-agent problem. If you, the principal, want someone else, your agent, to do something for you in risky conditions, and your agent has other interests, dislikes risks, and acts in ways you cannot monitor, even the best contract you can devise lands you in trouble. For a general study of this, see J. E. Stiglitz, 'Incentives and Risk-sharing in Sharecropping', *Review of Economic Studies*, 1974.

Chapter 14

EMPLOYMENT AND INDUSTRIAL RELATIONS POLICY

Robert Taylor

T HE ROLLING back of trade union power and the creation of a more flexible labour market were the main objectives of Margaret Thatcher's employment and industrial relations policy. As prime minister she never disguised her dislike for the trade unions and their leaders. Her aim was to destroy once and for all the social settlement on industrial relations that had survived since the Second World War despite its mounting difficulties. Mr John Major – her own preferred successor – may have come from humble origins and been very much a self-made man with at least some personal experience of social deprivation and he was seen by some on the left as a humane Conservative. However, he appeared to share his predecessor's robust opinions about employment and industrial relations policy. During his period as Prime Minister Mr Major has proved to be less combative and more conciliatory at least in the style of his presentation of labour market strategy, but to a very large extent there has been a strong continuity of purpose and action from the years of Margaret Thatcher.

Indeed, in many ways Mr Major's policy has turned out to be far more explicit and uninhibited than anything devised during the course of her own incremental 'step by step' programme. This approach had started in May 1979 under the benign direction of Mr Jim Prior as Employment Secretary with the avowedly modest aim of tilting the balance of power away from trade unions and towards employers. But the policy was transmogrified increasingly after 1987 into an aggressive offensive designed to neuter the trade unions in the workplace and undermine collective bargaining as well as promote a flexible labour market based on individualistic values. The creation of such a labour market, free from 'unnecessary' restrictions on the employers' unilateral right to manage and the encouragement of workplace acquisitiveness was coupled with further legislation to weaken the trade unions and reinforce what has become one of the most legally regulated industrial relations systems in the western world. The exclusionist strategy towards the trade unions adopted with more firmness in the final years of Mrs Thatcher became Mr Major's employment policy agenda during the early 1990s.

There was no evidence to suggest such inherited policies aroused any serious difference of opinion inside Mr Major's Cabinet. On the contrary, as the years went by ministers seemed to grow more, not less convinced about the success of the government's employment strategy in improving Britain's competitiveness in world markets. The Prime Minister may have sounded emollient and he was readier than Margaret Thatcher to meet delegations of trade union leaders and listen to what they had to say. But this did not mean that he was prepared to seek a new partnership with the trade unions over anything substantial. On the contrary, like his predecessor, he could see no obvious public policy-making role for the trade unions. In his opinion, they should concentrate what limited role they had on assisting companies to improve their productivity and reduce their unit costs and abandon any political pretensions they might still harbour.

THE EMERGENCE OF THE UK
LABOUR MARKET MODEL

The most coherent statement of the government's policy was contained in 'People, Jobs and Opportunity', a document published in February 1992. It argued Britain already had a 'headstart' for 'the decade of fierce international competition', thanks to the labour market achievements of the 1980s.

> Business became more efficient and productive; enterprise flourished; people at work began to assert themselves as individuals and to take advantage of widening opportunities and choice. The tide of collectivism – the drift towards a world where the workforce was treated as an undifferentiated mass with identical interests and objectives – was turned back. There was a new emphasis on the role and importance of the individual employee in business performance.

> We can and must build on these successes in the 1990s. We must widen even further the choices and opportunities for people at work. We must stimulate enterprise and encourage the trend towards individual initiative in every aspect of working life. There is a new recognition of the role and importance of the individual employee. Traditional patterns of industrial relations, based on collective bargaining and collective agreements, seem increasingly inappropriate and are in decline.[1]

Due emphasis was given on the need for employers to extend employee involvement through better communications, profit sharing and employee share ownership schemes. This outlook became the core of Mr Major's labour market strategy.

From the Prime Minister downwards, ministers liked to lecture their European Union colleagues and President Bill Clinton's administration in the United States on the 'success' of the British approach to employment policy and the folly of having the kind of social regulations familiar in most mainland western European countries. At the March 1994 jobs summit conference of the G7 countries (the main industrialized market economies) hosted in Detroit by Mr Clinton, both the Chancellor of the Exchequer, Kenneth Clarke, and employment secretary David Hunt made it clear that they believed they had nothing to learn from the employment experience of other western countries. Apparently the virtues of the so-called British labour market 'model' were self-evident for all to see.

'Our experiences and our achievements were very positively received,' Mr Hunt told a meeting of the Industrial Society on 17 March 1994, shortly after his return from Detroit. 'Everyone wanted to hear about the way we have managed to get unemployment to start to fall so quickly after the end of a recession; about our plans for a modern apprenticeship scheme and about the way our employment service leads the world in providing an individual service for all unemployed people.'[2] A special unit inside the Department of Employment has sought to sell the virtues of the 'new' system abroad, particularly among the emerging market economies of eastern Europe.

Whether such complacent triumphalism reflected the real condition of the British labour market, where the official monthly unemployment benefit claimant total stayed between 2.5 million and 3 million for most of Mr Major's years in office, was first another matter. For much of the period since December 1990 Britain's official unemployment total, as a proportion of the workforce, has remained higher than in most other European Union countries except France, Spain and Italy. It is true some labour market indicators looked impressive. Britain's strike statistics were especially low. In 1992–93 the country experienced the smallest number of disputes and working days lost since such data was first collected in 1891. The so-called British 'disease' of needless industrial conflict that gripped newspaper headlines in the 1960s and 1970s had been exaggerated at the time. Now it had all but disappeared. It is not evident, however, that this improvement was due to Mr Major's industrial relations strategy and reflected a new harmony in the workplace. The ferocity of the second recession in ten years in curbing shop-floor militancy and the severe difficulties for trade unions imposed by accumulated laws on organizing strikes may have had much to do with vanishing disruption. Moreover, the increase in the level of earnings continued to remain close to and often above the retail price index, suggesting most workers in work were able to protect their living standards and therefore had no good reason to indulge in industrial conflict. Comparative international strike statistics for the early 1990s suggested worker militancy was in sharp decline across most of the western world. In the strike league table of the Organization for Economic Cooperation and Development, Britain was half way down, still recording higher conflict figures than Germany, Sweden, the United States and Holland.

Earnings statistics continued to stay much higher than the policy-makers would have liked even if the underlying rate through 1993 and into 1994 was around 4 per cent which was the lowest level since before the 1967 devaluation. The increase in average weekly earnings in manufacturing was higher than in almost all the UK's industrial competitors. There was some evidence of an improvement in unit labour costs from the second quarter of 1993 but productivity growth seemed more to do with a further shake-out of industry than to any fundamental reform of working practices on a wide scale. Indeed, there were some signs to suggest the productivity differences between the UK and its main competitors were no longer closing from the late 1980s. The contrast between political rhetoric and social reality had never looked wider than in the area of Mr Major's employment strategy. But the government's delusion that Britain was enjoying a supply-side miracle which the rest of the world was watching with breathless admiration motivated much of the government's behaviour after November 1990.

FURTHER MARGINALIZING OF THE TRADE UNIONS

The political pressure for further labour legislation began to build up from the moment Mr Major walked into 10 Downing Street. The ambitious Michael Howard – appointed Employment Secretary by Margaret Thatcher – had made it clear in the House of Commons earlier in the year that the 'long process of industrial relations reform' had reached its conclusion with the 1990 Employment Act.[3] But now he discovered more important reforms of industrial relations law were needed to improve the labour market's efficiency. In July 1991 he published proposals which he believed were necessary to achieve that objective. 'Important as the achievements of the legislation of the 1980s have been, it would be wrong to assume that the process of reform is completed and that the progress which has been made is sufficient or permanent,' argued the green paper. 'The government believe it is necessary to consolidate and build on what has been achieved over the past twelve years.'[4] The need for further industrial relations legislation – argued the Department of Employment – derived from the 'pressures on British business to become more competitive' as a result of the completion of the Single European Market by the end of 1992. 'If our unit wage costs increase faster than those of our competitors in the markets of the world the inevitable consequence will be lost jobs and a lower standard of living. We simply cannot afford to risk slipping back into the inflationary pay settlements, low productivity and strike prone industrial relations of the 1970's.' Apparently the seven substantial pieces of labour law which had already been introduced over the previous decade under Margaret Thatcher were insufficient to create the conditions for Britain's future economic success.

Most of the proposals presented for discussion in Mr Howard's green paper in the summer of 1991 became law just over two years later in the Trade Union Reform and Employment Rights Act. These involved placing further restrictions on the ability of trade unions to call strikes. In future all pre-strike ballots of trade union members would have to be distributed and returned by post and they would have to be independently scrutineered. Employers would have to be notified by the union of the calling of each ballot. If a majority of workers supported industrial action in a postal ballot, employers would be entitled by law to seven days' written notice of the intent of a call for any workplace disruption and identification of the workers involved.

Workers in future would have a legal right to join a trade

union of their choice 'in circumstances where more than one union organizes employees of similar qualifications and occupations'. This meant an end of the TUC's 1939 Bridlington rules that had regulated inter-union rivalry over recruitment and representation in order to ensure workplace stability. Each individual worker in future would also need to give his or her consent to the deduction of their union subscription from their pay by their employer under the so-called 'check-off' system. The green paper suggested a worker's consent should be given annually but this was extended to once every three years in the resulting legislation. The certification officer was also to be given powers to make investigations into a trade union's internal activities that might involve 'serious or widespread irregularities in the conduct of its financial affairs or a breach of its rules relating to financial affairs' even if there had been no complaint from a trade union member about such a matter. Customers of public services were to be provided with the legal means to restrain unlawful action if an employer was unwilling to act or 'act quickly enough' in cases where 'the citizen may be defence-less' or when 'he is the specific target'. This last proposal was strengthened by inclusion in Mr Major's one Big Idea, the Citizen's Charter.

It is true the government did not legislate on all of the July 1991 proposals. Ministers at least heeded outside advice and decided not to change the law 'to encourage employers and unions to give proper consideration to the merits of making collective agreements legally enforceable'. But there was little evidence of support for the rest of what was being recommended even among employer organizations except for the right-wing Institute of Directors who made no secret that its ultimate objective was the removal of all legal immunities from trade unions in industrial disputes. The lack of enthusiasm from most employers for yet a further round of industrial relations legislation failed, however, to cool the ardour of Mr Major and his ministers. The proposals for more changes in employment law were re-emphasized in the Conservative party's 1992 general election manifesto and after Mr Major's victory Mrs Gillian Shephard, the new Employment Secretary, backed up by her deputy, the enthusiastic neo-Thatcherite Michael Forsyth, lost no time in pushing them through Parliament in the 1992–93 session.

Indeed, the final measure went much further than the 1991 green paper in seeking directly to weaken the power and influence of the trade unions. When the Court of Appeal upheld the case of a *Daily Mail* journalist who complained against Associated Newspapers that he had been unfairly discriminated against when he refused to accept a financial inducement as the precondition for agreeing to his union's derecognition by management, the Department of Employment inserted an amendment during the Bill's House of Lords stage which made it perfectly legal for an employer to discriminate, 'for the purposes of pay and conditions, providing the action was reasonable in the circumstances' between those workers who had agreed to a personal employment contract and those who wanted such matters to be covered by a collective agreement negotiated by an independent and recognized trade union. This change seemed to undermine the last vestiges of a trade union's right to organize and it was not surprising that the TUC decided in 1993 to lodge a formal complaint about the amendment to the International Labour Organization in Geneva.

A further sign of the clear hostility of Mr Major's government to organized labour was manifest in its symbolic gesture in the 1993 act to replace the original terms of reference for the Advisory Conciliation and Arbitration Service by deleting any suggestion that the tripartite organization existed to 'encourage the extension of collective bargaining' as part of 'good industrial relations'. The government also antagonized ACAS with the suggestion that the service should charge its customers for conciliation and arbitration. In fact, ACAS fought successfully to avoid such an imposition though the Department of Employment reserved itself the power to overrule the service on the charging question in future if it so wished.

Mr Major displayed his personal contempt or perhaps thoughtless insensitivity to trade unions in innumerable petty ways. In December 1992 the government decided to abolish the National Economic Development Council, that legacy of tripartism established by the One Nation Tory, Harold Macmillan, thirty years earlier. It is true its meetings had already been cut to four a year under Mrs Thatcher and the secretariat had its activities trimmed back to the bone. But the NEDC's sad demise came as a serious blow to the trade unions and many larger employers. It was not just a talking shop but a useful body, particularly at sector level, in encouraging employers and trade unions to work together on the problems of industrial innovation and competitiveness.

In March 1994 it was Mr Major alone who made the personal decision not to appoint a trade union leader to the governing body of the Bank of England. Ever since the bank's nationalization in 1946 it had been an unwritten tradition to do so. But despite entreaties from the bank's Governor, Mr Eddie George, in support of the reappointment of AEEU general secretary Gavin Laird for a third four-year term, the Prime Minister rejected the suggestion and refused to appoint any other trade union leader as a replacement for Mr Laird. Mr Major insisted any available positions on the bank's governing body should go to candidates whose 'individual expertise' would be directly useful to the bank.

The Prime Minister also refused to agree to end the ban on trade unionism at the government's Communications Centre at Cheltenham, imposed in January 1984 by Margaret Thatcher on grounds of defending national security. Efforts were made during 1993 to try to secure a compromise settlement of the issue in the face of a threat of censure on the government from the International Labour Organization but Mr Major insisted workers at GCHQ would face a possible conflict of loyalty between the state and a trade union if they were allowed to join trade unions again.

The Major government's hostility towards the trade unions was also seen in December 1992 when it was announced that state funding for trade union postal ballots as well as trade union training and health and safety at work courses was to be phased out within four years. Such financial provision by government had been an important element in Mr Jim Prior's industrial relations strategy under Mrs Thatcher before 1981.

The government's huge Deregulation Act in 1994, which provided ministers with controversial enabling powers and promised to scrap 450 items of red tape, contained anti-union provisions as well. A clause would allow a company to select employees for redundancy even if it contravened 'customary arrangements' or 'agreed procedures'. This would abolish the hallowed industrial relations principle of 'last in first out'. The government thought the previous position was 'unnecessarily restrictive' because any employer who selected workers for redundancy could face a possible charge of unfair dismissal before an industrial tribunal. There was also a provision in the Deregulation Act to make it easier to remove obsolete health and safety at work provisions though only after consultation with the Health and Safety Commission. 'Employers ought to have flexibility to adapt to current circumstances,' the Department of Trade and Industry argued. According to the TUC this was just another kick in the teeth for good industrial relations. But the government made no attempt to remove trade union nominees from the Health and Safety Commission and it accepted their continued presence on the other remaining public bodies like the Commission for Racial Equality and the Equal Opportunities Commission.

The election of Mr John Monks as Trades Union Congress general secretary in September 1993 to replace Mr Norman Willis brought a new change of direction in the TUC as it began to reorganize as much more of a campaign lobbying organization and abandoned many of its old pretensions of being an Estate of the Realm, demanding a direct voice in government policy-making. The arrival of a young, shrewd and conciliatory figure at the head of Congress House who made it clear to ministers that he wanted to develop a constructive engagement with them compelled Mr Major and his colleagues to respond amicably to what he had to say, even if they had no intention of going back to the close relations that used to exist between the TUC and post-war governments before Margaret Thatcher came to power. Mr David Hunt, the Employment Secretary, ruled out any return to what he regarded as the discredited corporatism of the 1970s, but even he spoke of a 'new' if limited future 'partnership' between the trade unions and government.

MAKING THE LABOUR MARKET
FREER

Marginalizing the trade unions in the name of individual freedom was coupled with more government dismantling of labour market regulations that were said to hamper productivity and competitiveness. The most controversial was the government's decision in 1993 to abolish the country's twenty-six statutory tripartite Wages Councils which had laid down minimum wage rates for 2.5 million low paid vulnerable workers in non-union sectors of the economy. This move aroused widespread condemnation not just from the trade unions but also from many pressure groups concerned with its social consequences. Not even Margaret Thatcher had gone so far, preferring just to exclude workers below twenty-one years of age from Wages Council awards under the 1986 Wages Act. The end of the Wages Councils was supported strongly by large private service companies such as Trust House Forte, Grand Metropolitan and the Burton group. The fear was that far from enabling employers to create more job opportunities, the removal of any form of legal protection for low paid workers would lead to a further erosion in the level of their earnings and an increase in their exploitation by unscrupulous employers. It is true that by 1993 the Wages Councils had come under considerable criticism because of their ineffectiveness, although this was due mainly to the government's deliberate underfunding and cutbacks imposed on the inspectorate (its number fell from 158 in 1979 to a mere 54 in 1992) who had been employed to enforce the pay awards on hostile employers. But the complete removal of any form of state regulation to protect the low paid from the harshness of the segmented labour market marked the demise of what had once been an important element of British social policy, introduced as long ago as 1908 by Winston Churchill, then President of the Board of Trade in a Liberal government.

Industrial training under Mr Major also turned out to be very much a continuation of Margaret Thatcher's approach. The establishment of eighty-two employer dominated Training and Enterprise Councils in England and Wales and Local

Enterprise Councils in Scotland was completed in 1991 to replace the old tripartite system that had been administered by the now defunct Manpower Services Commission. These new bodies – described in the 1992 Conservative general election manifesto as 'the most significant peacetime partnership between government and industry this century'[5] – were given the responsibility of meeting the training needs of local labour markets with the provision of £2.8bn a year of taxpayer's money. As unaccountable quangos under the control of employers, the TECs have remained a focus for national concern though many of their critics complained they have not enjoyed enough freedom from Whitehall scrutiny, particularly over the use of their operating surpluses. Whether in the long run the TECs will make any noticeable difference to the lamentable shortage of quality training in Britain remains problematic. So much of the government's labour market strategy has been conditioned by the demands of the Treasury for a tighter control over public expenditure and there is little appetite among many employers for a more interventionist strategy by the state to make them give a higher priority to training the unemployed. In 1994 David Hunt, the Employment Secretary, announced the government intended to introduce a modern apprenticeship scheme for young workers, a tacit admission that in the wake of the collapse of the traditional apprenticeship system during the 1980s the introduction of the Youth Training scheme had not proved to be an unmitigated success. The new programme, however, was initially to be a cautious experiment and involved a mere 20,000 youngsters in England and Wales. When the scheme was to be expanded the government said it hoped half of the participants would achieve level three national vocational qualifications. In 1994 32 per cent of all young workers achieved that level of expertise and the government set a target of half of them by the year 2000. Contrast this with Japan where 80 per cent of young people reached a comparable achievement level in 1986, the same figure as in France, according to the National Advisory Council for Education and Training. It was a further example of the government's *ad hoc* and timid approach towards what looks like being Britain's permanent training crisis.

Mr Major's years as Prime Minister saw a substantial rise in the number of people claiming unemployment benefit. When he came into office the figure stood at 1.85 million people, 6.1 per cent of the labour force and it peaked at just over 3 million at the beginning of 1993. The big shake-out for the second time in less than ten years brought large-scale redundancies across many traditional industries such as engineering, auto production, steel, shipbuilding and the railways. The most dramatic manpower cutbacks came in the coal mines. When the hapless President of the Board of Trade, Michael Heseltine, announced in October 1992 that the government supported British Coal's decision to shut 31 pits and make 30,000 miners redundant because of lack of demand for coal, he raised a firestorm of protest across the country and forced the Cabinet to stage a short-term retreat to prevent a Conservative backbench revolt that threatened the government's Commons majority. The resulting review of the coal industry did not even provide a temporary reprieve. By the time it was published in March 1993 the mood of national defiance had ebbed away and the closures took place amidst apathy and despair on the coalfields. By the beginning of 1994 there was hardly anything left of the mining industry to privatize.

But the demise of King Coal was perhaps not the most significant feature of the recession of the early 1990s. More serious for the Conservatives was the fact that the personal experience of unemployment was no longer confined to the ranks of manual workers. The 'downsizing' of companies to face the competitive challenge of global markets began to affect everybody, from senior management down to the shopfloor. Moreover, the recession hit the relatively affluent south east of England and London much more severely than other regions of the country. This was a new phenomenon and although it failed to cost the Conservatives the 1992 general election, it did suggest that Professor Kenneth Galbraith's 'culture of contentment' might have proved to be shortlived, at least in Britain.

EUROPEAN TROUBLES

Mr Major and his colleagues have never enjoyed a completely free hand in making employment policy. Much to their chagrin they found themselves increasingly ensnared in the European Union's social affairs agenda, with a growing number of unwelcome social directives emanating from the European Commission that needed to be inserted into British employment law. Hardly any of those which required the passing of domestic legislation were in tune with the government's flexible labour market strategy. Indeed, they reflected a philosophical approach to social policy which drew much of its inspiration not (as many Conservatives suggested) from Marxism or social democracy but social catholicism, from Pope Leo XIII's encyclical *Rerum Novarum* and not Karl Marx's *Das Kapital*.

The Prime Minister liked to boast he had won a famous victory at the heads of government summit in Maastricht in December 1991 when he secured an 'opt-out' for the UK from the social chapter of the new treaty that turned the European Community into the European Union. 'Game, set and match' was how he boasted of his personal triumph.[6] Apparently Britain was going to escape from further social directives that might emerge inside the EU after the implementation of the 1989 Social Charter and its forty-seven strong itemized social action programme. The country's competitiveness would not be obstructed by needless regulation. 'I have no objection to other member states deciding to hobble their competitiveness, if that is what they want,' declared employment minister, Michael Forsyth.[7]

But the government's comforting belief that Britain could insulate itself from the consequences of European social policy turned out to be sheer self-delusion. Indeed, over a wide front ministers found themselves in retreat before what they saw as a hostile EU social policy offensive. In some areas Mr Major and his colleagues had to swallow their doubts and agree to legislate in ways that strengthened the rights of employees in the workplace. The continental European concept of the citizen worker began to infiltrate its way into the fabric of Britain's common law legal system.

The most noticeable assimilation of the EU's social affairs agenda was made in the 1993 Trade Union Reform and Employment Rights Act. These involved the introduction of the legal right to fourteen weeks' maternity leave starting up to six weeks before the expected date of childbirth, regardless of length of service and the number of hours worked by an employee; the need for a statement of particulars for every worker written into their employment contract; and the implementation of health and safety at work provisions that provided workers with the legal right to refuse to work in unsafe conditions without facing dismissal by their employer. Perhaps the most serious EU interference with the government's employment policy came with its action over the UK's failure to implement the 1977 Acquired Rights Directive on the transfer of undertakings from one ownership to another. Under the 1993 act the government accepted that this directive did not just apply to commercial ventures, ensuring that the existing contractual terms and conditions of employment of a public sector worker would be upheld in the event of privatization. It was also agreed that under redundancy consultation procedures employers will be required by law to consult their employees, with a view to reaching agreement. Those ingredients in the 1993 Act strengthened the individual rights of workers and added some unspecified burdens on to business. They offered 'some small consolation by adding not insignificantly to the employment protection of workers in a manner that may provide additional means to resist employer-imposed changes to working conditions'.[8]

But on other employment issues the UK government tried to resist the pressures coming from Brussels. Employment Secretary David Hunt denounced the EU's working time directive in 1994 that laid down a forty-eight hour maximum working week and launched a challenge in the European Court of Justice against its enforcement. He was also derisive about the Young Workers' directive designed to limit the hours of sixteen to eighteen year olds. Ministers made it clear they would fight all the way against any changes demanded from the EU requiring a qualified majority of votes on the Council of Ministers that went beyond narrowly defined health and safety questions. But there were increasing signs of trouble for Mr Major across a wide range of social issues – sex discrimination in the workplace; collective redundancies and social protections for part-time workers as well as in the emerging threat of the creation of mandatory consultative and information arrangements for transnational European companies. The cumulative build-up of the EU's social programme – with more likely to come after 1996 – suggested the UK government would find it increasingly difficult to preserve intact its own flexible labour market agenda in face of the pressures from Brussels and increasingly from the adverse judgments made by the European Court of Justice in Luxembourg.

On the other hand, ministers convinced themselves they were winning the wider political arguments inside the EU on the merits of their employment strategy, especially when it seemed to be showing signs of success during 1993–94, as the claimant totals of those without a job began to fall slowly month by month. Unfortunately for Mr Major and his Cabinet colleagues, however, it was hard to discover any governments in the European Union who were noticeably impressed by Britain's alleged employment achievement. Indeed, the official comparative statistics provide no evidence to suggest their sceptical attitude was mistaken, for this country's jobless figures were very much in line with those elsewhere inside the EU. Most of the other EU countries tended to share the more interventionist views of EU president Jacques Delors and the EU's social affairs directorate, who believed a substantial 'social dimension' was required to complement the free single internal market established by the 1992 project. But to most Conservatives – One Nation Tories as much as neo-liberal Thatcherites – the very idea of a 'social' Europe was nothing less than subversion designed to destroy the supposedly free and dynamic labour market they were intent on creating in Britain. The exaggerated virulence of their attacks on Mr Delors and the EU Commission reflected an irrational failure on their part to recognize just how limited and pragmatic were the changes the EU wanted to introduce.

The government's defence of its labour market model from malignant continental influences seemed likely to degenerate into an increasingly bitter war of attrition with Brussels. Ministers drew some limited comfort from what they saw as a much more realistic attitude being adopted by other EU members in making the western European economy more competitive on global markets than was spelt out in Mr Delors' White Paper published in December 1993. A number of EU countries – France, Spain and Italy – modified their own labour market regulations to make them more flexible, which Mr Major and his colleagues could cite as evidence of a more sensible attitude being adopted elsewhere in the EU. But such reforms did not mean that any other country except Britain was prepared to champion the kind of neo-liberal employment strategy experienced in the United States during the Reagan-Bush years.

It is true that the UK government's own admiration for the American employment system fell short of actually launching a direct assault on the existing social benefit provisions of the welfare state for the unemployed or disadvantaged. As Mr Major's government explained in its document to the Detroit jobs summit, 'Labour market reform does not mean dismantling social protection. The UK believes a flexible labour market needs to be underpinned by a strong welfare state which targets help on those who need it most and gives people incentives to work'.[9] In this respect the policy was in tune with the underlying British tradition of voluntarism. 'The UK has never had a universal system of legal provisions determining terms and conditions of employment; these have rightly and consistently been for employers and employees, rather than legislation, to determine,' opined the UK government's contribution to the debate in Detroit. The labour market reforms carried out by the Conservatives had to be appraised against the background of a tax and benefit system and 'wide range' of legal rights that 'protected the welfare of individuals in the labour market'.

But Mr Major's increasing anger and frustration with the EU was due primarily to his realization that the main thrust coming from Brussels on social affairs threatened the durability of his party's longer-term employment and industrial relations policy introduced since 1979. The EU's enlargement to include Austria and the Nordic countries looked likely to worsen rather than improve matters because all of them still maintain various forms of social corporatism that coordinate the state, trade unions and employers behind a strong consensus on labour market questions and they looked set to strengthen the EU's existing employment strategy which balanced the cause of business competitiveness with that of workplace social solidarity. There was no sign anywhere that the British labour market example is one that others really wish to emulate. On the contrary, other EU countries were anxious not to be seen moving too far in the British direction.

THE MAJOR LABOUR MARKET ACHIEVEMENT; AN ASSESSMENT

The self-imposed isolation of Mr Major's government on employment policy may not prove to be a lasting one. In his often desperate attempts to hold the rest of the EU at bay, the Prime Minister appears to have convinced himself that Britain needs a flexible labour market to survive as a competitive economy. This has meant an emphasis on the marginalizing of the trade unions, the encouragement of worker individualism in all its forms from employee share ownership and profit sharing schemes to the removal of as much social regulation as possible. But as Dr Neil Millward observed in his analysis of the 1990 government commissioned workplace survey, Britain's unregulated labour market could be seen by its critics as marking 'a reversion towards the type of economy that gave rise to the birth of trade unionism in the last century'.[10]

Such a pessimistic view was not, of course, shared by Mr Major and his Cabinet colleagues. They believe that they are well on the road to the creation of a flexible labour market that has become the envy of the world. But their employment achievement looked more ambiguous than such public optimism might suggest. Unemployment continued to remain stubbornly high and the small net increase in jobs in 1994 was due to a growth in part-time and not full-time work. In December 1993 there were 700,000 fewer workers in employment than there had been two years earlier. The government's own training provision remained modest, while the performance of the TECs continued to arouse doubts. The level of earnings remained higher than the rise in the retail price index.

Many observers did not share the bullish optimism of ministers, who talked up the success of the British labour market 'model' and believed it was mainland Europe and not the UK who needed to change employment strategies. But in practice the pressures from the EU were forcing Mr Major to adapt and refine his labour market policies in ways that he disliked intensely. The deep recession in Britain was also a severe handicap for the government's attempt to insist on ever greater labour flexibility in the workplace. Opinion surveys found there was a widespread fear of redundancy not just among the unskilled and disadvantaged but also through the once secure ranks of senior management. There was a greater social segmentation inside the workforce. This hardly looked like a labour market – to use Mr Major's phrase – that was 'at ease with itself'.

But ministers remained confident that their comprehensive labour market strategy was working with the growth of individualism, further weakening of trade unionism and collective bargaining and a new emphasis on entrepreneurial energies in the creation of more job opportunities. Increasingly the Conservative dream was to transform Britain into a 'tiger' economy on the pattern of the Asian Pacific rim countries such as South Korea, Malaysia and Taiwan. It was not a project that seemed likely to bring the country either social stability or widespread economic prosperity. On the contrary, Mr Major's employment strategy looked destined to encourage the emergence of a huge urban underclass in Britain, complete with the violence, social deprivation and despair that have made so many American inner city areas almost uninhabitable. It is an approach that has moved Mr Major's government far away from the kind of paternalistic One Nation Toryism that used to dominate the Conservative party's employment and industrial relations policies for so much of this century.

The Prime Minister may have talked calmly and occasionally with sympathy about the social consequences of the recession. After all, he knew from first hand experience what it was to lose a job and suffer the humiliation of being unemployed. But none of this made any noticeable impact on his government's employment and industrial relations strategy. In this policy area at least, prime ministerial words of compassion were often belied by harshness of executive action. The creation of a flexible, more deregulated labour market was one subject on which all sections of Mr Major's Cabinet could find common agreement. Mrs Thatcher's labour market strategy was indeed safe in their hands.

Notes

1. *People, Jobs and Opportunity* Cmnd 1810 (HMSO, February 1992) p. 5 and p. 11.
2. Department of Employment Press Release, 17 March 1994, pp. 2–3.
3. Hansard Parliamentary Debates, 29 January 1990 Vol. 166, col. 38.
4. *Industrial Relations In the Nineteen Nineties*, Cmnd 1602 (HMSO, July 1991) p. 6.
5. *The Best Future For Britain*, Conservative Manifesto 1992, p. 19.
6. *Financial Times* 3 December 1991, p. 1.
7. Hansard Parliamentary Debates, European Standing Committee B, 23 March 1994, col. 11.
8. Keith Ewing, 'Swimming with the Tide', *Industrial Law Journal*, Vol. 22, September 1993, p. 178.
9. The UK Approach: Competitiveness and Employment, HMSO, March 1994, pp. 6–7.
10. Neil Millward, *The New Industrial Relations?*, Policy Studies Institute, 1994, p. 133.

Part 3

POLICY STUDIES

Chapter 15

DEFENCE POLICY

Lawrence Freedman

M RS THATCHER waited for the results of the first ballot of the leadership contest on 19 November 1990 in Paris. The conference she was attending was one of great symbolic significance. Agreements were being signed to mark a new era in European security: a revitalized conference on security and cooperation in Europe, with revitalized conciliation and conflict-prevention mechanisms, an arms control treaty to cut back conventional forces in Europe, and a confirmation of German unification within NATO. It included an idea she had particularly favoured for a 'European "Magna Carta" guaranteeing political rights and economic freedom'. Mrs Thatcher observed that this marked 'the formal – though sadly not the actual – beginning of that new era which was termed by President Bush a "new world order" '.[1]

Thus, perhaps appropriately, Margaret Thatcher went out with the cold war. John Major came in with the central problem which had guided British defence policy for the previous four decades apparently solved. He also inherited a rather oddly named defence review, 'Options for Change'. This had been formally set in motion by Tom King on 22 July 1990,[2] in order to bring defence provision into line with the new realities. It led over the following years to the defence budget being reduced more sharply than at any time since the post second world war demobilization.

Yet while John Major presided over a sharp cutback in the armed forces, they were also unusually active during this period. In addition to the now long established Northern Ireland requirement, which continued to tie down up to 20,000 British troops, new demands emerged. That eventful month of November 1990 also saw the passage of UN Resolution 678 which permitted the use of 'all necessary means' to liberate Kuwait from Iraqi occupation. One of the decisions taken at the Cabinet meeting of 22 November at which Mrs Thatcher resigned was to send a second armoured brigade to the Gulf.

Little in John Major's political career had obviously prepared him for the role he soon acquired as war leader. His brief sojourn in 1989 at the Foreign Office had not been happy; the Treasury was more his natural home. The delicacy of the moment was one reason why at least one former Chief of Defence Staff declared himself appalled at the timing of the move to depose such a natural war leader as Margaret Thatcher.

Nonetheless, within weeks of becoming Premier John Major was leading a country at war, with 45,000 serving men and women engaged in Desert Storm (or Operation Granby to give it the official Whitehall title).[3] This number was to be compared with the 25,000 involved in the Falklands. In 1992 a humanitarian mission in Bosnia led to the despatch of 2,300 troops. Later more British personnel were involved with the no-fly zones and the support of the blockade of Serbia and Montenegro. A further 800 troops were sent to reinforce the ceasefire in early 1994.

The unstable combination of defence contraction and military activism was a natural consequence of defence policy being caught between pressures on public expenditure and a determination to continue to play a world role. This tension has been evident for much of the post-1945 period, with defence provision at times being raised to sustain commitments – most notably in the first years of the 1950s and 1980s – and as often commitments being scaled back in the light of reduced provisions.

The pressure was eased for John Major as a result of the evaporation of the Warsaw Pact, but it was given a new twist

with the emergence of a whole series of new demands connected with the post-cold-war turbulence which gripped all areas
within the Soviet Union's former sphere of influence. Defence
of the realm was easier than ever before: the challenge for
Major's government was to define the level of defence spending and the forms of military activity necessary to provide it
with freedom of manoeuvre in a more complex world.

It is impossible to answer the question 'how much is
enough' with defence without some view on what it is wanted
for. In the past the United States might have provided Britain
with the benchmarks necessary to at least sketch out an
answer, but the United States was also disoriented by the
strange new world of the 1990s. Britain's European allies were
as flummoxed, so it was not as if a European standard could
replace the Atlanticist. In these circumstances, with so much
uncertain and in flux, a clarity of vision when it came to the
redefinition of Britain's strategic interest was probably too
much to expect. However, without it, the clearest answer to
the question of how much defence is enough was inevitably
going to be provided by the Treasury.

CHANGING SOVIET THREAT

Until the end of 1989, British security policy revolved around
the presumption of an expansionist Soviet Union successfully
contained through NATO's policy of deterrence. British
defence provision was set at a level that could legitimize its
second-in-command place within NATO. As long as they were
not actually needed urgently on NATO duties, the forces
designed for this purpose could meet most other contingencies, especially after the withdrawal from 'East of Suez' at the
end of the 1960s. The problem was that the NATO standard
encouraged Britain to contribute something to almost every
task, taking on the appearance of an American force in
miniature, from the nuclear force down. This was a 'balanced'
force, but the balance reflected inter-service politics and
NATO command structures as much as military logic.

Resource constraints were always the most likely source of

upset in this balance, hence the occasional defence reviews which such constraints prompted. Fundamental political change did not prompt such reviews though it sometimes came as a consequence (as with the withdrawal from East of Suez). Even during the late 1980s, with Mikhail Gorbachev attempting to define a completely new basis for East-West relations – with Mrs Thatcher's active encouragement – defence policy rested on the proposition that good intentions could be transitory but capabilities were for the long-term. However positive Mr Gorbachev's words, the Soviet Union could revert to its bad old ways. It could not be precluded that Mr Gorbachev was simply a more modern and PR-aware version of a traditional Soviet leader, attempting to lull the West into a false sense of security. Foreign policy could be optimistic: a prudent defence policy remained pessimistic. In 1990 Mrs Thatcher could declare that the Soviet Union was no longer 'an enemy' while still warning of 'false springs'.[4]

July 1990 saw the first draft of 'Options for Change'. Previous defence reviews could revolve around the question of whether enough of the right things were being done to deter the Soviet threat. Without a Soviet threat 'Options for Change' was faced with the awkward question of whether there was anything left that the country really needed to defend against?[5]

Saddam Hussein provided one sort of answer. (Perhaps as the previous review – 'The Way Forward' of 1981 – had been followed by the Falklands war, it should not have been so surprising that this review was followed by the Gulf war.) The Gulf war, at least temporarily, rescued the Ministry of Defence by providing a compelling reminder that, even without the traditional Communist menace, there could still be challenges to national interests and international order which could only be met by a substantial military response organized in concert with our major allies and with the blessing of the United Nations.

The Gulf confirmed that armed force might still be necessary, but not to the level required during the cold war years. So the reductions process continued, with each public expenditure round squeezing the defence budget further. By the start of 1994, British defence spending was scheduled to reach about 75 per cent of its 1986 peak level by 1996. At its peak defence had taken up over 5 per cent of GDP: it was now set to fall to some 3 per cent. Military personnel would decrease by a proportionate amount – to just under a quarter of a million. After the extra squeeze on defence spending in November 1993, the Ministry of Defence announced that it was looking to efficiencies in support costs to find the extra 3 billion pounds required by the Treasury over the next five years. Pointedly the government described this review as solely concerned with costs, and the announcement in July 1994 confirmed that it had only been support services, not front-line forces, that were to be cut. There was to be no reappraisal of defence commitments.[6]

Although the Labour party made play with the unemployment consequences of defence cuts, it appeared largely relieved that the government was taking the hard decisions in an area where it enjoyed charging the opposition with irresponsibility. Labour castigated the government by describing it as a Treasury-led review (as if this was something of a novelty) but it provided few ideas as to what a more strategic review might come up with.

In truth the attempt to generate a 'peace dividend' was inevitable in the 1990s. When Tom King first began to talk about his reforms in 1990 the catchphrase was 'smaller but better'. The emphasis was soon on 'smaller'. To make any sense 'Options for Change' had to mean ruling out at least some options. Could a strategic view be discerned guiding this choice of alternative, or was the exercise simply an across-the-board scaling down?

One obvious area of continuity was the strategic nuclear force. By 1990 much of the investment in the Trident replacement for Polaris had either been committed or spent, so that during the 1992 election no attempt was made by Labour to suggest that there was a financial case for exploring alternatives. The first Trident submarine was scheduled to enter service at the end of 1994. The government's only nod in the direction of the new situation, including participating in a flurry of post cold-war strategic arms control agreements between Washington and Moscow, was when Defence Secretary Malcolm Rifkind indicated that the new force would not carry the maximum number of warheads, but would be closer in total destructive power to the Polaris capability. (In practice this meant more warheads than Polaris but each of lower yield).[7]

However Rifkind also spelled out a much more restricted view of the role of nuclear weapons, taking care not to justify a continued capability by reference to new third world proliferators.[8] Every type of nuclear weapon in the British arsenal other than submarine-carried ballistic missiles was either eliminated or cut back. Short-range land-based systems (which were dual-key with the United States) were abandoned. So were nuclear depth bombs on both warships and maritime patrol aircraft.[9] With air-delivered weapons, the number of aircraft assigned to carry them was cut, and so were the number of We-177 free-fall bombs available for their use (by about half). Plans to replace the We-177 with a new stand-off missile were scrapped, leading instead to reliance on Trident for 'sub-strategic', minimalist strikes as well as the maximalist strategic deterrent.[10]

The Royal Navy was no longer to worry quite so much about a threat to Atlantic sea routes and relinquished some destroyers and frigates, and all diesel-powered submarines. The RAF also saw a cutback, but received support for the European Fighter Aircraft upon which its planning for the future was based. The biggest cutback was with the Army, with no case now for four divisions in Germany. The cuts inevitably threatened individual regiments, many with long traditions and some with royal connections. This was politically one of the trickiest defence issues faced by the government, though it was largely irrelevant in broad strategic terms.

Two divisions were kept in Germany, offered as the basis of a rapid reaction corps for NATO, the command of which Britain was anxious to gain. Both the Ministry of Defence and NATO remained fixated on the former Soviet Union. The fact that this was now the scene of great political convulsions provided little reassurance, for it created a risk that Moscow might act in wild and irresponsible ways. Authoritarianism might reassert itself, and, in reimposing its will internally, Moscow might also seek to reassert its power externally.

The limited cutback in Germany could be presented as a

prudent policy for the transition, though if there was still a serious risk of total war then the government might rightly be criticized for cutting too much too fast. Arguably as important in the maintenance of a semblance of a traditional NATO formation was the desire to reassert Atlanticism against the ideas current in 1991 during the lead up to Maastricht for a European defence entity.

Thus defence policy reflected a preference for the maintenance of as much as possible of the status quo in terms of the structure if not the size of the western alliance. With or without Thatcher, a Conservative government was not going to put the 'special relationship' at risk on behalf of vague notions of a common European defence – which anyway seemed to fail with every test. However this was not simply an institutional question: holding together a western alliance required a demonstrable capacity to meet the new external challenges of the post-cold-war world.

JOHN MAJOR AT WAR

The Gulf had proved to be far more suited to Margaret Thatcher's foreign policy style than the construction of a European Union. In the Gulf clear principles were at stake. It was an area of traditional British interest and influence. Her timely presence in the United States as the crisis broke in August 1990 had allowed her to use the opportunity to reforge the 'special relationship' with President Bush. The preoccupation of the previous months with the end of the cold war and German unification had suggested that Bonn was about to displace London as Washington's top ally. But Germany had nothing to offer in the Gulf. Even so, Mrs Thatcher had initially been cautious about committing too many ground forces, rather than aircraft and warships. She had gradually accepted that British influence on American policy depended on sizeable contributions to all elements of the forces arrayed against Saddam Hussein.

Treasury caution might have led John Major to resist war, because of the damage it might do to public expenditure projections, but by November 1990 the die had been cast. There were few basic policy decisions to be taken and, by and large, he seems to have been happy to leave these to Douglas Hurd at the Foreign Office. There is little evidence that he took much interest in the redeployment of British forces from the marine positions facing the Iraqi front lines to becoming part of the VII Army preparing to encircle the Iraqi Republican Guards which was the most important decision taken before the end of the year. (This move used up much of Britain's credit with the US Military.)[11]

Yet John Major was widely judged to have had a good war. He was helped by the enormous resources devoted to the campaign by the United States, which ensured that in no sense was this ever a 'close run thing'. British casualties were moderate, with the RAF suffering most through enemy fire as a result of the high-profile missions accepted by the tornado squadrons. The bulk of the land casualties were caused by an unfortunate attack by an American aircraft on a Warrior Fighting Vehicle as British troops moved forward, which resulted in nine being killed. The cost of the war was eased substantially – almost to nothingness – by contributions from the Gulf states, Japan and Germany.[12]

As with so much else, John Major's success as war leader stemmed from a favourable contrast with what might have been expected from Mrs Thatcher. Visiting the troops before the battle, his lack of bombast and general ordinariness went down well. There were not many testing moments during the war but the few there were passed without signs of panic. A bipartisan approach was followed, with Labour and Liberal leaders kept informed. Despite temptations, which many presume Mrs Thatcher would have found impossible to resist, there was no attempt to exploit the allies' victory with a quick 'Khaki election'. It was an IRA mortar attack that put him (and the War Cabinet) at risk in February 1991, but no one was hurt and his demeanour seemed to reflect a reassuring calmness rather than a lack of imagination.

The contrast with Mrs Thatcher was also evident in the first major initiative he took after the war. The defeat of Saddam Hussein had been followed by an insurrection which Saddam crushed ruthlessly. In the north of Iraq Kurds fled towards Turkey and Iran causing a horrendous refugee problem. Initially John Major, along with George Bush, apparently sought to deny that the Kurds were in any sense the West's responsibility. This was despite the encouragement that had been given (especially by Bush) to Iraqis during the war to rise up against Saddam. Whether or not an intervention by Margaret Thatcher on behalf of the Kurds caused a rethink, John Major's response was distinctive. Rather than coordinate a policy with Washington, he took the opportunity of an April 1991 summit in Luxembourg designed to reflect on the European Community's generally dismal performance during the war to launch the 'safe havens' initiative. This had the benefit of signalling his readiness to use Europe to develop new ideas.[13]

The next time Margaret Thatcher called for action on behalf of a persecuted people the response was less swift. As the Gulf crisis faded from view, the Yugoslav crisis took centre stage. By August 1991 there was major fighting underway in Croatia, with the Serb-dominated Yugoslav Peoples Army on the offensive. Soon the town of Vukovar was suffering a terrible siege. Again Thatcher called for action: this time the British government was unimpressed.

There were two factors involved: first there were grave doubts over whether those calling for intervention had seriously considered the full implications of sending troops into the middle of a vicious civil war. Second, it was unclear why Britain should get actively involved in a problem in the Balkans when it was so much closer to allies who had contributed little to the Gulf crisis. This reluctance to intervene continued through the even more vicious Bosnian war. When a ceasefire was agreed and a UN force was sent in early 1992 to Croatia the British contribution was minimal.

Nonetheless soon Britain found itself providing a major contribution to UN forces in Bosnia. The main reason for this was simply that Britain was one of the few countries capable of providing a major contribution. The two West European countries with a greatest interest in Yugoslavia – Germany and Italy – were both precluded for a variety of reasons, including historical, from getting involved. The United States had been only too pleased to take seriously European claims that the Yugoslav crisis did not require American participation. That really only left France and Britain with forces of the necessary quality and quantity available, around which a wider multinational force could be based. If Britain had not held the presidency of the European Council in the second half of 1992 it may have still resisted a contribution. In the event, holding back did not appear consistent with a desire to appear a full and responsible member of the Community, especially in the context of the major diplomatic initiative which led to the September 1992 London conference on the former Yugoslavia, and Britain providing former Foreign Secretaries as chief negotiators for the European Community (first Lord Carrington and then Lord Owen).[14]

So it was that 2,300 troops were despatched in late 1992. Ironically these became not so much a foundation for a firmer stand against Serbian aggression as a reason for not raising the military stakes too high. The vulnerable position of the British and French forces to Serbian retaliation became an argument for not adopting the measures canvassed by the Clinton administration from early 1993 (which, it should be noted, would not put American forces at risk) of air strikes and lifting the arms embargo which effectively denied the Bosnian government the right to self-defence.

Such resistance to American ideas led to some extraordinarily harsh transatlantic arguments. Gradually Serbian behaviour – especially in terms of the Bosnian capital of Sarajevo – made the air strikes option harder to resist. It was first mooted in August 1993. Serbian forces moderated their behaviour, but the issue arose again in February 1994, this time leading to an ultimatum. This was one of the moments of real crisis, when a situation is either going to get a lot worse or a lot better. Fortunately this particular moment of crisis forced both the United States and Russia into an active diplomatic role, leading to a series of political breakthroughs which had at the time of writing brought the Muslims and the Croats together and extracted some concessions from the Serbs. Britain was able to draw some credit in that the UN Commander on the spot, General Sir Michael Rose, was British and his tactics had enabled the UN to take full advantage of the improved diplomatic climate. Inevitably the logic of a more active UN role on the ground led to a greater requirement for troops. Having been reluctant to provide any more forces, the government found itself forced to do so to prevent the existing forces finding themselves dangerously extended with the new demands placed upon them.

In his memoirs John Major may claim that one of his greatest achievements was to prevent British forces from getting bogged down in combat roles in Bosnia and Somalia. In this the government has had the full support of the service chiefs, although in both cases there were rows with the United States, and in the case of Bosnia Britain has been left vulnerable to the charge of appeasing Serbian aggression. Even in its circumscribed, humanitarian form, the mission in Bosnia was a continuing drain on defence resources. So were the penny packets of forces through which token support was provided for other UN operations in which Britain declined to play a leading role. The Foreign Office remained keen to see Britain justifying its place as a permanent member of the Security Council through conspicuous support for Council-sponsored operations.

For the Army in particular this posed a predicament. To get involved in actions devoted to bringing peace and stability to turbulent parts of the world led to an enormous short-term demand for trained manpower – which was likely to endure because these operations have a notorious tendency to become semi-permanent. The demands of Bosnia were used to claw back a couple of infantry battalions from the originally planned cuts. In addition these operations were frustrating and often quite dangerous. The generals would far rather prepare their forces for armoured warfare.

Yet these actions were the main show in town. British troops, as a result of imperial traditions and contemporary experience in Northern Ireland, performed well in them. Not to get involved on the grounds that this was not the right sort of war and vital interests were not directly involved appeared to be missing an opportunity for exercising international influence and revived the unavoidable question of whether it would ever again be necessary to fight classic air, sea and land battles in which there is an unambiguous threat to the British way of life.

In practice, in the management of the competing claims of the immediate demands of peacekeeping (including Northern Ireland) and the long-term preparation for major war a continuous defence review was underway. Under John Major, British military policy moved into a curious phase. On the one hand the direct threats to national security had, at least for the moment, been eliminated. On the other hand, the indirect obligations had expanded dramatically as a result of a general presumption that the Western states, and especially permanent members of the Security Council, have broad responsibility for international order. More than ever, globalist aspirations rested uneasily with a determination to avoid direct approaches and to keep military liabilities to a minimum.

CONCLUSION

Has there been a Major effect on defence policy? Given the tumultuous international context the most surprising thing about this policy area has been the avoidance of controversy. With each successive cut in announced defence expenditure, the pro-defence group in the Conservative party has been aroused by reports of their likely severity, and even threatened to vote against the government, only to be pacified by the actual reductions being less than expected. Perhaps one reason for the ease of Major's passage in this area has been the disorientation of his main opponents. The Thatcherites are aware that the defence review was set in motion before Major took office and this is one area where Lady Thatcher's combative approach to international villains does not always appeal to her more nationalistic followers who have been generally pleased with Major's determination not to allow British troops to get directly involved in land combat. For its part the Labour front bench has been scared of appearing unpatriotic and has therefore taken a cautiously pro-defence and pro-interventionist line without making these questions a high priority.

Major himself has not made his mark on security policy.

It is hard to think of one significant speech on the issue, although both Douglas Hurd and Malcolm Rifkind have made a number of thoughtful contributions to policy debate. By and large, Major seems to have been happy to leave long-term policy formation to these two ministers, confining himself to occasional grandstanding when an issue comes up where he can see short-term political advantage – for example over safe havens for the Kurds in April 1991 or what was widely seen as a cynical relief operation for wounded children from Bosnia (known as Operation IRMA in honour of the girl whose plight prompted the operation – and claimed by cynics to stand for Immediate Response to Media Appeal). Good can come of such short-termism but it can betray a lack of a firm grounding for policy.

It is hard to see what an alternative British defence policy would have looked like, unless there had been a greater readiness to take risks with British troops' lives in the former Yugoslavia. With so much unclear, a clarity of vision was unrealistic to expect. It is a reflection on John Major's reputation that such clarity was neither expected nor was it forthcoming.

Notes

1. Margaret Thatcher, *The Downing Street Years* (HarperCollins, London, 1993), p. 842.
2. Hansard, 25 July 1990, cols. 470–473.
3. The British role is described in Secretary of State for Defence, *Statement on the Defence Estimates: Britain's Defence in the 90s*, Volume 1, (Cmnd 1559–I, July 1991); House of Commons Tenth Report from the Defence Committee, Session 1990–91, *Preliminary Lessons of Operation Granby*, (August 1991).
4. *The Times*, 6 August 1990.
5. The 1990 Defence Estimates warned that the 'defence planner' must keep in mind the 'darker' possibilities; 'he must look to possible mistakes and failures in the political scene, rather than successes'. Political shifts 'can happen – or be reversed – much faster than defence provision can be changed, run down or

re-built'. Secretary of State for Defence, *Statement on the Defence Estimates 1990*, Volume 1, Cmnd 1022–I (HMSO, London, April 1990), p. 17. The warning next year was that while the 'Soviet capability to mount a large-scale offensive into central Europe is diminishing' and so no longer puts the demands as before on NATO, risks were still faced though these were 'far less obvious and monolithic'.

> The Soviet Union remains an unstable military superpower, whose capabilities need to be counter-balanced if stability is to be preserved in Europe. These capabilities still present the most serious, if not the most immediate, threat to Western security.

Secretary of State for Defence, *Statement on the Defence Estimates 1991*, Volume 1, Cmnd 1559–I (HMSO, London, July 1991), p. 31.

6. See introduction to Michael Clarke and Philip Sabin, *British Defence Choices for the Twenty-First Century*, (Brasseys for Centre for Defence Studies, London 1993); Sherard Cowper-Coles, 'From Defence to Security: British Policy in Transition', *Survival*, (Spring 1994); Philip Sabin, 'British Defence Choices beyond "Options for Change" ', *International Affairs*, 69, 2, (1993); *Front Line First*, July 1994.

7. See speech by Malcolm Rifkind to the Centre for Defence Studies, 15 November 1993, reprinted in *Brasseys Defence Yearbook 1994*, (Brasseys, London, 1994).

8. Secretary of State for Defence, Rt Hon Malcolm Rifkind MP, *Intervention in Paris Symposium* (30 September 1992).

9. *Financial Times*, 16 June 1992; *Independent*, 16 June 1992.

10. See Lawrence Freedman, 'Britain and Nuclear weapons', in Clarke and Sabin, *op. cit.*

11. This is discussed fully in General Sir Peter De La Billiere, *Storm Command: A Personal account of the Gulf War* (Harper Collins, London, 1992).

12. Over £2 billion was received against a total cost for the war officially put at £2.5 billion. *Statement on the Defence Estimates 1991*, *op. cit.*

13. See Lawrence Freedman and Efraim Karsh, *The Gulf Conflict 1990–91*, (Faber, London, 1993), p. 423.

14. See Lawrence Freedman, ed, (*Military Intervention in Europe*, (Basil Blackwell, London, 1994), especially the article on Britain by Philip Towle.

Chapter 16

FOREIGN POLICY

William Wallace

THE MAJOR GOVERNMENT inherited from Mrs Thatcher a Conservative party more divided on foreign policy than on any other policy area. Mrs Thatcher lost office on the issue of European policy; John Major was elected leader partly because he was not seen to be either too Europhile or Europhobe. The new Prime Minister could be under no illusions that foreign policy would continue to be a difficult issue both in internal party terms and in adjusting to a rapidly-changing international environment. He came into office just after the unification of Germany, a development which his predecessor had done her best to hold back; with military action looming in the Gulf, to which Mrs Thatcher had committed Britain, under the American leadership she herself had urged President Bush to provide when Kuwait was occupied; and with preparations for an inter-governmental conference (IGC) scheduled for 1991 already well advanced.

The new Prime Minister had little prior experience or knowledge of foreign policy, and few known views on it. His brief – three-month – period as Foreign Secretary had represented a steep learning curve from a very low starting point, interrupted by his transfer to the Treasury. He differed from his predecessor however in a number of significant respects. A generation and a half younger, he was unmarked by the emotions or memories of the Second World War. He had no strong antagonism towards Germany, no particular affection for the United States. He showed no sign of identifying Britain's armed forces with Britain's sovereignty or international status; nor indeed of sharing Mrs Thatcher's passionate commitment to the defence of British sovereignty. First impressions were of a managerial Prime Minister, sympathetic to the 'Christian Democratic' European approach of Chris Patten, willing to rely on the experience and expertise of his Foreign Secretary (and rival for the leadership), Douglas Hurd, and wary of the pitfalls which this area contained for internal strife within his divided party.

'Europe' was the defining issue both for British foreign policy and for the internal party divisions which John Major inherited, because it had come to symbolize so many of the policy choices over which the Conservatives were split. Free market economics and closeness to the USA went together, reinforced by the personal closeness of Thatcher and Reagan and the intellectual (and financial) links between the think-tanks of the American and the British radical right. Industrial policy, preference for a more 'social market' approach, and greater warmth towards the European Community represented a different mind-set, and a different view of Britain's future, set out in Michael Heseltine's alternative 'manifesto' of 1989, *The Challenge of Europe: can Britain win?* The image of continental Europe as corporatist and authoritarian, and the English-speaking world as free market and free politically, had been the received wisdom of the intellectual right since Friedrich von Hayek and the wave of exiles from the occupied continent had spelt out their doctrines fifty years earlier.

More than that, competing interpretations of British national identify were at stake in the perceived choice of emphasis between a European and an Anglo-Saxon commitment. Mrs Thatcher had emphasized her resistance to any erosion of British national identity through European integration in her Bruges speech of September 1988. Michael Heseltine made clear his different perspective in the opening sentence of *The Challenge of Europe*: 'Britain's past is tightly spun into the history of Europe, and it is this web of influence that makes us what we are today.' 'There are those', he provocatively continued, 'who fear that in moving closer to Europe Britain will lose her identity. On the contrary, I believe that within Europe she will find a much greater one.'[1]

John Major had been the 'stop Heseltine' candidate of the Thatcherite loyalists. Yet he did not share their passions or their instincts. He took over from his predecessor Britain's commitment to act as the USA's staunchest ally in reversing the Iraqi annexation of Kuwait, and rapidly built up a relationship of mutual respect with President Bush. It was, however, a businesslike relationship between two managerial politicians, without the historical echoes which had marked the Thatcher-Reagan partnership. Antagonism to Germany had been a factor in Mrs Thatcher's downfall and a *leitmotiv* of the right, with Nicholas Ridley forced to resign earlier in 1990 when *The Spectator* had published his unvarnished views on what he saw as a German-dominated Europe. John Major, in contrast, moved immediately to build a partnership with the German Christian Democrats, declaring in a speech in Bonn in March 1991 that Britain intended to be 'at the very heart of Europe', working with its Conservative allies in other European governments. The warm relationship he developed with Chancellor Kohl was of a different order from the mutual antagonism of Kohl and Thatcher. For Kohl, too, part of the appeal of John Major was that he was not Mrs Thatcher; but Major clearly made a personal effort to transform the atmosphere, both between the two heads of government and the two parties.

It was however more difficult to transform the atmosphere within his own party. A central theme of Mrs Thatcher's period as Prime Minister had been the reversal of Britain's decline in international influence and status: the restoration of pride in Britain, through an assertive foreign policy with a nationalist flavour, harking back to memories of the Second World War. The sceptical tenor of her Bruges speech had set the tone for many in the younger generation of Conservative MPs as well as among older backbenchers, and re-echoed back from the constituency associations and the party conference. The Bruges Group had already become one of the most visible lobbies on the intellectual right, committed to maintaining a robustly mistrustful approach to the European Community. Commitment to her vision of foreign policy among her partisans had only been sharpened by their sense of betrayal in the circumstances of her departure, with Geoffrey Howe's resignation statement and Michael Heseltine's leadership challenge symbolizing the disloyalty of the pro-European 'wets' to the Thatcherite approach at home and abroad.

It was almost as difficult to transform the assumptions and expectations of the Conservative press. The *Daily Telegraph*, the unofficial 'house organ' of the Conservative party, had passed under the control of Conrad Black, a Canadian newspaper proprietor whose belief in the closeness of trans-atlantic Anglo-Saxon ties was matched by his admiration for both Reagan and Thatcher. In the *Sunday Telegraph* and *The Spectator*, which revived under his ownership to become the leading political weekly of the right, resistance to 'Europe' and admiration for the USA were underlying themes, often accompanied by suspicion of the 'Europeanizing' Foreign Office. *The Times* and *Sunday Times*, and their popular tabloid stablemates the *Sun* and the *News of the World*, had become under Rupert Murdoch's ownership both vigorously supportive of Mrs Thatcher and strongly anti-European; the *Sun* in particular propounded a nationalist populism in which anti-French and anti-German sentiments alternated. Both proprietors and their editors had maintained close relations with Mrs Thatcher and her circle, and filled their comment columns with contributions from the intellectuals she had encouraged. John Major, for them, was an unknown quantity, above all in foreign affairs; without a new composition on offer, they continued to play the tunes they had learned over the previous ten years.

There was, after all, no distinctive Major 'tune'; no new vision of Britain's place in the world to substitute for his predecessor's British Gaullism or Michael Heseltine's proposed shift towards Europe. John Major was a political manager rather than a visionary in style, whose interests were more domestic than international. Douglas Hurd, the Foreign Secretary on whom he relied for the active management of European policy in particular, was a diplomat by training, with long experience in foreign policy, who commanded widespread respect within both wings of the party. But he was also by instinct a manager rather than a visionary, a conservative in the classic sense who saw politics as a matter of incremental adjustment to external events rather than as the deliberate pursuit of defined objectives. An old Etonian who had started in the Conservative party as private secretary to Edward Heath, he attracted a degree of suspicion from the right as a member of the old 'establishment' they had come into politics to displace. With Heseltine back in the Cabinet, there was no personality on that wing of the party to propound an alternative perspective. The confusions of the Labour opposition on foreign and defence policy – again, above all on Europe – meant that no counterweight was offered from the left.

The first four years of the Major government in foreign policy were thus played out within a structural domestic political imbalance: between an ideologically committed and suspicious right within the government party and a managerial leadership, with a void on the left both within the party and across the floor of the House of Commons. In his first eighteen months as Prime Minister managerial approaches served John Major well. After the 1992 election, however, with the government's reduced majority giving the hard core of the unreconciled right the potential to defeat their own government by combining with the opposition, with the process of ratifying the Maastricht treaty proving far more difficult across the whole Community than expected, and from the end of 1992 with the re-established relationship with President Bush's Republican Administration replaced by the uncertainties of Clinton's Democrats, this primarily reactive, tactical, managerial approach became less and less sure. Vulnerable to the contradictory pressures of coalition-building with foreign governments in a rapidly-changing international environment, and coalition-maintenance within a party deeply reluctant to accept the implications of these changes for Britain, the Major government's foreign policy lost direction. By the beginning of 1994 it had become, as one official resignedly put it, 'a foreign policy directed from Number 12 Downing Street [the Whips' Office] rather than Number 10'.

THE FIRST EIGHTEEN MONTHS:
THE EMERGENCE OF A MAJOR STYLE

Coming into office in November 1990, the immediate foreign policy agenda was set by the Gulf crisis, the implications of German reunification, the unravelling of the Soviet empire, and the EC inter-governmental conference. British forces were already in the Gulf and Saudi Arabia, fully committed to an American-led operation to push the Iraqis out of Kuwait. The UN Security Council resolution to authorize the use of military force if Iraq did not withdraw before 15 January was adopted on 29 November, the day after Mr Major became Prime Minister. The British division in Saudi Arabia was already moving into place, the most substantial contingent of land forces from America's NATO allies, re-establishing Britain's 'special' position as the USA's most dependable ally.

Major's distinctive contribution to the Gulf crisis came after the expulsion of the Iraqis from Kuwait in January, when, contrary to expectations, Saddam Hussein remained in control in Baghdad while American and other forces were being rapidly withdrawn. Impressed by reports of the plight of the Kurds in northern Iraq, fleeing across the Turkish border as Iraqi troops were redeployed against them, and by arguments that the liberation of Kuwait should not have left minorities within Iraq still unprotected, he took the initiative in pressing for the establishment of 'safe havens'. Against a reluctant Washington, the British government gathered multilateral support through a special meeting of the European Council (on 8 April), sending British (and Dutch) marines and emergency aid to implement the strategy agreed. Ground forces were withdrawn from northern Iraq later in the year, leaving civilian UN monitors supported by air patrols mounted from Turkey; a limited increase in security for the Kurds, achieved through multilateral action largely on British initiative, the principles of state sovereignty modified by humanitarian concerns. Out of this initiative grew a wider emphasis within British foreign policy outside the OECD world which bore the marks of a Major style: an emphasis on more effective disaster relief and on 'good government' in the third world, replacing assessment of pro-western or pro-Soviet tendencies as criteria for bilateral aid and multilateral assistance.

Relations with Germany, the implications of reunification, and the politics of the Maastricht treaty revision were inextricably linked. The agenda for the inter-governmental conference had already been set by the Delors report on progress towards economic and monetary union a year before; but it was being transformed by the unexpected speed of political and security transmutation across Europe and the entry of a further 16 million Germans to the EC. The formal opening session of the IGC was held during the Rome European Council on 15 December 1990, barely a fortnight after Major had become head of government. In the Treasury he had of course been intimately involved in the politics of monetary cooperation, with the pound entering the exchange rate mechanism only in October 1990 in the midst of the embittered arguments which had brought down his predecessor. Memories of the previous IGC and of the controversies which had rumbled on within the Conservative party over the implications of the Single European Act inclined the party managers to approach this new exercise with extreme caution. What distinguished the British government's extreme position in the whole series of negotiations which led up to Maastricht a year later, one participant subsequently argued, was its determinedly minimalist position throughout: it wished the IGC to achieve as little as possible, and to present the treaty changes it proposed in as modest a form as possible.

A closer relationship with Germany was the key to successful management of these delicate negotiations, conducted while Mrs Thatcher toured the United States, attacking the federalist tendencies of continental governments and calling for a new Atlantic Community instead. John Major visited Bonn repeatedly in the early months of 1991, establishing a good personal relationship with the German Chancellor. But international developments were widening the IGC's agenda. US forces transferred from Germany to the Gulf were withdrawn from there to the USA, while Soviet forces were beginning to withdraw from the former East Germany. The

Belgian proposal in February for a second IGC on institutional reform (alongside that focused mainly on economic and monetary issues) was broadened on Franco-German initiative in April to cover foreign and security policy, the two governments struggling to adjust to the shifting balance in their relationship and to the reformulation of the Atlantic Alliance. That reformulation was being negotiated in parallel within the NATO framework, through a series of ministerial and official meetings culminating in a Brussels NATO summit in November, which approved a new 'Strategic Concept'.

Prime Minister John Major left the detailed negotiations within NATO and the IGCs to his Cabinet colleagues, above all to Douglas Hurd. Apart from his active dialogue with Chancellor Kohl and less frequent contacts with President Mitterand, his personal diplomacy took place within a wider compass, travelling in 1991 to Washington, to Moscow (twice), to Hong Kong and Peking as well as to Harare for a Commonwealth heads of government conference. Britain held the chair of the Group of Seven (of leading industrial countries) in 1991, thus enabling Major to act as a representative of 'the West' in negotiating the terms of financial assistance to the faltering Soviet Union. Gorbachev came to London for the July 1991 G7 summit, as a supplicant for increased aid. In contrast to Mitterand, Major's instinctive reaction to the attempted Moscow coup in August was to declare immediate support for Yeltsin. His subsequent visit to President Bush at his holiday home in Maine underlined the fact that Britain had re-established itself as the USA's natural *interlocuteur* in western Europe, after the period in 1989–90 when the Bush administration had deliberately signalled its priority for a partnership with Germany. From there he travelled to Moscow for talks with Gorbachev and Yeltsin, and then on to Peking; where, responding to criticisms within the British press and overruling the cautious advice of his officials, he admonished his hosts on their human rights record while negotiating with them on the future of Hong Kong.

At the Commonwealth conference in October Mr Major worked hardest to use this opportunity for dialogue between developed and developing countries to urge concerted pressure for completion of the GATT Uruguay round. Unlike his predecessors, he had few emotional attachments or inhibitions over Britain's Commonwealth connections; here, rather, was an opportunity to do business and for Britain to demonstrate its useful diplomatic role.

Negotiations within the European context, meanwhile, had been complicated further by the outbreak of fighting in Yugoslavia, with harsh words between Hurd and Genscher, the German Foreign Minister, over the immediate commitment of troops: the German demand for 'European' troops to be sent meant calling on the British and the French to send them, given the complications of German and Italian involvement in Yugoslavia fifty years before. The transformation of European security had also raised the prospect of further EC enlargement, implying consequences for EC decision-making which would require further institutional reform. By the time the Prime Minister became directly engaged in the final stages of the IGC, at the European Council in Maastricht in early December, the main compromises had been made. The balance between Atlantic and European foreign policy and defence cooperation had been struck at the NATO summit, with a Franco-American bargain over a 'European security identity' within the alliance; it remained for Britain and France to settle the fine print in the treaty over the relationship between Western European Union (WEU), NATO and the new European Union, with Germany as a moderating influence on both sides. On institutional reform, the British government sided with France against Germany, arguing vigorously for an inter-governmental 'three-pillar' structure to bring foreign and security policy and police and judicial cooperation within a single treaty framework, rather than the integrated Community accountable to a strengthened European Parliament for which Chancellor Kohl and his government had pressed.

The Maastricht package itself, and the style of the last stages of its negotiation, displayed most characteristically Major's preoccupation with party management rather than long-term objectives. Substantial concessions were made on the Europeanization of security and defence policy, and on the formalization of cooperation among police and intelligence services: significant inroads into British sovereignty, successfully concealed from the British press and the Conservative back benches and unnoticed by an ineffective parliamentary opposition. The line was held on institutional reform, at the cost of accepting the scheduling of a further IGC in 1996 to discuss the implications of enlargement, of progress towards EMU, and of revision of the WEU Treaty. 'We have four years,' Douglas Hurd reported back to Parliament, 'to demonstrate that the inter-governmental approach can work.'

The drama of the Maastricht Council was played out partly over British insistence on an opt-out 'Declaration' on the timetabled progress towards economic and monetary union, and partly over the proposed 'social chapter' of the treaty: a secondary issue for other governments, but one which went to the core of the ideological divide within the Conservative party. For free marketeers the inclusion within the treaty of entrenched rights for employees represented all that was corporatist in the construction of the EC. Against the resistance of the Dutch, the French and others, Chancellor Kohl now supported his young protégé in negotiating an acceptable compromise; which John Major at one point read over the phone to Peter Lilley, his social security minister, in London to check that it was acceptable to the Thatcherite wing of his government and party. The complex opt-out gained, Major and Hurd returned to London proclaiming victory for British objectives; though even then seven Conservative MPs voted against their own government in a preliminary debate on the Maastricht package the following week.[2]

All in all, the foreign policy team could look back on a successful transition after fourteen months in office. The New Year briefings for 1992 were upbeat, claiming (as the *Guardian* put it on 2 January) 'that Britain has emerged well from the past 12 months, with its influence undiminished by the removal of Mrs Thatcher'. Douglas Hurd, in a New Year article, pointed proudly to Britain's transition from the chair of the G7 group to that of the UN Security Council in January 1992, with the presidency of the EC Council of Ministers to follow in the second half of the year. 'In recent years Britain has punched above her weight in the world,' he concluded. 'We intend to keep it that way.' There were some more hesitant notes within the press, questioning whether 'globetrotting' and personal diplomacy could substitute for a redefinition of British objectives in radically altered international circumstances.[3] But the impression provided at home was of a government which commanded international respect, facing an opposition which had no foreign policy alternative to offer: an impression which, among many other factors, helped to carry the Major government to an unexpected victory in the April general election.

DOMESTIC CONSTRAINTS AND INTERNATIONAL UNCERTAINTIES: 1992–4

This sense of confidence persisted through the spring and early summer. In May the Queen formally addressed the European Parliament: a symbolic occasion which Mrs Thatcher had blocked throughout her period in office, dignifying a European institution which challenged Westminster's claim to untrammelled parliamentary sovereignty but to which the German government in particular attached political significance. Disregarding a renewed attack by Mrs Thatcher on 'Euro-federalism' in a speech in The Hague, the House of Commons approved the second reading of the bill to ratify the Maastricht treaty the following week. John Major then left for a four-day visit to Poland, Czechoslovakia and Hungary, pursuing his interest in a wider Europe that would in time become part of an enlarged Community, which was beginning to become one of his strongest personal foreign policy priorities. British reporting of Mr and Mrs Major's 'leisurely stay' at Camp David with President and Mrs Bush, in June – his fourth visit to the USA since taking office – was rapturous. The Bush-Major relationship, the *Sunday Times* noted, 'shows every sign of being as strong as Mrs Thatcher's with President Reagan'; though adding that 'the loss of Mr Bush from the White House would be a blow to Mr Major'. With the confidence born from an electoral victory 'from behind', Mr Major was even reported to have offered the President tips on electioneering.

From then on, however, the elements of this domestically-oriented foreign policy began to unravel. The Rio de Janeiro 'Earth Summit' to which Mr Major travelled from Washington saw the Prime Minister support a compromise which satisfied neither his free market critics nor the domestic environmental lobby. Meanwhile the Danish electorate had rejected the Maastricht treaty in a referendum, after a campaign in which Conservative 'Eurosceptics' had played an active part. Faced with renewed enthusiasm for opposition to the treaty on his own back benches, the Prime Minister announced that the process of ratification in the House of Commons would be suspended, a decision which made good sense in party terms, but which looked like weakness to governments on the continent. In August the Prime Minister announced Britain's willingness to contribute a military contingent to UN peacekeeping operations in Bosnia. Now formally as President of the EC Council of Ministers responsible for ensuring a concerted West European approach, Britain could offer only a reluctant contribution: made against the resistance of a number of leading Conservative backbenchers, sending a force half the size of the French without a clear mandate, which satisfied neither its French nor its German partners. At the same time Lord Carrington resigned as the EC's mediator in the former Yugoslavia, leaving John Major to chair a joint EC-UN conference (with Boutros Boutros-Ghali) in London which failed to agree much more than the appointment of Lord Owen to replace Lord Carrington, with the parties to the Yugoslav conflict pressed to make commitments which were never implemented.

Worse, at the beginning of September speculative attacks were mounted against the lira, the peseta and the pound within the exchange rate mechanism, in the politically uncertain conditions of the French referendum campaign on Maastricht. The lira was devalued on 13 September, while Norman Lamont as Chancellor of the Exchequer reaffirmed Britain's commitment to maintain sterling's current rate. A further bout of speculation the following week, during which a large proportion of Britain's reserves were expended, nevertheless forced the pound out of the ERM. The six-month EC presidency had been transformed from a triumph of British diplomacy to an exercise in damage limitation. The German government, preoccupied with the rising cost of integrating the former East German *Länder*, had urged the British and the French to accept an adjustment of ERM rates; British stubbornness had led only to British failure. John Major summoned an emergency European Council in Birmingham for 16 October, which struggled to work through a heavy agenda ranging from monetary cooperation to Bosnia to the completion of the ratification process.

Worse yet was to come. The government's attempt to proceed with treaty ratification, in the wake of the narrow approval in the French referendum and pressures from other countries, led to undignified scenes late at night in the House of Commons, with twenty-six Conservative MPs voting against their government and a narrow majority of three obtained only by personal prime ministerial persuasion among rumours of promises given and threats made.[4] Lady Thatcher was now a brooding presence in the background, encouraging 'her' partisans to resist the drift of government policy, attracting not only old loyalists, but many of the new 1992 intake of MPs who had come into politics during her long period of political hegemony. The Conservative press was beginning to turn against the government, on foreign policy as on other issues; the sustained bias of the *Sunday Telegraph* against the European Community indeed drove the Foreign Office to issue a series of detailed rebuttals of the stories it had published.

Worst of all, for a Conservative party which under Mrs Thatcher had warmed even more strongly to the Anglo-American relationship while insisting that the link with Europe was a matter of practical politics and hard bargaining, was the outcome of the American presidential election. The Major foreign policy team had consciously invited comparison with Mrs Thatcher over the previous year, emphasizing that they carried comparable weight in Moscow because they commanded comparable confidence in Washington. An element of hubris in Conservative Central Office, after successive election campaigns in which American

Republicans had advised their British fellow-travellers, had led the Conservatives to offer detailed assistance to the Bush campaign, focusing on negative techniques to denigrate their opponents. The most valuable negative campaign information from Britain would have been evidence that Governor Clinton had been involved in anti-Vietnam activities while a student at Oxford; and it emerged that, at the request of the Bush campaign, a search had been made of the Home Office files – without effect.

Visiting Washington in mid-December in his capacity as President-in-office of the European Council, John Major had to be contented with a twenty-five-minute phone call to President-elect Clinton while he paid his farewells to President Bush. A formal apology was made to the incoming administration about the excessive zeal of British Conservatives in assisting the losing Bush campaign. 'Mr Major's personal standing at present is not high either in the EC or in America,' the *Financial Times* reported, noting that the Prime Minister's visit to Washington went entirely unreported in the American press. When Mr Major returned to Washington in February 1993 for his first direct meeting with the new President, the anxious British press was filled with articles questioning whether the valued 'special relationship' was still a reality, and with comparisons between the Clinton administration's partnerships with Germany and France and its attitude towards Britain. 'It is certainly a help to the United States to have a generally complaisant junior partner,' the *International Herald Tribune* commented, 'but rather than fret about being on Mr Clinton's blacklist, Mr Major should get to work building up a new special relationship – with Britain's European partners.'

The costs of 'punching above our weight' were also beginning to cramp the government's international ambitions. Douglas Hurd was now fighting an increasingly public battle against the Treasury to protect the FCO budget from further cuts, while struggling at the same time to find the funds for a sharp increase in Britain's contribution to UN peacekeeping operations and for new diplomatic missions in the countries emerging from the former Soviet Union. Divisions within the Cabinet over the size and duration of the British commitment to Bosnia partly reflected resistance to a potentially costly open-ended operation. Lady Thatcher from the sidelines was now calling for more robust military intervention, while other senior Conservatives held to the line that this was a continental problem which was up to continental governments to manage.

The most distinctive international prime ministerial initiative of 1993 was perhaps John Major's active support for Manchester's bid to play host to the 2000 AD Olympic Games. His personal prestige was committed, lobbying the members of the International Olympic Committee and attending Manchester's presentation to the Committee. In the final stages of the competition with Sydney and Peking, the British government brought China's human rights record into the balance, adversely affecting the delicate negotiations over the future of Hong Kong with which the Prime Minister's close friend and Hong Kong governor, Chris Patten, was struggling.

Maastricht and Bosnia dogged the government's conduct of foreign policy throughout the year. Ratification was at last completed in July; but the frustrations of the right broke out at the Conservative party conference in a series of xenophobic speeches, including two from members of the Cabinet – Peter Lilley and, more surprisingly, David Hunt.[5] The Bosnian issue divided the Conservative party in three directions, with a generally passive line from the Labour opposition vigorously compensated for by repeated demands from the Liberal Democrat leader, Paddy Ashdown, for a more active policy. As the Clinton administration began to demand a decisive response to what it saw as continued Serbian aggression, so the uncertainties of British policy began to adversely affect transatlantic relations. A bitter row erupted in January 1994 over the American administration's issuing of a visa to the Sinn Fein leader, Gerry Adams. Once again, elaborate efforts were made to demonstrate that a special relationship still existed, with Mr Major invited to sleep overnight in the White House in February. But the issue of western policy towards Bosnia, one British minister privately commented, 'has been the real poison in the relationship'.

Without a clearly developed or publicly expressed view of British foreign policy and its adaptation to the transformed European order, the Major government had attempted to tiptoe away from Mrs Thatcher's Atlantic legacy while persuading its supporters that little fundamental had changed. After its initial successes, it found itself pushed by its unreconciled right and by the expectations of the right-wing press into a series of unsatisfactory and unsustainable compromises and contradictory positions. In February 1994 Douglas Hurd addressed a mass meeting of Foreign Office staff about the need for further cuts, in an effort to stem falling professional morale. After months of resisting any increase in its military commitment to Bosnia, the government then reversed its position under American pressure and in response to the televised performances of the British commander of the UN forces in Bosnia. In March, in the final stages of negotiations for Community enlargement with Austria, Sweden, Finland and Norway, a British government whose Prime Minister had made it clear that enlargement was one of his main international priorities determinedly blocked their conclusion, digging in on an issue – that of weighted majority voting – which could have been anticipated a year earlier. The impression given to its European partners was of a government which made foreign policy while looking over its shoulder at those behind it on the parliamentary benches, unable to manage the complex multi-level games of European and global multilateral bargaining because of its domestic infirmities. The circumstances in which John Major imitated the role of Mrs Thatcher in a celebrated Commons exchange, accusing the opposition leader of being 'the poodle of Brussels', only to climb down in Community negotiations – for lack of an alternative – the following week, only confirmed this impression.

The entire international context within which British foreign policy has to be made was transformed in the four years which followed the autumn of 1989. Mrs Thatcher's inability to adjust policy or rhetoric contributed to her downfall in the autumn of 1990. John Major attempted to alter the approach – and the personal chemistry – of Britain's relations with other West European countries in the course of 1991–92, most notably and successfully with Germany and with the German Chancellor, now Britain's most important foreign partner. In relation to the USA he successfully re-established with the Bush administration the personal rapport and security partnership which Mrs Thatcher had enjoyed with President Reagan. But neither he nor Douglas Hurd as Foreign Secretary attempted to explain to the Conservative party inside or outside Parliament, or to the Conservative press, the implications of the transformation of its international environment for British foreign policy. Nor did they venture any reformulation of national interests or objectives to fit these new circumstances. Playing different games in Westminster and in Brussels, caught unprepared by changes of regime in Washington and Moscow, they became less and less successful in bridging the gap between domestic expectations and external pressures. By the spring of 1994 John Major's government, twisting between continental pressures, uncertainties in Washington, the demands of a popular British general in Bosnia, and the unforgiving hostility of its own backbenchers, had no foreign policy: no sense of Britain's place in the world or how best to use diplomacy to achieve national objectives.

Notes

1. Michael Heseltine, *The Challenge of Europe: can Britain win?* (Weidenfeld, London, 1989). See also William Wallace, 'Foreign policy and national identity in the United Kingdom', *International Affairs* 67:1 (January 1991), pp. 65–80.
2. Stephen George, 'The British Government and the Maastricht Agreement', in Alan Cafruny and Glenda Rosenthal, eds., *The State of the European Community: the Maastricht debates and beyond* (Longman, London, 1993), pp. 177–192.
3. William Wallace, 'British Foreign Policy after the Cold War', *International Affairs* 68:3 (July 1992), pp. 423–442; Christopher Coker, 'The Special Relationship in the 1990s', *ibid.*, pp. 407–422.
4. David Barker, Andrew Gamble and Steve Ludlam, 'Whips or Scorpions? The Maastricht vote and the Conservative Party',

Parliamentary Affairs 46:2 (April 1993), pp. 147–166.

5. Barker, Gamble and Ludlam, 'The Parliamentary siege of Maastricht 1993: Conservative divisions and British ratification', *Parliamentary Affairs* 47:1 (January 1994), pp. 37–60.

Chapter 17

CRIME AND PENAL POLICY

Terence Morris

Behind the idea of a 'Major effect' to be compared with that of his predecessor, Margaret Thatcher, lies a question: what, if anything, has actually altered in Britain since those fateful days in late November, 1990 when she resigned as Prime Minister. Such changes in the configuration of social policies as there have been were altogether less immediately and overtly dramatic than the transformation in the leadership of the nation. In the field of penal policy there have been undoubtedly changes, but it can be argued that the most profound shifts in the direction of penal policy have occurred during these last four Major years. Beneath the surface of events, whose condition may vary from comparative calm to the raging turbulence occasioned by some crisis, there are at work many often conflicting currents of interest, while crime itself can be readily compared to the rising and falling of the level of the tide.

THE POLITICS OF CRIMINAL JUSTICE

I have argued elsewhere[1] that crime and penal policy were at the core of the consensus politics which formed the so-called 'post-war settlement' between the major political parties.

However, in the late 1970s crime became a focus of attention for the New Right, not only in Britain but notably also in the United States. In the context of the contemporary political rhetoric, public anxieties about burglary, car crime and the threat of being robbed on the street were not infrequently presented as being on a continuum of social ills which included the predatory activities of welfare scroungers and a long suffering citizenry being held to ransom by wildcat strikes. Traditional homespun solutions, often deceptively simple in their appeal to rationality and a dominant puritan ethic that rang reassuring bells for the traditional working class and those who aspired to its no less traditional suburban counterpoise, were contrasted with an intellectualized liberalism that spoke of treatment rather than punishment and welfare instead of just desert. Many traditional Labour supporters enthused over corporal and capital punishment, demonstrating what Lipset[2] once termed 'working class authoritarianism'.

Much of the success of the New Right in its various manifestations throughout the industrial world derives from its appeal to order in situations in which existing policies appear to be impotent in the face of lawlessness. There is no doubt that in the so-called 'Winter of Discontent' of 1978–79 much of this political rhetoric was illuminated by the events of real life. If crime was something that more people seemed to experience at first hand, albeit individually rather than collectively, then the random curtailment of public services by industrial action generated a wider, shared anxiety that the time-honoured conventions which guaranteed order and civility in social life were failing under pressure. It is not without significance that much of the extraordinary loyalty that Margaret Thatcher was able to generate among ordinary people almost certainly derived from the way in which she was projected as a charismatic figure who would, as well as cleansing the Augean stable, restore the traditional values and standards which were rapidly being lost. Yet, in the event, there is little to suggest that during her eleven years in office she was in any way specially engaged with the problem of crime or the shaping of penal policy. Her first Home Secretary, William Whitelaw, was in the tradition of the line of incumbents of that office stretching back through the years of the consensus to 1945; she distanced herself from the baiting that became a standing feature of the law and order debates at party conferences. Since the majority of Tory Home Secretaries since the war have been, if not always committed to reform, then at least to the *status quo*, most have had to pay a price in the currency of such public obloquy; only his successor, Leon Brittan, seemed to please. Douglas Hurd, with a Foreign Office background, slipped easily into the ministerial chair at Queen Anne's Gate, in turn dispensing an air of urbane wisdom and authority. Her last Home Secretary, David Waddington, for all that he had been identified as being a 'hardliner' on immigration issues, proved to be consistent to the Home Office tradition which attributed prisons with the aphorism that they 'are an expensive way of making bad people worse'.

PUBLIC ORDER OR CRIME CONTROL

Alone in the public sector, the police were in the early Thatcher years generously treated both in terms of pay and resources. As such, the policy had little impact upon crime levels, and the problem of the Thatcher years was that crime rose substantially and at a rate faster than under any other post-war government, Labour or Conservative. But it was not irrelevant to what was to become one of her intensely pressing concerns, namely the challenge to government presented by the miners' strike of 1983–84 during which the coordination of inter-force assistance at New Scotland Yard by the Association of Chief Police Officers gave rise to the concern that the creation of a national police service was imminent. Urban riots had underscored the problems of public order no less than the massive picketing in other industrial disputes and by the mid-1980s the phenomena of New Age travellers and *al fresco* pop music festivals had begun to create problems in the Tory heartlands of southern England. Hitherto, public order problems had been almost exclusively limited to the inner cities, still identified as the strongholds of municipal socialism. The reaction was the Public Order Act of 1986.

In the Thatcher years government concerns about conventional crime appeared overshadowed by the need to maintain public order. Indeed urban riots, disorders associated with industrial action or the extreme violence of the poll tax demonstrations in her last year of office suggested that public tranquillity was vulnerable as it had not been for more than a century.[3] There can be little doubt that at the end of the decade the police were incomparably better trained and equipped to deal with such contingencies than they had been at its outset when they drew on the experience of the police in Hong Kong.[4] But there was nothing to match this progress in other areas of police work. The rate of detection of reported crime actually began to decline, notwithstanding that more offenders were being apprehended. Offences notified to the police rose steadily throughout the decade from 2.5m in 1980 to reach just under 4.4m in 1990. A Home Office research report based on the 1988 British Crime Survey indicated that public confidence in the police had declined throughout the 1980s. What the average citizen wanted to see was not more policemen in riot gear on his TV screen, but more friendly bobbies on his street.

Nor on the prison front was there much about which to rejoice. Police cells had to take overflow populations and on 1 April 1990 Strangeways prison in Manchester erupted in an orgy of savage violence that was to last for no less than twenty-five days and become the longest, most vicious and most destructive prison riot in Britain in this century or any other. The repercussions for the remainder of the prison system, which was not spared from imitative disorder, were considerable and resulted in the establishment of an inquiry under the chairmanship of Lord Justice Woolf.

NEW MANAGEMENT: THE ARRIVAL
OF JOHN MAJOR

Though there are superficial similarities in the backgrounds of Margaret Thatcher and John Major, there are substantial divergences. She was a woman who had scaled seemingly impossible heights to become leader of the party and a figure on the stage of world history, appearing ever engaged in a series of titanic struggles in which she would emerge triumphant. In self-reference she assumed the regal plural. John Major appeared, at least at the outset, as the kind of man one would meet in the car park of any DIY store loading veneered chipboard shelves into his hatchback. In contrast to her hauteur, he exemplified the kind of common man whose image had been projected in a million advertisements embodying a reassuring approach to the kinds of things that trouble reasonable people, such as crime or injustice. It was entirely consistent with this image that one who could include in a speech to his party conference a reference to the need to improve the provision of 'comfort stops' on motorways for families with young children should also be committed to the notion of citizen's charters.

The first opening for this man of fairness and common sense came in March 1990 after the final collapse of the Crown case against the Birmingham Six. The Home Secretary, Kenneth Baker, who had gone to the Home Office on the same day that Major went to Downing Street, appointed the first Royal Commission for a decade to scrutinize the criminal justice system with a view to devising ways in which such miscarriages of justice might be avoided in the future. Grave public disquiet about so many serious cases had gone largely ignored during the Thatcher years and it was accepted that she herself had little time for Royal Commissions composed of the 'great and the good', preferring that policymakers should take the advice of those whose competence was self-evident from their success in business enterprise. The swiftness with which the Royal Commission was announced was indicative of Major's concern that something should be done to prevent a repetition of such injustices and an attempt at damage limitation where confidence in the courts and the judiciary was concerned. It came too late to prevent over a hundred members from putting down a Commons early day motion calling for the dismissal of the Lord Chief Justice, Lord Lane, who was unfairly targeted as the scapegoat for the shortcomings of the appellate system, though it successfully dissipated some of the political heat.

POLICIES FOR PRISONS

By the end of February 1991 Woolf's report on the Strangeways riot was published. It included the establishment of national standards of what prisons would provide by way of service to inmates and what would be expected of them in return, greater autonomy for prison governors and the coordination of the criminal justice system through Criminal Justice Councils that would operate on both a national and local basis. Much of what Woolf recommended was entirely consistent with the 'Charter' philosophy with which John Major had become personally identified. Seven months later the white paper, 'Custody Care and Justice: The Way Ahead for The Prison Service in England and Wales,' proposed the adoption of all but six of Woolf's suggestions, including the idea of a Criminal Justice Consultative Council.

But the government had another agenda for the prison system than that reflexively generated by riotous inmates. In August, Admiral Sir Raymond Lygo was appointed to head a review of prison service management and by December he had reported in favour of the prison service becoming an executive agency, a recommendation put into effect on 1 April 1993 under the directorship of Derek Lewis who came to prisons from television management. Such a move was entirely consistent with the Next Steps programme which had been inaugurated under Margaret Thatcher and of which John Major had always been an enthusiastic supporter. By contracting out work previously done in Whitehall it was believed that reduction in cost and improvement in service would go hand in hand. But for the government, prisons were beset by another problem: the power of the Prison Officers'

Association. Alone of all the public service unions which had flexed their industrial muscle in the late 1970s, the POA had evaded the gelding iron of the new industrial relations laws that had rendered so many powerful unions politically impotent during the Thatcher years. The solution to the problem of controlling what was perceived to be the Luddite element in the POA lay directly in the path of government policy; the move to agency status was concordant with the policy of 'contracting out' and all that it implied by way of new conditions of employment.

During Douglas Hurd's tenure at the Home Office it was suggested by certain enthusiastic admirers of 'private' prisons[5] in the United States that the time was ripe for experiment here. It is understood that he was unimpressed. But the movement of the prison system to agency status as a logical development of the Next Steps programme clearly indicated the advantages of contracting out the provision of custodial services and held the additional prospect of effectively breaking the long established ascendancy of the POA. Though at no time was this ever publicly proclaimed as an inclusive objective of moving the prison system further from the centre of government it could be regarded as a fortuitous consequence.

Under Kenneth Baker the movement towards the contracting out of prison services gathered momentum. In November 1991 it was announced that the new Wolds Prison on Humberside was to be run by the Group 4 company which already had the management of the Heathrow immigration detention facility; on 3 April 1992 the Wolds opened. Five days later Group 4 began its contract for the escort of prisoners and in spite of the fact that the first week embarrassingly produced no fewer than four escapes Baker's successors at the Home Office, Kenneth Clarke and Michael Howard, not only continued with that policy (the contract for London escorts, reputedly worth £96m, went to Securicor in December 1993) but moved towards the commercial sector for prisons with growing rather than diminished enthusiasm.

The next stage envisages inviting private companies to submit proposals for a tripartite package for the design, construction and management of a new generation of prisons. Again, this is a logical step towards resolving a paradox; while the pressure on prisons represents a growth in the effective demand for places, Treasury constraints on public expenditure make it impossible to envisage a massive prison building programme at the public expense. The second stage of contracting out will parallel the use of private capital in other major public construction projects. Meanwhile, the concept of 'market testing' has resulted in prison staff having to make competitive bids against the private sector for the running of existing prisons. At the newly rebuilt Strangeways the staff bid was successful.

SORTING OUT THE POLICE

In line with the underlying philosophy that the market should increasingly shape even those institutions for which contracting out was not yet in place and for which public divestment was not on the agenda, attention turned to the question of ranks and rewards in the police service. On 6 July 1992 Clarke announced the composition and terms of reference of an inquiry under the chairmanship of Sir Patrick Sheehy, Chairman of British American Tobacco, which was to report within ten months. The police feared that its intention was to provide a cover for cost-cutting exercises and especially the abandonment of the pay formula accepted following the report of Lord Justice Edmund Davies in 1978. Towards the end of the year leaks appeared in the press to the effect that the Home Office was, additionally, conducting a wholly secret in-house review of policing organization and accountability.[6] In the event, Sheehy's recommendations confirmed their worst fears. Performance related pay and fixed-term contracts were proposed alongside a reduction in the number of ranks. Whatever its merits as a management review – and there are aspects of administration which deserve closer scrutiny – the report was immensely damaging to the relationship between police and government and reflected a quantum change from the halcyon days of the early 1980s when the police enjoyed not merely the confidence but the largesse of the first Thatcher administration.

POLICY SHIFTS INTO REVERSE GEAR

Much of the closer engagement of government with criminal justice in the Major era has originated from a desire to provide better service and better value for money, albeit within a framework of ideas that stem from the central belief in the natural superiority of the market over all other devices for the allocation of resources in the public sector. It has been concordant with the spirit of the citizen's charters. But the most extraordinary feature of the period has been the way in which the direction of penal policy has changed, some would say by 180 degrees on to a reciprocal course. For apart from the Children Act of 1988, perhaps the most important and forward looking recent legislation in the Home Office field, there has been the Criminal Justice Act of 1991. Conceived in the last part of the Thatcher era, it went through its parliamentary stages in the first year of John Major's premiership. That its parentage was Civil Service rather than political is transparent, but for all that it was enthusiastically promoted by government, warmly accepted in Parliament and came into effect in October 1992. In essence, it sought to shift the emphasis of penal policy from custodial solutions to community based penalties which accorded well with the phrase 'punishment in the community'. Under the Act the use of imprisonment was restricted to offences that were 'serious enough'. There were new rules to discount the effect of previous convictions. Perhaps most novel was the move to the unit fine, a penalty based upon a combination of a numerical value accorded to the seriousness of the offence and the offender's disposable income.

In the autumn of 1992 Home Office ministers were speaking positively of the probation service as moving to the centre stage of criminal justice and funds being provided to accommodate the wider use of community penalties and bail hostels. But there was a climatic change on the way. Kenneth Clarke had succeeded Baker at the Home Office after the election in April 1992 and initially promoted the aims of the 1991 Act. But neither unit fines nor restrictions on the applicability of previous convictions were popular among the magistracy and anomalies were given great publicity although the original formulae for unit fines were capable of sensible amendment. By summer of 1993 the campaign against them in principle had been so successful that Clarke bowed to the pressure and these radical innovations were scrapped.[7] Just as he acceded to the pressures of the magistracy, so he seemed to shift away from emphasis on community penalties and back towards custody, proposing a new generation of secure training centres for twelve to fourteen year old offenders. In May 1993 he told a public meeting that he had no view on the size of the prison population which had been rising from the beginning of the year by an average of 17 per cent. Clarke's departure for the Treasury after the resignation of Norman Lamont resulted in the elevation of Michael Howard to the Home Office and the new policy shifted up a gear.

CALLING TIME ON THE CRIMINAL

By the summer of 1993, prison numbers were not only increasing but Home Office ministers seemed not to see this as a negation of the principles enunciated in the 1991 Act which the government had earlier promoted with such enthusiasm. Howard appeared to make little secret of the fact that he took a diametrically opposed view on the merits of prison from traditionalists such as Hurd and Waddington. It was the party conference that was to be the setting for perhaps one of the most notable speeches of a Home Secretary since the war, Howard setting out the now famous 27 points of policy for criminal justice. At the heart of this was the contention that 'Prison works!' The rhetoric at this time was nothing if not robust, employing other such popular ejaculations as 'Let's take the handcuffs off the police and put them on the criminals where they belong' and 'Yobs who break the law shouldn't be taken on holidays abroad ... Let's get them picking up litter and scrubbing off graffiti.' They echoed the sentiments of many perfectly reasonable but otherwise exasperated citizens who felt that it was about time someone 'called time' on the perpetrators of increasing public incivility. Thus the Conservative conference of 1993 became in effect an advertisement hoarding for the forthcoming bills on Criminal Justice and Public Order and the Police and Magistrates Courts which were to be published in December. Howard was not the only minister to make a speech at Conference which seemed to echo the concerns of the 'reasonable' voter. References in other speeches to single mothers and feckless welfare claimants seemed to give consistency to the 'time is up' approach to those whose predatory and parasitic activities were sapping the vitality of Britain.

A PERSONAL ROLE

In contrast with his predecessor, it can be argued that John Major has been much more closely identified with the direction of policies broadly concerned with the process of social control, including control through welfare. As early as February 1993 he was saying[8] that crime, which he identified as a characteristic of socialist-governed inner cities, could not be explained in terms of affluence and poverty and it was '... insulting to those families who may face all the problems of unemployment and yet do not resort to crime', maintaining in the Commons the following day that 'There is no excuse for crime. Society is not to blame and individuals are.'

Although the evidence must remain circumstantial, it is not implausible to suggest that the hand of the Prime Minister was more often giving a touch on the tiller of criminal justice policy throughout 1993 than was ever the case with Margaret Thatcher.

This shift in policy needs to be scrutinized in two dimensions; that of political opportunism and that of amending policy to fit changing circumstances. Politics, as Bismarck sagely observed, is the art of the possible. Given the need to repair the icon of government which had been damaged by the disunity over Maastricht and the desire to show that on the domestic front this was indeed a government of action, the themes of the 1993 conference developed around the Prime Minister's own proposals for a 'Back to Basics' campaign. The prominence of criminal justice issues reflected what must have been a rational decision taken on the advice of party managers, for no less damaging were the polls that indicated that the Tories were no longer clearly the citizens' choice as the party best able to deal with law and order. Thanks to the vigorous performance of Labour's shadow minister, Tony Blair, whose slogan 'Tough on crime and tough on the causes of crime' directly challenged John Major in his own kind of language, the recapture of this lost territory became essential.

LEGISLATION WITH TRIBULATION

It was the Police and Magistrates Courts bill that was first before Parliament in January 1994. Like its sibling, the Criminal Justice and Public Order bill, it was met with hostility from virtually the entire spectrum of reformers and many practitioners. Lord Taylor, who had succeeded Lane as Lord Chief Justice, criticized it in the Upper House and at a public meeting of *Justice*, the British section of the International Commission of Jurists, the following day; Lords Callaghan (Labour) and Carr and Whitelaw (Conservative), all previous Home Secretaries, contributed to its hostile reception, not least due to the way in which the bill proposed substantially greater Home Office powers in the appointment and control of the proposed new Police Authorities. That part which dealt with the pay and conditions of the clerks to magistrates – incorporating centralized control by the Lord Chancellor's Department and fixed term contracts – received no warmer a welcome.

The Royal Commission on Criminal Justice had, meanwhile, come up with a series of proposals that were not to everyone's liking, reaffirming the so-called 'right to silence' but recommending the removal of the defendant's until now inalienable right to elect jury trial.[9] But, more importantly, it suggested a Criminal Cases Review Body to remedy some of the defects of the appellate system that had been exposed so prominently. The Criminal Justice and Public Order Bill (for good reasons) made no reference to the review body and eschewed the abolition of the right to elect jury trial. It did, however, propose to do away with the 'right to silence' although this, in common with a number of other proposals, was subsequently modified during the passage of the bill. Just as it had become clear that by the end of 1993 many of the complex issues raised by the Runciman Commission on Criminal Justice were fast fading from public consciousness, it became equally clear that for all the government had sought its advice when it came to legislation it intended to be eclectic in choosing what it determined to be acceptable.

The bill as published contained many powerful and (some would argue) reactionary provisions, making life much more difficult for groups such as non-violent hunt saboteurs and well nigh impossible not merely for the so-called New Age travellers and weekend 'ravers' but for those who account themselves true gypsies. The number of amendments that have appeared combined with the significant number of government concessions to critics together suggests that both bills were drafted under pressure and not always with sufficient anticipatory political intelligence gathering as to the likely strength of the opposition. The inclusion, for example, of provisions for secure centres for juveniles to be managed by the private sector has earned the wrath of the penal reform pressure groups.

By the spring of 1994 the great designs that had been sketched out at the party conference in October 1993 were undergoing drastic amendment. As the Back to Basics campaign was driven on to the reef of sexual irregularity, government spokesmen feverishly maintained that the basic morality implied in its title was not individual and sexual but essentially social, citing the need to reduce crime and public incivilities generally. The passage of the two bills embodying the proposals outlined to such acclaim by the conference delegates was difficult from the outset. But what was more serious was that the tide of crime had, until 1993, continued inexorably to rise throughout John Major's tenure of office. At the end of 1990 the figure of recorded crime stood at 4.3m; for 1992 the corresponding figure was 5.6m, but the rate of increase appeared to be slowing substantially. However, in 1993 the publication of data from the British Crime

Survey of 1992 indicated that the real level of crime (as a result of under-reporting by victims) was nearer to three times the official figure. Other data suggested that the rate of increase was now less of a problem in the socialist dominated urban locations than in rural areas. Moreover, the clear up rate continues to fall; between 1990 and 1992 from 32 per cent to 26 per cent.

The figures published early in 1993 indicated that there had been a slight fall in recorded crime. Such variations must be interpreted with caution. According to a recent poll, public confidence in the ability of the police to deal with crime has diminished and while the precise effect of this on incentives to report crime is difficult to quantify it cannot be discounted. Just as those engaged in the black economy do not send their returns to the Department of Trade, so the experiences of many victims who do not, for a variety of reasons, wish to become involved with the police is lost to public view. There is no reason to ignore the fact that the victim survey data still indicate a true figure in excess of 15m.

As far as crime in general is concerned, the evidence suggests that both the predominant types of crime and the increased lawlessness of the last decade are best understood in terms of the long-term changes in British society that have been taking place for almost twenty years.[10] Juveniles and young adults are almost certainly responsible for most serious crime and there is reason to think that the growth of poverty that had been associated with the economic and social changes of the period may have made a contribution, certainly in the specific context of youth unemployment. But the underlying changes have been more fundamental; the progressive weakening of the traditional social bonds of family and community and the final transformation of the traditional function of state primary and secondary schools from one of pedagogically oriented social control to one of competitively – and socially divisive – oriented acquisition of knowledge and skills. The role of the Victorian Board School, which persisted as a model for primary education well into the present century, has been rapidly forgotten. Its high walls and oaken gates and the omniscient vigilance of its 'School Board Man' guaranteed that the children of the 'Lower

Orders' were constructively incarcerated for a critical portion of the day. It is the virtual disappearance of a range of auxiliary agents of social control from park keepers to bus conductors and school attendance officers which has left the police overexposed and inadequately resourced to deal with the problems of crime.

In that it is impossible to legislate for morality, however fervent the desire to return to 'basics', criminal justice policies can do no more than attempt to regulate the worst excesses of social misconduct. But to do so, they must have some reasonable chance of hitting their target and unfortunately, the bulk of the legislation now in progress can only hope to bear upon those who have already been discovered by the process of successful prosecution. This is no more than a very small proportion of those who are committing offences. For this reason it is more likely that the effect of the new direction of John Major's penal policies will be to satisfy those who nourish an enthusiasm to make offenders suffer, irrespective of whether the outcome is a reduction in crime or not. The judgment of historians of criminal justice on the legislation of the 1993 session may well be that it was reflexive rather than reflective in character; the broom may have been wielded with vigour but arguably to little ultimate effect. Dame Partington and Sisyphus had much in common.

MAJOR EFFORT BUT LITTLE EFFECT

All the signs are that the rapid alteration of course in criminal justice legislation has been determined by considerations that are political and subjective rather than deriving from a longer-term strategy. From the summer of 1993 to the spring of 1994, the problem facing John Major was increasingly – and ironically – one of political survival. Although the arcane mysteries of Maastricht and voting rules in an enlarged EU were the source of wounds within the Tory party, they are issues which at best mystify the electorate and at worst bore it to inanition. Its anxious concerns about the economy – and it sees tax increases more clearly than green shoots – and the especially personal fears of becoming the victim of redundancy or crime – or both – seemed curiously unaddressed. The heady draughts of political rhetoric which in 1993 flowed from conference hall to living room by way of the medium of television were long since drained. They had encouraged a belief that this transparently sensible man, with concerns no different from a million others of his class and generation, was, with his team, at last going to sort out the muggers, the burglars, the rapists and those odiously recalcitrant juveniles who, it would seem, the more often they offended the more they were indulged with a welfare version of Danegeld. Whatever the therapeutic merits of sending juvenile offenders on safari or steamer journeys down the Nile, such practices have a distinctly Erewhonian flavour.

The reality is that any speedy and immediately visible improvement in the crime situation is most unlikely to occur, no matter how resolute new policies may be. In this history is a cruelly disappointing if truthful teacher, for severity of punishment without certainty of detection can be as ineffectual as it can be the source of injustice. Similarly, increasing resort to carceral solutions for social problems is often equally lacking in effect but ruinously expensive. It is not enough simply to identify the cause of crime as criminals; crime of the kind that afflicts Britain and much of the post-industrial world reflects an altogether deeper malaise. It presents a complex, multi-faceted problem which demands carefully considered action. Like the conduct of foreign wars, it is probably best prosecuted in an atmosphere of political cooperation rather than inter-party competition.

Notes

1. In *Crime and Criminal Justice in Britain since 1945* (Blackwell for ICBH, Oxford, 1989).
2. Seymour Martin Lipset, *Political Man: Essays on the Sociology of Democracy* (Doubleday, New York, 1959).
3. For Margaret Thatcher such people were, in truth, the 'enemy within'.

4. See Northam, G., *Shooting in the Dark: Riot Police in Britain* (Faber and Faber, London, 1988).

5. In speaking of 'privatization' in this context its must be understood as being quite different from, say, the sell-off of public utilities such as gas, electricity, water or telephones. There is a distinction between the contracting out of the management of state owned prisons and contractual agreements on the part of the Prison Service Agency with prison companies for the incarceration of prisoners. Privately owned prisons in which inmates are incarcerated under contract represent a third variant.

6. See Robert Reiner, 'Police and Public Order' in Catterall, P. and Preston, V., eds., *Contemporary Britain: An Annual Review* (Blackwell for ICBH, Oxford, 1993) for further discussion of the constitutional implications of this secret inquiry.

7. Yet he was holding the line on unit fines as late as 6 May, only a week before the announcement that they were to be scrapped, telling a meeting of magistrates that he was in favour of the system but that it needed refining.

8. At the Carlton Club on 2 February 1993.

9. Mode of trial would thus be at the discretion of the magistrates where there was an option between summary trial and trial on indictment.

10. When Margaret Thatcher maintained at the time of the Brixton riots that 'nothing could excuse' them, she was speaking in accord with the old French proverb 'qui s'excuse, s'accuse'. There is nevertheless, an important distinction to be drawn between causal explanations and moral judgements, nothwithstanding that causal explanations may appear to be morally unacceptable.

Chapter 18

HEALTH AND SOCIAL POLICY

Howard Glennerster

WHAT'S THE TUNE?

Is there anything that could be said to constitute a Major social policy theme? If one exists it is difficult to pick out. That is partly because at the end of the Thatcher period her government passed a series of very distinctive policy measures, such as the reform of the National Health Service, which it has fallen to the Major government to implement. To this extent there has been a theme tune but it was not composed by Mr Major. His main contribution was to add a coda, 'The Citizen's Charter' announced at a press conference in July 1991. It was to set specified performance targets for public services, including the social services. This initiative reflected a belief that his government's distinctive contribution should be to improve the standard of public services, a very different stance from that taken by Mrs Thatcher who distrusted the capacity of any public service to provide satisfaction.

The attitude of the two Prime Ministers to the National Health Service encapsulates this different philosophy. In the last television interview he gave in the election campaign of 1992 Mr Major showed most passion and sincerity talking about the National Health Service, what it had meant to his own family, supporting the principles on which it was based.

It was a performance that Mrs Thatcher could never have achieved or have wanted to. He chose as Secretary of State for Health Virginia Bottomley, a knowledgeable and a similarly committed supporter of the NHS. Here, then, is one theme.

However, midway through his premiership, at the Conservative party conference in 1993, Mr Major allowed certain members of his orchestra to start experimenting with another tune altogether. Such improvizations lead to a diverting little movement variously called 'Back to Basics' or 'family values blues'. This movement is reviewed in chapter 20 of this book by Ruth Lister; it did not make the main theme tune any easier to appreciate.

At the same time a really serious counter-theme began to emerge. The Chief Secretary to the Treasury, Mr Portillo, who was in charge of public expenditure, announced a fundamental long-term review of social policy and the level of public spending that was to begin in 1993 and take at least two years to complete. The Secretary of State for Social Security, Mr Peter Lilley, unusually for a spending minister, made it clear that he supported such a move and would be doing his utmost to cooperate and fundamentally rethink the role of social security. His claims that social security spending would go on rising in an unsupportable way[1] were challenged by independent analysts.[2] However, both political parties were being forced to face up to the inconsistency of their basic positions on social policy. The Conservative party were pledged to *reduce* taxation while the fundamentals of demography and the economics of social provision were tending to expand the need to spend. Merely maintaining the existing level of services into the next century would mean increasing taxation by 5 per cent of the GDP in the next fifty years. The circle could not be squared except by steadily reducing the standard of service – in higher education by cutting spending per pupil, in social security lowering the basic pension relative to average earnings. Such pressures on standards were contrary to Major's central goal of service quality.

The Labour Party was struggling with equally unattainable ambitions and its attempt to find a way out, the report of the Social Justice Commission, was to be published in the autumn of 1994.

This rumbling portent of thunder was growing through 1994. In March 1994 the Adam Smith Institute, who gave us the poll tax, published their manifesto for Conservative social policy entitled *The End of the Welfare State*.[3] At the time of writing, this had not yet become the dominant opinion but it makes any review of the period, at this stage, provisional.

Another rumbling theme that was also exposing basic conflicts related to Europe. Historically the EEC had had little or no effect on UK social policy. However, many of those on the continent of Europe and especially in the bureaucracies take the view that the logic of a single market requires harmonization of social legislation. Countries with low social benefits and labour costs have some kind of unfair advantage and Britain falls into that category. Those countries with high benefits will attract benefit recipients: social dumping. This logic lay behind the move to add a social chapter to the Maastricht treaty. It was opposed by the Major government on the grounds that it would increase labour costs and governmental interference. Countries ought to be free to compete with whatever form of social policy they think most effective, hence the determination of the British government to opt out of the social chapter, an objective Mr Major achieved. Europe would continue to play a small part in UK social policy. We cannot understand Mr Major's social programme without a backward look at Mrs Thatcher's legacy. It set Major's own agenda to a significant degree. Then, the outcome of the NHS reforms are discussed because they encapsulate the essence of his wider philosophy.

MRS THATCHER'S LEGACY

Fiscal tightness and rebound There is no doubt that Mrs Thatcher's decade was a decisive one for social policy. She altered the terms of debate but it was not until the end of her period in office that distinctive legislative changes were placed on the statute book.

There was no reduction in the share of the nation's income devoted to social spending. There *was* an end to the century long rise in that share. This was achieved despite the substantial rise in spending needed to finance growing unemployment benefits and left services such as health in a serious situation. Public opinion moved more and more clearly in favour of spending extra on social services, notably on health and education.[4] This legacy caused its own reaction. In the run-up to the general election of 1992, when Major was Chancellor and then Prime Minister, the Conservative government permitted two relaxed public expenditure rounds which for a brief period allowed the NHS to grow faster than at any time since the 1960s. It was a process that had to be reversed yet again in Clarke's 1993 new autumn budget.

A strong central state It is wrong to think of Mrs Thatcher's government as one that reduced the role of the state in social policy. It did the reverse. Moreover, it concentrated state power more decisively at the centre.[5] In education a National Curriculum politicized an area of life previously excluded from explicit day-to-day party politics. The new grant maintained schools were to receive funds directly from central government. In health much closer central accountability was imposed on regions and districts and local representatives were excluded from these agencies. The result was to focus political attention on central government even more than in the past.

Greater inequality Perhaps the most important legacy of the 1980s were the sharp divisions that began to appear in the social fabric. Incomes of those in the labour market began to diverge more sharply than at any time since the Second World War. Unemployment rose to levels not known since the 1930s and on top of that the government deliberately reduced the tax burdens on the higher income groups and increased them on lower incomes. The poorest families became worse off in this decade.[6]

Such trends, at least as far as incomes are concerned, were not confined to the United Kingdom. Nearly all western societies have experienced growing inequality, beginning with the United States in the early 1970s, followed by the UK in the late 1970s and other countries later still.[7] This reversed at least a century of gradually equalizing effects of social policy on society.

Thus, social policy under any government is having to spend more and run harder to secure the same safety net. The reasons for this are basic economic ones.

Increasing public sector efficiency In the early part of Mrs Thatcher's period no really fundamental changes in social policy took place. Council house sales and the right to buy were significant but not revolutionary. The Fowler reforms to social security that came into effect after 1988 were immensely complex but their net effect has proved minimal.[8] It was not until 1988–90 that there was a glut of really important legislation which rivalled that of the years 1944–48 in significance.

Under the 1988 Housing Act alternative landlords could take over individual council properties with the agreement of the tenant, or estates or the whole of a council's stock of houses. Under the 1988 Education Act schools could opt out of local authority control and parents had free choice of schools that became funded on a formula basis, depending on the number of children attending. In effect, this introduced a system of parent-based or voucher funding. The 1990 National Health Service and Community Care Act turned district health authorities into purchasing agencies, losing their managerial responsibility for hospitals and taking on instead the task of contracting for health services with competing hospitals. Similarly social service departments were to become purchasers of care for their elderly and disabled populations.

Taken together this legislation was the biggest break with social policy tradition since 1945. It had several common threads:

1. the devolution of budgetary responsibility to schools, to care managers in social service departments, to housing estates, and to general practitioners.
2. the notion of introducing competition between public service agencies to obtain public funding: for example, hospitals having to gain contracts from district health authorities.

3. the capacity of public agencies to free themselves of local political control; housing estates could become owned and managed by housing associations, schools could become grant maintained directly by central government, social services contracted out to private agencies.

This collection of 'quasi market' reforms[9] were intended to improve the efficiency of these services short of full privatization. All of this legislation predated Mr Major but in many ways it encapsulated his philosophy and that of the centre left of the Tory party. At the time the National Health Service reforms were being discussed in 1988, those on the right of the party were advocating privatizing the NHS or at least moving it to a position in which the private sector could play a large role. However, even Nigel Lawson, who describes himself as Tory Radical, shows in his account of his period as Chancellor[10] that he became convinced that the NHS, as a public institution, was good value for money and that the private market was not the appropriate solution for health care. The efficiency advocates therefore won the argument in the end, suggesting that the public funding of the NHS should continue but that its provision could be improved by introducing competition between NHS hospitals. Clarke, Major's supporter, and later Chancellor, was a strong advocate of this approach.

Thus, Major was comfortable with this set of late Thatcher social legislation as he was not with the poll tax. To a very large extent it set the framework for social policy in the Major era. Of that group of measures it is the reform to the National Health Service that best exemplifies the Major theme tune and, no doubt, how he would like to be judged. Legislated in 1990, the health reforms were introduced in April 1991 and have provoked much interest abroad.

THE HEALTH SERVICE REFORMS: AN ASSESSMENT

In 1987, when the Conservative Party was elected to power for the third time, there was no hint that the National Health

Service was about to undergo its most fundamental reform for a generation. The NHS was not unpopular. Indeed, it was, and is, considered one of the most successful of all British social institutions. Dissatisfaction did increase substantially in the 1980s as the regular surveys of British social attitudes show but, 'Far from reducing allegiance to the NHS, dissatisfaction appears to fuel demands for extra expenditure and attention'.[11] The NHS was not expensive by international standards. Health took less of the UK's GNP than almost any other European country (5.6 per cent in 1989 compared to an OECD average of 7.6 per cent). Yet levels of health outcomes in the UK population were similar to those of neighbouring countries. It was and is a remarkably cost effective institution in *macro*-economic terms. The government aimed to preserve free, or almost free, access to health care and to keep tax based finance, but use competition between providers of the service to obtain more health gains and more consumer satisfaction *within* a tight budget. 'The principles that have guided it [the NHS] for the last forty years will continue to guide it into the twenty first century.'[12]

THE REFORMS

The central idea that underpins the new NHS is the distinction between the purchaser and the provider of services. The latter compete for the contracts set by the former. There are, however, two kinds of purchaser and each embodies a different model of purchasing. First and of central importance are the district health authorities. They are funded on a formula basis from central government and have the task of determining the health needs of their populations and purchasing services for them from the most suitable providers. Patients have no choice of purchaser unless they move into another area.

The exceptions are those patients who belong to a family doctor who has decided to become a GP fund-holder. These are the second type of purchaser. Groups of GPs with more than 7,000 patients can opt to become purchasers for a range of non-emergency hospital services, outpatient clinics and community health services. About a third of the population were covered by such family doctor purchasers in 1994. The closest analogy is the Health Maintenance Organization in the United States.[13] Hospitals and community services can opt to become independent trusts with their own governing bodies, receiving capital from central government, employing their own staff on their own contracts and terms of service. They compete for contracts from the District Health Authorities and GPs. By 1994 the great majority of hospitals had become trusts.

RESULTS

The government itself supported no comprehensive programme of evaluative research on the reforms it had initiated. It was left to the King's Fund to finance a series of projects designed to do that.[14] Other limited evidence is available. In what follows it is discussed under three main headings:
- Impact on expenditure;
- Impact on health service processes;
- Impact on equity in health care.

IMPACT ON EXPENDITURE

We have argued that the 1991 changes were not designed to reduce spending but to help government sustain a tight control on the health budget. In fact, in the short run, they had the opposite effect. The proposed reforms proved so unpopular politically and with the medical profession that the government were forced to increase the health budget to buy off this opposition. The changes themselves also involved higher long-term costs. Contracts, rather than vague understandings, require negotiation before the contract is set and monitoring and contract compliance after it. They need information, not least financial information. Many more managers and financial systems and accounting and contract staff had to be employed.

The combined result was to increase the budget taken by the NHS in the years before and immediately after the reforms were introduced. Indeed, for a period the NHS budget rose at rates not seen since the 1960s. (See Table 1.) The reduction in waiting lists and the other benefits the government claim for the reforms cannot be easily separated from this spending background. In the most recent public expenditure announcements[15] health spending is to be restrained again, back to the kind of rates of increases that sparked off the changes in the first place. For this reason, if no other, it would be wise to suspend judgment on the reforms.

Table 1: National Health Expenditure control totals

Year	Real expenditure Increase % on previous year
1989/90 White Paper	0.8
1990/1 Preparation year	4.1
1991/2 1st year	6.8
1992/3 2nd year	6.2
1993/4 3rd year (est)	1.3
1994/5 4th year (plan)	0.8
1995/6 5th year (plan)	0.5
1996/7 6th year (plan)	0.5

Source: HM Treasury

IMPACT ON HEALTH SERVICE PROCESSES

To work a market, quasi or not, would need:
- a clear divide between purchaser and provider;
- competition between providers;
- competition between purchasers;
- adequate information for purchasers;

- freedom to let the market work.
- a way to link the government's strategy to purchasing intentions.

Few of these conditions hold.

THE PURCHASER/PROVIDER SPLIT AND COMPETITION

In practice, this distinction is not as clear as the ideal suggests.

At the outset, in 1991, most hospitals remained 'district managed units' making the role of the districts very confused. The rapid spread of trusts is remedying this. Nearly all hospitals will have trust status by 1995.

The reforms freed districts from the pressures of managerial problems such as nurse grading reviews and labour disputes in the hospital laundry and concentrated their attention on thinking about local health needs and priorities. Hospitals and other providers have been left with the clear responsibility to manage themselves. Hospital trust status does seem to have focused the minds of those running hospitals on the need to survive and win custom. In particular, it has lead clinicians to take more financial and managerial responsibility.

However, the reality of this split is still far from clear or fully realized and the purchasing function remains undeveloped.

- Since 1961 government policy has been to build large district general hospitals to serve most of the needs of the district. District Health Authorities were set up to run them. Thus in most districts there exists one dominant provider that has traditionally had close links with the district and its officials.
- District officials are, in the end, responsible to politically appointed masters and want to minimize political embarrassment likely to follow from decisions not to contract on a large scale with the local hospital. A 'contractual relationship' does not transform that political reality.

- In all health care markets the purchaser is always in a weak position compared to the producer. Contracting skills are at a premium and the detailed medical knowledge required to bargain on equal terms with a hospital consultant in his or her specialism is simply absent. Those doing the contracting are often inexperienced and poorly equipped to do the job. They have to rely on the providers to tell them what is needed.

One evaluation of purchasing in the West Midlands concluded:

> Evidence from our project over the last three years suggests that purchasers were still trying to get to grips with the basic information they required to assess health care needs and make rational decisions concerning the choice of provider – based on quantifiable measures of quality, reliable data on prices, and, importantly, local opinion. But in addition, purchasers are only just beginning to grapple with the underlying methodologies of priority setting, the construction of contracts and the information implications of monitoring contract performance.[16]

Probably the main deficiency of the reforms to date is, therefore, the weak contracting capacity of districts. The government came to recognize this.[17]

GENERAL PRACTITIONERS AS PURCHASERS

Fund-holding GPs only have responsibility for purchasing non-emergency hospital care and community services, about 20% of the relevant budget. Since 1993 their purchasing powers have been extended and include community services such as district nursing.

Within that range of services GPs do seem to have done a better job of purchasing. They have been more prepared to diversify providers, to challenge hospital practices and demand improvements. The reasons go to the heart of the original debate. GPs are closer to patients than districts are. They see patients before they go into hospital and after they come out. They hear about their complaints. They, as doctors, stand to be affected by delays in treatment to their patients who are, as a result, more of a burden on their time. GPs have medical knowledge and status to confront hospital doctors in contracting. In short, with GPs as purchasers the information balance is more equal. They also have the motivation to contract on patients' behalf.[18]

On the other hand GPs are less well informed about area wide trends in disease and analyses of the kind that are necessary to decide where to place an accident and emergency centre. GPs also vary enormously in their competence to perform the purchasing task. The optimal boundary line between district or area wide purchasing and GP lead purchasing has probably still to be found.

IMPACT ON EQUITY IN HEALTH CARE

Though not explicitly stated as a goal in the government's white paper, equity and equal access are deep in the public's perception of what the health service is there to deliver. In the past forty odd years since the service was created it has succeeded in reducing the inequalities in the spread of GPs and hospital resources between regions.

We have argued that GP fund-holders are more effective purchasers of more regular hospital care than districts. If that is so, patients of fund-holders will get better and quicker treatment. This is seen to be unfair and the fund-holding system has come in for much criticism, which seems perverse, unless the critics believe in the principle of equal misery. The logic lies in extending the benefits of GP-based purchasing to all practices. The Conservative government seemed to be moving down that road in the summer of 1994.

CONCLUSIONS

John Major's period in office essentially did nothing to solve the basic dilemmas facing social policy in the UK. Electoral popularity and a nice-guy image were achieved by releasing the brakes on social spending in the early 1990s. That produced an unsustainably high public sector borrowing requirement and forced a party pledged to reduce taxation to increase it substantially in the autumn 1993 Budget.

The reforms introduced by the Thatcher administration to improve the efficiency of education, health and housing providers were having their impact. Yet the gains in quality were no match for people's rising expectations. The return to the harsh budgetary limits of the mid-1980s announced in the Clarke budget of November 1993 were producing the same problems for the NHS in 1994 as they had in 1987–88. Apart from the initial interest of Mr Major in his 'Charter for quality' in public services, no discernable 'Major effect' in social policy is evident. The dilemmas remain. So, too, do the policies of the Thatcher period. The new theme of more fundamental change in Britain's welfare state, seems out of character and probably outside his term as conductor. That tune will fall to the younger generation of Conservatives to elaborate.

Notes

1. UK Department of Social Security, *The Growth of Social Security* (HMSO, London, 1993).

2. J. Hills, *The Future of Welfare: a guide to the debate* (Joseph Rowntree Foundation, York, 1993).

3. M. Bell, E. Butler, D. Marsland and M. Pirie, *The End of the Welfare State* (Adam Smith Institute, London, 1994).

4. P. Taylor-Gooby 'Attachment to the Welfare State' in R. Jowell et al *British Social Attitudes, 8th Report* (Gower, Aldershot, 1991).

5. H. Glennerster, A. Power and T. Travers, 'A New Era for Social Policy: a New Enlightenment or a New Leviathan?', *Journal of Social Policy*, vol. 20, Part 3 (1991).

6. Hills, *op. cit.*
7. K. Gardiner, *A Survey of Income Inequality over the last twenty years: How does the UK compare?* LSE Welfare State Discussion Paper No. 100 (LSE, London, 1993).
8. M. Evans, D. Piachaud and H. Sutherland *The Fowler Reforms* LSE Welfare State Programme (forthcoming).
9. J. LeGrand and W. Bartlett, *Quasi Markets and Social Policy* (Macmillan, London, 1993).
10. N. Lawson *The View from No. 11 Memoirs of a Tory Radical* (Corgi Books, London, 1993), p. 616.
11. Taylor-Gooby *op. cit.*, p. 40.
12. *Working for Patients* UK DoH 1989, para 1.2..
13. H. Glennerster *Implementing GP Fundholding* Open University Press Milton Keynes 1994.
14. R. Robinson and J. LeGrand, *Evaluating the NHS Reforms* (Kings Fund Institute, London, 1994).
15. Department of Health, *The Government's Expenditure Plans 1994–5 to 1996–97* (Cm 2512, 1994).
16. Appleby et al. in Robinson and LeGrand, *op cit.*
17. Department of Health, *Expenditure Plans 1993–4 to 1995–6* (HMSO, London, 1993).
18. Glennerster et al, *op. cit.*, 1994.

Chapter 19

EDUCATION POLICY

Peter Scott

T HIS CHAPTER on the education policies pursued during
the Major years will attempt to do three things. The first
is to articulate an apparent contradiction. Since John Major
became Prime Minister the government has retreated on key
issues of educational policy; yet education appears to be closer
to the heart of the government's concerns than it ever was in
the days of Margaret Thatcher. The second is to highlight the
main changes which have taken place in education policy since
Mrs Thatcher fell from power. The third is to consider the
various interpretations which are offered of the overall
balance of these policies.

THE THATCHER INHERITANCE

The legacy of Margaret Thatcher was less clear-cut in education than in many other areas of social policy – ironically so for
two reasons. First, Mrs Thatcher's first Cabinet office in the
Conservative government of 1970–74 had been as Secretary of
State for Education and Science. Secondly, education was an
inevitable arena of confrontation in the war between the
allegedly progressive 'establishment' and its traditionalist
critics (in effect an unstable coalition of genuine conservatives,

neo-conservatives who were often lapsed liberals and neo-liberals committed to market solutions). When Margaret Thatcher resigned as Prime Minister in October 1990, her educational revolution was incomplete.

That revolution had not got under proper way before the mid-1980s. A number of reasons can be suggested to explain this slow start. One is that, although Mrs Thatcher's spell as Secretary of State had not left her with happy memories, or high opinions, of the Department of Education and Science (DES), her instinct does not seem to have been to give the reform of education a high priority after her election victory in 1979. Perhaps there was an initial wariness about becoming embroiled. It was probably only to be expected that a Prime Minister whose only other Cabinet experience had been as Secretary of State for Education and Science, not one of the great offices of state, should not have dwelt on this earlier association. Certainly the choice of Mark Carlisle as her first Secretary of State for Education and Science does not suggest that education was intended to be an active front in the early Thatcher revolution.

A second reason is that this revolution was primarily intended to be in economic, industrial and industrial relations policies. Its animating morality was that of the market – sound money, low inflation, tax cuts, free labour markets. Later came the leap into large-scale privatization and 'review' of the welfare state which were the logical extensions of these free-market objectives. But the moralizing typical of American neo-conservatives and their 'moral majority' allies was not a strong feature of Thatcherism in the early and middle years. Education policy, therefore, was for a long time a peripheral item on her government's agenda.

Schools and universities became embroiled because they were part of the corporatist, producer-dominated, anti-competitive world which denied the efficacy (and morality?) of the market more than because they were ideological bastions of liberal or otherwise 'left' values. Initially education was drawn in as an inevitable aspect of the efforts, first, to weaken local government, which explains the inexorable transfer of power from local education authorities to governing bodies, and secondly to enhance consumer choice, which explains a clutch of early Thatcherite policies such as the assisted places scheme and the publication of examination results. Overtly ideological policies were more tentatively pursued. The Schools Council was abolished but other targets of traditionalist anger such as the Open University, the Council for National Academic Awards and the Social Science Research Council survived (although the SSRC had to abandon its pretensions to be 'scientific' and settle for becoming the Economic and Social Research Council).

However a third, and perhaps the most persuasive, reason for the Thatcherite revolution's slow start in education is the arbitrariness of high politics as expressed through the contrasting styles of successive Secretaries of State for Education and Science. Between 1979 and 1986 there were only two Secretaries of State. The first, as has already been mentioned, was Mark Carlisle who made little mark. For example, the infamous 1981 university cuts seemed almost to pass him by. The second was Keith Joseph, who had been influential in the rejection of Butskellite policies by the Conservative party in the mid-1970s and so a key progenitor of Thatcherism. His move to the DES, therefore, should have been a signal that education was moving up the political agenda. But it turned out differently. Reforms were mooted but not implemented. Some hinted that Joseph had gone native. Others, more plausibly, pointed to the difficulty he experienced in reaching decisions. Perhaps even more pertinent is the fact that education was Joseph's last job. His career, and reputation, were already made when he arrived at the DES.

Since 1986 there have been four Secretaries of State, two appointed by Mrs Thatcher (Kenneth Baker, John MacGregor) and two by John Major (Kenneth Clarke and John Patten). All had careers still to make. All held office at a time of increasing political velocity – briefer ministerial tours of duty, a higher premium attached to presentation (the glossier the better), a sound-bite policy environment with an insatiable appetite for instant initiatives, frequent white papers, annual bills. Three – Baker, Clarke and Patten – have been activists, although with very different measures of success. Only MacGregor exemplified a return to the less frenetic, 'listening' style typical of the Carlisle-Joseph era at the DES. It is significant that much of the Thatcherite revolution in education was concentrated in the final years of her premiership. In legislative terms the bulk of these reforms, the most prominent of which were the National Curriculum and grant-maintained (or opted-out) schools, dates from the Education Reform Act of 1988, eleven years after her first election victory and only two years before her fall.

THREE CHARACTERISTICS OF EDUCATION POLICY

The education policy pursued by John Major's administration has three characteristics, all of which can be traced back to its awkward Thatcherite legacy. The first is that, because the educational revolution had only got under proper way in the late 1980s, the impetus of these reforms has carried through into the 1990s unabated. Kenneth Clarke's 1991 decision to abandon the binary system in higher education by allowing the polytechnics to become universities flowed inexorably from Kenneth Baker's 1987 decision to free the polytechnics from the control of local education authorities and establish them as free-standing corporations. Clarke's decision to free further education colleges from LEA control was clearly an attempt to clone the successful polytechnic policy of four years before. John Patten's decision to establish a funding agency for schools, to oversee the slowly but steadily growing number of grant maintained schools, followed from the government's determination to encourage as many schools as possible to opt out of local authority control. Alternative administrative and funding arrangements had to be made if the policy was to be credible.

The second characteristic is that, because so many of the detailed elements in the late-Thatcher educational revolution had been devised in a hurry, substantial revision has been required, notably in the National Curriculum and its apparatus of accompanying tests. Part of the reason was that the teacher unions organized a successful boycott of the proposed tests. The Major government had to bow to superior political *force majeure* represented by this threatened boycott. However part of the reason was that, in order to establish the National Curriculum, corners had been cut. In particular subjects 'content' elements demanded by traditionalists had been combined with 'process' elements preferred by progressives to produce an over-loaded curriculum. The purposes of the national tests prescribed at the various key stages had become muddled. Comparative, summative or diagnostic? The mid-1980s argument between norm-referenced and criteria-referenced examinations, which these tests had been designed to foreclose, re-emerged in oblique and confusing forms. So significant revision became inevitable. Whether this revision is better described as an inevitable process of bedding-down, which all reforms require, or as a retreat from some of the fundamental principles established by the last Thatcher administration in the late 1980s will be discussed later in this chapter.

The third, and final, characteristic is that, in some crucial respects, the education policy of the Major government has gone beyond the Thatcherite agenda. The most blatant example is the way in which education has got caught up in the Prime Minister's apparently much misunderstood (and much redefined) 'Back to Basics' campaign launched at the 1993 Conservative party conference. One reason for this is that, as the Prime Minister has been obliged again and again by a prurient media to say what 'Back to Basics' is *not* about (i.e., the sexual habits of Conservative politicians), he has been forced back on to less contentious – or, at any rate, less self-destructive – themes. Prominent among these has been the responsibilities of schools for inculcating respect for received morality and traditional institutions (like the family and the Conservative party but not the Church of England or the universities!). The banal effect has been to make the shift to schools-based teacher training, and religious and sex education, second-order questions despite the passion they arouse, key planks in the 'Back to Basics' platform.

As a result, education policy may have been given an exaggerated prominence on the government's moralistic agenda. This seems to have coincided with the personal agenda of John Patten who was the first Secretary of State to believe that the determination of good-and-evil, rather than the administration of education as a public service, headed the list of his responsibilities. At a conference in Oxford in January 1994 he insisted: 'Values lie at the heart of education and schools should teach them'.[1] As Secretary of State he devoted a disproportionate amount of his effort to these apparently second-order questions – religious and sex education – precisely because, for him, they were first-order questions. Mr Patten often left detailed administrative announcements to his junior ministers, particularly his influential Minister of State, Baroness Blatch, preferring the broad sweep of moral pronouncement.

However this account which emphasises the essential contingency of the government's incorporation of education in its 'Back to Basics' crusade is not the only one available. An alternative account would emphasize instead Thatcherism's comparative disinterest in moralizing and steely commitment instead to the 'morality' of the market. To the extent that Majorism represents a retreat from the uncompromising free-market project associated with Margaret Thatcher, there may be a need to construct alternative ideological foundations for a redefined Conservativism. Read in this light 'Back to Basics', in education policy and elsewhere, can provide those alternative foundations. Less austere economic policies, particularly with regard to taxation and public expenditure, may need not only to be cloaked by Citizen's-Chartist rhetoric stressing customer satisfaction but also balanced by a sharp tilt to the moral right on questions of social policy and individual responsibility.

THE IMPACT OF KENNETH CLARKE

The Major years began with a period of administrative activism in education policy, although this was due far more to the new Secretary of State, Kenneth Clarke, than the Prime Minister himself. In the final years of the Thatcher premiership the Number 10 Policy Unit, under Brian Griffiths, a former City University professor, had in effect usurped many of the policy-making functions of the DES. After her fall the department was back in charge. Mr Major demonstrated a dutiful but distant interest in education policy, unlike the passionate intensity of his predecessor which more than made up for her comparative lack of interest in education in her early years as Prime Minister.

Within six months of his appointment Mr Clarke had published two white papers which changed, perhaps for ever, the map of further and higher education.[2] Further education colleges were removed from local education authority control. This decision was the culmination of two distinct policy strands. The first, more blatant but in the long run less significant, was a continuation of the Thatcherite prejudice against local government. The second was the desire to promote a 'training revolution', which went back at least as far as the mid-1970s when Labour was in power and had long been promoted by the Department of Employment and its various agencies and quangos, from the Manpower Services Commission through the Training Agency to the Training and Enterprise Councils and the National Council for Vocational Qualifications.

In his second white paper Mr Clarke announced that the polytechnics would become universities with full degree-awarding powers, so ending the binary policy articulated by Anthony Crosland in the mid-1960s and the binary distinction between universities and other institutions of advanced education which was very much older.[3] The decision to break the links between further education and local government was limply opposed and the decision to promote the polytechnics was widely supported. Both perhaps reflected deeper currents of educational change which owed comparatively little to the surface turbulence of party politics – the inevitable abandonment of an anachronistic view of further education colleges as technical high schools, and the equally inevitable evolution towards a mass system of higher (or, better, post secondary) education.

But in policy for schools, the key arena, Mr Clarke displayed a less sure touch. It is difficult to escape the impression that the complex issues raised by the introduction of the

National Curriculum and its accompanying tests bored him. Moreover, this was sharply contested territory, unlike further and higher education where an unacknowledged consensus prevailed. The paradoxical outcome was that, in the twelve months after the fall of Mrs Thatcher and under a Secretary of State widely regarded as on the 'left' of the Conservative party, Thatcherites came to occupy some of the commanding heights of curriculum reform. Duncan Graham, a former chief education officer, and Philip Halsey, a career civil servant, stepped down in the summer of 1991 as chairmen respectively of the National Curriculum Council (NCC) and the School Examinations and Assessment Council (SEAC). They were replaced by David Pascall, a Shell manager and former Number 10 Policy Unit member, and Lord Griffiths, head of the unit who had been especially close to Mrs Thatcher.

The logic of these changes which appeared to grant Thatcherites a degree of influence over education policy which they never enjoyed while Mrs Thatcher was Prime Minister was obscure. One possible explanation is that Mr Clarke was simply following Lyndon Johnson's political maxim, that it was better to have potential Thatcherite critics pissing out than in. Another, more intriguing, explanation is that the ideologically-inspired Thatcherite agenda and Mr Clarke's own populist blokeish agenda had much in common. This convergence was demonstrated early in 1992 when the Secretary of State commissioned a report on primary education from the so-called 'three wise men' – Robin Alexander, professor of primary education at the University of Leeds (who had undertaken research which appeared to support the case for a more traditional approach), Chris Woodhead (then chief executive of the NCC and now the chief executive of the School Curriculum and Assessment Authority [SCAA]) and Jim Rose, chief inspector in HMI.[4] Mr Clarke's intention, which he made little attempt to conceal, was to de-bunk the progressive orthodoxy established in the mid-1960s in the wake of the Plowden report. In fact the report did little more than tweak the middle-of-the-road practice of most primary schools. But it served Mr Clarke's political purposes.

However the element of ideological calculation which lay

Concerned with practical rather than theoretical consequences

behind Mr Pascall's and Lord Griffiths' appointment and the three-wise-men report can easily be exaggerated. In an important sense Lord Griffiths' move to the SEAC was demotion, exile from Downing Street to Notting Hill. Mr Clarke was to display his canny pragmatism again later in 1992 when Her Majesty's Inspectorate (HMI) was replaced by the office of Standards in Education (Ofsted) and Eric Bolton, a robust but discreet critic, retired as senior chief inspector. HMI had long been suspected by Thatcherites of being 'the enemy within'. Its brisk abolition appeared to offer further evidence of the advance of the Thatcherites. But this interpretation is difficult to reconcile with Mr Clarke's appointment of the vice-chancellor of London University, Stewart Sutherland, as part-time successor to Professor Bolton. Professor Sutherland is now to be replaced by Chris Woodhead.

The – brief, as it turned out – ascendancy of Mr Pascall and Lord Griffiths over the National Curriculum's policy apparatus, therefore, was an ambiguous and even accidental phenomenon. Clearly the Secretary of State was impatient with the muddle created by the overlapping functions of the NCC and SEAC, a structural flaw inherited from the Education Reform Act. Mr Graham and Mr Halsey may have been blamed. The appointment of Sir Graham Day as chairman of the Teachers' Pay Review Body perhaps indicated a liking for crisp and relatively apolitical managers. But, if the intention was to appoint brisk efficient (and ideologically disengaged) managers, the choice of Mr Pascall and Lord Griffiths made little sense. In any case the muddle continued. Administrative tensions were *made worse* exacerbated by ideological ones, as orders specifying the detailed content and attainment targets in subject after subject under the National Curriculum accumulated. When Mr Clarke moved to the Home Office and was replaced by John Patten at the DES after the 1992 general election, the ingredients for the debacle over testing a year later were already in place.

disastrous collapse or defeat

THE ARRIVAL OF JOHN PATTEN

John Patten inherited a department itself caught up by administrative change. Its close oversight of the new funding councils created to manage the newly corporate FE colleges and now unified higher education system meant that the department had acquired detailed responsibilities which previously had been undertaken by either local education authorities or 'buffer' bodies like the University Grants Committee. The growth in the number of grant maintained schools (250 in May 1992, 500 eleven months later and 850 by April 1994) made it imperative that the department adapt its structures, and generate appropriate expertise, to meet this challenge too. On the other hand an Office of Science and Technology (OST) was established under William Waldegrave and the department lost its responsibility for the research councils. As a result the DES became the Department for Education (DFE). Its centre of administrative gravity shifted decisively towards schools. Some observers saw in the OST the embryo of a Ministry of Higher Education and Science.

However, John Patten's most urgent priorities, personally and politically, lay elsewhere. The white paper on schools, published in July 1992, and the ensuing Education Act of 1993 covered two broad areas.[5] The first was measures to encourage more schools to opt out of local authority control and, because the government now had to acknowledge that large-scale opting out would inexorably erode the capacity of local authorities to determine the pattern of schools, to establish a Funding Agency for Schools and also to make provision for 'Education Associations' to rescue failing schools. The second was to merge the NCC and SEAC into a single body, the School Curriculum and Assessment Authority, with the intention of leading to, in John Major's own words, 'greater rigour, simplicity and clarity of approach'.

The first area has led to few political difficulties (so far). Sir Christopher Benson was subsequently appointed chairman of the FAS. But, four years after John Major replaced Mrs Thatcher as Prime Minister, the agency has yet to begin work on a substantial scale. Also the development of a funding system for grant-maintained schools to replace historic budget-levels inherited from local education authorities has so far been tentative and provisional. The overwhelming majority of schools, although they now benefit from significant budgetary devolution, continue to be maintained by local education authorities. Whether the DFE and the FAS between them can create a viable administrative and funding structure for more than 20,000 schools remains unclear. The crucial transition from grant-maintained schools being a ginger-group minority to becoming the majority sector has yet to be made. Perhaps that will be the crisis of the late 1990s in education policy, to match the early-1990s crisis over the National Curriculum, although the slow pace at which schools are voting to opt out may delay this problem well into the next century.

However, encouraging schools to opt out has already had unanticipated reverberations in the independent sector. The re-invention of direct-grant schools, a rough-cut metaphor which describes perceptions of grant-maintained schools, means that middle-class parents are no longer faced with a stark choice between 'going private' and the local comprehensive. Grant-maintained schools appear to offer an attractive, and economical, middle way. The government's decision to abandon the initial restriction which prevented grant maintained schools (re)introducing selection for a five-year period will probably increase their competitive edge. Also the publication of examination league tables has reduced the independent schools' comparative market advantage. The gap between state and independent sectors can be seen for what it is – not as wide as historical prejudice suggests.

Even under Mrs Thatcher the Conservatives' education policy suffered from divided aims: should its objective be to strengthen the independent sector as an alternative to state provision, or to create an internal market among state schools, so raising standards through competition? The assisted places scheme and the City Technology Colleges (CTC) programme were designed with the first objective in mind. But after the Education Reform Act the second came to predominate, largely because these earlier efforts were seen as marginal. In the Major years the tension between these two objectives has become sharper. The Prime Minister's pre-occupation with improving public services through the Citizen's Charter, and the origins of both Mr Clarke and Mr Patten on the 'left' of the party have increased the emphasis on improving state schools at the expense of aiding the independent sector. Efforts to revive and broaden the CTC experiment through the Technology Schools initiative have underlined the Major government's comparative neglect of independent schools.

THE CRISIS OVER TESTING

However it was the crisis over the National Curriculum (and, in particular, national tests) which preoccupied, and at times threatened to overwhelm, John Patten during the spring and summer of 1993. It began when the teacher unions, with the discreet but delighted connivance of the beleaguered educational 'establishment', were provoked into a counter-attack by what they saw as the advance of the Thatcherites within the educational 'quangocracy'. Under Mr Pascall the NCC, aided and abetted by SEAC under Lord Griffiths, appeared to be determined to upset the delicate ideological balances within the National Curriculum apparatus contrived, para-doxically, by Mrs Thatcher's last two Secretaries of State, Kenneth Baker and John MacGregor. Mr Patten's tactless tampering with National Curriculum requirements, notably in English, and his peremptory instructions to reduce the proportion of course work in assessments seemed to offer proof of this counter-revolution. The SEAC's administrative fumbling over the pilot tests for fourteen-year-olds in 1992 provided the spark.

The result was to create a united, and consequently effective, opposition to the government – no mean achievement, given the chronic divisions between head teachers and classroom teachers and between National Union of Teachers (NUT) and National Association of Schoolmasters/Union of Women Teachers (NAS/UWT). The unions instructed their members to boycott the regular tests due in June 1993. Their motives, of course, were mixed. The NUT had consistently opposed the government's educational policies. Its critics accused it of resisting all change and of nostalgia for a lost world of teacher independence (and NUT power!). The more conservatively inclined NAS/UWT opposed, not the National Curriculum and testing as such, but the burden particularly the latter placed on teachers. It was on this issue of heavier work loads that the NAS/UWT successfully defended a legal challenge by the government which had argued that the threatened boycott was 'political' and therefore not a genuine trade dispute. But paradoxically what united the teacher trade unions was their rivalry. Their endemic competition for members meant that none could afford to acquiesce in the imposition of policies which rank-and-file teachers bitterly resented.

Through the spring and early summer Mr Patten and his colleagues at the DFE struggled to regain the initiative – wielding the stick (writing to the chairmen of all school governing bodies reminding them of their statutory duty, and commissioning opinion polls in the vain attempt to demonstrate the public's backing for the tests); and also offering a carrot by asking Sir Ron Dearing, the chairman-designate of SCAA, to undertake an urgent review of the National Curriculum and testing. Neither worked. The teachers were unimpressed by Mr Patten's threats and concessions. Very few fourteen-year-olds were tested in 1993. Not since Mrs Thatcher backed off from her first confrontation with the miners (only to exact exemplary revenge two years later) had trade unionists successfully faced down the government.

However the concessions offered by Mr Patten took much of the heat out of the conflict, because they were so substantial, even if they failed to persuade the unions to call off the boycott straightaway. In effect the Thatcherites were removed from the commanding height of curriculum reform. Neither Mr Pascall, who made little attempt to conceal his disappointment, nor Lord Griffiths was made chairman of the SCAA, the successor-body to the NCC and SEAC. Instead the job went to Sir Ron Dearing, a former civil servant and chairman of the post office. Sir Ron's experience of high-level educational policy-making had been as chairman of, first, the

Polytechnics and Colleges Funding Council and then as chairman-designate of the new Higher Education Funding Council for England. He came, therefore, from the consensual arena of further and higher education rather than the contested terrain of schools. Moreover, he had those apolitical administrative skills which Mr Pascall and Lord Griffiths disdained.

The task Sir Ron had been set was to 'slim down' the National Curriculum and to 'simplify' its accompanying tests. He produced an interim report in the summer of 1993, after extensive consultation with any and all interested bodies, itself a significant shift of political style, even a reversion to more consensus-building policy-making. He published his final report in December 1993.[6] The Dearing recipe was to reduce the core compulsory elements within the National Curriculum, freeing 20 per cent of teaching time to be used at the discretion of the school, and also to make National Curriculum Orders less prescriptive. Tests would be simplified and the time needed to administer them reduced. The thicket of attainment targets would also be pruned. Significantly the Dearing review took a more balanced view of the contentious issue of teacher moderated assessment. Above all, Sir Ron argued for a period of consolidation and stability, a five-year moratorium on further changes in the National Curriculum.

With the exception of the NUT, which remained committed to a root-and-branch opposition to all testing, his review was widely interpreted by the teacher unions, correctly, as an appeal for a truce in the curriculum wars. Its recommendations were accepted by the government with revealing haste. The restlessness (and radicalism?) of curriculum reform was abandoned. Mr Patten had to endure the jibe that he had been rescued by Sir Ron – indeed, that Sir Ron rather than he was really responsible for devising the government's education policy. However he was not entirely responsible for the debacle. It was his predecessor Kenneth Clarke, presumably with the endorsement of either the Prime Minister's office or the Cabinet who had appointed Mr Pascall and Lord Griffiths to the NCC and SEAC, who had failed to act decisively to rationalize the bureaucracy of the

National Curriculum (in marked contrast to his decisive actions in further and higher education), and who had ignored until it was too late the dangers posed by the emergence of an overloaded and over-politicized curriculum.

'BACK TO BASICS'

The 'Back to Basics' campaign which developed after the 1993 Conservative party conference perhaps provided a convenient smokescreen behind which Mr Patten could retreat, abandoning any attempt to use the National Curriculum as an instrument of ideological correction while making moralizing speeches. Instead more limited goals were pursued. A new education bill was introduced, the third since John Major became Prime Minister, aimed at traditional Tory targets – student unions and teacher training. The attempt to reform student unions foundered once more, revealingly as the result of a revolt by Conservative peers which cruelly underlined Mr Patten's diminished authority.

The parallel attempt to reform initial teacher training by establishing a separate Teacher Training Agency (TTA) barely succeeded. Even this success was likely to be short-term, for at least three reasons. First, the establishment of the TTA owed far more to the sound-and-fury of old ideological battles than to significant divergence of views about initial teacher training. There was little opposition to an extension of schools-based training. The only argument was about the balance between schools and departments of education. The TTA was likely to get in the way of a sensible resolution of this argument. Second, it introduced a heightened spirit of partisanship into the previously consensual arena of further and higher education. The agency's authority was discounted in advance by the widespread assumption/accusation that it would be packed with Mr Patten's friends. Could it succeed in rolling back the progressive tide, or the tide of mediocrity, where the abolished Council for the Accreditation of Teacher Education (CATE) had failed? Thirdly, the establishment of the TTA went against the grain of unification which has been the dominant theme of the government's post-school policy.

JOHN MAJOR'S RECORD

The final section of this chapter will review various interpretations of the development of education policy since John Major became Prime Minister. In doing so it will attempt to answer the question, Is it possible to distinguish education policy under Mr Major from education policy under Margaret Thatcher? Some interpretations have already been hinted at. One stresses the continuity of policy between the two periods. Education policy under Major was an extension of education policy under Thatcher, in a double sense. First, the momentum built up in the last years of Mrs Thatcher's premiership continued into the Major period. Secondly, the Major government had to cope with the consequences of mistakes made between 1987 and 1990, such as the overloading of the National Curriculum and the awkward demarcation between the NCC and SEAC.

A second interpretation emphasizes the contingencies of high politics. The Major years can be divided into two distinct phases in education, both coloured by the personalities of successive Secretaries of State. The administrative activism of Kenneth Clarke stimulated radical structural changes, but the underlying tensions within the National Curriculum were ignored. The next phase was dominated by John Patten's moralizing tendencies which were no substitute for the political street-fighting capacity he needed so badly, and so conspicuously lacked, in the crisis over testing. A third interpretation offers a dialectical account of the contrast between Thatcherite and Majorite education policies – the former preoccupied by efforts to dismantle the corporatist structures of the education 'establishment' and to introduce the disciplines of the market; and the latter by a renewed emphasis on traditional standards, both narrowly educational and more broadly patriotic, in a paradoxical mixture of (neo-conservative?) 'Back to Basics' and one-nation

Toryism. None of these interpretations is wholly satisfactory, although all may have glints of the truth.

The answer to the central question – what is the difference between Major and Thatcher in education policy? – remains obscure. In one sense it may be unanswerable because arguably it is based on a false premise, that in education as in social policy generally (and, more broadly, in politics) the 1979 election was a watershed. But in the *longue durée* of education policy, beneath the histrionic turbulence of 'Thatcherism', the impression is as much one of continuity as of counter-revolution. The backlash against an open and progressive curriculum began not with Mrs Thatcher's election success but with Lord Callaghan's Ruskin speech three years earlier. Regardless of the political complexion of the government, schools have increasingly been made scapegoats for comparative economic decline and the decay of old-fashioned patriotism. Similarly the erosion of the power of local education authorities is not a novel phenomenon. The long march from early nineteenth-century voluntarism and localism to a late twentieth-century national system is an aspect of deeper structural change. The attack on local education authorities in the 1980s and 1990s follows their decisive subordination to national direction in the 1960s. If this long view is taken the transition from Thatcher to Major is a minor event.

In another sense an attempt can be made to answer this question by referring to Lady Thatcher's own, although retrospective, account of the unfinished educational revolution and comparing this account with the achievements of the Major government.[7] The first item in her agenda was the need to quicken the pace of opting-out by schools. The model she explicitly offered was that of National Health Service trusts (although there is evidence, most notably in Nigel Lawson's memoirs, which suggests when Prime Minister she shied away from root-and-branch restructuring on the NHS model, hoping instead that piecemeal opting-out by individual schools would ginger up the local authority sector).

As has already been indicated her hopes of wholesale opting-out have so far been disappointed. There is little sign that, in the foreseeable future, the dominant organizing principle will become the grant-maintained rather than the local authority maintained school. But the Major government did what it could in the 1993 Education Act to bribe schools to become grant maintained and to tie the hands of those campaigning against opting-out. The turning-of-the-tide against opting-out in recent parental ballots is probably a symptom of a wider disenchantment with a decade-and-a-half of Conservative rule.

The second item was the reform of teacher training, reducing the power and influence of (allegedly) leftist, mediocre and impractical teacher educators. This objective has been tackled in the latest Education Bill.

The third item of unfinished business according to Lady Thatcher concerned the universities. While claiming credit for improving their managerial efficiency, she admitted that she had not given sufficient weight to considerations of academic freedom. When she left office, Brian Griffiths was working on a privatization plan intended to free universities from Treasury (and thus DES/DFE) control. It is difficult to know how seriously to take this still-born plan. Certainly it would have represented a tardy conversion to university autonomy by a Prime Minister under whose administration the concordat which governed relations between universities and the state had been abruptly abrogated, as just another corporatist abuse. The aspiration also had more than a whiff of earlier madcap IEA-inspired privatization schemes.

In this respect the Major government has not followed its lost leader's testament. Far from enhancing university autonomy, the abolition of the binary system and promotion of the polytechnics have led to the emergence of an extended higher education sector under, in Anthony Crosland's words when he introduced the binary policy in the mid-1960s, 'greater social control'. Universities and colleges are subject to detailed planning by the funding councils and are wide-open to 'market' pressures – the worst of both worlds, some might argue, or in the *patois* of a more recent politician, a double-whammy. It is tempting to see in this unified sector, responsive to social and 'market' demands, an expression of Mr Major's commitment to a classless society and the contractual state (at any rate as reflected in the vapid rhetoric of his multifarious 'charters').

But this interpretation is probably no more plausible than the conclusion that, at the eleventh hour, Lady Thatcher had become a convert to university autonomy. So the apparent gap between Thatcher and Major policies on higher education is perhaps more apparent than real.

The revolution in education allegedly begun by Margaret Thatcher remains unfinished by John Major – partly because, if a revolution at all, it had deep roots going back to the Callaghan government (and the divided and diminishing traditions of English education); partly because it is unfinishable, in the sense that politicized prescription often cannot be translated into administrative practice however intense the ideological will. Yet education remains one of the few arenas in which the Major government has a record which out-tops that of Mrs Thatcher's long administration.

Notes

1. John Patten, Speech to the Oxford Conference on Education, 4 January 1994. Department for Education Press Release, 1994.
2. Department of Education and Science, Department of Employment, Welsh Office, *Education and Training for the 21st Century*, 2 vols. (HMSO, May 1991).
3. Department of Education and Science, Scottish Office, Welsh Office, Northern Ireland Department, *Higher Education: A New Framework* (HMSO, May 1991).
4. Robin Alexander, Jim Rose and Chris Woodhead, *Curriculum Organisation and Classroom Practice in Primary Schools* (HMSO, January 1992).
5. Department for Education and Welsh Office, *Choice and Diversity: A New Framework for Schools* (HMSO, July 1992).
6. Ron Dearing, *The National Curriculum and its Assessment* (final report), (School Curriculum and Assessment Authority, December 1993).
7. Margaret Thatcher, *The Downing Street Years* (Harper Collins, 1993) pp. 597–99.

Chapter 20

THE FAMILY AND WOMEN

Ruth Lister

INTRODUCTION

Women and 'the family' do not constitute a discrete area of policy, especially in a country with neither an explicit policy nor a departmental minister with formal responsibility for such matters. For a rounded assessment of the implications of the Major years for women and families the reader, therefore, needs to take account also of other domestic social and economic topics covered elsewhere in this collection. In particular, while this chapter will focus on families with children, of growing importance for families (and women) are the rise in the number of older people and the community care policies directed towards them. (See Chapter 21.)

It should also be noted that men, as well as women, live in and have responsibilities to families. The nature of these responsibilities and how well men are – or are not – meeting them have recently begun to be the subject of some public discussion. As such, they are part of a wider, increasingly intense, debate about changing family patterns in general and the perceived threat to civilized society of the onward march of lone parenthood in particular.

The Major years have been characterized more by the growing political salience of a discourse around the 'breakdown of the family' than by any coherent policy response to a

set of family trends more or less common to western industrialized societies. This chapter therefore first briefly outlines
these trends and the debates surrounding them as well as the
dilemmas they raise for a post-Thatcherite Tory government,
before looking at actual policy developments since 1990.

SOCIAL AND ECONOMIC TRENDS

John Major came to power at the end of a decade in which a
number of long-term trends in family and women's employment patterns had accelerated.

In line with most members of the European Union, the
number of marriages was down and the rate of cohabitation
was up. Although cohabitation remained a prelude to marriage in most cases, for a growing minority it had become an
alternative. The proportion of women aged eighteen to forty-
nine who were married had fallen from 74 per cent in 1979 to
61 per cent in 1990. Conversely, the proportion of women in
this age group cohabiting had increased from 11 per cent to
22 per cent over the same period. (By 1992, the figures were
59 per cent and 21 per cent respectively.) A rising proportion
of second marriages has meant that step-families have
become increasingly common.

The proportion of births outside marriage more than
doubled during the 1980s to nearly one in three by 1992, of
which three-quarters were registered to both parents at the
same address. The overall birth rate has been falling and the
child-bearing years have become increasingly compressed.
Again, despite considerable variations between countries, the
trends follow a wider western European pattern.

Divorce has also been increasing in most European countries although the main escalation was during the 1970s. By
1991, for every two marriages in Great Britain there was one
divorce – the highest rate in Europe.

One politically sensitive consequence of these trends was
the rapid rise in the proportion of families headed by a lone
parent (nine out of ten of whom are women) from 12 per cent
in 1979 to 20 per cent in 1990 and 21 per cent by 1992. The

biggest increase was amongst single, never-married, mothers. The proportion of lone parent families increased in all the main ethnic groups but there remain considerable variations between them. By the end of the 1980s, the UK was estimated to have the highest proportion of lone parent families in the EU.[1]

Proportion of families headed by a lone parent (per cent)

Family type	1979	1990	1992
Lone mother	10	18	19
single	2	6	7
widowed	2	1	1
divorced	4	7	6
separated	3	4	5
Lone father	2	2	2
All lone parents	12	20	21

Source: OPCS, General Household Survey 1992 (HMSO, 1994)

Nineteen-ninety marked the first year in which the classic household of married couple plus children was overtaken by single person households as the most common type. By 1992, they represented 24 per cent and 27 per cent of all household types respectively compared with 31 per cent and 23 per cent in 1979. Again, there was considerable variation between ethnic groups.

These changes in family patterns have been paralleled by fundamental labour market trends, which have contributed to a revolution in women's labour market participation. Between the end of the 1970s and the beginning of the 1990s, the proportion of married women with children in paid work rose from 52 to 63 per cent. Among those with children aged under five the increase was from 27 to 47 per cent. However, over the same period the proportion of lone parents in work fell from 47 to 42 per cent. One consequence was a politically sensitive growth in reliance on social assistance from 38 per cent to 70 per cent of all lone parents between 1979 and 1992.

During the 1980s, women's share of total employment rose throughout the European Union but the trend has been particularly marked in the UK where women are now set to outnumber men in the labour market. However, it is a labour market which is still segregated along both vertical and horizontal lines and in which the majority of jobs open to women have been low paid and part-time (for a diminishing number of hours). The UK has the second highest proportion of female part-time workers in the EU (though part-time work is much less common among ethnic minority women). It also boasts the highest earnings gap between women and men.

The revolution in women's participation in the labour market has not been matched by any significant change in men's participation in the home and family. The 'new man' remains hard to find and men continue to work longer hours on average than in any other EU state.

At the same time, men's full-time employment has been diminishing and high unemployment continues to have a damaging impact on family life and living standards. The gap between two-earner and no-earner families has widened and overall the 1980s were marked by a disastrous growth in family poverty. Between 1979 and 1990–91, the proportion of children in households below average income rose from one in ten to just under one in three. Women, as the managers and shock-absorbers of poverty, will have borne the main brunt of this increase in family hardship. The proportion of total income going to families with children fell from 37 per cent in 1979 to 30 per cent in 1990. Over the same period there was a marked increase in the number of homeless families, although the trend did begin to turn in the early 1990s.

FAMILY POLITICS

Tory preoccupation with 'the family' surfaced at intervals during the 1980s, having been prominent in the run-up to the 1979 election. However, apart from a leaked document from the government Family Policy Group which suggested various ways of encouraging families to reassume their responsibilities, it was not until the end of Mrs Thatcher's reign that she really focused on the issue. Her memoirs revealed her growing belief that strengthening the 'traditional family' was the only way to get to the root of crime and other social problems. A similar message was being articulated by the right-wing think-tanks, most vociferously the Institute of Economic Affairs (IEA) Health and Welfare Unit which had as its central project 'to restore the ideal of the two-parent family'.[2] At the same time, the discourse of the 'dependency culture' was shifting its target from the male unemployed to female lone parents.

The coming to power of the more ideologically pragmatic John Major signalled a softening of this discourse and concern about 'the family' remained relatively low key. This was all to change in 1993, widely seen as the year in which 'the breakdown of the family' hit the top of the political agenda. On the one hand, the James Bulger murder and media coverage of a spate of 'home alone' cases raised public concerns about the nation's children and parental responsibility for them. On the other, growing anxieties about crime and incivility, linked by many to lone parenthood, were seized by the right as a potent weapon in their battle for the direction of the Tory government.

The defining moment, after a summer in which the political rhetoric concerning lone parents crescendoed, came at the 1993 Tory party conference. Here ministers vied with each other in their moralizing attribution of a range of social ills to lone parent families despite, it emerged later, their possession of a Cabinet briefing paper which challenged their arguments.

Major did not himself join in this orgy of lone parent-bashing and later in the year was reported to have reined back his Cabinet colleagues when it became apparent that their vilification of lone parents had not struck the expected chord with the electorate. Nevertheless his end-of-conference 'Back to Basics' rallying cry was widely interpreted as a victory for the right and was welcomed by his predecessor as signalling that 'Thatcherism is alive and well'. His subsequent attempts to disassociate 'Back to Basics' from moralizing about the family, in the face of a series of embarrassing lapses from family values amongst his colleagues, were not wholly credible given that family respect and responsibility figured prominently in his original articulation of 'Back to Basics'. The whole tone had been to counterpose family-based common sense against the supposed politically-correct orthodoxies seeded in the permissive 1960s.

Nineteen-ninety-three was also marked by a public outcry over the Child Support Act, with absent fathers portrayed in the media as the oppressed victims of a punitive state out to fleece them for every last penny. Less prominent were the beginnings of a debate about men's behaviour, as fathers, partners and the main perpetrators of crime, and about the implications for men's role and identity of the demise of unskilled full-time 'male' jobs. At the end of the day, though, it was primarily women – and in particular lone mothers – who were the main butt of the ideological crusade to reassert the primacy of the traditional two parent family.

This crusade was not without its dilemmas and contradictions for the Tory party. As Margaret Thatcher recognized in her memoirs, there is a difficulty in squaring an ideological commitment to reducing the influence of the state with intervention in the 'private' sphere of the family. A growing tension also emerged between the Tory commitment to a free enterprise society and increasing concern amongst some of the right about the impact of such a society on families and communities.

A particular dilemma concerned the proper place of mothers and, in particular, lone mothers. On the one hand, traditional Conservative thinking accorded primacy to mothers' place in the home, and community care policies were predicated on assumptions about the availability of, primarily female, carers. (See Chapter 21.) On the other hand, the 1990s had been hailed by Sir Norman Fowler and others as the 'decade of the working woman' because employers looked to women to supply their labour needs. Behind this slogan there was also the fact that the slump in labour force participation amongst lone mothers meant a bigger social security bill. The resolution of this dilemma lay in an official stance of neutrality.

FAMILY POLICIES

1. *Employment, women and families*

While this stance remains, under Mr Major there has been something of a shift away from Mrs Thatcher's antipathy towards the working mother. After his initial faux-pas of an all-male Cabinet, he has emphasized his support for women's promotion in the workplace through the encouragement of women to senior public appointments and his public backing for Opportunity 2000, an employer-led initiative to help women break through the 'glass ceiling'. After the 1992 election, Gillian Shepherd, then Employment Secretary, established a top-level working group to advise her on how to address the difficulties encountered by working women.

These difficulties were, however, exacerbated for many women by the Major government's continued commitment to labour market deregulation symbolized by its final abolition of the Wages Councils, highlighted by Mr Major himself as an example of how his government surpassed Mrs Thatcher's in its radicalism. Four-fifths of workers covered by the Councils were women; the Equal Opportunities Commission predicted a consequent widening of the wages gap between women and men as a result of the harmful impact of other deregulatory policies on women's pay and conditions.

The EOC's calls for new, stronger, clearer and more accessible legislation on equal pay and sex discrimination continued to be rebuffed on the grounds that the government believed that voluntarism was the best approach so as not to burden employers and threaten competitiveness. (The limits of such an approach were, however, evident from the lack of progress, in the face of recession and employer resistance, recorded in the second report of Opportunity 2000.)

Voluntarism has also continued to be the hallmark of the government's approach to resolution of the difficulties faced by mothers trying to juggle paid work and family responsibilities. As a result, the UK continues to lag behind most other countries in the EU in the support provided for working parents and to resist European Commission attempts to regulate in this area.

The 1992 manifesto summed up the government's child care policy: 'We shall continue to encourage the development of child care arrangements in the voluntary and independent sectors'; local authorities would be asked to ensure that the standards for which they are now responsible under the Children Act would be 'applied sensibly'. Building on the approach taken by the Thatcher government, though with greater emphasis on the needs of working mothers, funds have been made available to promote the provision of pre-school and after-school care by the voluntary sector and employers have been exhorted to make more provision. For their part, a group of major employers, under the banner of Employers for Child Care, called upon the government to increase funding for child care and to set a national framework and standards.

John Major made the issue of pre-school provision his own when, at the end of 1993, he declared that he wanted 'over time to move to universal nursery education'. This followed growing media coverage of the US evidence of the positive impact of quality nursery education on the later development and propensity to criminal behaviour of children and young people, prompted partly by the espousal of universal nursery education by the National Commission on Education which reported in 1993. However, by Easter 1994, there appeared to be some back-tracking from the Prime Minister's commitment which had not received a very favourable reception from his Education Secretary, John Patten.

A minor, but politically significant, initiative has been the introduction of a child care allowance, worth up to £28 a week, for certain parents claiming family credit and related benefits. This measure was explicitly designed to make it easier for lone parents and other low income mothers to take full-time paid work (defined for social security purposes as sixteen hours or more a week).

The development of accessible child care services is one of the provisions contained in the recommendation on child care adopted by the Council of Ministers in 1992 to enable women and men to fulfil their work and family obligations. Another is the promotion of flexible leave arrangements. Like the Thatcher government before it, the Major government has resisted attempts by Brussels to place obligations on member states in this area. It managed to water down the directive on the protection of pregnant women at work so as to minimize the improvement it had to make to maternity leave and pay. In the event, it introduced more generous reforms under the directive than expected, although they still leave the UK with the worst maternity provision in the EU.

The Major government also blocked an attempt to reactivate a directive on parental leave originally obstructed by its predecessor. It took a similarly negative stance on the working time directive and on attempts to introduce directives to regulate the employment of part-time and temporary workers and to extend to them employment and social security rights. (However, a ruling by the House of Lords in 1994 has now required it to treat part-time workers the same as full time, under European law, with regard to employment rights.)

2. Income Maintenance

'Accepting responsibility for yourself and your family and not shuffling it off to the state' was one of the 'basics' extolled by Mr Major at the 1993 Tory party conference. It reflected a central theme of social security policy from the mid-1980s onwards: the need to promote self-reliance as opposed to dependency upon the state. One of the clearest examples of the attempt to shift the boundary between public state and private family responsibility for income maintenance is afforded by the Child Support Act (CSA). The CSA was very much Mrs Thatcher's baby but Mr Major's government was responsible for its parliamentary passage and enactment and for defending it against an onslaught of criticism.

Described by the Social Security Select Committee as 'the most far-reaching social reform to be made for 40 years',[3] the Act effectively shifted a significant proportion of the bill for maintaining lone parent families (mothers as well as children) from the state to absent fathers. It was supported by a number of social security changes designed to encourage lone mothers into full-time paid work. An additional, Cabinet level, review of the position of lone parent families, designed to reduce their reliance on the state still further, has not, as yet, produced the cutbacks in social security some had feared.

Instead, an early product of Lilley's social security review was the proposed replacement of unemployment benefit, paid for twelve months, by a job-seekers' allowance, paid on a contributory basis for only six and at a lower rate to those aged under twenty-five. This reduction in entitlement for young people is but the latest in a long line of cutbacks during the 1980s designed to increase young people's dependency on their families. It also represents a further erosion of married women's right to an independent benefit, for only a minority of them will qualify for income support instead. At the same time the equalization of the pension age at sixty-five was finally announced.

The one main policy reversal executed by Major concerned child benefit where his personal commitment to the allowance contrasted with his predecessor's hostility. Frozen since 1987, child benefit's future beyond a further election, when the government would not be hamstrung by a manifesto pledge, looked distinctly tenuous. Already as Chancellor, Major had partially broken the freeze and, once Prime Minister, not only was a further increase announced but also the index-linking of the benefit. This was the first time such a commitment had ever been made. The 1992 manifesto promised that 'child benefit will remain the cornerstone of our policy for all families with children. Its value will increase each year in line with prices . . . [It] will continue to be paid to all families, normally to the mother, and in respect of all children.' However, a series of leaks has suggested that child benefit's longer term future is once again uncertain as the right's influence over social policy has strengthened.

Another change of direction has been the effective phasing out of the married couple's tax allowance in contravention of the earlier principle that the tax system should pay 'regard to the special relationship and responsibilities that exist within marriage'.[4] The demise of the allowance is, however, consistent with a more general trend in fiscal policy since the late 1970s, away from recognition of family responsibilities through the tax system, the latest example being the reduction in tax relief on maintenance.

3. Family policies and policies affecting families

John Major marked the International Year of the Family by appointing Virginia Bottomley, the Health Secretary, to coordinate family policies. Without a Cabinet committee to chair, however, the appointment was seen as carrying little weight.

The contrast between government preoccupation with 'the family' and the failure to institutionalize a family policy is not new. On the one hand family values and parental responsibilities are invoked in support of a range of policy initiatives; on the other no attempt is made to assess the impact of policies on families through the kind of family impact statements the Conservatives promised when in opposition. Criminal justice and education policy provide examples of the former; policies on homelessness, travellers and immigration exemplify the need for the latter.

The Criminal Justice Act 1991, which imposed new responsibilities on the parents of children before the courts, including liability for fines imposed on young offenders, is being strengthened by the Criminal Justice and Public Order Bill which, in turn, includes further powers to fine or even ultimately jail the parents of young offenders who fail to comply with court orders. Parental responsibility was also the theme of the Parent's Charter (echoing Mr Major's own reference to parental responsibilities as citizens in his Foreword to the Citizen's Charter) which is supposed to have been sent to every household.

Similarly, new guidelines on sex education in schools, which has been made voluntary, advised that the emphasis should not be on explicit sex education but on 'the value of family life', to the dismay of the Department of Health.

A white paper on adoption law placed strong emphasis on the married couple as the ideal family unit for adoption; it also gave rise to some confusion as to whether homosexual couples would be allowed to adopt – the answer appeared to be no, although single homosexuals would be considered. With regard to homosexuality generally, Mr Major made an important symbolic gesture in meeting Sir Ian McKellan of Stonewall but then voted against the equalization of the age of consent.

Pro-family members of the Conservative party (and, it has been reported, the Cabinet) have opposed the green paper proposals for the reform of divorce law which would allow divorce after a year, after mediation, on the main grounds of irretrievable breakdown rather than fault. This approach was seen by them as inconsistent with the government's family values stance.

Inconsistencies have also been highlighted, from outside the Conservative party, between the emphasis on prevention in the Children Act 1989, which provides the framework for government policy on children, and the impact on children of many of its policies.

Of particular concern have been the likely implications of proposals to reform homelessness legislation which currently primarily protects families with children. The genesis of the proposals lay in the right's mythology that young women get pregnant in order to acquire council accommodation. Although the lone parent factor was played down in the consultation document which finally emerged, lone parent families, who it has been estimated are eight times as likely to be homeless as other households, will be disproportionately affected. Fears have been raised of a return to the situation exemplified by *Cathy Come Home*, with homeless families unable to find permanent accommodation; of an increase in the number of children defined as 'in need' under the Children Act; and of women finding it harder to escape domestic violence.

Similarly, Save the Children has warned of the impact on travellers' children of the provisions in the Criminal Justice and Public Order Bill to repeal the Caravan Sites Act 1968. A prospect of frequent moves and insecurity will, it has been argued, damage children's health and education. A disregard for the family life of minority groups has also been a feature of immigration policy under the Conservatives, the latest example being the Asylum and Immigration Appeals Act 1993.

Critics have argued that such policies contravene the UN declaration on the rights of the child to which the UK is a signatory. The UK's first progress report to the UN has been criticized as complacent and misleading and has been compared with the more honest and self-critical reports submitted by some other governments. The government's refusal to appoint a statutory Children's Rights Commissioner has also been contrasted with initiatives taken in other countries in response to the declaration.

CONCLUSION: A MAJOR EFFECT?

Many forces have helped to shape changes in the position of women and families in the 1990s. Underlying trends, more or less common to western industrialized societies, have continued; the dictates of European law have required a number of changes in the face of government resistance.

As the right reasserted its power in the government, it increasingly made the running in the promotion of a discourse of traditional family values. Although Mr Major restrained ministers' attacks on lone parent families, his 'Back to Basics' credo was essentially supportive of their stance. The impact on working women of his enthusiastic embrace of Thatcherite deregulation policies outweighed his more sympathetic stance towards working mothers.

The rehabilitation of child benefit represents the one unambiguous example of John Major's personal stamp on policy, although whether or not it will hold remains to be seen. For a time it looked as if a commitment to universal nursery education might provide another, but it would now appear that that personal undertaking could go the same way as the similar one made by Mrs Thatcher back in 1972, in the face of fears about its public spending implications.

Overall, the Major government has worked within the context of the agenda set by the Thatcher government, sometimes extending it, occasionally softening it. It is more likely to be remembered for the 'moral panic' about the state of the 'family' and the backlash against lone parent families that it helped to unleash, together with the legacy it inherited in the form of the Child Support Act, than for any distinctive policies of its own directed towards families and women.

Notes

1. J. Roll, *Lone Parent Families in the European Community* (Family Policy Studies Centre, London, 1992).
2. D. Green, Foreword to N. Dennis, *Rising Crime and the Dismembered Family*, (Institute of Economic Affairs Health & Welfare Unit, London, 1993), p. viii.
3. Social Security Committee, *The Operation of the Child Support Act* (HMSO, London, 1993), p. v.
4 HM Treasury, *The Reform of Personal Taxation* (HMSO, London, 1986), para 3.14.

Chapter 21

COMMUNITY CARE

Jane Lewis

THE NATIONAL Health Service and Community Care Act came into force in 1990, but implementation of the community care provisions was delayed until April 1993. Thus the main direction of the new policy was laid by the last Thatcher government, which saw the introduction of a new paradigm of administration for the social services, whereby finance was separated from provision and market mechanisms were introduced into the public sector. However, the new community care policy has been refined and implemented entirely within the first Major government and its effects will in all probability be associated with him.

Embedded as it is in the social services departments of local authorities, community care has not been one of the high welfare spending fields of the post-war years, nor has it attracted huge public support in the manner of the health service. However, it has assumed a much higher profile and greater policy significance in the 1980s and 1990s, and the first part of this chapter explains why. The rest of the chapter suggests that there are fundamental tensions in the new community care policy and that these are affecting implementation. If the new community care policy stumbles badly, then there will be knock-on effects for the health service, primarily in the form of 'bed-blocking', which will cause difficulties for ministers. Headlines about the lack of

provision in the community for the mentally ill have already
proved politically sensitive during the past year.

THE PRESSURE FOR A NEW
COMMUNITY CARE POLICY

Community care has been something of a 'motherhood' issue
in the thinking of both the political left and right. During the
1960s, left-wing academics, notably Peter Townsend, made
moving pleas for the deinstitutionalization of elderly and
mentally ill people, although Richard Titmuss sounded what
has become a well-known note of caution. Referring to the
way in which the term community care conjured up 'a sense
of warmth and human kindness, essentially personal and
comforting', Titmuss warned that good community care
would not be cheap.[1]

In fact little progress was made in making a reality of
community care between 1957, when the Royal Commission
on the Law Relating to Mental Illness and Mental Deficiency
first used the term, to the end of the 1980s. Even the meaning
of the term was far from clear. For example, local authority-
provided institutional care became the health authority's
community care. During the 1970s cumbersome joint planning machinery between health and local authorities failed to
shift resources from the National Health Service to local
authorities. There was no change in the percentage of domiciliary and day care expenditure on the elderly as a proportion of total expenditure by social services departments
between 1973 and 1985. Nor after the economic crisis of the
early 1970s did those budgets expand sufficiently to take
account of demographic change.

Local authority social service departments have always
tended to be the Cinderella service providers within the welfare state, rocked by child care scandals and dealing with a
primarily poor and disadvantaged population. However,
their role in providing community care received new impetus
during the 1980s. The main reason was to be found in the
publicity accorded the demographics, which showed that by

the year 2001 the number of people aged over seventy-five was projected to rise by 30 per cent and the percentage of over-eighty-fives was set to double. The first Thatcher administration put considerable emphasis on the importance of the informal community care provided by kin, neighbours and friends, suggesting that '[c]are in the community must increasingly mean care by the community'.[2] Ironically at the same time changes in the social security system in 1981 and 1983 effectively gave an open-ended grant to those entering private or voluntary homes. This resulted in an enormous (138 per cent) rise in the number of private residential beds and a huge increase in cost to government in terms of the board and lodging allowance, which rose from £10m to £1000m between 1980 and 1989. As the Audit Commission commented in 1986, the encouragement that had been given to a particular kind of community care – private residential – had been 'perverse'.

As a result of the Audit Commission's report, Sir Roy Griffiths was invited to document the finance of and arrangements for community care, which he did in 1988. Griffiths recommended making local authorities clearly responsible for developing and delivering community care. Immediate reaction to the report expressed the belief that it would not find favour with ministers because of the powers it proposed to give local government. However, the report could be read as advocating considerably greater central control. Griffiths wanted to establish firm ministerial responsibility for community care, which would ensure the specification of objectives and the resources to match them. While Griffiths was anxious to avoid central government 'prescription' he nevertheless envisaged central government providing the 'framework' within which local authorities would operate. He recommended that a specific grant set at 40 or 50 per cent of agreed local spending be made available to LAs on the submission of community care plans which were judged to provide satisfactory evidence of local needs, collaborative planning and the promotion of a mixed economy of care. In other words, financing was to be linked to planning and was to serve as the lever for securing implementation.

The legislative framework that followed Griffiths' report

made clear government's determination to terminate the open-ended social security commitment to funding residential care. The care element of social security support to residential and nursing homes was transferred to local authorities in the form of a special transitional grant. It was clear that government intended to promote a 'mixed economy' of care in which local authorities became 'enablers' rather than providers. But the 1989 white paper, 'Caring for People' abandoned both Griffiths' idea of making political accountability at the centre explicit and, more significantly still, the link between planning and resource allocation. It can be argued that the responsibilities Griffiths sought for local authorities have remained, while central government's responsibility for making sure that resources are consistent with objectives has not (the House of Commons Health Committee took up this issue explicitly in 1993).

Griffiths has insisted that the community care changes are first and foremost about management change. His insistence on the political neutrality of his proposals is in line with similar claims for the 'new public management' more generally, with its stress on accountability, results, competition and efficiency. However, academic commentators have suggested both that the new managerialism has served to transform local/central government relations, extending the decentralization of production and the centralization of command made possible by the revolution in information technology from the private sector to the public, and that the ideas of the new managerialism will inevitably be subject to political manipulation in the context of local authorities. Thus while the new community care policy has presented local government with a large expansion in its role, at odds with the contraction of almost every other sphere of its activities, it may turn out to be a mixed blessing.

TENSIONS IN THE NEW
COMMUNITY CARE POLICY

The broad direction of the new community care policy introduced in 1990 was clear. Government wished to move the provision of community care from the auspices of the National Health Service to the local authorities, and associated with this, from institutional to domiciliary settings. The community care changes were intimately linked to the 1990 health reforms in that it was proposed virtually to end continuing care under the NHS. However, while NHS care is free at the point of delivery, that provided by social services is not. Government also wanted to move from public provision to a more mixed economy of care, and to shift from a provider-led service to a needs-led service.

The main idea promoted in the government documents immediately preceding and following the 1990 National Health Service and Community Care Act was that of making sure that services fit users' needs. Similar claims have been made in a number of European countries where changes in systems for providing care for elderly people have also taken place. In the British context, the idea of 'user-centredness' has also accompanied the introduction of 'quasi-market' systems in the health, education and housing services as well as in community care since 1988. The 1989 white paper asked local authorities to establish the clients' (or as they became in this document and the subsequent official guidance, 'the users') needs and to devise ways of meeting them that secured users the greatest possible choice and independence, which it was believed would also improve quality and secure cost effectiveness. It may be argued that there are a number of fundamental tensions within the policy objectives which local authorities will have difficulty reconciling.

The white paper listed six objectives. The first of these – to promote the development of domiciliary services and to enable people to live at home where possible – appears to reconcile the concerns of users and carers with those of government about the cost of residential care (because domiciliary care is believed to be cheaper). This objective focuses on the situation of only one client group, elderly people (because of the open-ended social security commitment to this group) and assumes that there are people in institutional care who should not be. However the evidence on this is conflicting. The Committee of Public Accounts suggested that if appropriate domiciliary services had been available, only 77 per cent of those entering institutions would have needed to be admitted; and Price Waterhouse's study of one-third of residents in Hampshire's residential homes came up with a figure of 86 per cent. However, Sinclair et al. drew attention to the difficulty of concluding that less residential care was necessary, and Henwood concluded from her review of the evidence that comparatively few people are inappropriately placed in residential care.[3]

The 'independence' objective also implicitly assumes that it is possible to keep people (again, implicitly elderly people) out of institutional care. However, the research literature has been quite clear as to the extent to which this requires substantial investment in the management of change and specifically in the development of rigorous care management, which may in turn be expensive. The effects of merely increasing community care resource inputs (home helps, respite care or whatever) alone have been shown by the Personal Social Services Research Unit (PSSRU) to be few and weak. Authorities must also tread a fine line between promoting independence and autonomy on the one hand, and protection on the other.

Finally this first objective assumes that elderly people want to remain at home. This may be so, but there has been very little research as to what elderly people want. The character of the vastly increased demand for residential care during the 1980s is hard to determine. In effect people were only able to 'choose' residential care because this was what social security monies would pay for. However, two-thirds of the 103 elderly people interviewed by Allen et al. said that they did not feel they would have been able to stay at home, even with extra help.[4]

The second objective – to prioritize support for carers – represented acknowledgement of the strong campaign, particularly by the Carers' National Association, to put carers' needs on the political agenda. Research has shown clearly that the presence of an informal carer significantly lessens the chance of someone receiving statutory personal social services. Their 'cheapness' reflected their previously hidden policy status.

The third objective – stressing the importance of assessment and care management – reflected the findings of the Personal Social Services Research Unit. But the white paper made no mention of the importance the PSSRU also attached to targeting, which in focusing attention on those in greatest need is also likely to reduce the numbers of cases to which authorities will respond.

Assessment is linked to making services needs-led. It has been a common criticism of social services that they have been preoccupied with delivering a limited range of services, rather than responding to what clients actually need. Nevertheless, it was surprising to find the concept of need so centrally placed in the new approach to community care. Need has always been subject to disagreement from a variety of points of view. Economists have tended to see it as impossible to measure and have put their faith in 'wants' which can be met through the market. New Right theorists have tended to dismiss the idea of need as inherently paternalistic. Certainly it is a 'contested' concept and inevitably so given scarce resources. In the context of community care, the needs of users and carers may be pitted against one another, as well as being contested by the authorities.

Assessment was one of the few specific duties laid on local authorities by the act. However, the act made clear that it is the local authority who will decide whether and how to meet need. The process of assessing need thus encapsulates the tension, unacknowledged in the white paper, between identifying need and allowing choice on the one hand, and rationing on the other. The possible conflict between the needs of user and carer is also unacknowledged. The 1990 Guidance advised: 'local authorities also have a responsibility to meet needs within the resources available and this will sometimes involve difficult decisions where it will be necessary to strike a balance between meeting the needs identified within available resources and meeting the care preferences of the individual'.[5]

The fourth objective – to promote the independent sector – reflected the pressure from the private and voluntary homes lobby and opposition to local government, as well as an ideological commitment to market mechanisms and the principle of separating purchaser from provider. This objective seeks to break the local authority's monopoly provider status and requires a set of market conditions that often do not exist.

Stimulating non-statutory providers was also seen as central to promoting user choice and cost effectiveness. The evidence on the latter is equivocal. Achieving greater choice depends in large measure on the kind of social care market that exists or can be created. One large private or voluntary sector organization contracting with the local authority does not increase choice. Consumer choice requires competitive purchasers, that is, alternatives to social services departments. However, the government rejected this model because it would have been less able to control costs. The policy guidance following the white paper made clear that it is intended that choice should consist in increasing the range of providers and the menu of services the social services staff (not the user) can choose from. In a report prepared for the Joseph Rowntree Foundation in 1992, Alvin Schorr wryly pointed to 'cognitive dissonance' around the issue of choice: 'true choice depends . . . on whether the care that is preferred will be paid for'.[6]

The idea of making services needs-led is not therefore the same as making them user-led. The 'quasi-market' in social services differs from a real market on both the supply and demand sides. The supplier is not necessarily out to maximize profits, nor is the ownership structure necessarily clear. On the demand side, consumer purchasing power is not expressed in cash (purchasing is not financed by the consumer, but by taxes), nor is it the consumer who exercises the choice in purchasing. The academic research on the phenomenon of quasi-markets is important for understanding the dimensions of choice that are offered. The user is not offered the possibility of 'exit' from the system, and this highlights the importance of the 'voice' s/he has via the assessment, care planning and complaints procedures.

The fifth object – to clarify the responsibilities of the agencies involved in community care – acknowledged the large amount of comment on the historical difficulties in securing joint planning and working. For community care to become needs-led it had also to become 'a seamless service'. The white paper and subsequent guidance stated the government's intention to move away from the idea of joint planning as it had emerged in the 1970s and to build instead on the new enabling framework: 'The government proposes to base future national policy on planning agreements rather than joint plans'.[7]

The other main duty laid on local authorities (in addition to assessment) by the act is to consult other agencies in the production of community care plans, with the emphasis on agreeing who should do what for whom, when, at what cost and who should pay. However, given that finance was not in the end linked to an obligation to work together, doubts have been raised, for example, by the House of Commons Social Services Committee, as to whether there are strong enough incentives in place to outweigh the risks and difficulties.

The sixth objective – to introduce a new funding structure – addressed the central concern of government to cut costs by removing the perverse incentive in favour of residential and nursing home care, but this implied a rapid rundown in support for the independent sector, which ran counter to government's parallel objective to promote this sector.

There are thus tensions inherent within these objectives and between them. Most important is that between the focus on the needs of users and carers and the resource constraints, which has been expressed in the effort to establish assessment procedures that are needs-led on the one hand, balanced by strict priorities and eligibility criteria for service on the other. The tension between meeting the needs of carers as well as users has become particularly stark in relation to the eligibility criteria for service. Neither user nor carer has final say in the community care market place. They may be more involved in the assessment process, but 'empowerment' does not extend to free choice of service. Only a voucher system could secure this, which was effectively what the social security system had provided in respect of residential care during the 1980s, but which proved much too expensive. The Independent Living Fund, which operated from 1988 to 1992, did much the same in that it gave disabled people money to pay for care. Its costs also spiralled, from £5m in 1988 to £97m in 1992. The fundamental tension between needs and resources means that there must in the end be strong constraints on user choice.

There is a second tension in the expectation that the creation of enabling authorities will increase choice, given that it is not the user who chooses the service; a professional buys on his behalf. Both the policy guidance and the views of academic commentators have concurred in arguing both that choice of service should be brought as close to the user as possible (in other words, budgets should be devolved), and that the range of providers should be increased in order to make services more responsive to users' wishes. However, both budget devolution and changing the pattern of service provision have raised difficult issues for authorities.

Third, the injunction to social services departments to become enablers and to inject quasi-market principles into social service provision may not sit easily with the parallel injunction to work more effectively with health authorities in particular. The guidance denied any possible tension between promoting a mixed economy of care and quasi-market principles on the one hand, and a 'planned economy' on the other. However, Wistow and Henwood have asked whether non-statutory provision can be incorporated into a planning framework and Hunter has warned that increased competition might be inimical to the trust necessary to develop a seamless service.[8] At the very least, the cultures of health and local authorities continue to be very different, and to some extent the introduction of quasi-market principles into the two services has exacerbated these differences.

Social services departments have been obliged to reconcile the tensions inherent in the new community care policy as best they can. But the process of implementation has also necessitated major internal reorganization within departments (involving the separation of purchaser and provider functions) at a time of severe financial stringency, with detrimental effects on morale and, in some places, on strategic capacity. The new purchaser/provider division has entailed a shift in power relationships and concomitant anxiety on the part of groups of staff, who may feel concern about job security (particularly providers) and/or the precise nature of their roles and tasks (particularly social workers). The substantial reorganization in SSDs is the backdrop for the attempts to reconcile major tensions in the new policy.

IMPLEMENTATION – PROBLEMS AND PROSPECTS

Full implementation of the 1990 act was delayed until April 1993. The shift from a provider-led to a needs-led system, involving the separation of purchasing from providing represented a huge organizational and cultural change for social services departments. Many frontline workers were favourably disposed towards the central idea of user-centredness in the new policy, but one year on disillusion is rife and morale low.

The process of assessment has been central to establishing a needs-led service. But the design of assessment forms has proved difficult and the fear that the process may become mechanistic has refused to go away. The official guidance insisted that assessment should not be performed by providers because they had 'a vested interest in supplying that service',[9] but this cast the role of the social worker into doubt. There has also been great pressure on social services departments to perform assessments quickly, especially in cases of hospital discharge, where government is concerned to prevent 'bed blocking'.

Given the inherent tension between need and resource constraints, social services departments must revise their charging policies (something that has yet to bite), prioritize need and determine eligibility for service. Setting priorities throws the issue of carers' needs into sharp relief, because, logically, it is difficult to prioritize a client for the purchase of service where the carer is showing no imminent failure to cope. In most authorities need is prioritized on the basis of professional judgment as to the existing degree of risk, dependency and statutory responsibility. The District Audit has promoted the idea of needs-led budgeting, which requires SSDs to define levels of need as low, medium and high; to estimate the numbers of users at each level; to define the care components for each level of need; and to agree and cost standard service levels. This amounts to a determination of priorities at the macro-level and enables the authority to work out how many clients it can afford to provide particular services for; eligibility criteria are then set accordingly.

It is possible to see a definition of need emerging from the assessment process. Need is being linked firmly to dependency and risk and hence to resources. The Audit Commission has urged authorities to set such eligibility criteria that they 'allow through just enough people with needs to exactly use up their budget (or be prepared to adjust their budgets)'.[10] Clients at the same level of deterioration may be accorded different priority on account of the willingness and ability of the carer to cope. Perhaps inevitably, need is translating into those whom SSDs cannot ignore. In the circumstances it is also inevitable that unmet need should have become a political issue. A letter from the Department of Health at the end of 1992 cast doubt on whether unmet need should be recorded: 'Practitioners will, therefore, have to be sensitive to the need not to raise unrealistic expectations on the part of users and carers'.[11] However, only by recording and acting on the gap between need and service can the aim of changing the pattern of service provision to make it needs-led be achieved.

Government offered relatively little guidance as to the mechanics of becoming an 'enabling' authority, the other main change necessary to implement the legislation. In December 1992 government decided that 85 per cent of the social security element of the special transitional grant had to be spent in the independent sector. However there are relatively few independent providers of domiciliary services, compared to residential homes. Both the official guidance and academic commentators consider the devolution of budgets as close to the user as possible to be crucial to the success of a competitive quasi-market in social services. However, the costs of trying to create such a market may outweigh the benefits. Multiple negotiations at local level are expensive and as provider 'cartels' develop, purchasing may have to be centralized. And as social services departments enter joint commissioning arrangements with health authorities they face the highly centralized purchasing arrangements common in the NHS.

CONCLUSIONS

The new policy of community care has been accompanied by copious government guidance and relatively little hard prescription as to implementation. This may be interpreted either positively to the effect that government has allowed for regional variation and local preference, or with a degree of cynicism prompted by the inherent tensions and contradictions within the policy which have made clear directions for implementation difficult. The government directives, particularly the 85 per cent rule, reflected the continued determination of government to make LAs into enabling authorities. There has been no slackening in government's resolve to introduce market mechanisms into the public sector; Major's policy has not deviated substantially from its Thatcherite origins.

In face of competing demands, local authorities have pursued very different implementation strategies. From the clients' point of view, it may be that fewer people end up receiving a better service. It seems inevitable that in the main only need defined as high risk/dependency will receive service. But this must be set against the growing proportion of elderly people in the population. 'Grey power' has not become a significant electoral variable in this country as it has in the United States, but the community care changes may have some long-term effect in this respect.

Social services departments have historically been 'doers' and the shift to enabling and purchasing is a major change. In addition, they are being asked to perform a tricky balancing act. The Department of Health wants more of a shift in the balance of resources towards non-residential care and further development of joint commissioning with health authorities, including GP fundholders. On the other hand, the Department also wants a degree of steady state. In particular, it is anxious to avoid market failure on the part of private residential homes and 'bed-blocking' in the NHS. Nor does it want any more publicity about too-rapid hospital discharge or lack of supervision of mentally ill people. To achieve change on the scale that is being demanded is a major challenge, but to accomplish it without noise may be impossible.

While there has been no significant alteration of course in this field under Major, it is becoming more evident how great a leap in the dark the new policy is. Central government has set clear guidelines and has taken steps to make sure that social care provision becomes a social care market, but on the ground LAs now find themselves facing the next wave of problems. Having separated purchasing from providing, how exactly do they structure and manage purchasing? The whole exercise is one gigantic pilot project and the results are hard to predict as the policy takes on a life of its own with the process of implementation. The first real test will come in a year's time with the end of the new money for community care in the form of the special transitional grant, possibly in time to make some impact on the next election campaign.

Notes

1. R. Titmuss, 'Community care: fact or fiction?', in *Commitment to Welfare* (Allen and Unwin, London, 1968), p. 104; lecture originally delivered in 1961.

2. Cmnd. 8173, *Growing Older* (HMSO, London, 1981), para 1.9.

3. I. Sinclair et al., *The Kaleidoscope of Care: a review of research on welfare provision for elderly people* (HMSO, London, 1990); M. Henwood, *Through a Glass Darkly. Community Care and Elderly People* (London King's Fund Institute Research Report no.14, 1992).

4. I. Allen, D. Hogg, and S. Peace, *Elderly People, Choice,*

Participation and Satisfaction (Policy Studies Institute, London, 1992).

5. Department of Health, *Community Care in the Next Decade and Beyond. Policy Guidance* (HMSO, London, 1990), para 3.25.

6. A. Schorr, *The Personal Social Services: An Outside View* (Joseph Rowntree Foundation, York, 1992), p. 22.

7. Cm. 849, *Caring for People. Community Care in the Next Decade and Beyond* (HMSO, London, 1989), para 6.10.

8. G. Wistow and M. Henwood, 'Planning in a mixed economy: life after Griffiths', In R. Parry, ed., *Privatisation* (Jessica Kingsley, London), pp. 32–44; D. J. Hunter, 'To Market! To Market!' A new dawn for community care? *Health and Social Care* 1, 3–10.

9. Department of Health, Social Services Inspectorate, Scottish Office Social Work Services Group, Care Management and Assessment, *Practitioners' Guide* (HMSO, London, 1991), p. 17.

10. Audit Commission, *Taking Care* (Audit Commission, London, 1993), para. 15.

11. C1 (92) 34, Social Services Inspectorate and Department of Health letter, 14/12/92.

Part 4

WIDER RELATIONS

Chapter 22

THE NATIONAL QUESTION

Andrew Gamble

T HE NATIONAL question is an ever-present but often neglected feature of British politics. Britain is a unitary state
but it is also a multinational state. Wales, Northern Ireland
and Scotland differ from England and also from each other in
their relationship to the United Kingdom and in the way in
which they are governed. There is not a single national question in British politics, but a Scottish question, a Welsh
question, an Irish question, and increasingly an English
question.

The Union between the different parts of the United
Kingdom has been a key factor in domestic British politics
throughout the modern period. The Conservative party is still
officially the Conservative and Unionist party, and at one
time earlier in the century was known simply as the Unionist
party. Preserving the Union between the different nations
that make up the United Kingdom has been one of the central
purposes of the party. In the period before 1914 some Conservatives were even prepared to act unconstitutionally in
order to defend the Union with Ireland.

At that time the Union was inseparable from the empire,
so that defence of the Union also meant defence of the
empire. One of the problems for contemporary Conservatives
is discovering a rationale for preserving the Union following
the disengagement from empire and the development of the

European Union. Multinational states are no longer common elsewhere in Europe, and the principle of national self-determination as well as the devolution of power to regions within the European Union has made the British state appear an anachronism, one of the last ancien regimes in Europe. Nationalists have not been slow to urge the break-up of the UK state.

Supporters of the traditional constitutional form of the Union regard the maintenance of the institutions of a unitary state as essential for preserving a British identity which can bind the different nations together. This British identity is under threat from the growth of nationalist sentiment. What being British signifies has become clouded in the post-war era firstly because the United Kingdom is no longer the centre of a British empire but a member of the European Union, secondly because the British state has been relatively unsuccessful in achieving its central policy objectives, particularly in managing the economy; and thirdly because the British population has become culturally and ethnically more mixed as a result of post-war immigration. The complex relationship between Englishness and Britishness has re-emerged.

TERRITORIAL MANAGEMENT

When he became Prime Minister at the end of 1990 John Major inherited two particularly severe, although very different, problems of territorial management, the first in Northern Ireland, the second in Scotland. A third problem was Wales, but it was on a smaller scale.

The two communities in Northern Ireland are two nations, each owing allegiance to a different state. Following a long period of relative quiescence Northern Ireland became a serious security problem for British governments after troops had to be dispatched in 1969 to contain the upsurge of sectarian violence triggered off by civil rights marches. The IRA re-established itself and relaunched its armed struggle against the British state. The security crisis prompted the suspension of Northern Ireland's devolved Parliament, Stormont, and the imposition of direct rule from Westminster. These steps severed the alliance between the Ulster Unionists and the British Conservatives. British policy since that time has been dictated by the twin needs to contain terrorism and promote a political solution involving both communities.

The Scottish problem is very different. The population of Scotland is not divided between rival nations, and has preserved under the Union its own institutions and its distinctive culture and civil society. The practical advantages of the union to Scotland however have dwindled especially with the disappearance of the empire, and the disadvantages of rule from Westminster have become more apparent. The demand for some form of devolution or Home Rule has steadily grown, while support for the Conservative party has declined. The problem facing Conservative governments has been that their mandate to rule Scotland derives from their majority in England. They have not had a majority in Scotland since 1955. This has been exploited by the other parties in Scotland and especially by the Scottish Nationalists who became a significant electoral force in the 1970s.

In Wales the Conservatives have also had to face the growth of nationalist opinion and the demands for a regional assembly. Wales was always more integrated into the United Kingdom than either Ireland or Scotland, but its distinctive cultural identity became the foundation for a nationalist movement which the Labour party sought to neutralize by establishing the Welsh Office in 1964, giving Wales, like Scotland, formal representation in the Cabinet. By recognizing Wales's separateness within the United Kingdom – Yorkshire did not have a Secretary of State – the creation of the Welsh Office made the case for devolution and a regional assembly stronger rather than weaker. But it also created a mechanism for giving Welsh needs and interests greater priority than the regions of England if the government so chose.

SCOTLAND

Little has changed in government policy towards Scotland and Wales since John Major became Prime Minister. He has been content to hold the line, seeking to prevent any further erosion in the Conservative position. The historical trend which has seen Conservative support in Scotland both in terms of seats and of votes halved since 1955 was not something that could be swiftly reversed. By abandoning the poll tax John Major removed one of the Scots' greatest grievances against the Thatcher government but the reason for the policy change lay in England rather than Scotland.

John Major had an opportunity at the 1992 election to reposition the Conservatives in Scotland by announcing Conservative support for a Scottish Parliament. The demand for the establishment of a Scottish Assembly had been endorsed by a broad coalition within Scotland during the 1980s and led to the establishment of the cross-party Scottish Constitutional Convention which included representatives of the trade unions, the Churches and the Labour party and the Liberal Democratic party. Among the opposition parties only the Scottish Nationalists had boycotted it, preferring to campaign on their demand for Scottish independence within the European Union. By 1992 the proposal for a separate Scottish Assembly, elected under a form of proportional representation and with substantial powers to raise taxes and to determine domestic policy in Scotland, had clear majority support within the Scottish electorate, including among many Conservatives who saw it as a way to blunt the advance of the Nationalists.

The Conservative leadership however decided to fight the election on a traditional Unionist platform, warning that there was a straight choice between the Union and complete independence. Ian Lang, the Scottish Secretary, was given considerable autonomy in developing this strategy, but it was also endorsed by Major. The Conservatives argued that an elected Parliament in Scotland with extensive powers, including the right to tax, would be incompatible with the party's traditional commitment to maintain the unity of the country. John Major declared in a speech at Glasgow: 'It is our party that supports the Union, not because it has always been good for us, but because it has always seemed right to us. Not always in our political interest, but always in that of our Kingdom and the countries within it' (Glasgow, 22 February 1992).

Ian Lang developed this point by arguing that any move towards Home Rule would so weaken the Union that it would be a slippery slope to full independence. During the election campaign John Major again endorsed this line and castigated the opposition parties for risking its destruction and playing into the hands of the Nationalists.

The result of the election was hailed as a great triumph for this strategy. In contrast to the rest of the UK, the Conservatives marginally increased their vote in Scotland and hung on to many seats which they had been expected to lose. (Their vote increased from 24 to 25.6 per cent and their seats from 10 to 11.) The result was not a decisive reversal in the trend of Conservative electoral decline (it was the third worst ever electoral result for the Conservatives in Scotland), but it did mark at least a temporary halt in their downward spiral, and gave the party a breathing space. The opposition's confident expectations that Conservative support would be reduced to such low levels that the government would be forced to concede the demands for constitutional change were disappointed. The problem of legitimating Conservative control of the Scottish Office with only minority support among Scottish voters and Scottish MPs remained, but it did not get worse.

Having signalled his commitment to the Union, John Major did move cautiously after 1992 to provide some reassurance to Scottish opinion. The Thatcherite attitude that the sooner the Scots embraced Thatcherism the better for them was relaxed. During 1993 a number of proposals were made to allow Scots to gain greater control over Scottish affairs. A blueprint for Scottish government was presented to the Cabinet in March 1993, followed by a white paper. These proposals stopped far short of the Scottish Assembly which the opposition parties wanted. They offered minor adjustments to the handling of Scottish business at Westminster, with the possibility of the Scottish Grand Committee (composed of the Scottish MPs) meeting sometimes in Edinburgh instead of London. The government also promised to take more account of the distinctive social and legal systems in Scotland.

Such initiatives made only very minor concessions to Scottish opinion. They strongly reflected Ian Lang's view that the union was best preserved by maintaining Scottish representation in the Cabinet. But they did signal a modest desire on John Major's part to heal the damaging rift which had opened between England and Scotland during the Thatcher years, and to let the Scots know that they were being listened to again at Westminster. One sign of this was the decision not to go ahead with full water privatization, as in England, but to set up new public boards outside local authority control to run the industry. Even concessions like these however did little to assuage Scottish opinion. Ninety-seven per cent of voters in the Strathclyde region rejected the plan on a 72 per cent turnout in a referendum organized by the Strathclyde Council in March 1994.

John Major's general impact on the Scottish question has been to lower the temperature, and to defuse some of the offence which was caused by the aggressive style sometimes adopted in the past by English Conservatives such as Margaret Thatcher and Nigel Lawson. Thatcher was puzzled why the land of Adam Smith was so resistant to the Thatcherite message, while Nigel Lawson castigated the dependency culture in Scotland. Thatcherites tended to see Scotland as a problem, a prime example of the British disease, with its large public sector housing, high subsidies, and highly unionized and overmanned industries. They would not accept that Scotland had a right to exercise different choices from England.

John Major did signal a different approach, but it did not embrace constitutional changes, only a difference in the way in which policies were implemented. Scotland was no longer to be treated as a possible laboratory for ideological experiments, but was to be regarded once more as a special part of the Constitution, with its own identity and concerns which needed to be respected. Conservatives were uneasily aware however that the erosion of Conservative support in Scotland ran deep, and that preventing further erosion in the future could be very difficult because in large parts of Scotland the

Conservatives had come to be regarded as an English rather than a Scottish party. Since both the Labour party and the Liberal Democrats were committed to setting up a Scottish Assembly, and were supported by a clear majority of Scottish opinion, the only way of averting future constitutional change was to ensure continued Conservative victories at British national general elections. As in some other areas of policy John Major's instinct was to play for time, hoping that Conservative support in Scotland could be rebuilt but without any clear idea of how that might be done.

WALES

One of the features of territorial management in the British state is that it creates institutions and procedures which give certain regions a degree of autonomy from central government policies. Secretaries of State for Wales and Scotland have traditionally enjoyed considerable freedom in determining a regional strategy. In the 1980s this often meant that these territories were protected from the full rigour of Thatcherite policies by Secretaries of State such as George Younger in Scotland and Peter Walker in Wales.

In Wales this process was taken one stage further when Peter Walker was appointed Secretary of State in 1987. Walker had been a close ally of Heath and was a persistent critic of Thatcherite economic policy. He used his powers to launch an effective industrial strategy for Wales of a kind which English regions were denied. By the 1992 election the Conservatives were happy to present Wales as one of their greatest success stories, although it had been achieved by methods of government intervention which broke some key Thatcherite principles.

John Major continued this policy towards Wales by appointing David Hunt as Secretary of State, whose attitudes were close to those of Peter Walker. In 1993 however he appointed John Redwood, a leading Thatcherite. The appointment did not signal any desire on John Major's part for a change in policy towards Wales, but only the vagaries of

Cabinet reshuffles. Major needed to bring Redwood in to keep the Cabinet balanced, following Lamont's departure, but also wanted to promote Hunt.

Redwood has been careful to continue the broad lines of policy established by his predecessors. He has used his office to make policy pronouncements on a wide range of national issues, but not to pursue a Thatcherite agenda in Wales. In this he follows a traditional Conservative instinct: the best way to preserve the union is not to concede devolution of powers to regional assemblies, but to use central powers of the unitary state to create a policy space in which the distinctive needs and interests of Wales and Scotland can be recognized and accommodated (at some financial cost to the rest of the country). Major made no significant change to this traditional Conservative approach and continued to give his Secretaries of State considerable discretion over how they developed policy.

NORTHERN IRELAND

Northern Ireland was a much more intractable problem than Scotland, and has been a constant preoccupation of modern British governments since 1969. The most significant development since 1990 was the signing of the Downing Street Declaration in December 1993 between the British and Irish governments, in a bid to start a peace process which would end the sectarian violence by both the Republican and Protestant paramilitaries.

This declaration was hailed by many commentators at the time as the most significant initiative which any British government had taken for twenty years – since the Sunningdale Agreement in December 1973 – and there was also agreement that John Major's involvement was crucial. He gave the initiative great prominence, both in a speech at the Lord Mayor's banquet and in the Queen's Speech in November 1993, ahead of other matters such as the 'Back to Basics' programme with which he had tried to re-establish his authority at the party conference in October. By identifying himself personally with the initiative in this way he signalled its importance.

The new initiative showed many continuities with previous policy on Northern Ireland. In the search for a political solution in the past the British government had been prepared to hold secret talks with the IRA and to seek common ground with the Irish government, indicating a readiness to override the Unionist veto if necessary. Both these features were present in the 1993 initiative.

When Major became Prime Minister the Northern Ireland problem remained deadlocked. The level of IRA and UVF violence had been contained during the 1980s, but the capacity of the IRA to carry out spectacular attacks such as the bombing of the Cabinet's hotel in Brighton in 1984, remained undiminished. A series of atrocities continued through 1991, 1992, and 1993. Some of the worst incidents took place during 1993 while secret talks about peace were proceeding. On 20 March an IRA bomb in Warrington killed two children and injured fifty-six people. On 24 April an IRA bomb in the city of London killed one, injured forty-seven and caused damage estimated at £1 billion. On 23 October an IRA bomb in the Shankill Road killed ten people and injured fifty-nine. A revenge UVF atttack on the Greysteel pub on 30 October killed seven people. These events and the revulsion they caused helped to speed efforts to find a new formula to end the violence.

Political initiatives in Northern Ireland have been built around three complex relationships; firstly between the two governments in Dublin and London; secondly between the British government and the constitutional parties in Northern Ireland; and thirdly between the British government and the IRA. Internal talks between the constitutional parties were intractable because the Unionists always sought to block any political moves which involved either Dublin or the IRA, while the Social Democratic and Labour party (SDLP) insisted on Dublin being included.

Major's task in developing a new initiative was eased by developments that had taken place under his predecessor. Thatcher had been an instinctive Unionist and was an implacable opponent of the IRA, as she showed during the

Maze hunger strikes in 1980, but she was still prepared to sign the Anglo-Irish Agreement in 1985, despite Unionist outrage, because she recognized the practical advantages of involving Dublin in the search for a political settlement which would help to isolate the IRA in Northern Ireland.

John Major's first step was to explore once again the possibility of an agreement between the constitutional parties in Northern Ireland. Repeated attempts had been made by the British government since the suspension of Stormont in 1972 to set up internal talks to persuade the constitutional parties to agree a political framework for the governing of the province. These talks had always foundered because the nationalists demanded arrangements that guaranteed them a share in power while the Unionists would not accept any dilution of Northern Ireland's links with Britain. Under John Major a further attempt was made. Talks were arranged by the Northern Ireland Secretary, Peter Brooke, under the chairmanship of Sir Ninian Stephen. After the 1992 election they were continued under his successor, Patrick Mayhew, but ended without agreement in the autumn of 1992.

The 1993 initiative tried another route. The constitutional parties were kept on the sidelines, while talks went on between the British and Irish governments and secret talks were resumed with the IRA. There had been earlier talks in the 1970s, but almost no contact during the 1980s. The date when the talks recommenced is uncertain. The IRA claim the first contacts took place in 1990, before Margaret Thatcher left office. The British government insists that there were no contacts until a message was received from the IRA in February 1992. What is certain is that the talks, which were held during 1993, were lengthy and detailed, and were a significant factor in making possible the Downing Street Agreement in December. Given the sensitivity of these talks John Major's personal endorsement of them was essential.

Suspicions that contacts between the IRA and the government had resumed grew during 1993, but the government resolutely denied it. On 1 November 1993 John Major told the House of Commons that talking to the IRA 'would turn my stomach over. We would not do it.' Leaked documents showing that there had been contacts since the previous

February were released on 27 November and forced the government to its considerable embarrassment to admit that there had been talks. It issued its own account backed up by forty pages of documents, and vigorously contended that while there had been talks there had been no negotiations, as the IRA claimed, and that the talks had only commenced at the IRA's instigation. The government claimed that the IRA had sent a message on 22 February 1993 which stated, 'The conflict is over but we need your advice on how to bring it to a close.' The British government's response four days later was: 'We understand and appreciate the seriousness of what has been said. We wish to take it seriously.'

While both sides preferred to put their own gloss on what had happened, the significant development was that the talks had taken place at all. It seems unlikely that Thatcher would have sanctioned them. These direct contacts with the IRA took place alongside the Hume-Adams dialogue which began after the Warrington bombing on 20 March which involved protracted discussions between the leader of the Social Democratic and Labour Party and Sinn Fein and produced its own detailed set of proposals that Downing Street claimed to know nothing about, but which were clearly one of the factors making the Downing Street Declaration possible. They were a further sign that the IRA might be willing to enter into serious negotiations about peace. Intelligence reports from MI5 about the debates within Sinn Fein and the IRA may also have been a factor in persuading the government to take such a bold initiative.

A further factor which made the Declaration possible was the new government in Ireland, which brought Dick Spring and the Irish Labour Party into coalition with the nationalist Fianna Fail under Albert Reynolds. A new political impetus in Dublin coincided with John Major's willingness to sanction a fresh approach from London. The cost in both lives and money, and the apparent pointlessness of the long struggle with the IRA, had created a mood of weariness in the British government and a strong desire to find a way of ending the conflict and getting rid of the Irish question from British politics once and for all.

The text of the Declaration which was signed on

16 December was notable chiefly for its vagueness and generality, but the serious purpose behind it was clear enough. The strategy of the two governments was to find a form of words which would reassure the two communities in Northern Ireland that their legitimate national aspirations would be safeguarded, while going far enough to provide the IRA with a reason for terminating its armed struggle and, after an interval, entering negotiations on the future of Ireland as a legitimate constitutional party.

The substance of the agreement therefore turned on whether the Irish government would agree to change Articles 2 and 3 in the Irish constitution which claimed Irish sovereignty over the whole territory of Ireland, and whether the British government would acknowledge the aspiration of the Irish people for a united Ireland to be a legitimate one. A further IRA demand was that the British government should not only accept the aspiration but should 'join the persuaders'. This implied that it would actively campaign to persuade the Unionists to join a new federal state in Ireland. Lloyd George had pledged the same in 1922.

The final wording fell short of what each side wanted. The Irish government only promised to review its constitution as part of a comprehensive settlement of the Northern Ireland issue. The British government accepted that Ireland could be united if the people of Ireland one day wanted that, but stopped short of saying that a united Ireland would be the most desirable outcome, or of promising to seek to persuade the Unionists.

Sceptics concluded that the Declaration really said very little that was new, and argued that the IRA was unlikely to accept it. The initial signs after the signing were not promising, and new bomb attacks and sectarian murders resumed in 1994. If John Major and Albert Reynolds had hoped that it might bring peace by Christmas, and that their boldness would reap a swift and dramatic reward, they were disappointed. But the declaration certainly opened a new phase in the Northern Ireland problem. It signalled that the Irish and British governments were prepared to build on the Anglo-Irish Agreement and extend their cooperation, and that they would seek to establish peace through the cooperation of the IRA. Indeed

one common view of the talks with the IRA and the subsequent Declaration was that the two governments were
endeavouring to split the IRA, by bringing into the constitutional process the elements around Gerry Adams, while
isolating hardline cadres in the Ardoyne and South Armagh.

Such a strategy was fraught with risk, because it required
an effective surrender by the bulk of the IRA, an implied
admission that the long struggle had failed, and that the
Unionist community could not be coerced into a United
Ireland but could only be cajoled to join over a much longer
period. The gain for the Nationalists was largely a symbolic
one. It was an acknowledgement by the British government
that it had no intrinsic claim to make upon the territory of
Ireland and would be as happy for Northern Ireland to be
reunited with the Republic of Ireland as it would for it to
remain in the United Kingdom. The crucial phrase in the
Declaration to which many commentators drew attention
was the assertion that Britain 'had no selfish strategic or
economic interest in Northern Ireland.' One of the last Conservative Unionists in the House of Commons, Nicholas Budgen, asked the Prime Minister whether the British
government had a strategic interest in Wolverhampton. John
Major evaded the question, but the point was well made.
Northern Ireland was defined more clearly than ever before
as a territory that was not an integral part of the British state,
and might under certain circumstances be transferred to
another sovereignty.

This admission had long been implicit in British policy,
and had been foreshadowed by Edward Heath at the time of
the Sunningdale Agreement and by Margaret Thatcher at the
time of the Anglo-Irish Agreement. Once Britain and Ireland
were both members of the European Community a re-
evaluation of the strategic and economic importance of maintaining British sovereignty over Northern Ireland was bound
to be made. Since the point of the European Community was
to establish common rules throughout its area, the interest in
the British state retaining exclusive sovereignty over a dis-
puted territory within the Community presented an anomaly.
European Union made British Union less important.

THE ENGLISH QUESTION

John Major endorsed the traditional Conservative approach to the Union, even though it was clear that this approach was not halting the growth of nationalism, or winning back support for the Conservatives in Wales, Scotland, or Northern Ireland. The union is no longer the pillar of Conservative politics that it was. As it has weakened so the English question has become more central. For John Major the national question in British politics has been increasingly about England.

The resurgence of a more assertive English nationalism is only partly a reaction to the assertion of nationalisms in other parts of the United Kingdom. Despite continuing differences between North and South in voting behaviour and in prosperity, England continues to lack the kind of strong regional identities which have political consequences. English nationalism has been fuelled primarily by resentments stemming from the loss of empire, from membership of the European Union, and from the problems of a multi-cultural and multi-ethnic society.

Ever since Enoch Powell demonstrated the possibilities, many Conservatives have hankered after a more assertive cultural Conservatism which, while avoiding racism, would proclaim and defend the values of English culture and insist that these values be given priority. They see the Union under threat from resurgent Celtic nationalisms on the periphery while England is in danger of losing its distinctive identity through attempts to impose the alien practices and values of a multi-cultural society and of a federal European Union.

John Major has resisted the pressures from this wing of his party, but at the expense of not being able to define clearly what an English identity is. Over Europe his policy has often been determined by the need to hold his party together in the face of its deepening divisions. Over race he has reaffirmed the Conservative commitment to a multiracial and multicultural society, as shown for example by his support for John Taylor, the black Conservative candidate at Cheltenham who encountered hostility from a section of his local Conservative Association.

Major's experience as a Brixton councillor gave him an insight into the problems of the ethnic minorities which few Conservative leaders obtain, and he consistently refused to give any support to those elements in his own party who wished to use the race card as part of a revived English national identity. The lead he gave on ethnic issues was generally liberal, aimed at reassuring the ethnic communities that they had a full part to play in British society, but his period in office still saw a worrying increase in ethnic tensions, and signs of a backlash in some white inner-city communities.

CONCLUSION

John Major proclaimed himself a strong believer in the British Union, but his approach to the national question in British politics was substantially different from that of his predecessor. He represented a pragmatic, common-sense English nationalism. He was happy for the British Union to continue if that is what the other nations wanted, but he was not the kind of politician who believed in the principle of the Union so strongly that he would take steps to coerce others to remain within it against their will. On both Scotland and Northern Ireland he made a clear commitment that should a majority in either ever wish to depart the Union the Westminster government would not stand in their way.

John Major's impact on the Scottish question was minor. He did not take the opportunity to revive the earlier support which the Conservative party under Edward Heath had given to the principle of devolution of powers to elect assemblies in Wales and Scotland. He continued the strong centralist line of Margaret Thatcher, and allowed his Secretary of State, Ian Lang, to set policy. But unlike Thatcher, Major did appear to recognize the grave damage to the Union and to the Conservative interest in Wales and Scotland which her assertive English nationalism was inflicting. There was a noticeably softer and more conciliatory tone, and the separateness and special interests of Scotland in particular were once more realized. John Major, however, had no great new project to put before the Scottish people to explain why they should continue to support a centralized Union rather than seek a Parliament of their own. Although a very different personality from Thatcher he appeared, like her, a very English politician, with no special appeal outside the English heartland. His period as Prime Minister has done little to re-establish the Union on a secure basis or to re-establish the fortunes of the Conservatives in either Scotland or Wales.

His main impact has been on policy towards Ireland. It is too soon to say whether the 1993 peace initiative will ultimately succeed. The early signs were that it would not. The verbal concessions that had been made seemed not to be sufficient to persuade the IRA to abandon the armed struggle against the British state. But the agreement is still likely to be viewed retrospectively as a milestone in Anglo-Irish relations. It brings significantly nearer the prospect of a united Ireland, by distancing Britain from a long-term role in Ireland, and embracing wholeheartedly the principle of collaboration with the Irish Republic to resolve the problem of the two nations in the North. Through this agreement John Major demonstrated that while the Conservative party still proclaims itself a Unionist party, in practice little is left of the old Unionist faith.

Chapter 23

MASS MEDIA

Colin Seymour-Ure

WHEN ASKED about a 'Major effect' to do with mass
media, one might be forgiven for assuming the ques-
tioner meant an effect *on* John Major, not one caused *by* him.
He was the victim, as time went on, of a slither of publicity
disasters – about policies, colleagues and his own leadership.
Gut loyalty of tabloid papers such as the *Daily Mail* and the
Sun gave way to calls for his replacement before doom struck
at the next general election. Even the smooth progress of
policy about the future of broadcasting was coarsened by the
accident (itself caused by press exposure) of his chosen minister, David Mellor, having to resign after an affair with an
actress.

GOVERNMENT RELATIONS WITH THE MEDIA

There are deeper reasons, however, why one might expect the
effect of any Prime Minister on mass media to be limited. For
media are not a traditional policy field in Britain. Broadcasting policy hid for decades behind the innocuous figure of
the Postmaster General; and still in the 1990s it lurked,
bizarrely, in a 'Heritage' ministry. Governments' preference

was for framework legislation, which left arm's-length bodies such as the BBC and Independent Broadcasting Authority (now Independent Television Commission) to get on with the job. For the press, there was not even framework legislation but a policy of 'no policy'. Papers were subject to the same laws as everyone else. These might have strong effects, like Mrs Thatcher's industrial relations laws; but they were a part of broader policy goals, not of direct and explicit press policies.

In general, then, it may be said that there are policies in a variety of fields (including trade, competition, taxation, security, civil rights, industrial relations), which affect media among other organizations; and, secondly, that there is a smaller range of specific media policies, notably about broadcasting. But there is no overarching, coherent media policy. Even a strong Major effect on media, therefore, would be different from the possible effects, say, on Health or Defence.

One of the most distinctive features of media, furthermore, is their entanglement with day-to-day government and politics, including the procedures of democratic accountability. John Major himself is much more likely to have become absorbed with media relations in this form – striving to keep his footing in the slither of disasters – than in high policy. During the 1980s there was indeed a 'Thatcher effect' of this kind. Bernard Ingham, Mrs Thatcher's press secretary, became one of her very closest advisers. Other advisers, on anything from personal grooming to campaign strategy, were sometimes prominent in her entourage (and subsequently in the honours lists). Downing Street news operations were probably managed more effectively than at any previous time, certainly since television intruded into politics. John Major, by contrast, seemed woefully ineffective. In the media policy areas, similarly, the Major government followed trends which, insofar as government influenced them at all, were set by Mrs Thatcher.

THE IMPACT OF THE 1990
BROADCASTING ACT

Mrs Thatcher's stamp was set especially strongly on the shape of ITV. John Major took office after the passage of the 1990 Broadcasting Act, and its fruits, widely regarded as rotten on the tree, were still being borne in 1994. Douglas Hurd, the minister ultimately responsible at the time, described the act later as 'one of the least successful reforms' of the Thatcher years.[1] Mrs Thatcher was convinced that ITV was inefficient, too rich and over-regulated. The key reform was the introduction of an 'auction principle' to the bidding process by which the sixteen franchises were periodically allocated. Applicants were to estimate what they could afford to pay the Treasury annually out of their advertising revenue and submit a sealed bid. Frantic lobbying by broadcasters persuaded David Mellor, the junior Home Office minister in charge, to strengthen the bill's 'quality threshold', which bidders would have to pass before the cash test was applied.

The act made many other changes. The national networking system was replaced, to give smaller companies and independent producers more chance of showing their programmes outside a single region. Ownership of ITN was broken up. Channel 4 was to sell its own advertising. Companies were to buy 20 per cent of their programmes from independent producers. A new Channel 5 franchise was to be awarded. The Independent Television Commission was to have a 'light touch'. All this, and much else, was supposed to embody 'deregulation'. Yet the act emerged three times as long as the previous legislation regulating ITV, and with more detailed prescriptions.

The most newsworthy product of the act came nearly a year after John Major took office. On 15 October 1991 the ITC faxed to applicants its decisions about the franchises starting on 1 January 1993. (See Table 1.) Thirty-seven applications had been submitted for the fifteen regional franchises and three for the national breakfast time licence. In three regions the existing franchisee was sole bidder. One of these, Central TV, knowing the position, bid a derisory £2,000. Carlton, in contrast, bid £43 million to win the comparably

Table 1: ITV franchises (bids in 1992 prices; viewing figures
represent total possible audiences)

Region	Winner	Owners	Losers
National Breakfast 54.8m viewers	Sunrise TV Bid £34.6m	LWT (20%)/Scottish TV (20%)/*Guardian* and *Manchester Evening News* (15%)/Walt Disney (15%)/30% to be placed	TV-am (incumbent, £14.12m) Daybreak TV (£33.3m)
London weekday 10.57m viewers	Carlton Television Bid £43.2m	Carlton Communications (90%)/*Daily Telegraph* (5%)/Rizzoli Corriere della Sera (5%)	Thames (incumbent, £32.5m)/CPV-TV (£45.3m, failed quality)
London weekend 10.57m viewers	LWT (incumbent) Bid £7.58m	Institutional investors, directors	London Independent Broadcasting (£35.4m, failed quality)
South and Southeast 5.044m viewers	Meridian Broadcasting Bid £36.5m	MAI (65%)/Central TV (20%/Selec TV (15%)	TVS (incumbent, £59.8m, overbid)/Carlton (£18.1m)/CPV-TV (£22.1m, failed quality)
Midlands 9.2m viewers	Central Independent Broadcasting (incumbent) Bid £2,000	Carlton (19.4%)/D. C. Thomson & Co (19.2%)	Unchallenged
North West 6.33m viewers	Granada Television (incumbent) Bid £9m	Granada Group (100%)	North West TV (35.5m, failed quality)
Yorkshire 5.43m viewers	Yorkshire Television (incumbent) Bid £37.7m)	Institutional investors	White Rose (£17.4m)/Viking (£30.1m, failed quality)
East of England 3.858m viewers	Anglia Television (incumbent) Bid £17.8m	Institutional investors	Three East (£14.1m)/CPV-TV (£10.1m, failed quality)
Wales and the West 4.298m viewers	HTV (incumbent) Bid £20.5m	Phillips & Drew (9.5%)/FMR Corp (6%)/Barclays Bank (7.6%)	C3W (£17.8m)/Merlin (£19.4m, failed quality)/C3WW (£18.3m, failed quality)
South West England 1.52m viewers	Westcountry Television Bid £7.8m	Assoc. Newspapers (20%)/Brittany Ferries (15%)/South West Water (20%)/Trilion (10%)	TSW (incumbent, £16.1m, overbid)/TeleWest (£7.3m, failed quality)

Region	Winner	Owners	Losers
Northern Ireland 1.4m viewers	Ulster Television (incumbent) Bid £1.02m	Institutional investors	TVni (£3.1m, failed business plan)/ Lagan (2.7m, failed quality)
North East 2.852m viewers	Tyne Tees Television (incumbent) Bid £15.1m	Institutional investors	North East Television (£5m)
North Scotland 1.095m viewers	Grampian (incumbent) Bid £720,000	Local businessmen	C3 Caledonia (£1.13m, failed quality)/North of Scotland TV (£2.71m, failed quality)
Borders 629,000 viewers	Border Television Bid £52,000	Local businessmen	Unchallenged
Central Scotland 3.557m viewers	Scottish Television Bid £2,000	Chase Nominees (8%)/Scottish Amicable (7%)/ Phildrew Nominees (6.7%)/Bank of Scotland (6.6%)	Unchallenged
Channel Islands 135,000 viewers	Channel Television (incumbent) Bid £1,000	Channel Islands Communications (100%)	C13 (£102,000, failed quality)

valuable London weekday franchise from Thames. (No one working on the bill, presumably, had thought of this eventuality.)

In addition to Thames, three companies lost their franchises. TVS (south and south east) lost to Meridian, TSW (south west) to Westcountry TV and TV-am (breakfast) to Sunrise TV. TVS and TSW had both put in the highest bid and passed the quality threshold, but the ITC did not think they would be able to afford actually to implement their plans. Four of the surviving franchisees won by submitting top bids. The other five survivors, including Granada, were luckier, in the sense that they were outbid, but by companies who failed the quality test.

TV-am seemed the most upset among the losers. Its bid trailed two competitors by £14 million to £33/£34 million. The irony was that Bruce Gyngell, its flamboyant Australian chairman, had made a fan out of Mrs Thatcher, and thereby helped to entrench the auction principle, by his determination to eliminate overmanning and by his success in strike-breaking. 'When I see how some of the licences have been awarded,' Mrs Thatcher wrote in a personal letter, which Gyngell pulled out of his pocket and read in an after-lunch speech, 'I am *mystified* that you did not receive yours, and heartbroken. You of all people have done so much for the whole of television and there seems to be no attention to that. I am only too painfully aware that *I* was responsible for the legislation.'

Those results typify the unsatisfactory nature of the 1990 Broadcasting Act. Equally Mrs Thatcher's reaction typifies her own characteristic involvement in the direction of reform. John Major, when the corresponding issue of reform of the BBC arose, gave little sign of a comparable concern.

The franchise winners were scrutinized carefully in the first year of operation for signs of the lower programme quality which critics feared as an inevitable consequence of the auction system. Sure enough, the ITC's 'Performance Review' of the companies' first year made some scathing criticisms, notably of Carlton ('unimpressive ... well below expectations') and GMTV, the renamed Sunrise. GMTV was given a formal warning, which meant that if its service did not improve it could face a substantial fine the next year. As a result of the franchise bids, nearly one quarter of ITV's advertising and sponsorship revenue in 1993 – some £360 million – was paid to the Treasury, on top of the companies' normal corporation tax. This was a little more than the total income earned by Channel 4, so it could be rightly claimed that the government was taking out of the ITV system a sum sufficient to run an entire channel. Some at least of that money might otherwise have been used to pay for higher quality programmes.

OWNERSHIP IN BROADCASTING

Judgements about quality were inevitably subjective. Of more practical import to the Major administration by the end of 1993 were the linked questions of concentration of ownership within the ITV system and cross-ownership with other media. Both questions appeared to be subject to a dramatic change of mood, which owed little to the government. From its start in 1955, the ITV system had excluded companies from owning more than one franchise. The 1990 act relaxed this rule, after a moratorium, only to the extent of permitting joint ownership of one small and one large franchise. Cross-ownership between press and ITV companies had been permitted at the start, to protect newspapers from a possible drain of advertising revenue to the new medium; but the ITC's predecessors had limited strictly the scale of involvement. The 1990 act set this at 20 per cent.

What confronted the Major government with a novel issue was the self-interested (but not necessarily inaccurate) claim by the ITV industry that companies were increasingly operating to such an extent both in international television markets and in multimedia markets (cable, satellite, etc.) that they would not be able to survive unless permitted to amalgamate. Already European, Japanese and American giants such as Bertelsmann, Fininvest (Berlusconi), Time Warner, Bell Atlantic, Viacom and Sony dwarfed the largest British broadcasters. The force of this claim was sufficient to overcome even the Labour leadership's conventional hostility to media concentration.

The government's first step was to relax the ITV takeover rules in November 1993. This permitted Carlton to take over Central and Meridian to join with Anglia in 'friendly' deals; while Granada won LWT after a hard-fought hostile bid. Earlier, Yorkshire had already been given approval to take over its small neighbour, Tyne-Tees. Peter Brooke, David Mellor's successor as National Heritage Secretary, then announced on 3 January 1994 a review of the rules on cross-ownership, with results expected in about a year.

Cross-ownership was potentially much the more contentious issue than take-overs. The ITV franchises were hedged with programme requirements to protect regional interests, news services and so on. For decades the BBC had operated as a national programme provider, and public expectations about scale and concentration of TV ownership had none of the historic connotations of a 'free press' operating in an open market. Besides, Mrs Thatcher was widely regarded as having loaded the ownership rules in favour of Rupert Murdoch, whose robust attitude to the print unions and initiative in launching Sky satellite TV had impressed her. While the 1990 Broadcasting Act limited press groups to 20 per cent of terrestrial TV and so-called domestic satellite TV companies, it placed no restrictions on cross-holdings with *non*-domestic satellites. Into this category the BSkyB service controlled by Murdoch conveniently fell. Decades of rhetoric, by no means all of it from the left, about the parlous effects of media concentration upon the cultural and political health of the nation, seemed now to have no resonance at all. It was a sign of the changed nature of public debate since the Thatcher years that a government would confront this issue without a great cry from its opponents and a major public inquiry. It was difficult to see, while awaiting the outcome of Peter Brooke's review, that there would be anything distinctive about the Major administration's approach.

BBC CHARTER

Renewal of the BBC's Charter (the document which, with its licence, provides its legal authority) was another opportunity for the Major government to make a distinctive impact. The Charter is renewable every ten to fifteen years, and to some extent policy about the BBC is always a kind of continuous dialogue, affected by developments that do not happen to fit that cycle. A debate about the future of the compulsory licence fee (£84.50 in 1994), the BBC's guaranteed core funding, had been continuing since Mrs Thatcher set up a committee under the economist Sir Alan Peacock in 1985, to consider the various alternatives. Mrs Thatcher hoped the committee would damn the licence fee. But instead they decided it was the least unsuitable form of supporting a national public service broadcasting system, and it withstood a battery of ingenious proposals for advertising, sponsorship, subscription and taxation revenues. Peter Brooke, presumably with John Major's consent, announced fairly early in the consultation phase, in November 1993, that the licence fee would remain after 1996. The BBC, in other words, was not to be privatized. This decision set the terms for the rest of the argument about its future.

The formal debate within the BBC itself was conducted through fifteen task forces, with a crescendo of meetings that included a hugely expensive summer retreat, provoking ribald comment, in a Cotswold country hotel. The outcome was a glossy eighty-eight page document, *Extending Choice* (BBC, 1992), which promised more efficiency, a clearer role for the Governors (who legally *are* the BBC) and a new complaints system. Its reinterpretation of the founding principles of public service broadcasting proposed concentrating on 'a set of clearly defined roles that best complement the enlarged commercial sector'. This was an important admission. Right up to the launch of satellite broadcasting, the BBC's assumption had been that 'if it's broadcasting, the BBC does it'. Now, it foresaw a core role as supplier of news and information, as stimulator of the national culture (including sport and entertainment), and as provider of educational and overseas programmes. The more frilly-knickered aspects of life would be left to commercial channels.

DIVERSIFICATION IN BROADCASTING

Many such developments were already in train, including the new twenty-four-hour satellite TV World Service (WSTV), initially beamed at Asia in a series of local partnership deals, and the hit repeat satellite channel, jointly owned with Thames TV, called UK Gold. Radio 3 was gently popularized, to combat the success of the national commercial station, Classic FM, launched in September 1992. Most controversial inside the BBC was the managerial reform known as 'producer choice'. This was intended to cut costs by allowing producers to buy programme services not only in house but on the open market. It was introduced amidst confusion, frustration and ill will.

The Future of the BBC, the green paper published by the Heritage Secretary, Peter Brooke, at about the same time as Extending Choice, was limited mainly to stating the issue: what should be the aims of public service broadcasting in the future; what services should the BBC provide; how should they be paid and accounted for?[2] It seemed likely, though, that with the BBC moving managerially in a 'privatized' direction, under its tough new Director General, John Birt, Charter renewal would not involve the kind of wholesale reform and dismemberment that would probably have followed from abandonment or modification of the licence fee.

PRESS OWNERSHIP

The Major administration's attitude to the press also followed lines set by Mrs Thatcher. Her government did not seem interested in the structure and pattern of ownership. Papers would carp – and might seriously affect the careers of ministers such as Cecil Parkinson and Leon Brittan – but they played the right tunes at the right times (general elections, the Falklands war, the 1984 coal strike). Mrs Thatcher's chief interest was in the industry's famously bad labour relations, which in the extreme case had kept The Times newspapers off the news stands in 1979 (at management's initiative) for a whole year. Her government's legislation about secondary picketing, in particular, helped Murdoch after he moved his newspapers overnight to Wapping in 1986 and sacked production staff in the traditional unions. That victory made easier the foundation of papers such as The Independent and transformed the profitability of others.

The consequences of the Wapping revolution were still working themselves out during the Major administration. Moreover, national newspapers remained in a long-run declining market, and individual titles, as always, were likely to find themselves financially strained. The Observer, for example, was weakly positioned in the Sunday market and was bought by *The Guardian* group in 1993 after a struggle with *The Independent*. *The Independent* itself, lacking the cushion of conglomerate ownership, needed major injections of capital in 1994, after competition from the other broadsheets (themselves improved, ironically, by standards *The Independent* set) ate into its circulation. Among the tabloids, the big splash was caused by Robert Maxwell's mysterious fatal plunge from his yacht into the waters of the Azores on the night of 5 November 1991. The collapse of his labyrinthine businesses forced the Mirror Group newspapers into receivership and heavy cost-cutting. The papers' traditional support for the Labour party also seemed in question. On the other hand Rupert Murdoch's *Today* showed signs of moving in Labour's direction.

PRESS AND PRIVACY

Content more than ownership apparently concerned John Major. With the collapse of the Soviet system and the reform of the Official Secrets Act in 1989 (though it was still far from a freedom of information measure), interest was shifting to the problem of privacy. This showed up in chaotically high libel damages, mainly for private-life allegations against showbiz stars and the super-rich, such as Elton John. The royal family too were exposed by telephoto lens and electronic bug in intimate activities reflecting difficulties in their marriages. The Queen referred publicly to 1992 as an *annus horribilis*, and she may have had tabloid intrusions partly in mind.

In an earlier decade a right to privacy might have been legislated on a wave of sympathy for the royals. But some of these stories, however squalid the means by which they were obtained, were accurate and showed their subjects in a less than attractive light. Beyond this, the third category of prominent victims of intrusion was politicians themselves. David Mellor's exposure by electronic bug in 1992 was the first and most sensational example. In his resignation speech he talked ironically of the 'alternative criminal justice system' run by the media.[3] Norman Lamont, when still Chancellor, found details of his credit card transactions made public. Michael Mates resigned as Northern Ireland minister in June 1993 after being hounded for his friendship with the Turkish Cypriot businessman, Asil Nadir, who jumped bail of £3.5 million. Six months later Tim Yeo was forced by constituency pressure to resign as a junior environment minister because of an extramarital affair (which included fathering a child). Press reporting of the suicide of MP Stephen Milligan in February 1994 included arguably gratuitous detail of solitary sexual practices, which certainly must have added to the distress of his family and friends. In January 1993 John Major himself became only the fourth Prime Minister this century (the others being Lloyd George, Churchill and Wilson) to start a libel case. He did so in order to scotch rumours about his relations with a caterer, Clare Latimer. These had been reported obliquely for months before being aired explicitly in an obscure magazine, *Scallywag*, and then in the *New Statesman and Society* on 29 January. (Both cases were settled out of court.) If the government moved to protect privacy, it would thus be conveniently easy for the media to cry that ministers were doing so chiefly to protect their own skins.

The groundwork for legal protection had been laid in 1990 in a report on privacy by a Home Office committee headed by David Calcutt, QC.[4] This proposed making a criminal offence out of such activities as unauthorized recording and photographing on private property, or electronic surveillance, if done with intent to publish and not in the public interest. Calcutt also suggested giving the press 'one final chance' to prove that voluntary self-regulation could work. If the Press Council did not reform itself into an effective body, with a twenty-four-hour complaints hot line, a comprehensive code of practice, and the authority to get it obeyed, then a statutory tribunal should be introduced, with powers of restraint and compensation.

The government gave the press eighteen months – till about the end of 1992. The press did indeed set up a Complaints Commission and a code. Its credibility soon took a knock, however, over the royals. First came publication of

Princess Diana's intimate phone conversations, the so-called 'Squidgy' tapes, in August 1992. Next month came reports of the existence of the 'Camillagate' tape of pillow-talk phone calls between the Prince of Wales and Mrs Camilla Parker-Bowles. The Complaints Commission Chairman, Lord McGregor, publicly attacked newspapers for having 'dabbled their fingers in the stuff of other people's souls', only to find ample evidence that the Princess, if not the Prince, had connived in the dabbling.[5]

Sir David Calcutt had meanwhile been asked to produce a follow-up study, published in January 1993 as a *Review of Press Self-Regulation*, just as transcripts of the 'Camillagate' tape were becoming widely reported. Calcutt largely repeated his recommendations, but John Major made it clear, nonetheless, that he continued to be against statutory controls.[6] A private member's bill about press responsibility and a Commons National Heritage Select Committee inquiry into press intrusion gave opportunities to sound parliamentary opinion. In November 1993 the Cabinet decided to give the press one further year's grace – notwithstanding the *Sunday Mirror*'s publication of pictures, sneakily obtained with hidden cameras, of Princess Diana, wearing a leotard, working out in a private gym. The Prime Minister was said to have agreed by now in principle to a legal right to privacy, but only if it did not just affect prying journalists.

GOVERNMENT MANAGEMENT OF THE MEDIA

Some idea has already been given of the government's bumpy ride with the media. John Major had the misfortune also to change his tone at the end of a Downing Street TV interview in July 1993, and then to see his private criticism of Cabinet colleagues as 'bastards' spread across the front pages. The microphone, alas, had still been running. The *Daily Mirror* offered readers a 'dial-a-tape' service. When it was banned by the telephone watchdog ICSSTIS (Independent Committee for the Supervision of Standards of Telephone Information

Services), they offered free copies of the tape instead.

This episode epitomized John Major's inept media management. Such a judgment needs making with caution. It does not automatically follow that his perilously low poll ratings occurred because of, rather than despite, Downing Street news management. What makes someone perceived as a good media performer, too, is difficult to predict. John Major may not have handbagged interviewers in the manner of Mrs Thatcher; but that did not mean his blander style was not attractive to audiences. Supporters persisted in contrasting his warmth and leadership qualities in private with the feebler public versions. It is difficult, even so, to believe that the connection between the government's unpopularity and its many presentational mishaps was wholly fortuitous, rather than one of cause and effect. Poor news management dogged such episodes as the decision to leave the ERM (September 1992), the plan (rapidly rejigged) to close thirty-one pits (October 1992), the many disputes about the Maastricht treaty, the trade mission to Japan in September 1993 (dominated by leadership crisis stories and not by selling-for-Britain stories), and the confusions of 'Back to Basics' (winter 1994).

DOWNING STREET PRESS SECRETARY

One problem was the lack of a more assertive press secretary at Downing Street. John Major took with him from the Treasury Gus O'Donnell, an academic economist turned Treasury spokesman, who was already working for him as press secretary while he was Chancellor. O'Donnell always had very good personal relations with the press. He went through the routines effectively and developed such practices as the formal mini press conference outside Number 10. But he inevitably lacked the gravitas of his predecessor, Bernard Ingham. Ingham's authority had accrued with time: he served Thatcher for all but her first few months in office. It gained too from his background as a provincial and Fleet Street journalist, before he joined the civil service. Above all, as Mrs

Thatcher put it in her memoirs, he became 'an indispensable member of the team'.[7] He spoke in her name with an almost ministerial voice.

O'Donnell could match little of this. In comparison with Ingham's, his lobby briefings were said to be anodyne, diffident, and often to lack any clear steer as to the direction of government policy. Much more problematically, he not only lacked a 'ministerial' voice (which many genuine ministers had resented in Ingham), but he failed to find ways of 'straddling the difficult divide between government and party business', as the BBC political correspondent put it.[8] By temperament and experience he was less adept at countering or deflecting the politically loaded probings of the tabloid journalists. Even his farewell dinner at Number 10 in December 1993 got a bad press for the Prime Minister because of the selective guest list, from which most of the tabloids were excluded.

Most Downing Street press secretaries have been either primarily civil servants or primarily journalists – in the case of Wilson's two appointees, political journalists. For a prime minister with Major's leadership problems, a press secretary with strong political instincts and an experienced news sense would have had a better chance of success. Yet when O'Donnell returned (as he had wished) to a senior job at the Treasury, another mandarin was chosen to replace him. This was Chris Meyer, formerly head of the Foreign Office news department and lately in a senior post at the Washington embassy. His media experience was perhaps more appropriate than O'Donnell's, but he was basically in the same mould.

O'Donnell had not been backed up, either, by a minister with responsibility for media relations – a kind of Ingham with a real ministerial voice. This was a device used by a few earlier prime ministers, notably Harold Macmillan, who appointed first Charles Hill and then Bill Deedes. Their role included regular press briefings and contacts with editors and broadcast executives. In Mrs Thatcher's administration, the Prime Minister herself had been characteristically effective in her dealings with such people; consulting, confiding, entertaining them in her Downing Street flat, and occasionally dining with proprietors such as Conrad Black and Rupert

Murdoch. John Major stepped up his use of such tactics (which were hardly novel) after the 1992 election – but with less favourable results. According to one well publicized story, the editor of the *Sun* on one occasion ostentatiously put the phone down on him. The record increasingly showed that, despite his efforts, John Major simply lacked the skills necessary to cajole or browbeat press barons and broadcasters into putting his desired interpretation on events.

The outcome was that by the spring 1994 the press was still predominantly Conservative – but not Majorite. Unlike Mrs Thatcher, John Major lacked foul weather friends. One might have expected this to be more true before the 1992 general election than after it, for the election gave Major his own mandate. In fact, however, press support seeped away after 1992. In the election itself press partisanship had followed the usual lines. Only two out of eleven national daily papers campaigned for Labour. Neil Kinnock could not be blamed for attributing Labour's defeat partly to the Conservative barrage, as did the *Sun* in a famous post-election headline ('IT'S THE SUN WOT WON IT' – 11 April 1992). The link, again, was difficult to prove, although the final attacks certainly coincided with the late swing to the Conservatives.[9] In the last ten days, John Major's own campaign came to life for the press, once he changed from stagey bar stool chats with pre-selected audiences 'in the round' to his 'soapbox', plonked on constituency street corners. The *Sun* immediately published a double-page spread, with a DIY expert's picture-by-picture guide on how readers could build their own soapbox. No one, surely, will have done so. But the article typified the *Sun*'s oblique, upbeat treatment of the campaign.

CONCLUSION

Having pulled off a rather unexpected win, John Major rapidly found victory turn sour, particularly after the ERM debacle. The BBC, bludgeoned by reorganization, Thatcherite pummelling and the prospect of Charter renewal, was

Table 2: National Daily Press

Name of Paper	Owner (1990/94)	Circulation ('000)	Preferred result, General Election April 1992
Daily Express	United Newspapers (Lord Stevens)	1,381	Con. victory
Daily Mail	Associated Newspapers (Lord Rothermere)	1,742	Con. victory
Daily Mirror	Mirror Group Newspapers (R. Maxwell till Nov. 1991; in administration, since)	2,503	Lab. victory
Daily Star	United Newspapers (Lord Stevens)	745	No endorsement (coverage mostly pro-Conservative)
Daily Telegraph	Hollinger (C. Black)	1,015	Con. victory
Financial Times	Pearson (Lord Blakenham)	300	Not a Con. majority
Guardian	Scott Trust	405	Lab. victory; more Lib. Dems.
Independent	Newspaper Publishing	292	No endorsement
Sun	News International (R. Murdoch)	3,947	Con. victory
The Times	News International (R. Murdoch)	468	Con. victory
Today	News International (R. Murdoch)	577	Con. victory

Circulation figures: Audit Bureau of Circulation, February 1994.

cautious in its coverage of the government. ITV was busy coming to terms with franchise renewal. But the press could let rip. By June 1993 William Rees-Mogg was writing in *The Times* that the Prime Minister 'would probably have to go'. Soon two of the bedrock Conservative tabloids, the *Sun* and the *Daily Mail* (now under a less loyalist editor, Paul Dacre) turned strongly against him. Major steadily lost support both in the broadsheets and the tabloids during the winter and spring. 'WHAT FOOLS WE ALL WERE', said a *Sun* headline early in 1994: John Major had 'all the leadership qualities of a lemming' (14 January); while the *Daily Mail* talked in the same week of his 'shilly-shallying' and 'jeopardizing his prime ministerial future'. Even the *Daily Telegraph*, traditionally the loyallest Conservative broadsheet, acquired in June 1994 a Deputy Editor, Simon Heffer, well known for his vituperative assaults on John Major in the *Spectator* (especially over Europe). The *Sunday Telegraph* and *The Spectator* had been hostile from early on and now other Sunday papers joined the attacks. Only the *Daily Express* and *Sunday Express*, for the time being, remained as the foul weather friends the Prime Minister so desperately needed. No other Conservative Prime Minister had been attacked so extensively and in such terms since before the Second World War.

Two factors, therefore, were striking, as John Major reached his fourth anniversary in office. One was the Prime Minister's apparent reluctance to challenge the continuing pressures towards media concentration and cross-ownership. This was all the more astonishing in view of the declared hostility of Rupert Murdoch's papers, notably the *Sun* and *Sunday Times*, and their part in the events fuelling the privacy issue.

Underlying this latter issue, secondly, was a shift in the nature especially of tabloid coverage of public affairs. Eighty per cent of voters read a tabloid in 1994, compared with fewer than half in 1970, before the *Daily Express* and *Daily Mail* had adopted tabloid format. Colour, high quality printing and graphics, trends in design – even the unconscious influence, perhaps, of TV – seem to have pushed coverage in these papers further along the tabloid path of sensation, oversimplification, stereotype and, above all, personalization. The *Sun*, *Daily Mirror* and *Star*, in particular, were barely *news* papers at all by 1994, in the historic sense and in their coverage of politics. Increasingly they were magazines, published daily because that is what their readers were used to and because the supply of advertising supported it. Not even Mrs Thatcher and Bernard Ingham could have done much about that. But when such papers decided to go for the government, it was only natural that they would go not for the jugular but for the crotch. This made it even more essential that, if the Prime Minister himself was ineffective as a manager of news operations, he must appoint someone at ministerial level who was. For if there was a Major effect to do with media, it was an impact felt, not made.

Notes

1. *The Spectator*, 6 November 1993.
2. Cm. 2098, *The Future of the BBC: a consultation document.* (HMSO, London, 1992).
3. 212 HC Deb. 6s. c.140, 25 September 1992.
4. Cm. 1102, *Report of the Committee on Privacy and Related Matters* (Chairman, David Calcutt QC). (HMSO, London 1990).
5. *Independent*, 13 January 1993.
6. *Ibid.*
7. Margaret Thatcher, *The Downing Street Years* (Harper Collins, London, 1993) p. 20.
8. Nicholas Jones, *The Guardian*, 17 January 1994.
9. David Butler and Dennis Kavanagh, *The British General Election of 1992* (Macmillan, London, 1992), p. 208.

Chapter 24

THE ARTS

Robert Hewison

JOHN MAJOR AND THE DECENT LIFE

On 19 November 1993 *The Bookseller* commented:

> Budget Day approaches with doleful inexorability, and the
> book business, which should be putting all its resources into
> fighting its way out of recession, is instead fighting off a tax that
> would hurl it into a condition considerably worse than reces-
> sion. Why it should face this prospect is surprising: John
> Major's accession to the premiership was heralded by hopes of
> a future less acrid, less divisive, more appreciative of the quality
> of people's lives than we had seen under Margaret Thatcher.

The Bookseller is not a journal much concerned with
politics, nor are most people for whom the arts are important
especially close observers of the political scene. Yet whenever a
political issue arose during the Major years that directly
affected them – in *The Bookseller*'s case it was a renewed
threat of the imposition of VAT on the book trade – their
response was the same surprise, and the same disappointment.
John Major was seen as a relief after Margaret Thatcher, his
ordinariness a stabilizing influence following an extraordinary
decade of revolution. Thatcherism had aggressively harried
the arts into adopting the values of the enterprise culture;

Majorism was expected to allow them to live at greater ease with themselves, to regain their accustomed, slightly left of centre position in the national consensus.

The public persona of Mrs Thatcher's successor encouraged this view. His first official prime ministerial portrait, by Peter Deighan, showed him in jacket and slacks, leaning informally against a bookcase. That the book in his hand was more likely to be *Wisden* than his favourite novelist, Trollope, gave assurance, though he was no stranger to culture: didn't his wife Norma write books about the opera? The painting, with its clear light and banal naturalism seemed intended to illustrate Major's personal message in the 1992 Conservative manifesto: 'That, I believe, is the way we all want to live – a decent life in a civilized community.'

Where Mrs Thatcher had viewed support for the arts largely in terms of national prestige, Major's conception of cultural identity was altogether more intimate and comfortably nostalgic. In a speech in 1993, given on – of all days – St George's day and to – of all people – the Conservative Party European Group, he was happy to evoke his England with his speech-writer's borrowings from George Orwell: 'the long shadows falling across the county ground, the warm beer, the invincible green suburbs, dog lovers and pools fillers ... old maids bicycling to Holy Communion through the morning mist'. But the absurdity of that final image revealed the distance between the ideal and the reality. Few old maids felt they could bicycle safely at any time of the day, and even Holy Communion had become a source of division. Major's talk of a classless society and a nation at ease with itself was an admission of the menace of their grimmer, and more concrete opposites: a society divided between ever richer haves and more destitute have-nots, a nation that had lost its direction and its sense of identity. The question was whether Major could restore the consensus that the Thatcherite machine had smashed so determinedly that even those who had set it in motion no longer had it under control.

MAJORISM'S FACE TO THE ARTS

Consensus, culture and a shared sense of identity are the shaping elements of national consciousness. People judge the quality of life by the harmony of this triad. One way for Major to convey his concern that people should be able to lead a decent life in a civilized community was through the state's provision for the material expressions of culture: the arts and heritage. To that end, he made a significant change in the structure of government, and he introduced a new, and potentially transforming, source of funding. Yet the disappointment and disharmony remained.

Under Mrs Thatcher, the arts and heritage had been kept on deliberately short commons, as they were weaned from what one of her arts ministers, Richard Luce, had called 'the welfare state mentality' that had encouraged them to expect steadily expanding subsidy. The arts had responded by becoming more entrepreneurial, by relying more on the box office and business sponsorship, but Thatcher had not created the economic conditions in which they could independently flourish. The recession at the end of the 1980s placed many companies once more in severe fiscal danger, with large deficits, and little hope of reducing them by enterprise alone.

In a sense, Major's concern for the arts was detectable even before he came to power, for it was under his brief Chancellorship that the first of a series of substantial increases in arts and heritage spending was announced: in 1989 a 12.9 per cent increase to £540 million for 1990–91. In 1990, under Major's first Chancellor Norman Lamont, this rose again, by 14 per cent to £560 million for 1991–92; in 1991 by 8.9 per cent to £610 million for 1992–93. Within this overall allocation the Arts Council's grant-in-aid rose by nearly 20 per cent over three years. There were other signs of prime ministerial patronage. In order to celebrate Britain's presidency of the European Community from July to December 1992 – an ironic decision in view of the machinations over the Maastricht treaty – £6 million was spent on a nationwide celebration of British and European culture. On the last day of Parliament before its dissolution for the 1992 general election, the government announced it would give English National Opera £10.8 million towards the cost of acquiring the freehold to its London home, the Coliseum. As Timothy Renton, Major's first minister for the arts, commented shortly before the launch of the Conservative manifesto: 'Majorism has a kindlier face towards the arts.'

THE DEPARTMENT OF NATIONAL HERITAGE

That manifesto contained two significant initiatives in cultural policy. While both Labour and the Liberal Democrats were already committed to strengthening the function and status of an arts ministry, there was surprise when the Conservative proposal proved yet more radical. A new department of state – named, after the election, the Department of National Heritage – would be created, led by a minister of Cabinet rank. It is possible to trace the origins of this department to the creation of the former arts ministry, the Office of Arts and Libraries, out of the Libraries and Arts Department of the Department of Education and Science by Mrs Thatcher in 1979. Indeed, her first arts minister Norman St. John-Stevas had Cabinet rank, by virtue of also being Chancellor of the Duchy of Lancaster, but Major's fully-fledged department of state was an unexpected stroke. It had never been thought, for instance, that the Home Office would surrender its role as regulator of broadcasting and the press to another ministry, or that cultural policy could expect a permanent place on the Cabinet agenda. It was here, with the creation of a new department of state, that Major signalled most clearly his concern for the quality of life, and a break with the attitudes of his predecessor.

The Department of National Heritage was intended to be, in the first Secretary of State David Mellor's phrase, more than 'the Office of Arts and Libraries on wheels'. To the OAL's responsibility for the performing arts, museums and galleries, and the National Heritage Memorial Fund were added English Heritage from the Department of the

Environment, sport from Education, film from Trade and Industry, and tourism from Employment. By focusing the former peripheral activities of half a dozen ministries, Major was shaping the 'big beast' that Mellor, in his informal, 'unstructured conversations' with the Prime Minister before the election, had argued should have both financial and political clout. Mellor would also have liked to have detached the British Council and the BBC World Service from the Foreign Office, but these were ambitions too far.

Not only did this create a cultural budget approaching £1 billion, one of the department's first tasks (which it successfully wrested from the Home Office) was to devise a National Lottery for good causes which would provide an entirely new source of funds for charities, sport, the arts, heritage and a Millennium Fund which, in the words of the 1992 manifesto, could 'restore the fabric of our nation'. This restoration was metaphorical as well as literal. It would mean that Britain met the millennium in style, and pay for various British versions of the *grand projets* that had been created in socialist France during the 1980s.

Until the National Lottery Act was passed in October 1993 Mrs Thatcher's residual Methodism had ensured that Britain was the only country in Europe without a state lottery. The probable proceeds when the lottery came on stream at the end of 1994 were uncertain, but likely to be substantial. At a minimum estimated turnover of £1.5 billion a year, with half going in prizes, a percentage for administration and profit for the commercial operator and a smaller amount going in tax than the Treasury would have liked, the five areas to be catered for by the fund could each expect £70 million a year. The money was intended for capital projects, and was not to be treated as public expenditure. The department was to continue to distribute grant-in-aid to the forty-five different non-departmental organizations (such as the Arts Council) to which it was patron. When the National Lottery reached its potential turnover of £5 billion a year, the Department of National Heritage, with a core staff of no more than 270, would be rich and powerful indeed and the arts, now part of a broader 'cultural industries' strategy, would play a central role in the restoration of the Conservative manifesto's 'Brighter Britain'.

THE MINISTRY OF FUN TURNS SOUR

Although the preliminary work of devising the Department of National Heritage was done by a small group of Conservative sympathizers who acted as advisers to the arts minister, Timothy Renton, it was plain that it was shaped to the tastes of Major's friend and ally, David Mellor. Mellor was an acknowledged enthusiast for the arts, especially music, and football. He had served briefly as arts minister under Mrs Thatcher before being promoted to Chief Secretary to the Treasury as his reward for his part in Major's successful campaign for the leadership. There he was able to act with generosity towards the arts during the period before the 1992 election. Although he did not choose its title – he has said he is not a 'heritage man' – Mellor was plainly delighted with his new department of state, the first such creation (apart from the Northern Ireland Office) since Harold Wilson's Department of Economic Affairs in 1964 – a somewhat unfortunate precedent. In order to cover the 'heritage' aspects of its responsibilities, Robert Key was appointed as parliamentary under secretary.

The department became quickly known as 'the ministry of fun', but the joke turned sour when in July 1992 Mellor was revealed to have been having an affair with an actress, Antonia de Sancha. Mellor's immediate offer of resignation was rejected, and he appeared to be riding out the scandal with the strong support of the Prime Minister, when in September there were fresh allegations that he had broken rules of ministerial conduct over free holidays from the daughter of a senior member of the Palestine Liberation Organization. The Prime Minister's loyalty could not save his friend, and the scandal, quite beyond Major's responsibility or control, early laid his administration open to the accusations of sleaze and corruption from which it never recovered.

This personal disaster was also disastrous for policy. However abbreviated Mellor's view of the arm's-length principle that was supposed to keep government and the arts at a distance, however much he chose to indulge his own enthusiasms, Mellor would have provided the new department with an identifiable personality, and would have had the access to the Prime Minister that his friendship gave him. Mellor's replacement was Peter Brooke, recalled from the back benches after serving as Secretary of State for Northern Ireland until a diplomatic gaffe on Irish television caused him to be replaced following the 1992 election. Describing himself as having 'fairly conservative tastes' – principally picture collecting – the fifty-nine-year-old Brooke *was* a heritage man, but was not ambitious for himself or his department in the way that Mellor had been. The extra security he required as a former Northern Ireland minister made it difficult for Brooke to act as Major's ambassador for the arts. The view of his political adviser Dominic Loenhis was: 'He believes the quieter you are, the more successful you can be. He is no Jack Lang.' Brooke's lecture to the Royal Fine Art Commission in December 1992 appeared to confirm this. 'We are not about to enter the era of Ludwig of Bavaria, or Louis XIV,' he warned.

To complicate matters, in the post-Lamont reshuffle in 1993 the junior minister, Robert Key, was replaced by the right-wing Iain Sproat. As a backbencher in the 1970s he had vigorously campaigned against the introduction of Authors' Public Lending Right, for which he would now be responsible. Some of Sproat's public and private pronouncements were a severe embarrassment to Brooke, and as talk of a 1994 summer reshuffle increased in volume there was speculation that either one or both men would leave the department. Major had many more important things than this clash of temperaments on his mind, but there was one other disposition that he had made where personality affected policy. His choice of Chief Secretary to the Treasury was the decidedly 'dry' Michael Portillo, who appeared to revenge himself on the more liberal Mellor by bearing down on the Department of National Heritage's budget allocation.

The new responsibilities of the department made comparisons with the former Office of Arts and Libraries impossible, but the first autumn statement of departmental budgets for the following year, £990.54 million, was a severe disappointment to the new department. In his new capacity as a columnist for *The Guardian* Mellor said the department was among the worst hit as the result of the very tight 1992 spending round. An immediate consequence was that the system of three-year 'indicative' funding for the Arts Council, introduced in 1989, was abandoned, and instead of the previously indicated 3.5 per cent increase, the Arts Council received a below the rate of inflation increase of 1.8 per cent for 1993–94, with the prospect of real cuts in future years.

Under Brooke, the ministry of fun became for a while the department of nothing happening as its permanent secretary, Hayden Philips, a Treasury high-flyer chosen by Mellor, sought to weld the disparate units of former ministries into a coherent whole. It was his estimate that it would take three years to see 'real added value' from the department. The National Lottery Act and the subsequent appointment of a Millennium Commission to oversee that part of the fund (with Brooke and Michael Heseltine as the government ministers on the nine-person commission) was the department's biggest achievement.

The attitude taken to the politically sensitive issues of statutory regulation of the press and the future of the BBC appeared to be 'wait and see'. The extension of Marmaduke Hussey's chairmanship of the BBC in 1991 and John Birt's move up from deputy director general to director general in 1992, appeared to be producing the cultural revolution from above intended by their original appointments under Mrs Thatcher. The BBC responded by reiterating its commitment to what it defined as artistic quality (a heavy investment in drama, *Middlemarch* being the most notable and culturally defining result). The dissatisfaction created by the 1990 Broadcasting Act appeared to make the department reluctant to tamper with the method of financing the BBC, and the licence fee, which Mrs Thatcher would have liked to have abolished, was given a new lease of life to run until the end of the century.

In May 1993 the department did at least acquire an identifiable geographical personality, when it moved into offices in Cockspur Street, just off Trafalgar Square. Behind the listed, 1929 neo-classical façade of the former Royal Bank of Canada lay a typical 1980s interior tricked out in developer's post-classical, leading to an atrium with waterfall, weeping fig tree and glass-sided lift. The location was curiously appropriate for a department that had chosen English 'heritage' rather than Stalinist 'culture' for its title: a restored façade and an ersatz interior.

MAJORISM AND THE ARTS COUNCIL

The Arts Council of Great Britain was only one of forty-five dependent organizations that had to forge a relationship with the new department, but it was the biggest. While the first arts ministry of any kind was the creation of Harold Wilson in the 1960s, the Arts Council, born out of the wartime Council for Encouragement of Music and the Arts, had for far longer acted as the institutional definition of what were officially recognized as 'the arts'. The BBC had more cultural influence, and was a far greater patron of actors, writers, designers, composers and musicians, yet the Arts Council was officially, as opposed to unofficially, charged with responsibility for the nation's cultural identity. What happened to the Arts Council was therefore of symbolic as well as practical importance.

Under Thatcher the Arts Council, like other institutions that were devoted to maintaining the consensus – the universities, the BBC, the national museums and galleries, all the Quasi-Autonomous Non-Governmental Organizations that undertook so much of the state's work at arm's-length from the government of the day – had been subjected to external pressure through funding restraint, and internal reconstruction by the appointment of political sympathizers. When Mrs Thatcher resigned in 1990 the Chairman of the Arts Council, Peter Palumbo, was given a peerage in her personal honours list. The Arts Council had responded, first under Sir William Rees-Mogg and then under Palumbo, to the managerial demands of the enterprise culture. Yet since 1989, when a former head of the Office of Arts and Libraries, Richard Wilding, had delivered a report on the relationship between the Arts Council and the Regional Arts Associations, the Council had been forced through a series of unwelcome changes.

Wilding had concluded that not only did the Arts Council lack 'vision', the system by which both it and the Regional Arts Associations (which received on average 90 per cent of their funds from the Arts Council) frequently subsidized the same organization was a wasteful duplication of effort. Wilding proposed the reorganization of the RAAs into fewer, and less local authority-dominated Regional Arts Boards, which would take over all but thirty of the Arts Council's clients, leaving the Council to care for the major national companies, touring and innovation. Although the intention was to create an integrated system that would give the Arts Council a large say, no bureaucracy likes to lose areas of responsibility to others or be reduced in size. There followed a long period of disruption and uncertainty as arts ministers came and went and the tide of what was officially called 'delegation' ebbed and flowed. The plan, according to the former, and most celebrated chairman of the Arts Council, Lord Goodman, 'for practical purposes spelt the end of the Arts Council'.

The cause of delegation was taken up enthusiastically by Major's first minister for the arts, Timothy Renton, especially when he discovered that Palumbo had been going behind his back to deal directly with Mellor at the Treasury. (Again, the breaking of the Palumbo-Mellor connection was of consequence for the arts). Shortly before the 1992 election Renton floated the possibility that Britain's national companies could be dealt with directly by the government, and the rest handled by the Regional Arts Boards, thus hinting at the abolition of the Arts Council that he was publicly to call for in 1993.

Although the process was not completed until April 1994, a large measure of delegation went ahead, thus sharpening the appetites of the RABs. With the creation of the Department of National Heritage, the Arts Council found itself caught between the rock of the RABs and the hard faces of the civil servants of the DNH who were determined to prove they were an effective new department. While Brooke regularly reasserted the value of the arm's-length principle, the buzzword among his bureaucrats was 'accountability'. When, in an effort to prove it had the vision it was accused of lacking, the Arts Council spent eighteen months and half a million pounds on the 'strategy' *A Creative Future*, published in January 1993, the department quietly pigeonholed it.

At the beginning of 1994 the Arts Council calculated that it had spent £6 million since the delivery of the Wilding report on restructuring, relocation, redundancies and the cost of external and internal management enquiries. According to the Council's secretary general Anthony Everitt – his predecessor Luke Rittner had resigned in 1990 in protest at the proposals for delegation – the government 'in its clumsy efforts to make us more efficient has actually made us more inefficient through these endless interventions and ministers coming and going, each with a slightly different idea'.

Although the Arts Council was made the agency responsible for distributing lottery money to the arts when it came on stream, and so had a future of some sort, the final blow came in March 1993 when it was decided that the Arts Councils of Scotland and Wales, technically sub-commmitees of the Arts Council of Great Britain, would be funded directly by the Scottish and Welsh Offices. This decision, at least, may have had Major's hand on it, as a gesture of devolution to two of the Union's disgruntled members. From April 1994 the Arts Council of Great Britain ceased to exist, replaced by the Arts Council of England, reduced in size, power and credibility, with a former Conservative arts minister, Lord Gowrie, as its first chairman.

Majorism did not show a kindlier face to the Arts Council. Because of the devolution to Scotland and Wales, the Department of National Heritage's second annual budget allocation at the end of 1993 was smaller than the first, £967 million. Although the department claimed to have an additional £21 million at its disposal, for the first time in its history the Arts Council received a cash cut of £3.2 million, which Palumbo appeared to take as a personal slight. Faced with the prospects of this cut, which came into force in April 1994, the Arts Council of Great Britain spent its final year trying to prepare for cuts while at the same time reshaping policy along the lines outlined in *A Creative Future*. The results were a fiasco. A proposal to cut off completely the grants of up to ten regional theatres was effectively shouted down by the arts community; the invitation to an outside panel of experts chaired by Lord Justice Hoffman to select which of the three London orchestras should be promoted to stand beside the London Symphony Orchestra as a 'super-orchestra', while the other two lost their grants entirely, ended in similar retreat and confusion. At the beginning of 1994 Anthony Everitt took the opportunity of the impending arrival of a new chairman to resign as secretary general.

It is fair to say that the Arts Council of Great Britain's last year of existence was also its worst, and that it lost all credibility with the arts constituency. The Department of National Heritage exploited the arm's-length principle to stay clear of the debacle, yet it could not avoid being called to account. The brief period when arts funding had risen (though many would argue that this did no more than restore levels to their equivalent in 1979) decisively came to an end, with many companies technically insolvent because of their deficits. If this was a kindlier face to the arts, it did not feel like it to those about to go out of business.

JOHN MAJOR AND CIVILIZATION

In theory, the creation of the Department of National Heritage was a significant innovation, for at last a British government had acknowledged that it had a responsibility towards the spiritual and creative needs of its citizens, as well as their material ones. This alone shows a difference between the Thatcher and Major years. That this new department should go under the comforting, retrospective label of 'heritage' was a reflection of the civilizing reassurance that Major was hoping to bring. Yet in spite of the sums that were eventually to flow from the National Lottery, Major allowed his creation to suffer unnecessarily in the first spending round after its intro-duction. A relatively trivial increase in funds could have added significantly to the gloss that might have been put on his premiership, after the close-fisted years of Mrs Thatcher. Instead, a small act of meanness towards the Arts Council threatened to precipitate disasters elsewhere in the arts economy.

The unravelling of one of the major institutions of the consensus, the Arts Council, came about as a result of accidents of personality as well as acts of policy. But that the Department of National Heritage appeared to seek to prove its own virility by punishing an already weakened Arts Council showed that Major's government did nothing to halt the centralizing tendencies of the Thatcherite state as it filled the voids created by its own denial of democratic pluralism.

While administrations are in a position to manipulate the popular consensus, culture and identity remain largely beyond government control, and Major's attempt to reverse an all-pervasive feeling of decay was unsuccessful. Heritage was no answer to long-term national decline, as the confusion over 'Back to Basics' proved. Cricket and warm beer were weak symbols around which to rebuild national cohesion, especially when English cricketers were internationally so unsuccessful. A European arts festival was no resolution to the divisions over British versus European identity that tore the Conservative party apart. The attempt to turn the commemoration of the fiftieth anniversary of D-Day into a public relations stunt showed the extent to which a department devoted to 'heritage' had lost touch with history.

By the end of the 1980s the Thatcherite juggernaut had run out of control, bringing down the symbols of national identity: the cultural consensus, the Church, the Monarchy, and eventually the Conservative party itself. The arts were brushed aside in the crush. John Major was unable to pick up the pieces.

Chapter 25

SCIENCE

Tom Wilkie

A RADICAL DEPARTURE

Less than a month after John Major became Prime Minister, press reports started picking up suggestions from Downing Street that the machinery of government was to be reorganized and that the arrangements for civil science were to be part of these reforms. After the general election of 1992, Mr Major signalled a radical departure from his predecessor's policies towards science, engineering and technology by appointing William Waldegrave as Britain's first Cabinet-level minister for science since Lord Hailsham had held that office some thirty years earlier.

However, science was not to be Mr Waldegrave's sole portfolio. As Chancellor of the Duchy of Lancaster, he assumed responsibility for open government, the civil service, and the Citizen's Charter as well. It has been notable throughout Mr Waldegrave's term of office that his other portfolios have been the main focus of political and media attention. This runs contrary to the usual rule of thumb that political attention focuses on the expenditure of taxpayers' money; little public money is expended in relation to the Citizen's Charter, whereas the £1.2 billion allocated for the Office of Science and Technology (OST) spending on civil science in 1994–95 represents the main budget of Mr Waldegrave's department.

Scientific research has always represented something of a problem to Whitehall. It is clearly necessary in the late twentieth century that scientific advice should inform the business of government on issues of public policy ranging from AIDS to global warming; science, engineering and technology are also fundamental to modern industry (although the connection between the laboratory and the shop floor is neither direct nor easy to trace) and an active government must seek to promote the diffusion of science into industry. Finally, the pursuit of scientific knowledge is an intellectual discipline in which all civilized nations must, for the preservation and enrichment of their culture, allow talented individuals to engage, and this too is a legitimate responsibility of government. But science does not fit neatly into the administrative categories represented by the departments of state. Since the Science and Technology Act of 1965, 'pure' curiosity-driven research has been the part-time responsibility of a junior minister in the Department of Education and Science, while other departments commissioned applied research either from their own in-house research establishments or from outside contractors. Thus Mr Waldegrave's appointment represented a significant break with established Whitehall procedures. (It also represented an astute appropriation by Mr Major of parts of the technology policy which had been advocated by the Labour party during the general election campaign.) There is no doubt that the creation of the new post was a conscious decision on the part of Mr Major. However compelling the arguments (which will be examined in the next section) Mrs Thatcher would never have countenanced the change.

THE REASONS FOR CHANGE

Britain's presidency of the European Community in 1992 was the factor which crystallized the decision to centralize political control over government-funded science in this way. There had been growing dissatisfaction on the part not only of academic scientists but also of the managers of science-based companies that British science and technology was being crippled in terms of its representation in Brussels compared to the French and the Germans. Both these countries have strong central ministries for research and technology, headed by forceful politicians who have had a track record of securing national advantage in negotiations with the European Commission. In contrast, putting the case for British technology had been the responsibility of a junior minister in the Department of Trade and Industry while 'pure' scientific research, because it fell within the remit of the Department of Education and Science, went largely unrepresented.

In the domestic arena, there was a clear feeling that the budget for science suffered because it was not important to any Cabinet minister's political interest to preserve it. The three main spending departments were the Ministry of Defence, the Department of Trade and Industry, and the Department of Education and Science. Official secrecy has perpetually cloaked the details of how the Ministry of Defence has spent its budget for military research and development. Little of this money seems to have trickled down to stimulate innovation in the civilian economy or to enhance the cultural value of science. The Department of Trade and Industry's spending tended to be earmarked for specific industrial projects and in 1988, the department confused scientists and industry alike by announcing a sudden switch in its funding policies away from 'near-market' research. Within the Department of Education and Science, the Secretary of State naturally devoted his energies to schools and, during a time of constant pressure on his budget, science represented an easy and painless area in which to make economies.

The administration of science was thus diffuse, decentralized and uncoordinated. But Mrs Thatcher had consistently rejected all suggestions that science should be represented by a minister with Cabinet rank, even though the House of Lords select committee on science and technology had been pressing for such an appointment to be made. Her response had always been that as the head of government was herself scientifically trained and as she maintained a personal interest in science, there was no need for a ministerial appointment. However, unless a minister's personal interest is informed by considered advice from the civil service it can turn into personal caprice, and Mrs Thatcher's record brings to mind the unhappy and damaging influence of Frederick Lindemann, Lord Cherwell, an earlier scientist-politician who enjoyed considerable power during the premierships of Winston Churchill.

The creation of the OST owes a great deal to the character of the government's Chief Scientific Advisor: a down-to-earth Scots biologist, Professor William Stewart. His predecessors, during Mrs Thatcher's term, had not been notably successful but Professor Stewart, at first sight an unlikely figure in the corridors of Whitehall power, and the Cabinet Secretary, Sir Robin Butler, both became convinced that existing arrangements for the administration of civil science were inadequate. The prospect of Britain's chairmanship of the EC clinched the matter, for what senior minister would chair the science and technology meetings?

The creation of the new post and Mr Waldegrave's appointment were widely welcomed. But in the initial excitement, several factors were overlooked which have since come to acquire great significance. The first is that Mr Major's decision did not represent a bold new initiative so much as a step 'Back to the Future'. The OST is effectively a recreation of the old Department for Scientific and Industrial Research (DSIR) which came into existence during the First World War and whose abolition in 1965 was even more widely welcomed than the OST's creation a quarter of a century later. For the hard truth is, as discussed in *British Science and Politics since 1945*,[1] the DSIR was a failure: 'it had become clear that the task was too much even for a Minister as competent and energetic as Hailsham'. In August 1964, in one devastating phrase, *The Economist* dismissed the office of the Minister for Science as a 'palsied little creation'.

The historical parallels are profound and compelling. Hailsham's appointment was, like Waldegrave's, partly stimulated by the need to coordinate Britain's participation in international scientific projects, represented in the late 1950s by such things as the European Laboratory for Particle Physics (CERN) and the European Space Research Organization. But domestically, Hailsham was crippled because he had no responsibility for aerospace or electronics, nor could he properly coordinate the dissemination of scientific expertise out of the laboratory and into industry. These deficiencies in remit not only remain but have been exacerbated in the creation of the OST.

On its abolition, the DSIR was split, ultimately into five research councils answerable to the Department of Education and Science, to perform basic curiosity-driven research. The remainder of the DSIR became part of the Wilson government's Ministry of Technology which ultimately metamorphosed into the present Department of Trade and Industry. The existence of the DTI thus pre-empts budgets and areas of responsibility that were once part of the DSIR and from which Mr Waldegrave's OST is now excluded. If Hailsham's science ministry was truly a palsied creation, the geography of Whitehall will ensure that the OST is more feeble and sickly still.

The second factor overlooked at the time of the OST's creation was the risk that, notwithstanding the fact that many areas which should be within the remit of a revived science and industry department are off limits to the Office of Science and Technology, the new office might centralize and concentrate political control over those assets it does have. This is precisely what has happened.

THE WHITE PAPER – A CENTRALIZING AGENDA?

In the first few months after his appointment, Mr Waldegrave creditably got out and about, visiting laboratories and research centres, talking and listening to scientists. Since the scientific community had felt demoralized, ignored and, at times, derided by its political paymasters over the previous decade or so, such personal interest from a political heavyweight was heady stuff. Mr Waldegrave's stock rose still further when he ensured that the House of Commons hold a formal debate on science – the first such that the current generation of MPs could remember – and when he promised that the government would fully review its science policy and publish the first white paper on science since the 1970s. More than 800 written submissions went into the OST, public meetings were organized by the Foundation for Science and Technology, and by the Parliamentary and Scientific Committee.

When the white paper 'Realising our potential: A Strategy for Science, Engineering and Technology' was published on 26 May 1993, it too was widely welcomed.[2] It set out two basic themes: that science should contribute to wealth creation and to the quality of life. The first – the relationship between science and wealth creation – occupies almost the entire seventy-four pages of the document, whereas the role of science in contributing to the quality of life (presumably through such measures as the work funded by the Medical Research Council, intended ultimately to ameliorate disease and improve human health, or the work of the Natural Environment Research Council, on pollution, global warming, ozone depletion, and the like) is scarcely articulated. The emphasis is economic, one might say mercantile, to the exclusion of all else:

> The central thesis of this White Paper is that we could and should improve our performance by making the science and engineering base even more aware of and responsive to the needs of industry and other research users, and by encouraging firms and other organisations to be more aware of and receptive to the work being done in other laboratories, especially those of the science and engineering base.

There is little doubt that this fixation on science for wealth reflected the personal concerns of Mr Waldegrave. One plank of policy was to reorganize the research councils, and it is believed that Mr Waldegrave insisted the new chairmen should be drawn from industry. Changes to postgraduate education also appear to reflect deeply felt views on the part of Mr Waldegrave and his then junior minister, Robert Jackson.

To enhance the role of science in wealth creation, the white paper set out thirteen specific policies, 'designed to get maximum value for money from our annual public expenditure of some £6bn on science and technology':

1. The government's use of funds was to be made more transparent and an annual Forward Look was to be published each year to state the government's strategy.
2. A new cooperative exercise between industry and the scientific community, known as 'Technology Foresight' would inform government decision making. A second benefit of the exercise would be that it would foster better links between science and industry.
3. The Advisory Council on Science and Technology was to become the Council for Science and Technology.
4. Existing schemes for technology transfer would re-emphasize the importance of the interchange of ideas, skills, know-how and knowledge between the science and engineering base and industry.
5. There was to be easier access for small and medium sized firms to the innovation support programmes run by the Department of Trade and Industry (and its counterparts in Scotland, Wales, and Northern Ireland).
6. The existing research councils were to be reorganized. The Science and Engineering Research Council (SERC) was dismembered, with bits being hived off in two new councils: the Engineering and Physical Sciences Research Council and the Particle Physics and Astronomy Research Council. Other parts of SERC went to the Agricultural and Food Research Council which was reconstituted as a Biotechnology and Biological Sciences Research Council. The research councils were given 'mission statements' to make explicit their commitment to wealth creation and the quality of life. In addition, their management structures were modified to give each a part-time chairman (brought in from industry) and a subordinate full-time chief executive (who was to be a scientist).
7. The independent Advisory Board for the Research Councils (created in 1972 by Mrs Thatcher when she was Secretary of State for Education and Science) was abolished and a new post, of director general of Research Councils, created. Whereas the chairman of the Advisory

Board had always been a scientist of distinction, usually university-based and therefore independent of government, the new director general was to be a civil servant answerable to the permanent secretary and to the minister. The post was eventually taken up by Sir John Cadogan, a retired industrial research chemist.

8. The 'dual-support' mechanism for funding university-based researchers was to be maintained. This is the system whereby basic costs (salaries, heating, lighting, etc.) are met by the university from money granted by the Department of Education, while specific research projects are funded by grants from the appropriate research council.

9. Most of the government's own research establishments were to be privatized.

10. There was to be greater cross-department coordination regarding science and technology. However, the white paper was comparatively silent on how this, one of the most difficult aspects of science policy, was to be achieved.

11. Similarly, the British position in international science and technology programmes was to be better coordinated.

12. The education and training of post-graduate scientists was to be reformed, with fewer students being permitted to conduct original research leading to a PhD and more being sent on MSc courses.

13. There was to be a new campaign to spread the understanding of science, technology and engineering in schools and to the public.

PLUS ÇA CHANGE?

The more time that passes since its publication, the more the stature of the white paper seems to diminish. 'Realising our potential' now appears an extraordinary document, both in what it says and in what it leaves out. In those matters over which Mr Waldegrave has direct responsibility, the white paper reveals him to be *dirigiste* to a degree that is without precedent in the entire history of British governments' relationship with science. Yet in those areas where Mr Waldegrave had to use his political weight to attain his ends – where the scientific interests of the Department of Trade and Industry and the Ministry of Defence overlapped with those of the OST – the white paper is eloquently silent. Privately, civil servants are in no doubt that the MoD and the DTI defended their turf and saw off the OST. Although in introducing the white paper Mr Waldegrave declared that it would put science where it deserved to be, at the centre of the government's agenda, it is worth noting that 'Realising our potential' contained not a single proposal that would have required primary legislation. The government's business managers had made it clear in advance that they would not make time available for science policy.

Since the foundation in 1913 of the Medical Research Committee (later to become the Medical Research Council), government ministers have maintained a distance between themselves and the scientist at the laboratory bench. This principle was enshrined in the 'Machinery of Government' report produced under Lord Haldane at the end of the First World War and most memorably articulated in a Commons speech in 1920 by Christopher Addison, Britain's first minister of health. He pointed out that all ministers become committed to certain policies and that new scientific knowledge tends to undermine the basis for those policies. Ministers might then be tempted to suppress or divert the course of scientific research if the results were going to upset their policies. The only way to prevent this was by making the connexion between the administrative departments and the research bodies as elastic as possible and '*by refraining from putting scientific bodies in any way under the direct control of Ministers*' (emphasis added).

The first significant breach of that arm's-length relationship was made during the last Conservative government, under the premiership of Edward Heath, with the publication in 1971 of the Rothschild Report on 'The Organisation and Management of Government R&D', which brought applied research and development directly under departmental and therefore ministerial control. Mr Waldegrave was a member of the think-tank under Lord Rothschild whom he clearly regards as one of his most important mentors. It is therefore hardly surprising that he should have completed the centralizing work which Lord Rothschild began, by bringing curiosity-driven research also under the control of ministers. This *dirigisme* with respect to science has been characteristic of Conservative, not Labour administrations.

The white paper makes it quite clear that what science should be done and who should do it will be determined by ministerial fiat: the government 'intends that decisions on priorities for support should be much more clearly related to meeting the country's needs and enhancing the wealth-creating capacity of the country' and to this end the Research Councils 'will operate under the direction of the Chancellor of the Duchy of Lancaster'. Where successive governments over a period of nearly seven decades had nurtured and valued the creativity and individuality of scientifically talented individuals, now 'it is not realistic to expect that all research proposals deemed excellent in scientific terms can be supported. Nor can every individual with the potential to contribute good quality research be supported.'

In place of the traditional criteria of scientific merit and timeliness, the funding of scientific projects will now follow from the priorities identified in the 'Technology Foresight' exercise. Mr Waldegrave has written to more than 1,200 scientists and industrialists asking them to participate by nominating those areas which are most likely to be the economically important technologies of the future. The idea is remarkably reminiscent of the 1960s corporatist and now much-derided policy of trying to 'pick winners', except that the targets will not be individual companies or sectors of industry but the more diffuse concept of areas of fruitful technology. Whether technology foresight will be a success remains to be seen, although the criteria by which it might be judged a success or failure are unclear.

Mr Waldegrave did deliver when it came to the first public expenditure round after publication of his white paper. In what was a difficult year for all departments, he secured at least funding of £1,236.5 million for the research councils and the other elements of the 'science base' for which he was responsible. However, measured across government as a whole, the total spend on research and development has declined sharply in real terms during the term of successive Conservative governments. According to figures published in March 1994 by the Central Statistical Office, government spending on research and development fell in real terms from £4,952 million in 1981 to £4,043 million in 1992. Although industry and business has increased its spending by £1,500 million over the same period, industry's investment in research and development has been affected by recession and in 1992 was £500 million lower than it had been five years earlier. The overall decline has actually been disproportionately sharper than the downturn in the economy as a whole: gross domestic expenditure on research and development has fallen from 2.25 per cent of GDP in 1985 to 2.12 per cent in 1992. CSO figures are always a couple of years in arrears, so it will be some time before any financial measures of the effectiveness of the government's more industry oriented policy become available.

WAS THE CHANGE RADICAL ENOUGH?

Virtually all commentators are agreed that Britain suffers economically from the way in which the A-level examination system forces even the brightest of school children to specialize early. When faced with a choice, the majority drop science and are thus cut off from one of the most important driving forces of modern society and modern industry. The case was put forcibly by Sir Claus Moser, in his presidential address to the British Association for the Advancement of Science in 1990. But the white paper is largely silent on this topic, one of the most important, albeit indirect, ways in which science might contribute to wealth creation. Instead of serious structural reform, the OST sponsored a publicity drive for science, culminating in the launch of an annual 'National Science Week'. The first of these, coordinated by the British Association, was held in 1994 and was an unqualified success. But it seems unlikely that it will do more than scratch the surface of a deep-seated and peculiarly British problem.

More damaging still, the question might well be asked as to why Mr Waldegrave's office and not the Department of Trade and Industry has embarked on the exercise of harnessing scientific innovation to the nation's wealth-creating industries. A further question might be whether there is any real point in identifying areas of national scientific expertise which could contribute to wealth creation in a country which no longer seems to have the industrial capacity to benefit from such expertise. Britain no longer has a domestic mass-manufacturer of television sets or other consumer electronic goods; it has sold its largest car manufacturer to the Germans and the Japanese; it no longer has any significant British-owned companies manufacturing computers or electronic microchips; and most of its computer software industry (which depends entirely on the quality of individuals' scientific talent) has quietly been sold off to overseas owners.

To ask these questions is to approach what may be a central deficiency in the government's thinking. In common with virtually all its predecessors, Mr Major's administration has tried to use science policy as a proxy for an industrial strategy. Its free-market principles prevent the government from intervening in the affairs of industrial companies, yet it is hard to avoid the conclusion that there is some structural deficiency in the way British industry and its supporting financial institutions are organized which obstructs the growth of new, high-technology companies capable of contributing to the creation of national wealth well into the twenty-first century. Innovation resulting from scientific research is but one part of the process of wealth creation and it may be that, for reasons of ideology and departmental politics, the Chancellor of the Duchy of Lancaster has concentrated on the least important part. But that is a topic beyond the scope of this essay.

Notes

1. Tom Wilkie, *British Science and Politics since 1945* (Basil Blackwell, 1991).
2. *Realising our potential: A Strategy for Science, Engineering and Technology* (HMSO, 1993).

Chapter 26

SPORT AND LEISURE

Richard Holt and Alan Tomlinson

JOHN MAJOR'S ENTHUSIASM FOR SPORT

With a Prime Minister who, in response to BBC Radio 4's invitation, asks to take the Oval cricket ground to his 'Desert Island' and talks fondly of England as a land of 'cricket and warm beer', sport would seem to be a pursuit whose time has come. The authenticity of the Prime Minister's feelings is surely not in dispute. Major is no Harold Wilson, with a sudden and dubious-sounding passion for football as England wins the World Cup with an election in the offing. Major is the kind of chap one could imagine poring over an old *Wisden* in a quiet hour; not one for sport of the lone or the dangerous kind such as the rigours of ocean racing that gave Ted Heath a touch of glamour, an aura of 'our island race'. Major's sporting enthusiasms are unexceptional, he likes – even loves – our national winter and summer sports; supports Surrey County Cricket Club and Chelsea Football Club, pops up at the Test Match for an hour or two after lunch, apparently oblivious to the awful pressures of high public office, follows the play attentively, knowledgeably, a man momentarily 'at ease with himself'.

Just as the Queen is said to be at her best in the company of horses, so the Prime Minister seems to relax and relish the presence of sportsmen, inviting them to his folksy pre-election gatherings and commenting publicly on the passing of great or much-loved figures: the deaths of football heroes Bobby Moore or Matt Busby, for example, or most movingly of the cricket commentators John Arlott or Brian Johnston. When Major said of 'Jonners' that 'summers will never be the same', even those who distrusted everything else about him could hardly doubt the sincerity of his tribute – the very ordinariness of his sentiments, pastoral cliché perhaps, but nonetheless deeply felt, the voice of a generation that grew up listening to Test Match Special and the community nostalgia of BBC Radio 4's 'Down Your Way'. 'Jonners' was just the kind of cheerful, uncomplicated, decent citizen who inspired John's new vision of Britain; a Thatcherite nation of entre-preneurs, no doubt, but softened by a feeling for tradition.

As the corner shop was for Maggie, so the cricket pitch is for John. And as one of the Premier's central metaphors, this has assumed for sport a new cultural significance. Here is a certain idea of Britain – or rather of England, for Mr Major's sporting enthusiasms are very much of the Home Counties rather than the more removed English regions or the Celtic fringe; sport as affectionate patriotism and as a profound attachment to the community rituals and mores of the subur-ban culture of Britain, as it was, and in part remains. Major reveres the conventional pieties of Middle England, of which sport is one, cheerfully oblivious to the sneers of the chat-tering classes. Sport now commands a prominent place as part of our National Heritage, complete with a department and a powerful minister.

THE DEPARTMENT OF NATIONAL HERITAGE

The Department of National Heritage (DNH) was estab-lished in 1992, born of John Major's general election victory. The first Secretary of State with responsibility for the Depart-ment was David Mellor, until 'cultural internationalism and ... newspapers did for him', as the BBC urban affairs correspondent David Walker put it.[1] Mellor, writing his own tabloid by-line when saying how much he looked forward to being Minister for Fun, was genuinely excited at the conception of a ministry integrating cultural concerns. On BBC Radio, in conversation with David Walker, he demarcated the Conservative government's interest in culture from Stalinist state-led cultural policy: 'what we think is that there is a cultural dimension to life that the government has to have a role in promoting and facilitating, but that the whole aim of it is to allow the artist and the performer to follow their own inclinations.' The combination is clear here: cultural paternalism wedded to an individualism of direction and outcome.

Mellor's successor as Secretary of State, Peter Brooke, has stressed how the DNH can bring together different cultural spheres – arts, broadcasting, sports, museums/galleries, tourism – so that 'we can all take full advantage of being part of the same family'. Further priority for Brooke has been 'to put the extension of individual access to our heritage, culture and sport firmly at the top of our agenda'.[2] Brooke also acknowledged 'the importance of our fields of interest to economic regeneration'. So sport could be seen as a serious player in the national cultural game, and inflected as 'heritage' it conjured up an image of a glorious past worthy of retrieval and preservation. The Brits could certainly be competitive – but weren't they always civilized and jolly good sports?

LEISURE AND CONSUMER TRENDS IN THE 1980s AND 1990s

The years of Margaret Thatcher's premiership have been seen as important not just for political reforms and initiatives, but also for leisure itself. Trend analysts have identified six points which made 'The Thatcher years ... special for leisure': exceptional economic growth; a leisure ethos stressing high consumption – work hard, play hard; more money was sought by people for leisure; commercial provision was strongly encouraged; leisure lifestyles polarized haves and have-nots; and the rationale for subsidized leisure provision was challenged.[3]

The top ten market sectors in 1989 accounted for more than 75 per cent of all leisure spending, as Table 1 shows.

The Main Markets

Value of spending	1989		1979	
	£bn.	Rank	£bn.	Rank
Eating out	11.3	1	3.9	2
Beer	10.7	2	4.7	1
Holidays overseas	10.4	3	2.6	3
Do-It-Yourself	4.9	4	1.7	5
Spirits	4.6	5	2.5	4
Wine	4.5	6	1.6	6
Holiday Accommodation in UK	3.9	7	1.5	8
Sport	3.3	8	1.2	10
Television	2.9	9	1.6	7
Gambling	2.9	10	1.3	9
TOTAL OF ABOVE	59.4		22.6	
ALL LEISURE SPENDING	77.8		29.0	

Source: Leisure Consultants, 1990: p. 6

These top market sectors remain prominent in the 1990s. The ways in which people take their leisure do change: but there are notable continuities of the dominant markets.

Particular leisure markets which emerged or flourished in the 1980s were all domestic technologies with home-based applications: video hardware and software; computer games and applications; and electronic music equipment. The most interesting impact of many of these new consumer trends was upon leisure lifestyle: individual choice as to how and when and what to consume was made possible, the image of the isolated individualized consumer becoming an indicative one for the time. Sports participation – particularly in indoor sports – increased from 9.8 million adults in 1979, to 12.4 million and 13.2 million in 1984 and 1989 respectively, a 35 per cent increase. The expansion of public and private facilities made such growth possible, as did the provision of home-based inspiration: the video of the work-out, for instance, facilitating new forms of frenetic stay-at-home leisure.

Depsite the economic downturn in the 1990s leisure spending in the UK held its own in the economy. In 1989 leisure's market value was £78,512 million; in 1992 it was £92,816 million.[4] In 1992, sales of compact discs exceeded the number of cassettes sold for the first time,[5] confirming the impact upon leisure choices and lifestyles of some of the growth sectors of the 1980s.

The continuities in leisure activity outweigh the discontinuities. Comparing 1990 and 1994 figures on activities participated in at least once a week shows this clearly. Nearly everyone still watches television and reads the newspaper; around three-quarters continue to listen to records; about two-thirds read books, specialist magazines and watch video; one in two people drink alcohol at home, visit the pub in the evening, play with the children and do a bit of gardening. Between a quarter and a half of the population plays with pets, cooks for pleasure, does the football pools, pops to the pub at lunchtime, eats at a fast-food restaurant, and does exercises at home. Fewer people now take photographs (displaced by the camcorder craze) or attend religious meetings (10 to 20 per cent now, rather than a quarter to a half). Other activities engaging the energies of 10 to 20 per cent of people were knitting, hobby-sewing, billiards/snooker, voluntary work and aerobics. The 'home computer' was a newcomer to this list in the 1990s. Still popular, but attracting less than 1 in 10 of the population, were jogging, darts, evening classes and home beer/wine making. Leisure participation on a *weekly* basis showed few changes from 1990–94, then, with the home computer's rise to prominence confirming the impact of the growth technologies of the Thatcher years. In terms of weekly leisure participation, active sport continued to be very much a minority activity, though sport was prominent in several less active forms – gambling, and television watching, for instance. Leisure activities participated in less frequently than weekly showed that condemned cultures could revive. One in 3 went to the cinema at least once a quarter in 1990. This has risen to well over 40 per cent by

1994, a sign that technologies such as video might revive more public forms of leisure consumption rather than simply undermining them.

THE THATCHER LEGACY

Despite its minority base, sport can be seen as integral to the vision of civilized competitiveness, an anchor of tradition and fairness within a world buffeted around on the waves of the latest fads or theory. For John Major it is truly meaningful, certainly much more than a photo opportunity. For his predecessor it wasn't even that. Mrs Thatcher was the first Prime Minister since Churchill to be indifferent and on occasion openly hostile to sport. In her memoirs, *The Downing Street Years*, sport has hardly a mention. For her it was never more than a blunt instrument of international policy or just a plain social problem (and even then the Heysel tragedy is cited in terms of evidence of international diplomacy). She had tried to promote a British boycott of the Moscow Olympics as a protest over the Soviet invasion of Afghanistan (to reinforce the 'special relationship' with the USA) but this had backfired when sports organizations and athletes refused to see things the same way: 'Unfortunately, most of the British Olympic team decided to attend the Games, though we tried to persuade them otherwise: of course, unlike their equivalents in the Soviet Union, our athletes were left free to make up their own minds.'[6] Margaret Thatcher's account retrieves victory from defeat here, turning her own loss of face into the triumph of a wider political principle. Her period at Number 10 also coincided with the climax of the hooligan sub-culture around football which took up valuable police resources at home and brought shame and humiliation abroad. Mrs Thatcher demanded something be done and the scheme to introduce compulsory membership of 'clubs' and identity cards for supporters – perhaps the greatest single proposed change to the game since its inception – was the result. Fans mobilized a concerted opposition to this, and events overtook the idea with the Hillsborough tragedy and the Taylor report (perhaps explaining the lack of any mention of this episode in *The Downing Street Years*).

The recommendations of the Taylor report are now changing the landscape of the game for good. Swaying, jostling crowds, standing jammed together, packed into Ends like the Kop and the North Bank, for which one suspects Mr Major and Mr Mellor – his friend, chosen cultural aide and sporting lieutenant – shared a certain sentimental attachment – are replaced by all-seated audiences. After Mellor's fall from grace (clothed only in a Chelsea shirt, according to the tabloids that hounded him), he shifted adroitly from life as a powerful minister to the microphone and written word, hosting BBC Radio 5's Saturday evening phone-in, putting the case of the fan as consumer, a Citizen's Charter for sport, the new populism of the 1990s; and writing regular columns for *The Guardian* newspaper.

Margaret Thatcher – and protégés such as the minister for sport, Colin Moynihan – were no such cultural populists. The Thatcher legacy to British sport was a characteristic blend of occasional brusque interventionism within a wider framework of deregulation, which has had a profound influence on the 1990s. In particular, the sale of television rights in professional football to the highest bidder – on or off the networks – has been a shock. Promoting satellite television has had the effect of fragmenting the 'television sports' audience, although the process is as yet not very far advanced. BSkyB has said that its strategy for football is nothing less than the pure 'americanizing' of the sport with the creation of a Monday sports night with live football for those willing to put up a satellite dish and pay for the privilege. Sales of satellite dishes have been less than Rupert Murdoch would have wished, though, and one unintended consequence of BSkyB's coup has been that public houses and bars have acquired new audiences for the broadcasting of the live sports event. The logic of this deregulating development is to establish a monopoly over the top events and it must be only a matter of time before huge bids are made for Wimbledon or Rugby's Five Nations. Of course, the process of commercialization itself preceded the Thatcher years. Cornhill sponsored cricket and athletes were being given appearance money by Andy Norman before 1979. But the withering away of the amateur code which had ruled sport for a hundred years gathered pace in the 1980s. Its stars were a mixed bunch: Torvill and Dean, on the ice; Sebastian Coe, on the track; Steve Davis, on the green baize, as well as on the platform at the Tory party electoral rally; and cricketers Gower, Botham and Gooch – 'Essex Man' intermingled with representatives of an older ideal of fair play and bodily grace, from 'Gazza' to Gary Lineker.

Under Thatcher, then, it was not so much the application of the market to sport which was a novelty – except in terms of TV – as indifference to the paternalism that had character-ized the old order. Professional sport embodied to perfection the ideal of a meritocratic elite enriching itself through talent. Athletics, for instance, offered opportunities for unthought of scales of opportunity for the successful competitor; and the boomtime sport of the Thatcher years was snooker. Snooker millionaire Steve Davis and his Essex-based manager Barry Hearn embodied the Thatcherite dream. As Gordon Burn has memorably put it, 'The success of Hearn was a celebration of values at the core of Thatcherism; particularly the triumph of his own brand of popular capitalist enterprise'.[7]

In terms of participation in more physically exerting acti-vities squash and aerobics were the boom activities of the Thatcher decade; physical culture as yuppie competitiveness or image-led narcissism. Obviously this touched only a min-ority but a significant minority who went to the gyms and set the tone of sport. Alongside this a section of the left (still touched by the 1960s), progressive physical educationalists, and feminists denounced competitive games. More impor-tantly, government treatment of the teaching profession led to withdrawal of cooperation for extra-curricular activities including sport.

THE NATIONAL CURRICULUM DEBATE AND SPORT IN SCHOOLS

By the end of the 1980s, in the schools, sport, physical education and related areas were seeking survival strategies in the debate on the National Curriculum. The Physical Education Working Group set up in 1990 included Olympic gold medallist Steve Ovett and the black Wimbledon footballer John Fashanu. Neither was able to attend many meetings of the Working Group, but Education Minister Angela Rumbold, season ticket holder at Wimbledon Football Club, certainly achieved 'black street-cred' (her words) and man-in-the-street impact in the selection of Fashanu for this role, and of the anti-establishment figure of Ovett as the other 'sports' figure.[8] The Working Party was chaired by Ian Beer, Head Master of Harrow School, and with an alliance of the sports and the health lobbies, by 1994 physical education had secured a 'compulsory' place in the curriculum for all school pupils through the years of secondary schooling.

John Major pushed a Thatcherite fundamentalism still further in this area, encouraging sports minister Ian Sproat's zealous campaign for the 'reinstatement' and prioritization of traditional team games. The *Daily Express* political editor Jon Craig saw the drive to give all children regular daily exercise as a 'PE revolution, inspired by John Major's Back to Basics drive'.[9] Sproat spelled out the philosophy at the heart of this 'revolution' in an address to the Sportswriters' Association: 'When I talk about sport in schools I do not mean step aerobics, going for country walks and listening to lessons on the history of diets. These are all right in their way but they are not what I want. I want team games properly organized – competitive team games, preferably those sports we invented, such as soccer, rugby, hockey, cricket and netball'.[10] There was clearly the voice of the former school cricketer John Major in such a manifesto, though when this sort of commitment was reaffirmed in April of 1994 by the sports minister (in an 8,000 word paper to John Major, calling for the overhaul of the sporting curriculum), headlines and leader pages reminded the government that simple dogmatism over 'our' games was sure to generate a lively popular response, but could hardly guarantee a revival of national sporting fortunes.

For John Major, who bears a striking resemblance in speech and physical style (or lack of it) to that sporting hero of his premiership, Nigel Mansell – and like Nigel sometimes gives the impression of having greatness thrust upon him when he would be more at home in a conference of double glazing salesmen – the collapse of sportsmanship is a serious thing. Caught in a contradiction between the operation of the free market in sport and a vision of Britain as a decent, law-abiding place with a sense of 'fair play', John Major's line has been to accentuate (quite naturally) the positive and ignore the unacceptable face of commercialized sport, especially the question of drugs.

TOP-LEVEL SPORT AND LEADERSHIP CRISIS

The Olympics have been on the whole kind to Mr Major. No one really expected him or Bob Scott, who got a knighthood out of the failed bid, to bring the Olympics to Manchester for the millennium. But he was much more involved than was Thatcher during Manchester's previous bid: he went to Monte Carlo and did his best, not winning but taking part in true Olympic spirit and providing some generous funding for Mancunian sport facilities in the process.

Before that Barcelona provided a boost in the shape of gold medals for Linford Christie and Sally Gunnell, who gave some reassurance that Britain's athletic heyday of Coe, Ovett and Cram was not quite over. Several of the outstanding performers had the added attraction of being black, promoting a cheerful multiculturalism for the youth of the inner cities (so long the Achilles' heel of the Conservatives, pushing up crime and unemployment figures); and providing role models like Linford Christie, Kriss Akaboussi, Tessa Sanderson or Fatima Whitbread, whose famous 'wiggle' belied a keen business sense in alliance with the athletics entrepreneur Andy Norman.

Otherwise our rowers were remarkable and Olympic gold medallist Chris Boardman shot to fame with a DIY bike that seemed to show British self-styled inventive genius could triumph over the vast investments other nations were believed to put into sport. For the former Chief Secretary to the Treasury never let his love of sport overcome respect for the tradition of voluntarism and government parsimony that were the hallmarks of public policy on sport.

The 1994 Winter Olympics in Lillehamer saw the return of Torvill and Dean and with them the largest TV audience (over 20 million on the final night of their competition) for a sporting event in the Major era; when they were placed 'only' in bronze medal position, there was a hint of the deeply-held British belief that foreign juries were not quite impartial, but Jane and Chris won Gold from the crowd and the British viewing public.

The nation has been less inclined to indulge the failures of John Major. And his own Achilles' heel has so often been the new Europe. There must have been moments when the Prime Minister and the England soccer manager felt like consoling one another in the face of savage assaults from the popular press. While John was being mauled on the front page, Graham Taylor was pilloried on the back. In this the ascent of John Major neatly parallels the rise and fall of the most prominent sporting personality of his premiership. Graham Taylor was a nice man, too, unlike several of the other candidates for the England managership; better, it was said, than his predecessor with the media, more 'user friendly' in the computer jargon of the age; the fact that he had not really won anything at the highest level was brushed aside. When he chopped and changed the side, showing little vision or consistency, and having his share of poor luck, the media turned on him with a vengeance. He doesn't seem to know what he wants, they wailed, railing when he ignored them and despising him if he took advice that didn't work. During the debacle of the European Championships in Sweden in 1992 even Bobby Charlton, that supreme expression of the elevated working-class gent, decent Englishness and sportsmanship, was moved to protest. This wasn't good enough for England. But the FA wasn't really listening. They were honourable men. Graham was a well-groomed pragmatist who had to be given his chance. The Conservative party has a record of being rather less indulgent towards its lacklustre and ineffectual leaders.

Two of the most prominent clashes of personality and power during the Major years nicely encapsulate the sporting trends of his premiership. First, there was the Gower and Gooch affair in the national summer game. The dropping of Gower from the Test side seemed to be the final blow against a certain gentlemanly ideal of cavalier cricket in favour of the dour, fitness-based approach of the unshaven Essex man who had become England captain. Ironically, the chief victim seemed to be the classic effortless amateur, and Oxford man Ted Dexter, of glorious batting memory, trying to bridge the gulf that has grown up between the conflicting demands of style and performance. At one point he wholly abandoned rational explanations of the deficiencies of English performances, and (as chairman of the cricket test side selectors) attributed defeat to the movement of the planets. Tongue in cheek or not, this was basis enough for pundits and media to write obituaries to the memory of the gentleman amateur. Dexter's successor, the gritty Yorkshireman Ray Illingworth, symbolized the claimed 'classlessness' of Major's preferred society. Ian Botham had combined style and performance for a while but lacked the personal dignity to hold the England captaincy successfully, hounded as he was by the tabloid press on top of his own dismissive approach to the establishment. In the Major years the England captaincy continued its oscillation between the gritty old pro and the spiritual and social descendants of the gentleman. And so the mantle passed from Gooch to Atherton – the artisan amateur, of Manchester Grammar and Cambridge – and with it the continuing dilemma of a game and of men who were supposed to carry the weight of English dignity and expectation whilst slogging away in one-day matches in coloured pyjamas.

From the cricketing shrine of Lords to Tottenham Hotspur's home, White Hart Lane, is socially and culturally quite a long way. The Venables-Sugar affair was all media-hype and big money as the debts of Spurs accumulated in their bid to become a publicly quoted company. This brought in the taciturn Alan Sugar of Amstrad – who had made a fortune from the personal computer boom – in what seemed the dream ticket with Terry Venables, successful footballer, turned author, turned manager, turned pundit and bar owner. Money talked and Venables was pushed out under a cloud of press speculation about dubious loans, none of which has in the event stopped him from becoming the England football coach.

Old ethics may be inexorably on the wane, but Britain under Major has at least not reached the level of absurdity, sensationalism and degradation pertaining in the United States where a lawsuit permitted a competitor whose husband and trainer had admitted trying to cripple a rival to force the authorities to select her for the Olympic ice-skating team. How unlike the home life of our own dear Jayne and Chris, despite its edging, painful moments as revealed in a widely watched BBC 'fly on the wall' documentary.

Athletics had been ravaged by the scandal of Andy Norman's threats to the late Cliff Temple, *Sunday Times* athletics correspondent, who tragically committed suicide at the end of 1993. But all is not lost and much remains the same. Britain had the best golfer in the world for much of the early 1990s, but even the efforts of Cliff Richard and Stefan Edberg's coach Tony Pickard could not find us a really good tennis player. There was no England (nor any of the other three footballing nations of the United Kingdom) at the USA World Cup in 1994. But England's hosting of the next European Nations Soccer Cup will at least secure the Home Countries one place; and thirty years on from the last time England played at home, they might even win. But they may, like John Major, remain locked in a time-warp of traditionalist parochialism. As David Ginola, soccer player for Paris St. Germain put it in the very week that Major's Tory government was shuffling its way out of an isolated corner to the newly expanded European community: 'You chauvinists, you English, you remain closed in your little world and you learn nothing that way. We know all about the championships of other countries because we know they are as good as ours. But the English, oh no. You don't open your eyes or your spirits to anything beyond your shores'.[11]

CONCLUDING COMMENTS

John Major has certainly raised the political profile of sport and leisure. For Thatcher sport was little more than a troublesome irritant in the wider context of law and order debates, or a means to a diplomatic end. Major's innocent enthusiasm for spectator sport and the moral values of competitive games in schools was an example of his 'back to basics' philosophy of 1993–94, indicative of the vulnerability of his thinly thought-through populist posturing – for, despite public massaging and distorting of participation figures, the majority of the population has little time for participation in sport. The alleged sporting basics were never widespread back there in the first place. Major also backed culture and leisure-based initiatives: not just the Manchster Olympic bid but also the National Lottery, the contract for which was won by Camelot in May 1994. But Major's real impact on the sport and leisure field has been a rhetorical one.

In April 1992 John Major said that in fifty years' time 'Britain will still be the country of long shadows on county grounds, warm beer, invincible green suburbs, dog lovers and pools fillers'. He has used sport to evoke images of a distinctive national character and identity. Francis Wheen argued that 'the equation of a cricket or football team with Her Majesty's Government is a corker of a category-mistake'[12] but to deny the significance of sport and leisure themes to the Major government would be foolish. For in his freely-chosen use of sport as metaphor and ideological fodder, John Major has produced a lasting set of images not just of an idealized sporting life but of a frail political culture and vision.

Major's initiatives have been shot through with contradictions. Sport, and the 'heritage' emphasis in leisure, have been a source for the construction of simplistic certainties in times of deep uncertainty. Bryan Appleyard has pointed out the more specific political side to this paradox – amid backbench calls for the end of Major's premiership – in noting that 'a populist Eurosceptical rhetoric is the visceral, atavistic driving force of current British politics. John Major has to bow to its power with evocations of summer evenings and cricket as symbols of an irreducible England beyond the reach of Brussels'.[13] When England hosts the European Nations (Soccer) Championships during the summer evenings of 1996, no doubt John Major will follow it with his usual interest. But in what capacity? As Prime Minister presenting the trophy to Europe's best; or as a backbench celebrity pundit on the BBC or BSkyB?

Notes

1. 'Analysis', BBC Radio 4, 28 January 1993.
2. London Seminar of DNH, 18 June 1993.
3. Leisure Consultants, *Leisure Trends: The Thatcher Years* (Leisure Consultants, Sudbury, 1990).
4. These figures, and those comparing 1990 and 1993–94 data, are from Henley Centre, *Leisure Futures* – November 1990; Volume 4, 93, Volume 2, 94 (Henley Centre, London).
5. Social Trends, 24 (HMSO, 1994).
6. Margaret Thatcher, *The Downing Street Years*, HarperCollins, 1993, p. 88.
7. Cited in Alan Tomlinson, ed, *Consumption, Identity and Style: Marketing, Meanings and the Packaging of Pleasure* (Routledge, London, 1990). See also Gordon Burn, *Pocket Money – Bad-Boys, Business Heads and Boom-time Snooker* (Heinemann, London, 1986).
8. See Margaret Talbot, 'Physical Education and the National Curriculum: Some Political Issues', in Graham McFee and Alan Tomlinson, eds., *Education, Sport and Leisure: Connections and Controversies*, Chelsea School Research Centre Topic Report 3 (University of Brighton, Eastbourne, 1993) pp. 34–64.
9. *Daily Express*, 22 January 1994.
10. *The Guardian*, 28 January 1994.
11. *The Guardian*, 29 March 1994.
12. 'Play up, play up, and get on with the real thing', *The Observer*, 3 April 1994.
13. *The Independent*, 30 March 1994.

EPILOGUE

Dennis Kavanagh and Anthony Seldon

WHAT THEN has been the Major effect? Before answering the question one must first review some of the problems our authors faced in answering the four questions we posed to them, as set out in the introduction.

- In many spheres, continuity rather than change is evident because policy initiatives, and spending commitments, set in train before November 1990 are still working their way through the system.
- Changes of premier, and indeed government, can be exaggerated in importance. Our earlier volume, *The Thatcher Effect*, suggested in some areas that too much can be made of the importance of 1979. In education, James Callaghan's 1976 Ruskin College speech is more significant than 1979. On foreign and defence policy, changes of leader such as Gorbachev's emergence as Soviet leader in the mid 1980s, or Clinton's election as President in 1992, can matter more than a change of British Prime Minister. In economic policy, Britain's ejection from the ERM in September 1992 has been all important.
- The chapters have focused on the Major effect *on* policy, rather than on the effect *of* that policy. It will take many more years before judgments can be made about how successful government policies have proved.
- Distinguishing rhetoric from substance is difficult at this

moment in history. Major has spoken positively, for example, about the importance of manufacturing. It is difficult to assess how far this has translated through into policy impact.

THE IMPACT OF JOHN MAJOR

Major's personal influence can be detected on various spheres of policy. He has chosen to concentrate his effort on these areas, largely overlooking others, such as defence or agriculture, which are traditional Tory areas. Many listed below are John Major's initiatives, but some others come from his key advisers in Number 10, principally Sarah Hogg, Head of the Policy Unit. At this point it is not possible to distinguish their respective importance.

- Economic Policy. Major has laid great store by the reduction of inflation as a necessary prelude for economic growth. 'He has a deep hatred of inflation,' said one close aide.
- The Charters, and attempts to make the public service more accountable, are his responsibility. He played the key role in initiating and pushing through *The Citizen's Charter* (Cm. 1599) of July 1991 which set the agenda.
- Privatization. Major's keenness to extend private choice informs his drive behind further privatizations, and market-testing and contracting-out parts of the public service. (With the Post Office, however, unlike Clarke and Heseltine, he was cautious on privatization.)
- Ireland. Major has been very concerned to isolate the IRA, and try to bring a settlement to Northern Ireland. In this endeavour he has worked very closely with Cabinet Secretary Sir Robin Butler, repeating the close involvement Butler's predecessor, Sir Robert Armstrong, had in the 1985 Anglo-Irish Agreement.
- Social Security/Crime. Major had been a social security Minister (1985–87) and has strong views for example prevailing over Lilley to achieve equalization of pension provision; or his harsh pronouncements on social

workers getting back in touch with reality, or beggars being an eyesore, in May 1994. Major has been similarly keen to challenge what he saw as liberal thinking in the Home Office.

- Education. He has shown a strong interest in education reform, a subject neglected by Mrs Thatcher until near the end of her premiership. His influence can be seen for example in his pushing ahead with the new model apprenticeship scheme and GNVQs.

- Heritage. He wanted the Department of National Heritage, created after the 1992 general election, and has pushed for the National Lottery as a device for securing extra funding for the arts.

- Honours System and Openness. He dislikes class-based patronizing attitudes, feeling that he has suffered himself from them. He initiated the (albeit limited) opening up of the honours system in 1993/94 and more openness in government, seen in the publication of details about Cabinet Committees and Cabinet procedure in 1992, and the *Open Government* White Paper (Cm. 2290) of July 1993.

- Europe. Major is an instinctive European rather than an Atlanticist. He drove through the Maastricht process believing that Britain should be closer to the heart of Europe than did Mrs Thatcher. But he also wants a high degree of flexibility. Talk of a 'multi-track Europe' during the June 1994 European election campaign was more than merely a consequence of the need to hold his party together on the subject.

THE GOVERNMENT EFFECT

Authors produced very different answers to the overall question of the effect of the Major government. The table below grades the impact according to whether there was low, medium or high change.

Low	Medium	High
Parliament	Conservative Party	Civil Service
Labour Party	Local Government	Short-term voting
Defence	Ireland	Economic policy
Health	Law	Europe
Women/family	Industrial policy	Cabinet and policy-making
Community care	Financial sector	
	Labour market	
	Criminal justice	
	Foreign policy	
	Education	
	The arts	

The table evaluates changes in policy, not change in the
impact of policy. Items in the 'low' column are ones which
display little change from their position in the later Thatcher
years. 'Medium' areas display some significant changes, and
'high' important change. The Civil Service, voting patterns,
economic, European and Irish policy have all revealed some
radical departures from how they stood under Mrs Thatcher.

FORCES FOR CONTINUITY AND CHANGE

The chapters reveal some consensus about the factors that
have caused or retarded change. Again a table helps to clarify
the position.

Forces Against Change	Forces For Change
Prime Minister	Prime Minister
Conservative Party	Conservative Party
Civil Service	Think Tanks
Local government	Activist ministers
Economic position	
Small majority in Commons	
Unpopularity of government	
Lack of ideological cohesion	
Lack of press/intellectual support	
Public opinion	

Two factors appear in both columns. John Major has played an important role in accelerating change in certain areas, as itemized above, and retarding it in others. Demands from the party for continuity and consolidation, articulated at Cabinet level by Lord Wakeham, Tony Newton and Douglas Hurd, have acted against change. At a popular level this tendency found expression in the review of plans for pit closures after the 1992 annual party conference. But perception at the centre that the party faithful do not want to see the government become stale after the long years in office since 1979 resulted in the very activist 1992 party manifesto, *The Best Future For Britain*.

The balance of factors has been against change. Civil Service inertia resists all radical change, above all where directed against itself. The persistence of recession, the small majority in the House of Commons (21) after the 1992 election, lack of support in the country or a clear ideological thrust backed by media and intellectual opinion has further militated against change. Think tanks, although less dominant than under Mrs Thatcher, have pushed for continued extension of market disciplines, albeit against an open door. Activist ministers, principally Michael Heseltine, Kenneth Clarke and Peter Lilley, have all shifted the agenda within their various departments.

CONCLUSION

Studies of individual administrations can overlook the powerful forces for continuity – economic, demographic, financial, social, technological and institutional – all powerfully present from 1990. We hope that we and our authors have not succumbed too far to this trap in asserting that there has been a pronounced Major Effect, and one that merits more careful attention than it has so far received.

APPENDIX A

Chronology of Main Events

November 1990

27 John Major wins leadership election after resignation of Prime Minister Margaret Thatcher. He receives 185 votes (just short of 187 needed for an outright victory) and his opponents concede.

28 John Major becomes Prime Minister. Gus O'Donnell replaces Bernard Ingham as Press Secretary to the PM.

December 1990

Mrs Thatcher is to become President of the 'No Turning Back' group.

5 Sarah Hogg replaces Brian Griffiths as head of the Prime Minister's policy unit.

10 Judith Chaplin is appointed as Prime Minister's Political Secretary.

21 John Major goes to Washington for his first meeting as Prime Minister with George Bush.

January 1991

1 John Major's first New Year message as Prime Minister promotes his vision of an opportunity society while promising to continue the Thatcherite doctrine of privatization.

17 Air strikes signal the beginning of hostilities in the Gulf war. John Major's war Cabinet: Major, Hurd, King, Wakeham, Mayhew.

27 Poll shows John Major has highest personal rating of any Prime Minister since Winston Churchill.

February 1991

1 Brian Griffiths becomes Chairman of the Centre for Policy Studies.

March 1991

5 John Major meets Mikhail Gorbachev in Moscow.

8 Liberal Democrat victory in Ribble Valley by-election.

11 John Major has summit with Helmut Kohl in Bonn. He announces to German audience Britain would play a role 'at the very heart of Europe'.

12 Conservative Way Forward launched as a new Thatcherite pressure group in the party with Mrs Thatcher as President.

13 Labour overtake the Conservatives in the polls for the first time since John Major became Prime Minister.

21 Michael Heseltine announces the replacement of the poll tax with Council Tax.

April 1991

17 First draft treaty for European Union submitted. Britain dissents from it.

18 Sir Terence Burns is to replace Sir Peter Middleton as Permanent Secretary to the Treasury.

May 1991

13   Lords votes to reject the War Crimes Bill by 131 to 109. The government invokes the Parliament Act to pass the legislation.

2   In the local elections the Conservatives gain 245 seats but lose 1135 seats.

19   Major urges UN to enforce sanctions against Iraq as long as Saddam Hussein is in power.

June 1991

11   Bruges Group memo leaked to the *Evening Standard* criticizing the government's policy on Europe causes protest from all sides of the Conservative party.

17   Margaret Thatcher attacks moves towards federalism in a speech in Chicago.

26   Alan Budd appointed to replace Sir Terence Burns as Chief Economic Adviser to the Treasury.

27–28   EC Luxembourg Summit.

July 1991

16   BA announces that it is ending its donations to the Conservative party.

17   G7 meeting. President Gorbachev is in London after receiving an invitation from John Major.

22   John Major reveals his Citizen's Charter white paper. It includes plans for privatization of BR, the end of the Post Office monopoly, a passengers' and parents' charter and enhanced rights for individuals taking legal actions against trade unions.

September 1991

2 John Major becomes first Western leader to visit China since Tiananmen Square.

24 New draft EC treaty calls for new powers for the European Parliament, a common foreign policy and refers to a federal goal.

30 John Major rules out November election.

October 1991

1 Bill to replace Poll Tax with Council Tax introduced.

6 John Major makes clear Trident missile programme will proceed as planned.

12 Conservative conference opens at Blackpool. Major complains to BBC over alleged bias.

28 John Major pledges to increase number of women holding senior public appointments as he launches Opportunity 2000.

31 Queen's speech includes replacement of Poll Tax with Council Tax, the end of division between universities and polytechnics, the publication of league tables on school performance and more competitive tendering in local authorities.

November 1991

8 Sir Norman Fowler elected to replace the Eurosceptic Bill Cash as Chairman of the Conservative Backbench European Affairs Committee.

11 John Major's speech at the Mansion House shows his determination to do a deal on European economic and political union in the 8 December EC summit in Maastricht.

18 The white paper *Competing for Quality* identifies government services where competitive tendering is being considered.

December 1991

9–10 Maastricht Summit. Major claims triumph. He wins an opt-out for Britain at the later stages of the European Monetary Union. Britain rejects the social chapter which the other eleven members sign.

18–19 Two-day debate on Maastricht in House of Commons. Seven Conservatives vote against the government and 20 others abstain.

January 1992

1 In a speech John Major singles out the free NHS as a symbol of the caring post-Thatcherite society. He rules out any possibility of electoral reform.

February 1992

21 Richard Shepherd's bill to allow a referendum on Maastricht treaty is talked out of the Commons.

March 1992

11 John Major announces Parliament will be dissolved and a general election held on 9 April.

18 Conservative manifesto *The Best Future for Britain* is published.

26 John Major announces his disapproval of Scottish devolution.

April 1992

9   Polling day. The Conservatives win with a majority of 21. John
    Major promises 'classless society'.

10 The Department of Energy to be subsumed into the DTI.

12 Major completes Cabinet reshuffle. Kenneth Baker (Home
    Secretary) replaced by Kenneth Clarke, and David Mellor
    becomes head of the new Department of National Heritage.

13 Neil Kinnock and Roy Hattersley resign as Labour leader and
    deputy.

15 Sir Peter Levene becomes the PM's new adviser on efficiency.

May 1992

6   Queen's Speech opens new Parliament. It includes plans to
    privatize BR and British Coal, a national lottery, a bill to
    implement Maastricht and an extension of the Citizen's
    Charter.

7   In local elections Conservatives have net gain of 308 seats. Best
    result for seventy-three years.

10 Sir Norman Fowler replaces Chris Patten as chairman of
    Conservative party.

12 Queen speaks to European Parliament.

15 Margaret Thatcher attacks Maastricht in a speech in
    The Hague.

18 John Major publishes details of cabinet committees and sub-
    committees for first time.

20 Sir Marcus Fox defeats Cranley Onslow for the chairmanship
    of the 1922 Committee.

21   Bill to ratify Maastricht passes its second reading in the
     Commons, 376 to 92, with 22 Conservatives voting against.

June 1992

2   The Danes vote against Maastricht in a referendum.

3   More than 100 Conservative MPs sign a Commons motion
     calling for a fresh start in Europe.

5   In the dissolution honours, Thatcher, Howe, Lawson, Tebbit,
     Parkinson and Ridley go to the Lords.

12   Major makes speech in Brazil at the UN conference on the
     environment.

18   Irish referendum supports Maastricht.

25   Scottish affairs select committee is to be revived.

26   EC summit in Lisbon concerned with events in Yugoslavia and
     enlargement of community. John Major calls for review of
     Civil List.

July 1992

1   Britain assumes EC presidency for six months.

8   Hurd tells Euro-Parliament the aims of the British Presidency
     are the ratification of Maastricht, completing the Single
     Market, sorting out EC finance, a GATT deal enlargement,
     developing relations with Eastern Europe and tackling the
     problem of Yugoslavia.

10   Tim Collins appointed as Conservative Communications
     Director.
14   Government announces plans to start the privatization of BR.

18 John Smith becomes leader of the Labour party.

19 David Mellor's affair with Antonia de Sancha revealed.

21 Sir Peter Kemp's retirement announced as manager of the Next Steps initiative.

August 1992

1–2 John Major meets Andrew Neil, editor of the *Sunday Times*, to try to persuade him to call off his paper's attack on the government's economic policy.

26 Lamont announces that despite turbulence on foreign exchanges Britain will stay in the ERM.

27 3000th killing in Northern Ireland since beginning of the troubles.

September 1992

16 Black Wednesday – Britain pulls out of ERM.

17 Interest rates cut from 12 per cent to 10 per cent.

20 France narrowly votes in favour of Maastricht.

22 Interest rates cut from 10 per cent to 9 per cent.

24 David Mellor resigns as Heritage Secretary. Replaced by Peter Brooke.

24–25 Commons recalled for debate on sterling crisis.

29 John Major suggests the EC will be willing to back his call for the overhall of the ERM.

October 1992

1   New Criminal Justice Act comes into force.

7   Conservative party conference at Brighton. Leadership is
    criticized by the anti-Maastricht Lord Tebbit at start of the
    Conference.
    Lady Thatcher attacks Maastricht in an article in
    The European.

13 British Coal announce the closure of 31 pits.

21 Downing Street blames Tory Euro-sceptics for spreading
    rumours that the British government's five-week crisis had left
    John Major not eating properly and unsure of his friends.
    Sir Leon Brittan and Bruce Millan reappointed as Britain's EC
    commissioners putting end to rumours about Neil Kinnock and
    the job.

22 A poll shows only 16 per cent of people have confidence in
    Major and 77 per cent are dissatisfied with him.

23 Tomlinson Report recommends cuts and closures for London's
    hospitals.

November 1992

2   John Major claims he is 'The Greatest Eurosceptic in the
    Cabinet'.

4   Debate on Maastricht treaty in Commons: 26 Conservatives
    vote against the Government. Government majority is 3,
    despite Liberal Democratic support.

9   Three Matrix Churchill executives acquitted on charge of
    illegally supplying arms-related equipment to Iraq.

10 It is announced that Lord Justice Scott will head enquiry into
    Matrix Churchill affair.

21 John Major apologizes to Bill Clinton over help George Bush received for his failed re-election campaign.

23 Opposition stage full-day debate accusing John Major of misleading the House over the 'arms to Iraq' affair.

26 Details of Norman Lamont's credit card transactions leaked to press.

December 1992

11–12 EC Summit in Edinburgh foreshadowed by criticism from both home and abroad over Major's handling of the EC Presidency.

14 Major announces he will revamp domestic policy.

21 High court says British Coal acted unlawfully in proceeding with closure plans without consultation.

January 1993

1 Single European market comes into force.

13 First British death in Bosnia-Herzegovina.
The Treasury and Civil Service Select Committee criticizes the handling of economic policy during and since the September 1992 crisis.

21 House of Commons Select Committee on unemployment criticizes government for pit closures.

29 Libel writ issued by John Major and Clare Latimer after publication of allegations in the magazines *New Statesman* and *Scallywag* that they had an intimate relationship.

February 1993

3 Government announces revised defence cuts. Four infantry regiments threatened with merger saved.

11 John Major announces that the Queen is to pay income tax.

19 Judith Chaplin, Conservative MP for Newbury, dies.

March 1993

4 John Major announces plans to make the honours system more 'meritocratic' in the Commons.

8 Government defeated in division on a Labour amendment to the Maastricht Bill: 26 Conservatives vote for Labour amendment.

17 Lamont's Budget announces plans for VAT on domestic fuels.

18 Major announces 10 million poorer people will be helped to meet the cost of VAT on fuels.

April 1993

24 IRA bomb in City of London causes massive damage. One dead, 44 injured. Initial estimates predict £1000 million in damage.

May 1993

4 William Whitelaw calls Major's twelve months in office the worst for a government since 1945.

6 Overwhelming defeats in local elections. Conservatives lose control of 15 councils. Newbury by-election lost.

10 Government majority cut to 10 over VAT on fuel. Two Conservative MPs vote against the government.

18 Danes vote 'yes' in second Maastricht referendum.

20 Commons gives third reading to Maastricht treaty bill by 292 votes to 112. Forty-one Conservative MPs vote against the bill and 5 abstain.

21 Inflation at 1.3 per cent. Lowest figure for twenty-nine years.

27 Norman Lamont resigns as Chancellor of the Exchequer.

30 Tory MP Michael Mates linked with disgraced Polly Peck chairman Asil Nadir.

June 1993

4 Poll shows John Major's popularity is lower than any Prime Minister since polls began in the late 1930s – standing at 21 per cent.

9 Lamont's resignation speech reveals that Major rejected his earlier proposal to remove sterling from the ERM, and criticizes him for giving 'the impression of being in office but not in power'.

21 Michael Heseltine has a heart attack in Venice.
   EC Summit in Copenhagen.

24 Michael Mates resigns.

July 1993

5 Six Conservative MPs vote against government in House of Commons coal debate.

7 Poll shows only 14 per cent of people feel John Major is doing a good job.

12 Government majority only 8 in Commons vote on VAT on domestic fuel.

15 The Open Government white paper is published.

22 Government is defeated on Maastricht issue in Commons by 327 to 316. It calls a confidence vote.

23 John Major wins a Vote of Confidence.

25 Major reported to have described three senior cabinet colleagues as 'bastards'.

29 Conservatives lose Christchurch by-election. Swing of 35.4 per cent.

August 1993

2 Government ratifies Maastricht treaty.

16 A local government by-election gives the Liberal Democrats control of Dorset County Council. The BNP wins their first council seat, at a by-election in Tower Hamlets.

September 1993

18 Conservative Party is £18.6 million in debt.

20 John Major tells Conservative MPs to stop their 'stupid internecine squabbling' and show loyalty to the leaders.

23 John Major puts forward post-Maastricht blueprint for the EC firmly rejecting a 'corporate' power structure in favour of decentralized market solution.

October 1993

8 During the Conservative party conference at Blackpool, John Major launches his 'Back to Basics' campaign.

13 Christopher Meyer's appointment announced as John Major's Press Secretary replacing Gus O'Donnell.

25 Government reject deal with Sinn Fein. John Major says he doesn't do deals with people 'who plant bombs and kill people'.

November 1993

1   The EC becomes the EU due to Maastricht.

15 Edward Heath claims John Major's European policy is causing Britain 'immense harm'.
John Major warns Ulster Unionists that they may eventually have to talk to Sinn Fein if peace is to be achieved.

25 GATT World Trade talks enter final phase.

December 1993

11 EU summit in Brussels.

15 Downing Street Declaration signed.

22 John Major becomes the first prime minister to visit West Belfast since the start of the 'troubles'.

26 Tim Yeo, a junior environment minister, admits fathering a love child. 'Back to basics' comes under increasing scrutiny.

January 1994

8   Alan Duncan, a PPS, resigns after revelations of his cut-price purchase of a neighbour's former council house.

9   The Earl of Caithness, the aviation and shipping minister, resigns after his wife's mysterious suicide.

10   Revelations that David Ashby, Conservative MP, shared a bed with another man on holiday 'to save money'.

12   Poll reveals Labour party 12 per cent ahead in opinion polls.

13   Westminster Council, the Conservative flagship, accused of 'vote rigging'.

17   Major testifies to the Scott enquiry. He claims he did not know about the affair until 13 November 1992 and said he hadn't seen memos sent to his office concerning the affair.

29   Norman Lamont describes Major as 'weak and hopeless' in an interview in *The Times*.

30   Gerry Adams is granted a US visa.

February 1994

7   Stephen Milligan MP dies in mysterious circumstances.

27   John Major starts his visit to America. He meets President Clinton for talks in Pittsburgh.

March 1994

7   William Waldegrave, minister for open government, creates a furore by claiming that, in some situations, it is all right for a minister to lie to the House of Commons.

9   IRA mortar attack on Heathrow Airport.

28   Tony Marlow, Conservative MP, calls for John Major's resignation during Prime Minister's Question Time.

May 1994

5 The Conservatives lose 428 seats in the local elections and control of 18 councils.

12 John Smith, leader of the opposition, dies.

19 Michael Heseltine announces delay on Post Office privatization.

24 Competitiveness white paper published.

27 Major speaks in an interview in a Bristol newspaper about beggars on the streets.

31 Major speaks of a 'multi track' Europe.

June 1994

9 The Conservatives lose 14 seats in the European elections. They also lose the Eastleigh by-election. Majority cut from 17 to 15.

13 Major gives a press conference in the garden of No 10 in which he announces his intention to continue as PM and to have a reshuffle.

16 Norman Fowler announces he is to resign as Party Chairman.

24–25 Major blocks the appointment of Dehane as EC President.

July 1994

6 Broadcasting White Paper. Renews BBC charter for a further 10 years.

7 Major gives an up-beat speech to the 1922 Committee before the Summer Recess.

10 Anthony Bevins writes in the *Observer* that Major is now more
    in command of party and government than probably any time
    since 1990.

13 Civil Service white paper. Disappoints those who wanted more
    radical reform to top civil service, but maintains momentum
    lower down.

14 Front Line First. Defence review cuts £750m from defence
    budget.

20 Major reshuffles his government.

21 Tony Blair becomes leader of the Labour party.

October 1994

11 Conservative party conference begins at Bournemouth.

November 1994

28 Four years since Major became Prime Minister. Since 1945,
    only Attlee, Macmillan, Wilson and Thatcher outserved him.

APPENDIX B

Cabinet Office-Holders

OFFICE	28 NOV. 1990–09 APR. 1992	10 APR. 1992–26 APR. 1993	26 MAY 1993–20 JULY 1994	20 JULY 1994
Prime Minister	J. Major	J. Major	J. Major	J. Major
Chancellor of the Exchequer	N. Lamont	N. Lamont	K. Clarke	K. Clarke
Chief Sec.	D. Mellor	M. Portillo	M. Portillo	J. Aitken
Foreign Sec.	D. Hurd	D. Hurd	D. Hurd	D. Hurd
Home Sec.	K. Baker	K. Clarke	M. Howard	M. Howard
Leader, House of Commons	J. MacGregor	A. Newton	A. Newton	A. Newton
Lord Chancellor	Lord Mackay	Lord Mackay	Lord Mackay	Lord Mackay
Lord Privy Seal and Leader of Lords	Lord Waddington	Lord Wakeham	Lord Wakeham	Lord Cranborne
Chancellor of the Duchy of Lancaster	C. Patten	W. Waldegrave	W. Waldegrave	D. Hunt

OFFICE	28 NOV. 1990–09 APR. 1992	10 APR. 1992–26 APR. 1993	26 MAY 1993–20 JULY 1994	20 JULY 1994
Agriculture	J. Gummer	J. Gummer	G. Shephard	W. Waldegrave
Defence	T. King	M. Rifkind	M. Rifkind	M. Rifkind
Education	K. Clarke	J. Patten	J. Patten	G. Shephard
Employment	M. Howard	G. Shephard	D. Hunt	M. Portillo
Environment	M. Heseltine	M. Howard	J. Gummer	J. Gummer
Health	W. Waldegrave	V. Bottomley	V. Bottomley	V. Bottomley
Social Security	A. Newton	P. Lilley	P. Lilley	P. Lilley
N. Ireland	P. Brooke	Sir P. Mayhew	Sir P. Mayhew	Sir P. Mayhew
Scotland	I. Lang	I. Lang	I. Lang	I. Lang
Trade	P. Lilley	M. Heseltine	M. Heseltine	M. Heseltine
Transport	M. Rifkind	J. MacGregor	J. MacGregor	B. Mawhinney
Wales	D. Hunt	D. Hunt	J. Redwood	J. Redwood
Nat. Heritage	–	D. Mellor 25/9/92→ P. Brooke	P. Brooke	S. Dorrell
Chief Whip	R. Ryder	R. Ryder	R. Ryder	R. Ryder
Min. Without Portfolio (and Party Chairman)				J. Hanley

APPENDIX C

Notes on Contributors

Nick Crafts is Professor of Economics, University of Warwick.

Ivor Crewe is Professor of Government, University of Essex.

Lawrence Freedman is Professor of War Studies, King's College, London.

Andrew Gamble is Professor of Politics at the University of Sheffield.

Howard Glennerster is Professor of Social Policy, London School of Economics.

Robert Hewison is Arts Editor of the *Sunday Times*.

Richard Holt is Visiting Professor at the University of Leuven, Belgium.

Peter Jay is Economics Editor of the BBC.

Dennis Kavanagh is Professor of Politics at the University of Nottingham.

Simon Lee is Professor of Jurisprudence at Queen's University, Belfast.

Jane Lewis is Professor of Social Administration, London School of Economics.

Ruth Lister is Professor of Social Administration, University of Loughborough.

Terence Morris is Professor of Sociology, London School of Economics.

Peter Riddell is Political Columnist and Assistant Editor (Politics) of *The Times*.

Peter Scott is Professor of Education at the University of Leeds. Before that he was Editor of *The Times Higher Educational Supplement*.

Anthony Seldon is Founding Director of the Institute of Contemporary British History.

Colin Seymour-Ure is Professor of Politics at the University of Kent at Canterbury.

Peter Sinclair is Professor of Economics at the University of Birmingham.

Robert Taylor is Labour Correspondent of the *Financial Times*.

Alan Tomlinson is a Professor in the Faculty of Education, Sport and Leisure at the University of Brighton.

William Wallace is a Fellow of St Antony's College, Oxford.

Tom Wilkie is Science Correspondent of *The Independent*.

John Willman is Public Policy Editor of the *Financial Times*.

Hugo Young is Political Editor of the *Guardian*.

Ken Young is Professor of Politics at Queen Mary and Westfield College, London.

INDEX

Adam Smith Institute, 16, 34, 154, 156, 319

Adams, Gerry, 297, 395

Adoption law, 361

AIDS, 432

Alexander, Robin, 339

Allan, Alex, 160

Allen, Brady and Marsh agency, 37

Armstrong, Robert, 155, 163, 460

Arthur Andersen Consulting, 30

Arts Council, 420, 422, 425, 426, 427, 428, 429, 430

Ashdown, Paddy, 104–5, 118, 151, 297

Asylum and Immigration Appeals Act 1993, 362

Attlee, Clement, xi, 3, 83

Audit Commission, 367, 376

Authors' Public Lending Right, 424

'back to basics', 36, 41, 141, 311, 313, 319, 336, 337, 346, 347, 355, 356, 361, 363, 390, 412, 430, 452, 457

Baker, Kenneth, 30, 37, 134, 305, 307, 309, 334, 335, 343

balance of payments, 7

Banham, John, 91, 92

Bank of England, 58, 174–5, 183, 185, 187–8, 190, 193, 194, 235, 254

banks, 229–31

Baxendale, Presiley, 74, 132

BBC, 136, 400, 404–8, 414, 425, 426, 444, 445, 446, 456

Charter, 406–7

Radio 3, 407

World Service, 422

Beer, Ian, 452

Bell, Tim, 37–8

Benn, Tony, 150

Benson, Sir Christopher, 341

Biffen, John, 51

Bingham, Sir Thomas/Bingham Report, 125, 126

Birmingham Six, 123

Birt, John, 408, 425

Black, Conrad, 286

'Black Wednesday', 107–9, 116, 120, 152, 169, 177, 183, 185–6, 188, 192, 201, 223,

232–4, 237, 241

Blair, Tony, 55, 56, 150, 312

Blatch, Baroness, 92, 337

Blom-Cooper, Sir Louis, 131

Body, Sir Richard, 51

Bolton, Eric, 340

Bookseller, The, 418

Boothroyd, Betty, 59–60

Bottomley, Virginia, 43, 133, 134, 319, 361

Boyson, Sir Rhodes, 85

Bright, Graham, 160

British Airways, 34, 208

British Coal, 9, 36, 208, 258

British Council, 422

British Gas, 208, 211, 212

British Rail, 9, 22, 36, 60, 208

Brittan, Sir Leon, 134, 303

Broadcasting Act 1990, 401–4, 406, 425

Brooke, Peter, 30, 43, 59, 392, 405, 406, 407, 408, 424, 425, 446

Brown, Gordon, 55, 149

Bruce, Brendan, 37

BSkyB, 406, 450

Budgen, Nicholas, 51, 395

building societies, 231, 238–40

Burke, Edmund, 3, 10

Burns, Sir Terry, 71, 76

Bush, George, 262, 269, 275, 276, 283, 285, 287, 293, 296, 299

Butler, R. A., 3, 172

Butler, Sir Robin, 67, 74, 76, 434, 460

by-elections, 28, 39, 41, 47, 54, 56, 99, 100, 108, 111–4

    Christchurch by-election, 111–2, 118

    Eastleigh by-election, x, 114

    Newbury by-election, 111–2

Cabinet, 154–5, 161

    agenda, 165

    and public expenditure, 164

    Cabinet committees, 165–6, 461

    collegiate decision-making, restoration of, 161–6

    Cabinet government, 161–4, 166

    greater openness, 163, 166

    informality of political Cabinets, 165

    Maastricht Cabinets, 162

Caborn, Richard, 58

Cadogan, Sir John, 438

Calcutt, Sir David, 131, 410, 411

Callaghan, James, x, 3, 56, 102, 172, 201, 236, 312, 348, 459

Carers' National Association, 370

Carlisle, Mark, 334

Carlton TV, 401, 404, 405

Carr, Lord, 312

Carrington, Lord, 278, 294

Cash, William, 51

CBI, 34, 91, 155, 211

Central Policy Review Staff, 155

Central TV, 401, 405

Centre for Policy Studies, 16, 34, 154

Channel 4, 401, 404

Chaplin, Judith, 160

child care allowance/child benefit, 358, 360, 363

Child Support Act 1993, 356, 359, 363

Child Support Agency, 132

Children Act 1989, 358, 362

Citizen's Charter, 9, 10, 12, 22, 35, 65–6, 74, 95–6, 97, 124, 139–40, 143, 161, 199, 252, 305, 309, 318, 343, 361, 431, 450, 460

City of London/stock markets, 192, 202, 240–1

City Technology Colleges, 342, 343

Civil Service, 9, 22, 64–81, 93–4
  appointments system, 75–7
  Commons Treasury and Civil Service Committee Inquiry, 77
  contracting out/privatization of agencies, 66–8, 71–2, 74, 78, 80
  core Civil Service, 71–2
  cuts in, 79–80
  morale, 73–4
  parliamentary/public accountability, 74–5, 78–9
  politicization of, 77–8
  reforms, 64–7, 70–2, 73, 78, 79–81, 463
  trade unions and industrial action, 73, 136, 156, 254

Clarke, Kenneth, 9, 27, 41, 42, 43, 54, 72, 92, 157, 161, 163, 178, 187, 191, 192–4, 196, 207, 237–8, 249, 307, 308, 309, 310, 321, 323, 330, 334, 335, 337–40, 343, 345, 347, 463

Clarke, Tom, 55

Classic FM, 407

'classless society', 149

Clinton, President Bill, 248, 278, 287, 296, 297, 459

collectivism, 6, 7, 148

Collins, Tim, 38

Committee of Public Accounts, 370

Community Care Act 1990, 365, 366

consensus, 7

Conservative Party, 29–44
  and constituencies, 32
  and Europe, 23–4, 25, 26, 27, 32, 38, 42, 51, 117
  and industrial relations, 22
  and John Major, 9, 12, 21, 26, 27, 32
  and privatization, 22, 36, 49, 54–5
  and Thatcherism, 8, 11, 18, 26
  conferences, 32, 33, 35, 36, 41, 141, 336, 463
  CRD, 34–5
  disunity, 116
  European Group, 419
  finances, 29–32, 33–4, 37–8, 44
  leadership election, 44, 48, 85, 120n
  membership, 32
  morale, 41
  organization/organizational reform, 30–3
  percentage of vote, 27, 100, 104, 106, 111, 112–4, 145, 146–7, 233
  periods in office, 20, 28, 29, 44, 50, 61, 119, 145
  policy formulation, 34–5
  popularity/unpopularity, 38–9, 44, 99, 103, 105, 107, 109, 116, 117, 118, 152–3
  propaganda, 37–8

Tory rebels, 25, 39, 42, 52, 258
Constitution, 122–43
  Bill of Rights, 139–40
  constitutional role for law and
    lawyers, 124
consumer choice and rights, 12,
    15, 22, 139
Cook, Robin, 55
Council for National Academic
    Awards, 334
Council for Science and
    Technology, 437
Council for the Accreditation of
    Teacher Education, 346
Council of Ministers, 24, 358
council tax, 19, 86–7, 88–9, 158,
    173
Cradock, Percy, 155
criminal justice, 13, 157
Criminal Justice Act 1991, 309,
    310, 361
Criminal Justice and Public Order
    Bill, 312, 361, 362
Crosland, Anthony, 3
Crossman, Richard, 3
Curry, David, 91

Daily Express, The, 103, 117,
    416, 452
Daily Mail, The, 103, 253, 399,
    415, 416
Daily Mirror, The, 117, 233, 411,
    416
Daily Star, The, 117, 416
Daily Telegraph, The, 117, 286,
    416
Day, Sir Graham, 340
Day, Sir Robin, 125
Dearing, Sir Ron, 344, 345

Delors, Jacques, 261–2
Denning, Lord, 122
Department for Education, 338,
    341, 342, 344, 349, 432,
    433, 435, 438
Department of Education and
    Science see Department for
    Education
Department of Health, 361, 376,
    378
Department of National Heritage,
    421, 422, 423, 424, 427,
    429, 430, 445, 446, 461
Department of Trade and
    Industry, 314, 433, 435, 437,
    439, 442
Deregulation Act 1994, 254–5
Desert Storm, 270
Dewar, Donald, 55
district audit, 376
divorce, 352, 362
Dorrell, Stephen, 70
Downing Street joint declaration
    on Northern Ireland, 41, 56,
    142–3, 390, 392, 393, 394,
    395

Earth Summit, 294
Eastern Europe, 12, 249
Economic and Social Research
    Council, 334
Economist, The, 6, 231, 434
economic policy
  and industry, 7, 194, 199,
    209–10, 214, 220
  'balance' in public finances,
    188–9, 193
  balance of payments, 7
  budget deficit, 178

control of money supply, 7
disinflation, 177–81
ERM, 23, 108, 153, 155, 159,
    164, 169, 173–4, 177,
    181–6, 187–8, 202–3,
    214–5, 220, 224–6
fiscal policy, 173, 174, 178,
    187–8, 190, 215
growth record, 26, 176–7, 191,
    210, 220
incomes policies, 5, 6, 7
inflation, 5, 7–8, 26, 105, 158,
    173–4, 175, 176, 178, 182,
    186, 187–8, 190–2, 200–1,
    203, 223, 236
interest rates, 15, 105, 172,
    173, 179, 190, 194, 201,
    223, 226–8, 229–32, 233
international context, 12,
    178–9, 182–5
leading ideas in, 6–8, 13
macro-economic policies, 12,
    15, 108, 176, 191, 194, 200,
    207, 214, 220, 229
monetary policy, 173, 177,
    178, 187, 192, 215, 229
output/GDP, 179–81, 189–90,
    191, 193–4, 210
privatization, 7, 9, 10, 12, 15,
    22, 36, 209, 212, 214
public expenditure, 7–8, 15,
    164, 178, 179, 257
taxation, 7–8, 9, 13, 41, 54,
    113, 189–90, 193, 194,
    195–6, 212, 226–7, 229,
    238, 244
unemployment, 5, 26, 176,
    178, 179
union reforms, 8, 9, 22
economic recession, 14, 21, 99,

105, 116, 169, 178, 179,
    186, 188–9, 191, 192,
    197–8, 214, 216, 218, 220,
    223, 226, 228, 230, 233–4,
    237, 240–1, 243, 249, 258,
    265, 463
economic recovery, 26, 27, 113,
    116, 120, 190, 191, 194,
    216, 233
Eden, Sir Anthony, x, 3
education see schools; universities
education policy, 8, 10, 16, 157,
    159, 461
electoral behaviour, 99–120, 152
    demographic factors, 104–5, 146
    distrust of Labour, 105, 116,
        146, 152–3
    perceptions of Conservative
        competence, 105–6, 107,
        108, 152
    popular view of Major as
        opposed to Thatcher, 104
    preference of Major to
        Kinnock, 103
    regional variations, 106
    slump in government
        popularity, 107, 116–20
    traditional Conservative voters,
        101, 119–20
    women voters, 107
employment policies, 6, 7, 12,
    246–65
    and Wages Councils, 256, 357
English National Opera, 421
Equal Opportunities Commission,
    357
ERM (Exchange Rate
    Mechanism), ix, 15, 23–4,
    26, 39, 54, 55, 99, 108, 116,
    149–50, 153, 155, 159, 164,

169, 173, 177, 181–6,
    187–8, 192, 201–3, 214,
    215, 220,224–6, 244, 295,
    412, 414
European Commission, 357, 433
European Community (EC) see
    European Union (EU)
European Court of Human
    Rights/Justice, 136, 138, 261
European Economic Community
    (EEC), 319
European elections, 32, 37, 38,
    41, 42, 99, 114, 146
European monetary system
    (EMS), 23, 169, 182, 223
European monetary union
    (EMU), 292
European Policy Forum, 16, 68,
    75, 80, 155
European Union (EU), 12, 16, 19,
    23–4, 41, 138, 156, 158,
    196, 224–6, 248–9, 259–63,
    264, 275, 277, 286, 288,
    289, 291, 292, 296, 315,
    352, 353, 354, 357, 359,
    384, 386, 395, 396, 420, 456
    Britain's presidency, 432, 434
Evening Standard, The, 165
Everitt, Anthony, 428, 429

Fairbairn, Sir Nicholas, 57
Family Policy Group, 354
Feldman, Sir Basil, 31
Field, Frank, 58
Financial Times, The, 212, 233,
    296
Finkelstein, Danny, 155
Foreign Office, 73
Forsyth, Michael, 253, 259

Fowler, Sir Norman, 30, 33,
    36–7, 160, 163, 322, 356
France, 12, 183–4, 198, 210, 212,
    218–9, 226, 249, 257, 262
free market economics, 5, 6

Gardiner, Sir George, 42
Garrett, Tony, 31
GATT, 41, 157, 173, 194, 197–9,
    200
general elections, 8, 9, 11, 20–1,
    23, 27, 30, 32, 33, 34, 35, 36,
    37, 38, 46, 48, 66, 85, 145,
    151, 152, 188
    1992 general election, 103–7,
    145, 147, 152, 157, 158,
    159, 178, 233, 244, 258,
    460, 463
George, Eddie, 175, 254
Germany, 6, 174, 182–3, 184,
    186, 209, 210, 212, 218–9,
    224–5, 226, 232, 250
Gilmour, Sir Ian, 3
GMTV, 404
Goodman, Lord, 427
Gorbachev, Mikhail, 272, 290
Gould, Bryan, 150
Gow, Ian, 155
Gowrie, Lord, 428
Graham, Duncan, 339, 340
Granada TV, 403, 405
Green Party, 146
Griffiths, Lord Brian, 158, 337,
    339, 340, 343, 344, 345, 349
Griffiths, Sir Roy, 367, 368
Guardian, The, 92, 117, 233,
    292, 409, 424, 450
Gulf War/crisis, 19, 163, 233,
    270, 272, 275–7, 283, 285,

288

Gummer, John Selwyn, 30, 89, 91, 92, 93, 157

Gyngell, Bruce, 403, 404

Hailsham, Lord, 3, 127

Halsey, Philip, 339, 340

Hambro, Charles, 31

Heath, Edward/Heath government, x, 6–7, 90, 155, 227, 236

Hennessy, Peter, 163

Her Majesty's Inspectors, 339, 340

Heseltine, Michael, 3, 27, 43, 83–4, 85–6, 87, 88–9, 90–1, 93, 94, 97, 102, 118, 120n, 134, 157, 164, 187, 195, 207, 210, 258, 284, 286, 287, 425, 463

Hewitt, Patricia, 151

Hill, Jonathan, 36, 158, 160

Hilton, Brian, 65

Hogg, Sarah, 36, 158, 159, 460

Holland, Sir Geoffrey, 73

Home, Lord, x, 3

Home Office, 130, 131, 132, 303, 304, 305, 307, 308, 309, 310, 312, 420, 421, 422, 461

home ownership, 36, 146

Hoskyns, John, 155

Housing Act, 9

Howard, Michael, 42–3, 73, 89, 94, 142, 157, 164, 250–1, 310, 311

Howe, Lord, 3, 100, 102, 127, 163, 164, 172, 223–4, 286

Hunt, David, 43, 249, 255, 257, 260, 297, 389, 390

Hurd, Douglas, 3, 43, 73, 85, 92, 102, 163, 164, 187, 225, 275, 276, 281, 284, 286, 290, 291, 292, 296, 298, 299, 303, 307, 310, 463

Hussein, Saddam, 272, 275, 276, 277, 288

Hussey, Marmaduke, 425

Ibbs, Robin, 155

IMF (International Monetary Fund), 7

Independent, The, 92, 117, 233, 408, 409

Independent Broadcasting Authority *see* Independent Television Commission

Independent Living Fund, 374

Independent Television (ITV), 401, 404, 405, 415
franchise, 402, 405

Independent Television Commission, 400, 401, 403, 404, 405

Independent Television Network (ITN), 401

industrial relations, 208, 212, 220, 246–65

industry, 206–20
and training, 209, 218–9, 220, 256–7, 264
competitiveness, 208–9, 211, 212, 214–5, 216, 220, 227, 248
de-industrialization, 206, 217
industrial performance, 207
manufacturing productivity, 206–7, 209–10, 217, 220, 232, 247–8, 250

see also privatization; trade
    unions; industrial relations
inflation, 5, 7–8, 13, 14, 26, 169,
    173–4, 175, 176, 178, 182,
    187–8, 190, 191, 200–1,
    203, 223, 224, 225–9, 233,
    235–6, 460
Ingham, Bernard, 155, 159, 160,
    400, 414, 416
Institute of Contemporary British
    History, x
Institute of Directors, 156, 252
Institute of Economic Affairs, 6,
    16, 34, 154, 156, 355
Institute of Public Policy
    Research, 16
interest rates *see* economic policy
Inter-Government Conference,
    283, 289, 290, 291, 292
International Herald Tribune,
    296
investment, 7, 207, 209, 214, 218
IRA, 276, 384, 391, 392, 393,
    394, 395, 398
Italy, 232, 249, 262

Jackson, Robert, 436
Jenkins, Lord, 3, 172
Jopling, Michael, 62
Joseph, Sir Keith, 3, 7, 334
Judge, Paul, 30

Kaufman, Gerald, 78
Kemp, Sir Peter, 67
Key, Robert, 423, 424
Keynes, John Maynard/Keynesian
    economics, 6, 150, 151, 207
King, Tom, 269, 273

Kinnock, Neil, 21, 55, 103–5,
    110, 114, 148, 149–50, 151,
    414
Kiszko, Stephan, 123
Kohl, Chancellor Helmut, 285,
    290, 291, 292

labour market, gender divisions
    in, 354
Labour Party/governments, 6, 26,
    27, 33, 80
  and constitution, 139–40, 147,
    151, 153
  and Europe, 11, 51, 147, 150,
    152, 153
  and industrial relations, 11, 147
  and markets, 15, 148
  and public ownership, 8, 11,
    15, 147–8, 153
  and regional variations, 147
  and social chapter, 147, 153
  and taxes, 11, 15, 38, 106, 147,
    149, 150
  and trade unions, 8, 15, 148,
    150
  and welfare, 8, 151
  decline of, 122, 146
  in local authorities, 95, 96, 116
  in Parliament, 46, 49, 52–4,
    55–6, 57, 62, 145
  leadership of, 55–6, 152
  longevity in opposition, 145
  membership, 151
  modernizers, 11, 16
  new generation in, 150
  pact with Liberals, 152
  percentage of vote, 39, 41, 100,
    104, 106, 111, 112, 145,
    147, 151

policy changes in, 11, 147, 150

popular conceptions of, 105, 109–10, 116–7

shift to political centre ground, 11, 15, 149, 150, 153

structural changes, in, 148, 150

turbulence in, 116

unity in, 150

Laing, Sir Hector, 30

Laird, Gavin, 254

Lamont, Norman, 9, 26, 39, 42, 50, 55, 58, 85, 172, 178, 187–8, 189, 191, 192, 193, 195–6, 202–3, 225, 231, 232, 234–8, 294, 310, 390, 410, 420

Lane, Lord, 127, 306, 312

Lang, Ian, 386, 387, 388, 397

law, 121–42

advice to ministers, 133–5

European Union influence on, 137–8, 141, 259–61

judicial review, 135–8

judiciary, 121–3, 124–5, 140

law and lawyers as challenge to government, 121–3, 124, 125, 128, 136–7

miscarriages of justice, 122, 129

protectionism of legal profession, 127

reform, 129

Royal Commission on criminal justice, 122, 129–30

Lawson, Nigel, 3, 47, 162, 163, 172, 174–5, 177, 178, 182, 188, 195, 214, 223–4, 227, 228, 234, 243–4, 323, 388

Leigh, Edward, 43, 50

Leigh-Pemberton, Robin, 174–5

Levene, Sir Peter, 159–60

Lewis, Derek, 76, 306

Liberal Democrats, 39, 52, 54, 56, 96, 104–6, 110–3, 139–40, 141, 143, 146, 151

Lilley, Peter, 26, 43, 54, 157, 292, 297, 319, 360, 460, 463

Livingstone, Ken, 135

Lloyds of London, 241–3

Local Education Authorities (LEAs), 335, 348

local government, 9, 13, 195

accountability, 87, 88, 90

and Citizen's Charter, 97

and competitive tendering, 66, 84, 94

community care, 84

control of spending, 88–9

council tax, 19, 86–7, 88–9

elections, 32, 38, 39, 41, 56, 92, 96, 99, 100, 108, 110–3

Local Government Commission, 90–3, 97

management, 93–4, 95

poll tax, 8, 19, 83–5, 86, 89, 90, 93, 96

reforms/reorganization, 35, 84, 90–3, 94–5

Loenhis, Dominic, 424

London Weekend Television (LWT), 405

Luce, Richard, 420

Lyell, Sir Nicholas, 126–8, 142

Lygo, Admiral Sir Raymond, 306

Maastricht Treaty, 14, 24, 25, 39, 52, 53, 62, 129, 134, 182, 196, 225, 259, 275, 287, 289, 291, 292, 293, 294,

297, 311, 315, 319, 412, 420

Major, John,
    absence of a political
        philosophy, 3, 4, 13, 14, 22,
        23
    and British cultural identity,
        419
    and British union policy, 397;
        England, 396; Northern
        Ireland, 390, 391, 392, 393,
        394; Scotland, 386, 387,
        388, 397; Wales, 389
    and Cabinet, 14, 20, 25, 42,
        161–6, 461
    and the Citizen's Charter, 9, 10,
        22, 35, 65, 95, 139–40, 143,
        161, 460
    and the Civil Service, 64, 70,
        74–5, 76–7, 80–1
    and community care policy,
        365, 377, 378
    and the Conservative Party, 3,
        13, 19, 26, 30, 32, 36–7, 44,
        61, 102–3, 117
    and crime and penal policy,
        305, 311, 312, 313, 315
    and defence, 269, 270, 281;
        Gulf crisis, 276, 277;
        Yugoslav crisis, 279, 280
    and the ERM, 23, 108–9, 169,
        173, 182–3, 186, 201–3
    and Europe, 19–20, 23–4, 158,
        182–3, 194, 196–7, 259–63,
        264, 461
    and foreign policy, 283, 285,
        286, 287, 288, 290, 291,
        292, 293, 295, 296, 297,
        298, 299
    and free trade, 197–8
    and health and social policy,
        318, 319, 323, 330
    and local government, 83–5,
        88–9, 90, 93–7
    and the media, ix, 27, 32, 39,
        59, 117, 203, 233, 400, 404,
        408, 410, 414
    and open government, 22,
        74–5, 163, 461
    and Parliament, 47–8, 59, 61,
        62–3
    and privatization, 22, 70, 460
    and public opinion, 27, 32, 39,
        99, 100, 102–3, 107,
        109–10, 116–20, 149, 233,
        244
    and public services, 9, 10, 15,
        22, 64–6, 95, 159, 194, 199
    and sport and leisure policy,
        444–5, 450, 452, 453, 457
    and trade unions, 22, 156,
        246–7, 252–5
    as Chancellor of the Exchequer,
        172, 177, 178, 182, 186,
        201, 202, 224–5, 233, 243,
        420, 421
    as Foreign Secretary, 283
    as man of detail, 24, 183
    as Margaret Thatcher's
        successor, 18–9, 20–1, 22,
        24, 30, 44, 64, 96, 102, 107,
        174, 177, 203, 243–4,
        246–7, 459, 462
    as Whip, 19, 25, 47–8, 103
    background and political
        career, 3–4, 19, 20, 27, 47,
        83, 149, 246, 265, 397, 460,
        461
    personality, 3, 10, 13, 14, 17,
        18–9, 20–1, 24–5, 27, 39,
        43, 47, 102, 103, 107, 118,

120, 162, 202–3, 244

Major, Norma, 419

Mates, Michael, 42, 55, 58, 60, 86, 410

Mather, Graham, 68, 75, 156

Matrix Churchill affair, 123, 129, 132

Maxwell, Robert, 409

Mayhew, Sir Patrick, 126–8, 392

media, 399–417
  and Conservative policy, 37
  and the economy, 175, 187, 190, 192, 203
  and general elections, 103–4, 117, 120
  and John Major, 32, 39, 41, 103–4, 117, 203, 233, 400, 404, 408, 410, 414
  and law, 125, 131
  and Maastricht bill, 53
  hostility of Conservative press, 104, 117
  use by Conservatives in election campaigns, 38

Medical Research Council, 436, 439

Mellor, David, 26, 39, 42, 55, 59, 399, 401, 405, 409, 421, 422, 423, 424, 427, 445, 446, 450

Meridian TV, 403, 405

Meyer, Chris, 159, 414

MI5, 393

'Middlemarch', 425

Middleton, Sir Peter, 70

Millar, Sir Ronald, 14

Milligan, Stephen, 410

Ministry of Defence, 272, 273, 274, 433, 439

Mirror Group newspapers, 409

Mitterrand, President François, 290

Molyneaux, James, 56

Monks, John, 156, 255

Monopolies and Mergers Commission, 211

Moser, Sir Claus, 441

Mottram, Richard, 68, 76

Moynihan, Colin, 450

Murdoch, Rupert, 117, 286, 406, 408, 409, 414, 416, 450

McColl, Sir Colin, 75

MacGregor, John, 334, 343

Mackay, Lord, 126–8

McKellan, Sir Ian, 361

Macmillan, Harold, 3, 6, 102, 117, 172, 253

Nadir, Asil, 55, 60

National Association of Schoolmasters/Union of Women Teachers, 343, 344

National Commission on Education, 358

national curriculum see schools

National Curriculum Council, 339, 340, 341, 343, 344, 345, 347

National Economic Development Office, 9

National Health Service (NHS), 8, 9, 10, 22, 79, 118, 133, 318, 319, 321, 323, 324, 326, 330, 365, 366, 369, 377, 378

National Lottery, 422, 425, 429, 457, 461

National Lottery Act, 422, 425

National Union of Teachers (NUT), 343, 344, 345
NATO, 269, 271, 274, 275, 288, 290, 291
Natural Environment Research Council, 436
New Right, 5, 12
New Statesman and Society, 410
News of the World, 286
Newton, Tony, 43, 62, 163, 165, 463
New Zealand, 75
Norman, Andy, 453, 456
Northern Ireland, 123, 139, 141, 143, 280, 390–5, 460
Northern Ireland Office, 423

Observer, The, 408
O'Donnell, Gus, 159, 412, 413
Office of Arts and Libraries, 421, 424, 426
Office of Science and Technology, 431, 434, 435, 436, 439, 441
Office of Standards in Education (Ofsted), 340
oil prices, 225
'One Party', 31
Open University, 334
opinion polls, 27, 28, 56, 102, 117, 146, 149, 233
   Gallup polls, 100, 102, 103–4, 108–10, 113, 117, 119, 147
opposition parties *see* Labour Party; Liberal Democrats; etc.
'options for change', 269, 272, 273
Owen, Lord David, 278, 294

Palestine Liberation Organization (PLO), 423
Palumbo, Peter, 426, 427, 428
Parents' Charter, 361
Parkinson, Cecil, 41
Parliament, 27, 46–63
   and back-bench behaviour, 19, 46–7, 50, 53, 92, 99, 116, 146, 192, 258
   and European Union, 25, 42, 51–3, 56, 62
   and select committees, 34, 54, 57–60, 359, 368, 373
   government defeats in, 25, 39, 52–3
   government majority in, 14, 46, 48–9, 50, 52, 54, 61, 463
   House of Lords, 42, 47, 60–1, 92, 136, 146, 359, 433
   Maastricht bill, 49, 51–2, 53, 55, 56, 61
   opposition parties in, 55–6, 59
      see also Labour Party; Liberal Democrats; etc.
   televising of, 59
   Tory revolt in, 39, 46, 47, 49, 51–2, 53, 54–5, 61
Pascall, David, 339, 340, 343, 344, 345
Patten, Chris, 4, 30, 33, 36, 37, 164, 284, 297
Patten, John, 3, 43, 73, 157, 334, 335, 337, 340, 341–3, 344, 346, 347, 358
Pergau Dam, 28
Personal Social Services Research Unit, 370, 371
Philips, Hayden, 425
Physical Education Working Group, 452

Pirie, Madsen, 156

pit closures, 39, 49, 53–4, 211, 258, 463

Plant, Professor Raymond, 151

police, 303, 311, 312, 314

Police and Magistrates' Courts Bill, 60, 312

Policy Unit, 155, 158–61, 337, 339, 460

political agenda, 3–17

poll tax, 8, 19, 48, 83–5, 86, 89, 90, 93, 96, 102, 107, 113, 116, 158, 172, 194–5, 239, 304, 319, 386

polytechnics, 335, 338, 345

Portillo, Michael, 26, 43, 319, 424

Post Office, 9, 43, 208

Powell, Charles, 155, 160

Prescott, John, 55

Press Council, 410

Prior, James, 247, 254

Prison Officers' Association, 307

privatization, 7, 8, 9, 10, 12, 15, 17, 22, 36, 60, 66, 69, 147, 178, 206, 209, 212, 214, 220, 228–9, 238, 260, 460

public spending, 7–8, 15, 178

Rayner, Derek, 155

Reagan, Ronald, 12, 262, 284, 285, 286, 293, 299

Redwood, John, 26, 43, 389, 390

Rees-Mogg, Sir William, 415, 426

Regional Arts Associations, 426, 427

Regional Arts Boards, 427

Renton, Timothy, 423, 427

Reynolds, Albert, 41, 56, 393, 394

retail price index, 172, 227, 241, 250, 264

Ridley, Nicholas, 90, 163, 285

Rifkind, Malcolm, 273, 274, 281

Rimington, Stella, 75

Rittner, Luke, 428

Robertson, George, 55

Rose, Jim, 339

Rose, General Sir Michael, 278

Royal Air Force (RAF), 274, 276

Royal Navy, 274

Rumbold, Angela, 452

Ryder, Richard, 43, 163

Saatchi and Saatchi, 37–8

St John-Stevas, Norman, 421

Sancha, Antonia de, 423

Saunders, Martin, 30, 31

Save The Children, 362

Scallywag, 410

Scarman, Lord, 131

School Curriculum and Assessment Authority, 339, 341, 344

School Examinations and Assessments Council, 339, 340, 341, 343, 344, 345, 347

schools, 10, 16, 22
  and curriculum, 10, 13, 157, 321, 335, 336, 339, 340, 342, 343, 344, 345, 346, 347, 452
  and Education Act 1993, 341, 349
  and Education Reform Act 1988, 9, 322, 335, 340, 342
  and local budgets, 10
  and opting out, 10

and testing, 157
grant-maintained, 79, 321, 323, 335, 341, 342, 349
Schools Council, 334
Schorr, Alvin, 372
Science and Engineering Research Council, 437
Scotland, 147, 151, 386–9
Scott, Sir Bob, 453
Scott inquiry/Lord Justice Scott, 28, 74, 123, 124, 126, 128, 131–2, 140
Scottish Assembly, 386, 387, 389
Scottish Constitutional Convention, 386
Scottish Nationalists, 385, 386
Sedley, Mr Justice Stephen, 126
Sheehy, Sir Patrick, 308
Sheldon, Robert, 59
Shephard, Gillian, 252–3, 357
Silcott, Winston, 123
Single European Act, 24, 62, 182
Sinn Fein, 136, 297, 393
Skinner, Dennis, 150
Smith, John, 55–6, 110, 118, 141, 145, 149–50
social chapter, 51, 52–3, 147, 153, 194, 211, 259
Social Democrats, 11, 12, 51, 105, 116, 117, 118, 146, 150
Social Justice Commission, 319
Social Market Foundation, 16, 156
Social Science Research Council see Economic and Social Research Council
Somalia, 279
Soviet defence threat, 271–5
Spain, 12, 232, 249, 262
Spectator, The, 285, 286, 416

Spicer, Michael, 51
Spring, Dick, 393
Sproat, Iain, 424, 452
Squire, Robin, 86
Steel, David, 103
Stephen, Sir Ninian, 392
sterling, 7, 23, 54, 55, 116, 177, 181–6, 188, 223, 224–6, 227, 232–5
Stewart, William, 434
Straw, Jack, 55
student loans, 9
Sun, The, 117, 286, 399, 414, 415, 416
Sunday Express, The, 416
Sunday Mirror, The, 117, 411
Sunday Telegraph, The, 117, 286, 295, 416
Sunday Times, The, 186, 286, 293, 416, 456
Sutherland, Stewart, 340
Sweden, 6, 12, 250
Symons, Elizabeth, 73

taxation, 7, 8, 9, 12, 15, 16, 54, 113, 116, 118, 120, 189–90, 193, 194–6, 203, 212, 220, 229, 233, 243, 244
Taylor, Ann, 55
Taylor, Graham, 454
Taylor, John, 396
Taylor, Sir Peter, 124
Taylor, Sir Teddy, 51
Teacher Training Agency, 346
Tebbit, Norman, 30, 39, 42, 102
Television South-West (TSW), 403
Thames TV, 403, 407
Thatcher, Margaret/Thatcher

governments/Thatcherism, ix, x, 3–17, 18–27, 30, 32, 35, 37, 42–4, 46, 47, 53, 63, 65–6, 69, 74, 79–80, 83–5, 88–9, 93–4, 96–7, 100, 102–7, 118, 119, 120n, 122–3, 124, 127, 130, 133, 136, 140, 141, 146, 148, 149, 152, 153–66, 172–4, 176–7, 182, 188, 191, 195–6, 199, 203, 207, 209–10, 220, 223, 225, 227, 228, 234, 236, 238, 244, 246–7, 250–1, 254–5, 256, 261, 265, 269, 270, 272, 275, 276, 277, 283, 284, 285, 286, 289, 293, 295, 297, 298, 299, 302, 303, 305, 318, 320–3, 330, 332–5, 355, 365, 367, 388, 389, 391, 392, 393, 395, 400, 401, 404, 406, 408, 413, 416, 418, 433, 449, 450, 457, 461–3

think-tanks, 12, 15, 34, 124, 154, 156, 463

Thomas, Harvey, 37

Thorneycroft, Lord, 37

Times, The, 6, 286, 408, 415

Today, 117, 409

tourism, 446

trade unions, 6, 7, 8, 9, 13–4, 22, 116, 146, 156, 206
  and unemployment, 208
  bargaining power, 208
  decline of power, 246–7, 250–5, 263–4
  in Civil Service, 73, 136, 156, 254
  leadership, 212, 255

reforms, 208, 250–5, 260

Treasury, 23, 70–1, 89, 158, 164, 172, 188, 189, 190–1, 192, 229, 235, 270, 271, 273, 283, 289, 296, 308, 310, 319, 326, 349, 401, 404, 414, 422

Treaty of Rome, 24, 211

True, Nick, 158

Turnbull, Andrew, 160

TV-am, 403

TV-South (TVS), 403

Ulster Unionists, 56, 385

unemployment, 5, 14, 26, 39, 120, 147, 173, 176, 179, 207, 228, 232–3, 235–7, 249, 258, 263–4

United Nations (UN), 272, 277, 279, 280, 288, 292, 362

United States, 6, 10, 12, 38, 161, 226, 228, 231, 235, 239, 242, 248, 250, 262

universities, 333, 335, 338, 349

UVF, 391

VAT on domestic fuel, 39, 49, 54, 116, 118, 120, 189–90

Waddington, David, 303, 310

Wages Councils, 256, 357

Wakeham, Lord, 20, 43, 47, 162, 163–4, 165, 463

Waldegrave, William, 66–7, 163, 431, 432, 434, 435, 436, 438, 439, 440, 442

Wales, 389–90

Walker, Peter, 93, 389
Wall, Stephen, 160
Walters, Alan, 155
Ward, Judith, 123
welfare services, 5, 6, 7, 12, 15,
        16, 262
Western European Union, 291,
        292
Westland affair, 116, 118, 133
Wheeler, Sir John, 58
Whitelaw, Lord, 47, 60, 134, 155,
        163, 164, 312
Whitmore, Sir Clive, 73, 155
Wilding, Richard, 426, 427
Wilson, Lord, 3, 26, 102, 234,
        236

Winter of Discontent, 7, 107
Winterton, Ann, 49
Winterton, Nicholas, 49, 58
Woodhead, Chris, 339, 340
Woodward, Shaun, 38
Woolf, Lord/Woolf Report, 126,
        131, 135, 304, 306
'Working Together', 31

Yeltsin, Boris, 290
Yeo, Tim, 32, 41, 86, 410
Young, Sir George, 85, 86
Younger, George, 389
Yugoslav conflict, 270, 277–9,
        281, 291, 294, 297, 298, 299